UNBOUND

A Novel

Kara D. Wilson

Rowan Publishing

ISBN 979-8-218-57042-2 (print)

First Edition.

Title page image: 123rf.com/seamartini
Front cover: 123rf.com/ai-image-generator

Printed in the United States of America.

OTHER WORKS BY KARA D. WILSON

The Aurora Chronicles
The Empress' Consul
The Regent's Daughter
The Assassin's Apprentice
The Emperor's Raven
The Dragon's Son

The Falkrow Narratives
Rhys of Earth
Rhys of Quadrant Six
Ronan of Space

Cardinal Zero

Breach Effect

For my Mordecai

1

Thirteen

LEGS PUMPING UNDER HER, KELLICK looked over her shoulder and sneered at Simon. That seemed to annoy the boy as his face folded into a determined frown.

Kell ducked expertly under a new mast that was being transported between half a dozen men along the docks and then dodged a moving crate of fish and ice being escorted into town. When she looked back, she found Simon gone. Winded, she slowed momentarily to discern where her friend had slunk off to.

"Busy, Kell?" asked a beefy man carrying a couple of pails of chum.

"Hm? Oh, uh, no." Kell wiped the sweat from her forehead as she continued to search the docks. Where *had* Simon gone?

"Good, here ya go." The man, Hugh, passed her the buckets.

Despite her thirteen years, Kell was lean and muscled from manual labor. More often than not, she went shirtless like most of the young boys and men who inhabited the area. No one said anything—because they didn't know she was a girl. Of course, Kell never offered up that information. And with her short crop of brown hair frequently plastered with salt to the side of her head and curveless body, no one suspected otherwise.

Straining against the weight, she followed Hugh, who had retrieved an enormous crate of materials and now led the way along the water. The slip he stopped at was occupied by a rusting commercial fishing boat. Panting and muscles tensed, Kell boarded his boat and deposited the chum buckets on the deck.

"Great, great," Hugh muttered, wiping the sweat slithering down his temples. "Thanks. Much appreciated."

"Ambrose not around?" Kell asked, stepping out of the August sun into the shade of the helm tower. "He normally helps you with this kind of stuff."

Hugh ran his sausage fingers through greasy, salt-encrusted hair. "Haven't seen him since yesterday afternoon. Probably still out with Murray."

Kell offered what consolation she could. "Eh, he'll show up. He knows the market's tomorrow."

Hugh grunted in response and then passed her a wrinkled apple.

Pleased with her reward, no matter how meager it was, Kell glanced about the boat. "Is there anything else I can do?"

"No. Just tell Ambrose to head back this way if you see him."

She shrugged and, brandishing her prize, stepped onto the adjacent dock. She was about to bite into the fruit when she heard the rush of feet. Knowing what was coming, she threw the apple back onto Hugh's boat as Simon tackled her. His momentum carried her backward, and together, they toppled off the dock into the polluted waters.

"Damn it, Simon!" coughed Kell as soon as she came up to tread water. Her chest felt bruised.

Simon looked rather pleased with himself. With a smug smile, he splashed a floating fish head toward her and then swam for the docks. They struggled to pull themselves back up and then lay on the hot wood.

"I believe you owe me that apple," he said as they squinted against the azure sky and brilliant sun.

Kell kicked him and then sat up to ruffle the seawater from her hair. She was glad to be shirtless, otherwise it would have taken a lot longer to dry off. The supple rubber-soled slippers she frequently wore were more than capable of withstanding the constant wear and tear of work around salt water—at least for a while.

After surrendering her apple to Simon, Kell led the way to the wharf. She was glad when Simon shared half of the mushy fruit with her.

"Dad's in a bad mood. He's worried they're gonna increase taxes again," said Simon as they walked. "We don't have that type of money."

"Yeah, we're hurtin' too." Kell watched Montague reverse his little fishing boat out of its slip; she grimaced as the engine squealed and clacked. "The past few months have been the worst."

"And you know we're comin' up to the end of August. The tax collectors will be crawlin' along these docks with the regulators this Sunday after the market, sayin', 'It's your civic duty,' or 'Your services are compulsurray.'" Simon waved to Montague who had whipped the steering wheel to avoid hitting the stern of another boat and looked back to make sure he had missed it. "I hate them so much."

"What do you think they do with all that money they take?" mused Kell.

Simon shrugged. "Throw parties?"

She grinned. "Have enormous feasts?"

"Get drunk?"

"Eat fresh fruit and vegetables?" Her smile faded.

"Take a bath every day—in *clean* water?"

They fell silent as each fantasized about what the life of a regulator or civil servant must be like, what kinds of luxuries they surely enjoyed.

"You wanna know something?" Simon eventually asked as they meandered toward the end of the wharf. "You know how Jonas has been missing for about a week now?"

"Yeah?"

"Edmund says it's 'cus of the Munera. He overheard his parents talkin' last night. They said flyers went out in the Upper District talkin' about the games comin' back." He looked pointedly at her. "They're startin' to look for fighters."

Understanding what he was implying, Kell asked, "And what is their reason this time?"

"To celebrate the king's fiftieth birthday."

Kell scoffed and gazed out at the brackish water. Farther out at sea, inviting royal blue waters whitecapped. "So... Jonas was snatched, huh?"

"Somethin' like that."

"When are the games?"

Simon shook his head. "Edmund didn't say. Probably around the autumn equinox. I'm sure they'll want the day to be auspicious." He eyed her. "We gotta be careful."

"They're not takin' children," Kell retorted.

"Uh, Jonas was fourteen." Simon nudged her fondly. "Still, be careful. I don't want you gettin' snatched."

Kell passed him a warm grin before peering back out at the sea. She loved Simon. Although she had grown up with a ragtag group of dock urchins and had spent long hours working alongside them, Simon was hers.

His family owned a private fishing vessel a few slips down. And just like her, he had been raised along the docks, working to put money in his parents' pockets instead of going to school, as was common practice for the majority of children in the Lower District.

Simon was naturally inquisitive, intelligent—despite his inability to read and write—and had a strong sense of honor which, Kell suspected, he had learned from his father. He could be relied upon in a fight and did well to keep the other dock kids in check. Kell considered him a natural-born leader and enjoyed watching him scold the older youth who gravitated toward trouble.

With his brilliantly blond locks, bright blue eyes, and stubborn chin, he exuded confidence and, on occasion, charm. Kell had developed crushes on a number of the girls her age along the docks because she considered herself more male than female, but when it came to Simon, she was head-over-heels in love with the fourteen-year-old.

That evening, she finally returned to her home aboard *Polaris*, announcing her arrival by slamming open the rusting cabin door. Since her clothes were mostly dry, she moseyed into the small space and flopped down on her creaky bunk.

Tarquin peered around the corner of the narrow galley, his forehead dripping with perspiration. "Thought you'd gotten snatched," he muttered through his heavy, black beard.

"Naw, they don't want scrawny kids like me," Kell replied, lifting an empty bucket by the wire handle with her toes and depositing it among the stack of others.

"Don't be messin' around off the docks, yeah?" Tarquin disappeared into the galley but kept talking. "Lucerne down the way got picked up this afternoon for fraud."

Kell sat up. "Fraud? What's that?"

"When regulators claim you've been lying."

"About what?"

"About anything."

Kell studied the dingy, familiar floor. "Simon was sayin' the Munera's been called. Said that's what's happened to Jonas, that he's been snatched."

"Yeah, his parents have been askin' around for anyone who saw it happen. Either no one saw it or—the much more likely event—regulators threatened everyone into silence." The fishmonger leaned back out of the galley and set a dark eye on her. "I'm serious, Kellick. Don't be goin' where you're not supposed to be."

She nodded. "Got it."

Tarquin motioned to the latch-locked cabinet opposite the doorway. "Get the table set. We're five out from supper."

After a humble dinner of cooked fish, wilted greens, pockmarked carrots that Tarquin had cut mold off of, and lukewarm tea, Kell cleaned the galley while the aged sailor put the deck equipment away.

Their thirty-meter private fishing boat was old but in better shape than others along the docks as Tarquin fastidiously kept up its maintenance. Kell thought that with new layers of blue and white paint, their boat would look as nice as some of the vessels that sailed out of Eclat's Middle District port. But paint cost money.

The two-story cabin centered at the front of the boat provided cramped living quarters, but Kell knew nothing else. The top tier of the cabin contained the wheelhouse and helm as well as a collection of navigational and radio equipment. The lower cabin consisted of a small galley, three bunk beds, a small sitting area with a moveable table, a water closet, a fish hold, and a small engine room. On hot nights, Tarquin would leave the engine running until midnight to cool off its innards before silencing it to save fuel.

The boat boasted an assortment of nets stored on its deck, including ring nets and purse-seine nets that could collect sizeable amounts of fish and not break. Of course, Tarquin also had heavy-duty fishing poles and hooks to pursue larger individuals like sea bass, swordfish, and marlin, which were time-consuming to catch but sold for more at market. Buoys, ropes, barrels, and a gantry to draw the netting onto the boat crowded the middle and stern of *Polaris* and gave the vessel the appearance of organized chaos.

Eventually, Kell took a bucket bath on the rear deck and then headed for bed. With a sigh, she rolled over to watch Tarquin across the narrow aisle, his face illuminated by the dim light of the low-watt bulb situated near his bunk. "What time are we gettin' up?"

Tarquin pulled his shirt over his head to reveal a barreled, hairy chest and a large gut. "Four. We'll make a quick run up the docks for fuel and then head to the market. I'm leavin' the engines runnin' to keep the water goin' in the fish hold."

Kell watched the large man with worried eyes. "Simon says the regulators will come to the docks on Sunday with the tax collectors. Do... you know how much they will want?"

"Another five percent of our month's earnings." He sat heavily on his bunk. "That makes thirty-two and a half percent. We just don't—" He shook his head. "We gotta make it work." He threw her a nod. "G'night."

"Yeah." Kell turned onto her back and stared at the bottom of the bunk overhead, rubbing her chest where Simon had crashed into her. The spot beneath her right nipple hurt, ached. How hard had he hit her?

She stretched and then went to sleep. But her night was not restful. She tossed and turned and her stomach felt crampy, like her meal wasn't sitting well. Around two o'clock, she rose and scooted out of bed to go to the bathroom. Her lower stomach was tight and felt kind of hard to the touch. She quietly cursed the stale vegetables Tarquin had cooked as she sat on the toilet, bent over her knees. Because she hadn't turned on the light or else ruin her night vision, she finished her business in the dark. When she wiped, she felt something slick but thought nothing of it.

When Kell returned to her bunk, she saw a dark spot on the bed in her poor grayscale night vision. Frowning, she ran her hand over it. It was dry.

She must have left mud when she sat there earlier. With a shrug, she lay down with the promise to take care of it in the morning.

Tarquin's alarm went off at four. As he rose and readied for the day in the light of his bunk lamp, Kell watched him with bleary eyes. She was exhausted. Her stomach had hurt all night with little relief. Even now, it felt crampy.

"Come on," Tarquin muttered, rubbing his face. "Got work to do." He lumbered to the galley.

Kell sat up, pushed her hair around, and then swung out of bed. She stood with a stretch and then grimaced as she felt something wet slide down her thighs. Bewildered, she looked down to find a black trail of liquid staining the inner hem of her cutoffs.

She screamed and toppled backward into bed, frantically pulling at her pants to locate her injury.

Tarquin stumbled back into the bunk, wide-eyed. "What? What's wrong?"

"I'm hurt! I didn't know—Tarquin, there's so much blood. Where did it—" She pulled the belt of her cutoffs away and studied her blood-smeared legs.

Tarquin joined her, bearing a small flashlight. "What is it?"

"There's blood, everywhere." Kell stripped out of the cutoffs she had worn to bed and sat back nude, heart hammering, to evaluate herself. Tarquin flashed his light across her before shifting it to the floor. Kell looked at him, afraid and horrified. "What? What is it?"

He glanced at her, unbothered by her nakedness, and then sighed. "Hold on." He disappeared from the cabin. Kell heard him leave the boat.

Tears pooling in her eyes, she wiped the blood along her thighs with her cutoffs since they were already soiled and continued to search for the major wound she must have unknowingly suffered. By the time Tarquin returned, she had determined that she was bleeding from the secret spot between her legs.

Panicked and ashamed, she looked up as he reentered the cabin with Vera, Simon's mother. Kell hurriedly covered herself, alarmed. No one knew she was female. Vera's face reflected surprise and then understanding.

"Thank you, Tarquin," she murmured, still dressed in a ratty nightgown and her hair in disarray. "I'll take care of her."

Tarquin gave a soft grunt and then disappeared outside.

Kell pulled her thin blanket over her bloodied cutoffs so Vera could no longer see the blood.

The woman smiled and seated herself on the edge of Tarquin's unmade bunk. "I suspected."

"You knew… I was a girl?"

Vera shrugged.

"Have you told Simon?"

"No, no one else knows."

"Please don't tell him."

"I won't. Don't worry." Vera motioned to her. "You're bleeding."

Kell flushed, bearing down on the blanket. The woman's nonchalance made Kell think that perhaps she was overreacting. "Am I… dyin'?"

With a gentle smile, Vera shook her head. "No, you're not dying. Quite the opposite."

That confused Kell.

Simon's mother sighed and threw a disgruntled look over her shoulder. "Damn man. Not telling you anything. No, you're not dying. You're becoming a woman."

Kell relaxed a little. "Bleedin' means I'm a woman?"

"It means your body is changing. It's called a monthly. It will happen every month for the next forty years or so."

"What?" squealed Kell in horror. Vera nodded. "*Every* month?"

"Unless you become pregnant."

"Does it ever stop? Will I just keep bleeding constantly?"

Vera laughed. "No, no. You will bleed for four to six days and then it'll stop. Then it will start again the following month, usually around the same time. So, mark the date or the moon's phase so you won't be surprised."

"Do… all girls go through this?" Kell asked numbly.

"They do. When they reach your age, sometimes older, sometimes younger."

"But why?" cried Kell. "This is stupid. How am I supposed to-to do *anything* if I'm bleeding all the time?"

"Like I said, it's not all the time."

Kell stared at the blanket, a heavy weight settling over her. "What do I do? How do I keep other people from knowin'?" She looked at Simon's mother. "You go through it, right? How do I hide it?"

Vera stood. "There are ways. Let me get some supplies. In the meantime, try to wash up. Cold water only." The woman reached through the space between them and held out her hand. Kell hesitantly took it. "Welcome to the sisterhood, Kellick." Vera gave her a reassuring nod and then hurried from the cabin.

The sound of running water in the galley reminded her that Tarquin was waiting. Frowning, she stood, holding the cutoffs and blanket to her. Embarrassment and shame urged her to hide as she felt a slither of motion between her legs.

Momentarily, the water turned off and the fishmonger reentered the bunks with a bucket and rags. He set it in front of her and then left, closing the tiny cabin door behind him.

Humiliated but grateful, Kell left her soiled clothes and blankets and began washing the blood off her legs. When Vera returned, Kell was drying off. The woman set a small basket of supplies next to her on Tarquin's bed and then passed an appraising eye over Kell's naked body. "You're going to have to stop going shirtless."

Kell frowned, if possible, deeper. "Why?"

Vera motioned to Kell's chest. "You're starting to develop. Does it ache or bother you much?"

Realization clicked in Kell, and she nodded. Simon hadn't hit her hard. When she thought about it, both of her breasts had been sore for a while now. She had thought nothing of it. She hardly ever scrutinized herself; she had no real need to. Glancing down, she swallowed. Now that Vera had said something, Kell could discern the mild swelling in her bosom.

Tears filled her eyes once more as she contemplated the ramifications this had. She would never be able to go shirtless again. The others in their group would wonder why in the middle of August she still wore clothes. What was she going to do? What if they found out? What if *Simon* found out?

Vera must have seen the panic and defeat in her gaze because she passed the girl a calm smile. "You'll be fine. I promise. Hundreds of millions of women have gone through this for all of humanity. You'll adapt. But you will need to start covering up. I'll see if I can find you bandeaus to hide your, um, development." She cleared her throat and began taking items from the basket she had brought.

Kell awkwardly joined her.

"Most women use sea sponges," Simon's mother explained. "For us around the docks, they're easy to get a hold of and cost almost nothing. There are a few dealers along the docks—Evelyn and Sabina—who can get you exactly what you're looking for. I have a whole basket of them, so you can have these ones."

Kell scrutinized the soft, palm-sized sponges Vera had brought. They came in a variety of neutral colors and appeared to be exceptionally clean. Simon's mother passed her one.

"I've already boiled them. You can reuse them for five or six months before throwing them away. Make sure you keep them clean. You can just boil them for a few minutes. That should take care of everything—"

"What do I do with them?" Kell rolled the sponge in her hands. "Do I just…" She blotted herself a few times and then looked at Vera for validation.

Vera opened her mouth to say something and then sighed. "How much has Tarquin taught you about your body—You know what? Never mind. Let's get you into a belt and then I'll explain."

A few minutes later, Kell found herself sitting on her bare mattress wearing a rather uncomfortable belt that boasted clips along her back and abdomen to keep a washable cloth in place between her legs. Fidgeting in it, she listened as Vera explained female anatomy, menstruation belts, and how to use the sea sponges.

Lying back on her bed, Kell glowered overhead. She was done with the day—and it wasn't yet dawn.

There came a tentative knock on the cabin door, and Tarquin appeared. "We need to head out, Vera. You done here?"

"I am." Simon's mother stood, watching Kell slip into a worn shirt. She looked at Tarquin. "She's a woman now, Tarquin. She shouldn't be hanging around those boys anymore."

"Yours included?"

The woman scoffed and said, "This is just the tip of the iceberg, so to speak. I've promised to find her some bandeaus, but if you're wanting to keep her a secret, she's going to need clothes that don't reveal her bandeau or belt. Those ratty cutoffs she wears hardly cover her ass. I'm surprised she's not been found out yet."

Kell saw Tarquin's gaze darken. "But we're gonna keep it that way, aren't we?"

Vera slipped her basket onto her arm. "Yes, of course"

"Everyone thinkin' she's a boy keeps her safest."

"I'm well aware of the dangers womenfolk face working along the docks, Tarquin. I'm not going endanger dear Kellick. I'm only telling you this because you've done a piss-poor job of preparing her for what is to come." To Kell, she said in a softer tone, "If you need anything, only say it. I'm more than happy to help you or explain anything."

"Thank you, Mrs. Ashway."

Simon's mother winked at her and then left. Tarquin passed by the cabin doorway, waving for her to follow. Kell drew herself up, got dressed, and began helping the man prepare for market day.

2

The Market

TARQUIN MADE A RUN TO the fuel station along the harbor's west side to stock up for the week while Kell, still suffering from cramps, offloaded fish into crates and weighed and organized them for purchase. As the sun crept over the horizon and the skies turned from purple to pink, she felt her mood worsen. She was tired, angry at the injustice of having to suffer such a horrible indignity, and in pain. She wanted to lie down and sleep, but it was market day, and Tarquin needed her.

With stubborn resolve, she pushed through the pain, sometimes pausing as a particularly painful cramp crippled her. She kept her face devoid of emotion for fear others would guess what was happening and pretended that she was counting fish as she crouched along the dock. When Tarquin returned, he passed her hot tea and ordered her to sit and count the crates' contents as he finished her manual labor.

Grateful for the relief the tea brought but annoyed that Tarquin was taking pity on her, once the cup was mostly empty, she returned to work. Per Vera's suggestion, she wore a tatty, short-sleeved shirt that covered her beltline. Even as she strained to carry the crates of fish to the wheeled cart at the end of the dock, Kell became aware of how correct Vera was; she could make out the swell of budding breasts under the relatively thin shirt. She returned to the boat, retrieved a roll of emergency bandages, and bound herself. By the time she finished, she was sweating.

Around six o'clock, Tarquin picked up the loaded cart of fish and started for the market behind a stream of other merchants. Kell followed with a smaller cart, straining against it as she pushed it up the hill. The incline was the worst part of the trip; although it wasn't particularly steep, it was long, and trudging up it while pushing a hundred pounds of fish and fighting the uneven bricks was a challenge.

By the time they reached the top of the hill and turned onto Miller Road, Kell was panting audibly. She, along with several others, rested along the intersection and sipped water. Vera and two other wives distributed morning snacks of hard biscuits with jelly and tea.

"You feelin' all right?" asked Tarquin under his breath as Kell partook of the generous breakfast.

"Yeah, fine," she replied, glancing at Simon who was across the street cheerfully chatting with his father.

"You look, uh, tired."

"Yeah, I just pushed three times my body weight up a hill," Kell snapped. Tarquin busied himself by checking the wheels of his cart. After a moment, she muttered, "Sorry." He nodded but didn't say anything.

They were set up along Donahue Street by seven o'clock with the other merchants. As Kell wrote out the tally board and pricing, Tarquin hurriedly arranged the fish so they appeared aesthetically pleasing to passersby. Across the long street, Simon's family also prepared.

"Ooo, you've got a good selection today," Simon said, jogging over. "Is that swordfish?"

"Got it yesterday," replied Tarquin.

Kell tried to act normally, but her self-consciousness led her to be somewhat standoffish and awkward. As Tarquin turned to speak to a potential customer, Simon leaned into her and said, "You all right? You look rough."

Kell scoffed but tempered her response. "I'm tired. Didn't sleep much." Looking to change the subject, she peered eagerly down the street. "Seems like everyone's here this morning."

For as far as the eye could see along the apartment-lined street, vendors and merchants crowded the sidewalks with carts, trollies, crates, and baskets. Despite the early morning sunshine, the closed-off road teemed with throngs of customers and clients as well as the occasional regulator. The smell of fish was in the air, but the scents of sandalwood, fried foods, and fuel from farther down the street made it tolerable.

The sun was low in the sky but with the apartment flats around them, Donahue Street remained in the morning shadows.

Simon wiped his face and followed her gaze. "Fishin's good right now. The mussels have been at a peak for a few weeks. August market is usually a good one."

Suddenly spotting Hugh lumber into the street a short distance away, Kell asked Simon, "You seen Ambrose this morning?"

"Nah, I haven't. Still hasn't showed, huh?" Simon followed her gaze. "Feel bad for the guy. I know he's tired."

"Come on back over, love," Vera beckoned from across the street.

Simon flashed a smile at Kell. "See you later."

Kell watched him trot back to receive a light cuff from his father who had been trying to haggle with three people at once. Simon immediately turned to one of the customers and began the long-held tradition of aggressive bargaining.

For the next two hours, Kell tended to the large crowds that pressed in around their cart, often shouting over the cacophony to be heard. The street was full of people haggling, greeting one another jovially, and calling out wholesale prices. Market days were always a wild event, and though she loved how much money they earned, the mornings were brutal as families and restaurants fought for the best catches and produce.

Sometime around ten o'clock, a lull finally visited Tarquin's cart and Kell was allowed a few minutes to catch her breath. She was miserably tired, and now that the sun was overhead, she felt sweaty and gross—which was no different than any other day. But she could discern a new odor around her, which made her extremely self-conscious.

Squinting with a grimace at passersby, she considered leaving to go wash herself. But *Polaris* was several blocks away; she couldn't leave Tarquin alone for so long. She would have to tough it out until they returned to the docks.

Her gaze drifted across the street to Simon, who also appeared tired and sweaty. He was perched atop a precarious stack of empty crates. When his eyes found hers, he grinned and glanced at his mother who had her back turned to them. With a jerk of his chin, he jumped off the crates and then ducked past the family cart.

Realizing he was running off to take a break, Kell glanced at Tarquin. Unwilling to leave him without providing some excuse, she said, "I'm going to the toilet."

"Come right back," he replied without looking up from a complex hand-scrawled spreadsheet.

Kell hurried after Simon. She felt Vera's gaze on her as she followed him down the street. Free of her responsibilities, Kell shouted after her friend, legs pumping under her. Simon threw her a cheeky smirk before darting into an alleyway.

She turned down the delivery lane and immediately crashed into him. They both stumbled forward before Simon caught her. Kell turned to clobber him but stopped; Simon's attention was elsewhere. Following his gaze, she realized they weren't alone in the alleyway.

A group of teenage boys had cornered two girls. Kell squared off beside Simon, suddenly aware of how much more power she had because she looked and acted like a boy. The two girls cowering near overflowing trash bins appeared fierce but scared as the four teenagers around them cracked jokes and remarked on their poor-quality clothes.

"Hey!" called Simon, his voice raw with anger.

Deciding then and there that she and Simon were no match for four well-to-do teenagers, Kell sprang forward and pushed through the throng. "There you two are," she said. "Father's looking for you. He's called the regulators."

Kell took one of the girl's hands and passed her a furtive glance. The girl, who was no more than Kell's age, understood and allowed her to lead them through the group of boys. Kell lifted her chin as she passed one of the young men and caught his gaze.

He appeared infuriated that she had interrupted. Though his collared blouse, slacks, embroidered vest, and glossy shoes appeared to be of high quality and marked him as a merchant's son or someone from one of the upper districts, the expression on the young man's face was worn, raw. Purple bags of fatigue hung under his unusual amber eyes; his neatly trimmed black hair emphasized their unsettling color. He held her gaze for a long moment and then coughed theatrically. "Ugh, what's that smell?"

Kell felt her face flush but continued down the alleyway.

"A bunch of filthy fishmongers," the teen cawed. Relieved that *that's* what he was referring to, Kell hurried past Simon who herded the second girl back into the crowded street.

Once they were out of sight, Kell picked up the pace until they were two or three blocks away. Panting, she released the girl and passed an appraising eye over them. "You all right?"

The girl nodded. "Thank you for your help." She nudged her slightly younger companion. They appeared to be sisters.

"Oh, yes, thank you."

"Stay away from the alleyways," Simon said. "Where's your family cart?"

"Just around the corner," the first girl replied. "We can make it." She flashed Kell a smile, thanked them again, and then began weaving with her sister through the crowds.

"Those assholes," Simon cursed. "We coulda taken them."

Kell scoffed. "No, we couldn't have. They were four or five years older than us and had money."

Standing in the middle of the busy street, they watched the two girls disappear around an apartment building.

"Can't wait 'til I'm older," Simon continued. "Tired of not bein' any help to anyone. Can't lift the stupid mussel crates, can't haul in the anchor, can't rescue some scrawny girls—"

Heavy hands fell on their shoulders, startling Kell and Simon from conversation. Both turned to gaze up into the faces of three regulators in starchy, navy uniforms. Fingers moving to the hems of their shirts, one of the regulators, a man with oval glasses, whirled them around. "This them?" he asked, to Kell's horror, the wealthy merchant's son with amber eyes.

"Yes sir, that's them. I'm sure they ditched everything as they were running," the teen replied, his accent crisp. "I've got others who can vouch if you need to talk to them."

In a rage, Simon lunged at the black-haired teen. "You!"

As Simon wrenched the regulator in one direction, Kell ducked backward out of her shirt. At the moment, she didn't care who saw. She was more than scared of regulators; she was terrified. Tarquin had relentlessly hammered into her head the power they wielded and what they did to those they arrested.

For the first time in her life, she abandoned Simon and ran. In a dead sprint, she darted through the throngs of people until she saw Tarquin up ahead speaking with customers. With a whimper, Kell slid into the space beside him and crawled under the cart.

Tarquin was too calm and collected to let her sudden reappearance ruffle him, so he finished his transactions before leaning on the cart and asking, "What happened?"

"They got Simon," Kell managed, her hands shaking. "The regulators. They got Simon."

Tarquin reached under the cart and dragged her out by the arm. "Where? Where are they?" The abrupt change in the tone of his voice scared Kell.

She pointed down the street. "Down around the strawberry vendor."

"Jonathon! Vera!" Tarquin called, his deep voice a boom that seemed to shake the street. Simon's parents looked up, their eyes wide. Tarquin speaking in such a loud voice meant trouble. "Simon! They've got Sim—"

The navy caps of the regulators appeared over the heads of the crowd. Momentarily, they passed through with Simon handcuffed between them.

"Simon!" shouted his father, leaping over their cart and going to the regulators. The people along the street made room for the commotion, some pausing in their shopping to watch the encounter.

"Dad! I *swear* I didn't do anything!" cried Simon. Kell dropped below Tarquin's cart and peered at her friend from behind a fish's gaping mouth. "I swear it!" Her heart hurt hearing his desperation.

"What's he being charged with?" asked Jonathon as Vera and Tarquin joined them in the street.

"Thievery. He had an accomplice, but we can't find him," replied the regulator with spectacles.

Kell noticed Tarquin shift his body to block the man's peripheral view of her. "Simon's no thief."

"I've got four witnesses," the regulator coldly explained.

"No, Dad." Simon strained against the men. "Dad, I'm serious. We're being framed. Me and Kell, we helped these girls that were being ruffed up and then-then, the boys, they—We didn't do anything. We didn't steal anything. They're getting back at us—"

Kell dropped under the cart to look out from between the spokes of the wheel, panting. She had forsaken Simon; she had abandoned him. She should have been out there with him in handcuffs, pleading to Tarquin for help.

"Look, maybe we can work something out," Vera inserted gently, trying to diffuse the situation. "Perhaps you gentlemen require some fresh mussels? Fish even?"

The regulator looked at her abruptly. "Are you trying to bribe us?"

"Oh, God no. He's just a boy," Vera said tearfully. "Please, he's so young. Even if he did steal, it's not worth being arrested, is it?"

"From what we heard, he's a repeat offender," the bespectacled man replied. "If we let him go, he'll just continue."

"This is an outrage!" erupted Simon's father. "You know damn well he's not been thieving. You see us here every month. Why would he—"

"Sir, sometimes kids, especially those of your… background, aren't as well behaved as society would like them." The regulator motioned to his cohorts. "He's going to be booked. You can find him in the Lower District jail."

"No, please!" cried Vera, pulling at the regulator's uniform. "He's a boy. A child!"

"Mom? Dad!" Simon writhed in an attempt to free himself, but the men holding him were far too strong for the fourteen-year-old. His voice cracked. "Dad! Please!"

Kell left her hiding spot, shaking and crying. As the regulators marched Simon down the street, Vera wilted against her cart, sobbing. Jonathon kept pace with the men, arguing with them.

Simon struggled against his captors. At one point, Kell thought that he had managed to free himself, but the regulators grabbed hold of him and dragged him back into their custody. At that moment, his eyes fleetingly found hers. From over his shoulder, he gazed at her, a maelstrom of emotions between them.

"Simon," Kell finally whispered. "No, Simon." Her voice cracked as she started to call him. "Simon!" She staggered from behind their family cart and started numbly after the regulators. The world around her faded. All she could see was Simon looking back at her, tears running down his sweat-laden face. "Simon!"

"Kell, quiet," shushed Tarquin, taking hold of her and leading her back to their cart.

"No!" Kell planted her feet on the bricks to strain against him. "Simon!" she screeched, her voice reaching a new octave.

From deep within, she felt a kind of release followed by a swelling of adrenaline and energy. The windows of the apartments cracked and shattered in a roaring cacophony, causing the people underneath to cower or scatter. Sparks of fire erupted into existence and flitted with purpose to the wooden carts and crates like summertime fireflies. Fire bloomed with wrathful intensity and began consuming everything around it.

Screams and cries of panic rang out as the crowds turned to run.

"He's a User!" someone shouted.

Kell felt Tarquin's meaty arms around her as he hoisted her over his shoulder and started running down Donahue Street back to Miller Road. Horrified, Kell gaped as the fire spread to the apartment flats along the road. Though Tarquin had put distance between them, the heat that radiated from the rampant orange, red, and amber flames was hot.

More windows shattered as fire licked the adjoining apartments and exhausted great blasts of super-heated air. Thick tendrils of black smoke billowed upward to form a solid cloud that blotted out the sun.

Alongside them people ran, jostling one another and dropping precious items of produce and money. Even when they made it to Miller Road, the roar of the fire remained a swelling rumble. Large plumes of brackish smoke filled the air as citizens from neighboring buildings spilled into the streets to gawk.

Sirens from elsewhere within the city roared to life as steam-engine water trucks and bucket brigades clamored toward the inferno. At the bottom of Miller Road, most people who had been fleeing felt they had put enough distance between them and the conflagration to stop to catch their breaths. But not Tarquin.

Kell clutched him as he powered down the rest of the slope and raced to the harbor. His panting was audible and his neck was slick with sweat. The smell of fish and smoke on him was strong. Mouth open, Kell continued to gape at the enormous clouds of smoke that darkened the skies over the Lower District of Eclat.

What had happened? Where had the fire come from? She could hardly comprehend the scale of destruction they had just escaped.

"Tarquin!" shouted Montague from the docks. "What happened?"

Tarquin ran on, his grip on Kell becoming weaker.

"Hey! What's wrong?" Montague called. "What's going on?"

Kell watched over Tarquin's enormous shoulder as the expression on the old man's face deepened in concern. Montague hurried back into the cabin of his fishing boat. By the time they reached *Polaris'* slip, Montague was already zooming out to sea.

Tarquin finally dropped Kell along their dock, wheezing. He panted over his knees for a minute and then ushered her to the boat. "We're puttin' out," he huffed. "Get the ropes."

Shakily, Kell untied the dock ropes and coiled them neatly in their storage bins on the deck as she had done since she was a child. She had hardly stepped back onto *Polaris* before Tarquin revved the engine and gunned it in reverse out of the slip.

Kell leaned against the back wall of the cabin and gazed out at the sea, deeply afraid. Tarquin was always so collected. Nothing fazed him. Even when Henry, who owned the slip next to them, returned from a fishing expedition with half his arm missing, Tarquin had remained unruffled, unbothered. He exuded calm, as though his years as a veteran fisherman had prepared him for everything life could throw at him.

Violent squalls, illness, storm surge, monstrous waves, wind, blood, guts—nothing flustered him. He had always been a stoic rock of a man whose actions spoke louder than his words.

To see her beloved caretaker in such a frenzy frightened Kell and instilled in her a deep sense of dread. On the verge of tears once more, she sank to the deck.

Tarquin whipped *Polaris* around in the harbor with an expert hand and, ignoring the no-wake policies, accelerated hard out of the safety of the wave breaks. At full throttle, they powered through the blue waves due west, clouds of smoke gathering along the Lower District at their backs.

3

Captive

THE SUN WAS HIGH OVERHEAD when Kell finally found the courage to make her way to the wheelhouse. She found Tarquin slumped in the chair at the helm, his chin in his hand and his gaze set on the horizon.

Feeling as though she had done something wrong, Kell carefully approached him. Even from the side, she could discern his distress. His tan, bearded face was taut and his brows creased together. His lips were pulled tight and his body stiff.

Unsure of what to say, Kell quietly cleared her throat.

Tarquin didn't move or acknowledge her.

She shuffled into his periphery, but it became evident that he was lost in thought. "Uh, Tarquin?"

His gaze dropped to the ship's steering wheel before he looked at her. His brown eyes were liquid pools of grief, fear, and worry. Kell felt her throat tighten. "Yeah?" he grumbled.

"Where are we goin'?"

Tarquin drew a slow breath. "Avives."

"What's in Avives? That's a week's journey."

"A sanctuary."

She frowned; she hadn't expected that response. "Why are we goin' to a sanctuary? What's the sanctuary for?"

"For Users." Tarquin looked back out at the sea. "Like you."

Kell stood in silence, her mouth open. "You think I'm a User?"

Tarquin grimly nodded.

"But-but why would you think that? I'm not one of them!" Kell swelled with panic and anger. "Why would you think I'm one of *them*?"

"Because you are, Kellick."

She fell quiet.

Tarquin rubbed his face, suddenly weary, and sighed. "I've been waiting for this day… for years."

"But… why would I be a User? I'm… Kellick. Just Kellick." She looked at him. "My parents—You told me my mom died while working in the textile factory in the Middle District." As she spoke, Tarquin shook his head. "That you were… her brother…"

"I don't know where your mother is. I found you wrapped in a satchel atop some buoys and ropes at the end of my slip." Tarquin took another long breath. "Your mother was being pursued by regulators. I heard the commotion but didn't dare go out. I found you an hour or two later after they dragged her away." He finally looked at her. "I didn't know what to do. You were… an infant, a few months old."

"Maybe… she was a criminal or something," Kell argued half-heartedly, tears blurring her vision.

"It was the night after the Culling started. People were tryin' to get their kids out the city." Through pursed lips, he concluded, "Your mother was no exception."

Kell stifled a sob as she staggered back to the wall. "I'm not a-a User."

"I felt it in you, Kell," Tarquin said. "When I was holdin' you back. I felt it course through you, like some great spark. I almost let you go it scared me so bad."

Kell gaped at the floor. "So… I started the fire? I did… all that?" In her periphery, she saw Tarquin nod as he looked out the wheelhouse glass. "I did that? I did that…" Her voice grew small as she started to cry in earnest.

She had most certainly killed people. Because all the apartment flats, shops, and buildings were so close together, the blaze had spread. Even the brick edifices wouldn't be spared. The flames would consume the Lower District until there was nothing left.

For the next hour, they sat in silence, each in their own thoughts. Eventually, Kell slumped to the floor and slept, overcome with fatigue and emotion.

She awoke midafternoon to Tarquin speaking on the radio. Without moving from her position on the floor, she strained to hear what he was saying over the rumbling of the engine.

"We'll be in around Thursday afternoon should the weather hold, over," he said, pausing with the receiver pressed against his chin.

"All right, look for a chap with a large mustache along the eastern docks, over."

"Thanks, Brooks. Over and out." Tarquin returned the receiver to the dashboard and stayed poised over it in apparent thought.

Kell sat up and started to say something but felt the unpleasant sensation of liquid run around her thighs. Grimacing, she rose and, without looking at Tarquin, hurried to the cabin to take care of herself as Vera had shown her. She rejoined Tarquin later after washing in a bucket on the rear deck and stood beside him for a few silent minutes before finally asking, "What do you want for supper?"

"I don't care," came his somber response. "Whatever."

"Do we have anything left in the hold?"

He shook his head. All their catches, all their hard work, had been left in the cart on Donahue Street.

Kell wandered downstairs to the small ice box they had in the galley. Except for a few wilting greens—the ones she had accused of upsetting her stomach the night before—only condiments and herbs graced the bare inner shelves. Realizing she would need to catch their dinner, she headed for the rear deck and prepped two fishing poles.

The meager meal she managed to put together was eaten in silence that evening with only the hum of the engines to fill the distance between them. Kell wanted to ask more questions about her past but simply couldn't bring herself to broach the subject.

After dinner, she took the helm so Tarquin could bathe. When he returned, she returned the ship to his care. Standing next to the dashboard of simple instruments, she studied the purple horizon and the stars materializing overhead. "So, you're takin' me to a sanctuary in Avives?"

Tarquin nodded.

"Do I get a say in the matter?"

"No." He sat back in his chair and looked at her. "I'm takin' you to Abbey of the Sacred Tree. They only host children. You'll be safe there since it's run by the Church."

Kell leaned on the paneling. "I'm going to be a nun?"

"No, I've heard they'll provide you a safe place to grow up and will teach you." Tarquin frowned, glanced at her hands, and then sighed.

"What? What was that?"

"They only take Users who have been Bound."

"Oh, with those marks on their wrists?"

He nodded.

"Why not just have me Bound then?" asked Kell after a moment. "Just find someone to bind me, that way, I can't be a problem."

"It's not that simple," Tarquin growled, leaning on his elbow. "Bindin' Users is done by the government, usually when someone's born or when they're young. It's a tattoo. Besides, to the capital, you don't exist. You died the night your mother was arrested. I don't have any birth records or proof of name."

"Oh," was all Kell could say.

Tarquin bounced his leg as he thought.

"Do you know what the mark on Users' wrists looks like?" she ventured.

Tarquin nodded, continued to fidget for a moment longer, and then shifted his dark gaze to her. "We can draw it on you."

"But it'll come off."

"And you'll have to draw it back on." He stood and retrieved a well-used inkwell from a nearby drawer. "The mark of a User is two bands on either wrist. Go get one of the basting brushes from the galley."

Kell did as she was told and watched with interest as Tarquin dipped the long-haired brush into the ink and drew a fat but careful band around her left wrist. He had the steady hands of a butcher. He blew on it and then, holding her hand to keep her steady, circumscribed a thin line above the first band.

"It looks like that. You're gonna have to practice with your weak hand because if anyone looks too closely, they'll be able to tell. So, practice steady lines and don't expose your wrists."

A thought occurred to Kell and she looked at him. "Are you goin' to the abbey with me?"

"No. I gotta return to Eclat."

"But why? Why can't you stay with me?" Tears gathered once more in her eyes. Today seemed to be the day for crying.

"Because I'm a fisherman; I'm registered with the harbor master and the Department of Labor and Agriculture, remember? They check us monthly to make sure we're hittin' quotas."

"So? What would happen if you just disappeared?"

"Then my quota would be added to others' and a warrant for my arrest would be put out. I can't do that to our neighbors."

Kell glanced at him sheepishly. "But what if they saw me set the fire? What if someone knew it was because of me? Then they'd come after you for harborin' a User."

Tarquin nodded. "Yeah, they would."

"So, just stay with me! How would they know we didn't sink at sea? We can escape into the countryside or just sail around—"

"And leave Vera and Jonathon? Hugh and Montague? Edmond, Teague, and Lawrence? Let them take the repercuss'ns for me? No way." He scoffed. "I raised you better than that." When tears spilled down her cheeks, he sighed. "Don't cry. If we leave you in Eclat, someone will find out and they'll kill you or worse—take you to the Munera."

"But I can hide," she wept. "I'll hide real good and no one will ever find me."

Tarquin hugged her. "That's the exact reason I'm takin' you to the abbey. There will be someone there to help you. I know it." He squeezed her hard and then motioned her to the rear stairs. "Go on. Get to bed. Your shift starts at two o'clock."

Still sniffing, Kell retired to their shared cabin where she cried herself to sleep.

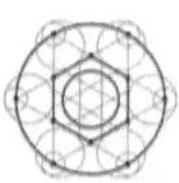

Simon glowered at the other inhabitants of his communal cell. Although the regulators had managed to drag him handcuffed beyond the inferno, they had not been able to safeguard him from the glass that had shattered over their heads. He sported varying degrees of cuts on his arms and a particularly nasty gash along his left cheek that had finally stopped bleeding. Without proper care, the laceration would scar.

The seven others in the cell with him had been brought in for a variety of grievances. What crimes they had committed didn't concern him. The two captives bearing black ink bands on their wrists, however, greatly worried him.

The two Users appeared bedraggled as they were clothed in rags. It was obvious they had been living in the ghettos, the shanty towns west of the docks that were known to house Users. They wore dirt and grime like a second skin and were so malodorous that Simon sought refuge in his shirt, which was heavy with smoke. Though they didn't appear dangerous, Simon knew they could easily kill any of them if they wanted.

Slumping against the wall, he recounted the events of the day, reviewing the most confusing pieces repeatedly.

How had Kell escaped the regulators?

What had caused the apartment windows to shatter?

How had the fire started?

Evening fell and the hustle and bustle outside the Lower District jail quieted. He waited for something akin to supper, but the cell's residents were offered nothing. Afraid, anxious, and angry, Simon withdrew into himself. His parents should have already been there to bail him out.

A thought occurred to him that made tears spring to his eyes. What if they hadn't escaped the fire? What if that was why they hadn't come? Simon wiped his eyes, determined not to let the others see him cry. When that didn't work, he pulled his knees to his chest and hid his face in his arms. There, he let the tears come, silent and heavy.

He didn't sleep that night. He couldn't. The jail cell was too humid and cramped. The weak fan that cooled the space creaked as it spun but not in a rhythmic way so as to lull Simon to sleep. It was sporadically noisy and offered little relief from the heat of the evening. Simon spent most of his time crying. He was glad when he heard a few other sniffles in the tense quiet of the night.

The following day was much of the same. They received two other people, but no visitors graced the facility. The captives were given half-rotten potatoes and wrinkled apples for lunch and nothing else for the day.

That evening, two of the prisoners began begging for water. Simon refused to be one of those poor souls. If he was going to die, he would do it with dignity. He wouldn't give the regulators the satisfaction of seeing him plead.

Later, the man seated beside Simon turned to taunting the Users. Simon wished he would shut up, but his neighbor continued, saying, "You could just bust us out of here. All of us. That's what you got that devil magic for, right?" The woman nearest the bars shushed him.

The next morning, the cell's captives were startled awake by a booming voice. Simon, who had finally dozed off sometime shortly before dawn, frowned and squinted against the harsh light that now streamed into the jail. Fresh air wafted through the small facility, providing much-needed relief from the odors within.

Simon, who was seated near the rear of the cell, watched as a burly man dressed in a starchy regulator uniform walked in, his cap under his arm. He carried a steaming cup of coffee whose aroma spread through the stale space. Simon had learned the day prior that the lieutenant was a relatively fair person as the officer had prevented one of his subordinates from abusing the Users. Of course, that didn't make Simon like him anymore, but it was good information to know.

The lean and grizzled man who followed the lieutenant, however, made Simon recoil. The predatory look in his keen, blue eyes frightened him. The tall man wore a knee-length brown vest over wrinkled pants and scuffed boots and nothing else. His tan chest and muscled arms were toned and bore shades of scars.

The lieutenant stepped before the cell. The lanky man joined him, rubbing his stubbly chin as he appraised the prisoners. "Well?" the officer asked.

The newcomer looked the prisoners over. When his eyes found Simon, Simon looked away. "I see some possibilities. Anyone come for them?"

"You know they haven't," the regulator replied.

"I'll give you three hundred for the lot of them."

"Naw, come on, Dockett. They're worth more than that." The lieutenant sipped his coffee. "We got two Users there."

"Yeah, street urchins. Why don't your mates pick up something of a higher class?"

"Like what?" asked the lieutenant coldly.

"I don't know. Something with more," Dockett waved a hand, "life. You bring me this shit—How is this supposed to entertain thousands? Look at 'em." Dockett leaned against the bars, his gaze falling on Simon once more. "But I see some potential in there." He sighed. "Four hundred. Final offer."

The lieutenant sighed. "Fine, yeah."

His eyes lingering on Simon, Dockett followed the lieutenant out of the jail to the front lobby.

"They're taking us to the Munera," a man across the cell whispered. "We're going to be in the games."

A shiver ran through Simon as he realized that his cellmate was right. No one had come for them which meant they wouldn't be missed. They were perfect candidates for the Munera.

A few hours later, a group of regulators accompanied by some swarthy characters returned. The cell door was pushed open, and the lieutenant ordered everyone to form a line. Once they were handcuffed in heavy shackles, the imprisoned were led single-file out of the cell, through the lobby, and onto the short staircase out front where the rear gate of a large truck welcomed them.

Although Simon squinted against the harsh August sun, he relished the freedom it instilled in him. It made him want to make a break for it.

Others must have felt the same because, in the next instant, one of the Users lunged from the line through the detail of scarred men. As the grungy prisoner staggered down the stairs, he raised a fist toward the guards. A puff of fire, like oil lighting in a burning pan, erupted briefly from his palm, causing the guards to dodge. The User ran.

Alarmed, Simon crouched behind the man in front of him. He could feel the heat on his face. The other prisoners also cowered in fear as they pulled away from the line to escape the heat of the attack. But the leathery guards seemed unfazed. Aside from avoiding the assault, they hadn't left their positions.

Movement in the back of the truck drew Simon's eye to Dockett. The tall man observed the escapee with annoyed patience and then sighed. "All right, go get 'em."

Two of his cohorts left their ranks, dashing after the User. Simon watched with morbid curiosity as they gave chase and easily tackled the User to the street. Although small plumes of fire tore through the air around them, the men appeared to be experts in what they did. A few minutes later, the User was returned to the line, worse for the wear.

"Yep," Dockett muttered. "All righty, let's get to it." He motioned to the first prisoners who clambered onto the truck's gate and trudged to the benches along the cabin's walls.

With each step, Simon considered running. He was faster than the User. He could disappear into an alleyway and slink into the shadows. He knew the streets better than them. As he approached the truck's gate, his body quivered in indecisiveness. This might be his only time to escape. The regulators had gone back inside and Dockett's guards appeared distracted.

Now, he would do it *now*.

Simon glanced at Dockett, expecting to see the lanky man pacing the innards of the truck. Instead, he met Dockett's eyes and Simon knew he had been caught.

"Yeah," Dockett said. "That's what I thought. Come on, kid. Up ya go."

Tears of frustration, humiliation, and anger filled Simon's eyes as he clambered into the truck. Because he was shorter than the adults and his hands were cuffed, he had a hard time with it. Dockett dragged him by the shirt collar and then pushed him roughly to a bench. Once everyone was seated, the man closed the gate and pulled the curtain down along the top.

The truck roared to life and took off, jarring its occupants into one another. As Dockett held onto a handle on the ceiling and surveyed his new captives, Simon tried to catch glimpses of the outside world beyond the rippling canvas curtain. How much of the Lower District had burned? Where were his parents? Had they survived? Where was Kell? What was he doing?

Stressed, weak, and angry, Simon sat back against the uncomfortable wooden beams of the truck's cabin. When it became apparent that they weren't getting out any time soon, he slumped against his neighbor and slept.

It was just before noon when the truck finally puttered to a stop. Beyond the curtain that Dockett lifted, Simon saw exquisite buildings of marble, gray brick, and fine wood as well as a beautifully kept avenue lined with gorgeous shade trees and bright gold and magenta flowers.

Dockett clambered out, returning the truck's occupants to the hot, dark cabin. Simon wiped his face and grimaced as he touched the dried blood along the gash on his cheek.

A few minutes later, the tailgate of the truck was pulled down and the curtains drawn aside. Simon could hear men talking but couldn't see them.

Instead, he gazed out at the otherworldly realm they seemed to have entered. Others also stood to gape at the luxury that was the Upper District of Eclat.

Instead of rusting automobiles that creaked and groaned and made any number of horrible sounds as they hummed along, glistening vehicles cruised by in near silence. Full baskets of petunias, lantanas, and verbena hung from buildings and along even the alleyway entrance where the truck had parked.

As Simon approached the gate, his eyes went skyward, following the grand gray-brick walls that extended countless stories overhead. The air smelled sweet, possibly of vanilla?

Utterly bewitched by the utopia into which he had stepped, he didn't realize the prisoners were being sorted until rough hands pulled him to a stop beside the truck.

"Put him with the other kids," a man with a clipboard said.

"No," called Dockett from the front of the truck. "He's with me. Put him with mine."

Clipboard Man shrugged and then motioned Simon toward Dockett. Swallowing, Simon hurried over to the two other captives Dockett had claimed—the man who had first said they were being taken to the Munera and a middle-aged woman with frizzy brown hair.

After a few minutes of chatting with his cohorts, Dockett started down the alleyway toward a pair of metal doors that appeared to be the side entrance of the adjacent building. Though the man had not said anything, it was implied that Simon and the other two prisoners were to follow.

Beyond the metal doors was a plethora of winding corridors illuminated by harsh fluorescent lighting. At first relieved to be in cool air, Simon quickly grew cold as his adrenaline faded. When Dockett ushered them out the back of the building, goose pimples spread across Simon's skin as the sunlight warmed him.

Behind the ornate edifice and situated behind enormous walls was a quaint courtyard that boasted stained wooden benches, beautiful trees loaded with lemons, and flowerbeds of well-maintained lavender. The aroma was intoxicating and uplifting. Mouth agape, Simon looked about in awe.

Sensing someone's gaze, he looked at Dockett who appeared amused. Realizing that perhaps he had given away too much information, Simon closed his mouth and rested his face in a stoic expression. Dockett grinned before leading them through an ivy-adorned archway on the other side of the courtyard. An older man wearing a forest green button-down shirt and black slacks met them in the doorway.

"You two," said Dockett, motioning to the other two captives, "go with him." To the senior newcomer, Dockett added, "They're in groups three and four."

The old man bowed to Dockett. "Yes sir."

"Send for Madam Parthemos as well. We'll be in the courtyard."

"Of course, sir."

The female prisoner passed Simon a fleeting look of fear and concern as she was led down an intersecting corridor. Dockett watched them leave before turning and heading back toward the courtyard.

Once the lanky man flopped himself onto the nearest polished bench, Simon took the time to further study his surroundings. He couldn't yet discern where they were, though it was obvious he had been taken to the Upper District of Eclat. Were they at a private residence? Or perhaps a government building? He had never seen a government building or a residence of such opulence, so both options seemed plausible.

"What's your name, kid?" asked Dockett.

Simon turned to regard him with disdain. "Why?"

"Because I asked."

"Simon Ashway."

"And how old are you?"

"Fourteen."

Dockett passed an appraising eye over him. "What'd you get arrested for?"

A soft breeze rustled the branches of the lemon trees, causing Simon to turn to look at them. "Some rich snobs framed me and my friend. Told the regulators we were stealing." He looked back at Dockett. "I'm no thief."

"So, what are you, boy?"

Simon considered him before answering, "Just Simon."

Dockett gestured to his face. "What happened?"

"Windows exploded or something before the Saturday market went up in flames. Regulators saved me from the fire but not the glass." Simon met his gaze. "What's your name?"

Dockett scoffed. "Naw, that's not how this relationship is gonna work. See, I picked you out and, if Madam Parthemos approves, I'm about to become your Lanista."

Simon frowned. "Lanista?"

"Even you street filth have heard—"

"I'm not street filth!" Simon interrupted.

Fury flashed in Dockett's eyes, and he stiffened like he was going to leap to his feet. After a moment, however, he relaxed and chuckled. "That attitude's either gonna get you killed… or get you applause."

"What?"

"As I was sayin', you've heard of the Munera, right?"

"Those stupid games where people kill each other?"

Dockett pointed at him. "And become rich."

Simon eyed him.

"Look, rich folk don't like to watch kids kill each other. It's no fun. They've got no skill or strength. So—"

"So what?"

Dockett stood, raised a long leg, and with a swift kick, caught the chain between Simon's shackles, dropping him to the ground hard. "Interrupt me one more time, boy, and I'll end your career right here."

"I hope *I* am allowed to interrupt you," came a melodic voice.

Dockett stepped back to allow Simon to stand. Fresh blood ran down Simon's reopened face wound; his arms and elbows bore stinging scrapes. Dockett bowed and politely greeted the woman, "Madam Parthemos."

Simon wiped off the blood running down his cheek with his shoulder and looked at the newcomer. With hair as black as a raven's wing and supple, ivory skin, Madam Parthemos was the most beautiful woman he had ever set eyes on. She wore a champagne-colored, floor-length dress that boasted numerous buttons along the spine and a light purple sash. Atop her head was a wide-brim hat adorned with fresh lavender and a matching ribbon. Her silky black hair was knotted in an elegant updo along the nape of her neck.

"Oh, Lord Dockett, always so polite." Madam Parthemos moved her stunning hazel eyes to Simon. "If you damage the property before it gets here, it's not worth as much."

"The damage happened before us picking him up." Dockett shrugged. "He probably got into a knife fight or something—"

"I told you, all the windows around us exploded," Simon interrupted before he could stop himself. Realizing his immediate error, he clamped his mouth shut and looked between Madam Parthemos and Dockett.

"Oh, I see." Madam Parthemos approached him. "You're wanting to take this one on, aren't you?"

"Is it that obvious?" asked Dockett sheepishly.

Madam Parthemos bent down to Simon's level. Her sweet, almost cloying, perfume wafted over him. "How do you know you won't kill this one?"

Simon blanched and looked at Dockett who was grinning. "I just have a gut feeling about him," the lanky man replied.

A smile crossed the woman's face. "Very well." She straightened herself and returned to Dockett. "You may have him. He pleases me."

Dockett bowed deeply. "Thank you. I won't let you down."

"See that you don't." She turned to leave.

Once she left, Dockett leveled an excited smile at Simon. "You're gonna make me rich, kid."

4

Avives

KELL PACED THE REAR DECK of *Polaris*, her gaze searching the horizon for something, though she knew not what. Their journey to Avives had been uneventful but tense. There was much she wanted to ask Tarquin, yet she couldn't bring herself to approach him.

She felt distant from the man and painfully alone. She didn't know what to expect in Avives—and neither did Tarquin. Supposedly, someone was going to meet them and take her to the sanctuary.

The last time she would see Tarquin would be at the docks. That terrified her and brought tears to her eyes every time she thought of it.

They would be in Avives by the afternoon.

"You packed?" asked Tarquin, emerging from the cabin.

"Yeah." Kell jumped onto one of their crabbing cages and seated herself there.

Tarquin watched her and then looked out at the blue waters. "I'm gonna," he cleared his throat, "miss you."

Unable to say anything or else she'd start to cry, Kell just nodded.

The large man lumbered awkwardly across the deck to her. "It's time you made your way in the world."

"At thirteen?" scoffed Kell, eyes misty.

"Uh, well…" Tarquin swallowed visibly. "You know what I mean."

There was a long moment of silence between them before Kell said, "I'll come back to you."

Tarquin fidgeted with a rope knotted around the side of the cage.

"I promise it. I'll come back to you. And I'll find Simon."

"Kell, don't be makin' promises you can't keep, all right? Life's got a way of plantin' you on courses you never knew you'd be followin'."

Kell hung a leg off the cage. "What happens if I can't learn to control the fire?"

"You will."

"But what if I can't?"

"Have faith in yourself." Tarquin held his hand out and helped her down. The moment her feet touched the deck, he swept her into an enormous embrace, squeezing her like his heart was about to explode.

Kell made a conscious effort to keep from bursting into sobs as she hugged him back.

A few hours later, they slowed to enter Nianola Landing, which was a bustling harbor filled with local and commercial fishing boats coming and going. The harbor was lined with predominantly whitewashed buildings that stood out against the vivid azure of the surrounding seas. Compared to Drayburns Harbor in the Lower District of Eclat, the waterfront was picturesque and beautifully quaint.

"Have you been here before?" Kell asked, leaning on the forward paneling in the wheelhouse.

"Just once, years ago. The buildin's weren't white though. Heard there was a pandemic a while ago. They whitewashed the buildin's with limestone to help get rid of it. Limestone kills disease." Tarquin scrutinized the harbor. "I'll bring us 'round to the eastern docks. Brooks said we're supposed to be meetin' someone named Alekos."

Kell drew a long breath. She didn't want to tell him she was scared. Tarquin had always taught her to overcome her fears, to look them in the face and charge forward, determined and unwavering. "Don't write," she finally said. Tarquin glanced at her. "You'll put yourself in danger."

The enormous man nodded, but Kell saw him purse his lips beneath his beard.

As they motored past dozens of boats, big and small, all of which were in far better condition than those at Drayburns Harbor, Kell retrieved her tattered duffle bag from their shared bunk. She hadn't packed much, just clothes, the feminine products Vera had given her, some rope, a knife, the ink and its inkwell, a fine brush, and a few toiletries.

Dressed in her usual cutoffs, a lightweight, long-sleeved shirt, and boat shoes, she appeared like any other dock boy. The fact that she had wrapped her breasts with the spare bandages they carried would remain a secret, at least until they were off the docks and at the abbey.

Lithely, she stepped off the boat and drew the dock ropes out of their designated buckets. With expert hands, she tied off *Polaris* and then retrieved her bag. Tarquin joined her as they disembarked.

A squat and tan middle-aged man with neat, black hair met them at the end of the dock. Dressed in the black habit of a clergyman, he appeared both regal and alarmingly stern. "Tarquin Fisk?"

"Yes sir, that's me." Tarquin offered his enormous hand.

"I'm Father Alekos Legotis. Is this the child?"

Tarquin placed protective, heavy hands on Kell's shoulders. "This is Kellick Fisk. My… nephew."

Father Legotis held his hand out to Kell. The moment Kell's palm was in his, he lifted her sleeve to reveal her wrist. Kell snapped her hand from the father's grip. "Good," Father Legotis said, "He's Bound."

"The climate's not too good in Eclat right now," Tarquin explained. "It's my understandin' that you can take him in and provide for him 'til he's older. That right?"

"Yes, so long as he contributes to the abbey, he should have no problem settling in." Father Legotis passed an appraising eye over Kell before turning to Tarquin. "As you discussed with Brooks, no mention of your or Kell's arrival will be made. You were never here."

Tarquin nodded. "Is there anything else I need to send with him?"

The father folded his hands behind his back. "Just his personal belongings. If all works out well, he'll be with us for a while."

"Oh, very good." Tarquin gestured to Kell and pulled her away from the father who politely turned his attention elsewhere. Tarquin lowered himself to her level. "Taught you to take care of yourself, I did. I'm not afraid; you shouldn't be either." He swept her into another hug.

Kell cherished his strength and the familiar smell. "I'll come back to you."

"Take care of yourself."

"Ready?" asked Father Legotis.

Kell gathered her bag and followed him off the docks. When she looked back, Tarquin was untying the dock ropes. Kell saw him aggressively swipe at his eyes.

"Kellick, that's an interesting name. Where's it from?" the father kindly asked as they walked along the wooden docks to the cobblestone road beyond.

"Don't know. My uncle didn't say."

"Isn't there a type of anchor called a kellick anchor?"

Kell smiled. "Yeah, there is."

"When you address a senior, you will speak properly and address them with sir or ma'am."

"Oh… all right."

Father Legotis glanced at her.

"Yes, sir."

To her surprise, the clergyman led her to a black, well-maintained automobile parked along the cobblestone road. He held the door open for her, and Kell slid into the front seat. Excited, she looked about eagerly. She had not once sat inside an automobile before. A horse cart, yes. A motorized vehicle, no. It smelled of polished leather.

Father Legotis got in, reversed the car, and then headed north from the harbor. Kell admired the whitewashed buildings, the menagerie of colorful flowers, and the vibrant blue and yellow murals that adorned the fronts of some of the shops.

"What made your uncle decide that now was the time to bring you here?"

Kell glanced at the clergyman. "Oh, the, uh, Munera was recently announced. So, that means the regulators have been lookin' to snatch people."

"What do you mean 'snatch?'" Father Legotis seemed genuinely concerned.

"The regulators have a quota to fill to supply the Munera with, uh… Users. So, they go around the Lower District lookin' for anyone doin' anything wrong. People's been goin' missin'."

"People *have* been going missing," corrected the father. "Well, that's concerning, to say the least. Your uncle was wise to reach out to us. Not many people know we take in Users. Have you had many problems with controlling your temper?"

Alarmed by the news, Kell hesitated. Is that what had happened?

"Ah, I see. That's fine." Father Legotis turned onto a brick street and continued down an avenue. "Many children who come to us have a hard time controlling their tempers. We'll make sure you won't be a danger."

"Oh, thanks."

"Thank you," the father corrected once more.

"Thank you, Father."

After some small talk about the recent weather and a delicious meal the father had recently partaken of, he pulled the vehicle into the round driveway of a grand, steepled building with enormous stained-glass panels. Kell pressed her face against the vehicle's window to gawk at the flying buttresses and arches. The surrounding grounds were manicured but austere. She had never seen anything like it.

Father Legotis led her not through the enormous front doors but through a hidden side entrance. From there, he ushered her into a small lobby, down a narrow breezeway, and into an adjoining building situated behind the magnificent church.

"We already have a room prepared for you. You'll be sharing it with two other boys. I'm sure they'll be glad for your company," Father Legotis explained over his shoulder.

Kell grimaced. Living in close quarters with other boys was going to be difficult. "Uh, Father?"

The clergyman paused in step to look at her.

"I'm… a girl."

Father Legotis appeared utterly shocked as he studied her face and then passed an eye over her shapeless body. "Oh… I—Hmm—I'm sorry. Your uncle said—"

"It's easier to be a boy around the docks than a girl," Kell explained.

"I see. Yes, I suppose it would be. My apologies. Allow me to—Oh, Freesia!" The father stopped a passing teenage girl with long, blond hair. Kell noticed that she had black bands tattooed on her wrists. "Would you tell Sister Lyla that we're in need of another bed in the girl's dorm?"

"Yes, Father."

As Freesia hurried off, Father Legotis led Kell down another corridor to a closed door. He opened it with a key and stepped aside to allow Kell to enter. "This is my office. Should you need anything while staying here, you need only to stop by."

The office was stately. Its walls were decorated with portraits of other clergymen as well as landscape paintings. Burgundy drapery framed an enormous arched window situated behind a polished mahogany desk that was cluttered with piles of papers. Large bookshelves that rose to the ceiling showcased a variety of books, manuals, and records.

"Let me just gather some more information about you and then I'll take you to the girls' dorm." Father Legotis seated himself in the plush chair behind his desk, picked up a pair of reading glasses, and began rifling through papers. Once he found what he was looking for, he drew an inkwell near him, dipped a pen, and looked at her. "What's your full name again?"

"Kellick Fisk," she replied.

"And you are how old?"

"Thirteen."

"Birthday?"

"May 15."

"Eh, what are the names of your mother and father?"

"I don't know. My uncle never told me. They died when I was very young."

"Ah, I see. My condolences." He scribbled on the paper. "And you were Bound when you were born or shortly thereafter?"

Kell frowned. "What do you mean?"

The father gestured to her wrists.

"Oh! Oh, yes. The week after."

"Mh-hm." Father Legotis continued to write for a minute before asking, "You worked with your uncle? He's a fisherman, correct?"

"Yes."

"Commercial or private?"

"Private."

"Life must have been tough making ends meet."

"Oh, uh, yes. It's been hard." Kell wasn't sure how much she should reveal, although it no longer seemed to matter.

Father Legotis read through several other papers, writing as he went, before setting them aside and going to the next. There seemed to be a lot of paperwork. Eventually, he set his pen aside and sat back. "All right, let's get you to the girls' dorm."

After locking his office, he ushered her down a passageway lined with windows into the next building. Up a flight of stairs and down a hallway they went until he stopped at a closed door. The father knocked tentatively; a woman replied. "Uh, yes?"

Father Legotis swung the door open to reveal a rustic office. Everything was light and open. A cushioned bench on the other side of the room accompanied by a lamp presented a fine reading corner. Plants of varying species hung in baskets and cluttered the floor near the enormous window on the east side of the room.

Behind a small, white desk sat a mousy woman with dark brown hair which was partially covered by a white veil. Seeing them, she stood with a soft smile. She was plump and had a way about her that made Kell gravitate to her. "And who is this young man, Father?"

"This young *woman*," corrected the father, "is Kellick Fisk. She's your new student."

"Oh! Goodness, please forgive me. I thought—You know, you look just like a boy." Sister Lyla stepped around her desk to reveal the long and plain petal pink dress that she wore. "Kellick, it's so very nice to meet you."

"Thanks, you too," replied Kell.

Father Legotis cleared his throat.

"Oh, uh, it's nice to meet you too," Kell corrected, glancing at him.

"Kellick will be staying with you for the foreseeable future. I'm sure you'll treat her like one of our own." Father Legotis passed a terse smile to Kell and then left.

"Oh, I'm so happy you've been able to join us, Kellick—"

"Kell, just call me Kell."

"My apologies. Kell."

Kell flushed, feeling guilty for having corrected such a sincere and utterly pleasant person. "It's fine."

"Come. Let's get you settled. You don't have to work tonight since it's your first day." Sister Lyla led Kell down the hall. "Everyone is expected to work here. In the mornings, before classes, you are to complete your assigned chores. After classes conclude in the afternoons, you may have free time before supper."

The sister stopped at a room at the end of the hallway and knocked.

"Yes?" came the reply.

"It's Sister Lyla. I have your new roommate," the sister called through the door.

The door opened to reveal a girl of perhaps fifteen. She peered at them through the tops of her brows, her head turned downward. Her enormous brown eyes reflected distrust.

"Kellick—I mean, Kell—this is Tori. She's from Eclat like you."

Tori looked between Kell and Sister Lyla and then said in a timid voice, "I'm sorry, Sister, but I'm not comfortable rooming with a boy."

"I'm not a boy," replied Kell. "See?" She lifted her shirt to reveal the bandages wrapped around her chest. Tori stepped away as Sister Lyla modestly pushed down Kell's shirt.

Sister Lyla smiled. "It's true. Kell is a girl. Father Legotis already vetted her. She's also Bound, like you."

Tori watched them from a few steps away and then, without saying anything, retreated farther into the room.

Sister Lyla opened the door. "So, this is where you'll be staying, Kell. I know it's small. I've been asking Father—"

"This is *wonderful*!" declared Kell, spinning in the middle of the room. Sister Lyla was right, of course. The room was small, but it was bigger than anything Kell had ever lived in, especially the cramped cabin she had shared with Tarquin all her life.

On one side of the room were two bunk beds. The top appeared to have been taken by Tori, so Kell assumed she would be assigned the bottom bunk. On the other side were two small oak desks and narrow bookcases already supplied with books, notebooks, inkwells, pens, and paper. A two-pane window took up most of the far wall, allowing natural light to illuminate the room. A single oak chest stood in the corner with a side panel large enough to hang a few articles of clothing. Although the floor—also oak—was mildly scuffed and worn, to Kell, it made her feel sophisticated.

"Oh, I'm glad you like it so," said Sister Lyla. "Well, I'll let you two get acquainted. Kell, if there's anything that you need, please don't hesitate to reach out to me. Supper is at five-thirty." She gave a little wave to Tori and then left, closing the door behind her.

Kell set her bag on her bed and walked around the room, delighted. It felt so fancy! Grinning, she turned to Tori who watched her from her desk. "Isn't this great? We came from Eclat and we're here!" Kell beamed. "I wish Tarquin was here. He'd like this. Simple but nice. He'd even fit in the bed—"

"Great?" interrupted Tori.

Kell stopped and looked at her.

"This is a prison." The girl looked at her fingers as she picked a cuticle. "You'll see."

"But… they're so nice."

"Yeah."

Her mood dampened, Kell sat on her bed. "What kind of stuff do you do here… that you don't like?"

Tori met her gaze, again through her brows, never fully raising her head. "You'll see."

5

New Lives

DINNER WAS A FEAST AND consisted of baked chicken, roast carrots and spinach, potatoes, and bread. Kell fell on the food with manners most unbecoming of a school-age girl but paid no attention to the horrified looks the others passed her. Once she helped clean off the tables, she took a gloriously hot shower, repainted her fake handcuffs along her wrists, snuggled into bed, and slept—hard.

The following morning after she dressed in her usual cutoffs and shirt, she followed Tori and some of the other girls downstairs to the rear courtyard where Sister Lyla assigned morning chores. Having already been awake for a few hours since she was on a fisherman's schedule, Kell was glad to have something to do.

Over the next hour, she swept, mopped, and polished the wooden floors, pleased that her bucket didn't slide around as it usually did when she was wiping down *Polaris'* decks. While she worked, she observed the other students. They didn't seem particularly unhappy or downtrodden. Some even joked and laughed as they went about their chores. But every once in a while, she would glimpse someone lost in thought, staring up at the sky or blankly looking across the expansive grounds. Determined to make the most out of her new home, Kell chalked up the behavior to coincidence.

After chores were completed, everyone headed to class. Both male and female students were schooled together, though they were separated by age. When she found herself in a classroom of twelve to fourteen-year-olds, she sat next to a group of talkative boys whose lively conversation immediately ended.

She grinned. "I'm Kell. What're your names?"

The pre-teens looked at her with a mixture of distrust, confusion, and alarm. "Are you… We haven't seen you around the boy's dorm. Are you new?" said one.

"Oh, I, uh," Kell glanced at the girls, "yeah, I'm new."

The boy who had asked shrugged and held out his hand. "I'm Mordecai. This is Mason and Fletcher."

Mordecai was a handsome boy of perhaps fourteen. He was just becoming gangly with arms and legs that seemed too long for his body. A mop of black hair hung over his brows, shading blue eyes. Though his face had yet to take on the squareness of adulthood, his features were pleasant to look at.

"Where're you from, Kell?" he asked.

"Eclat, the Lower District."

Mordecai nodded in understanding and then gestured to the taller boy named Mason. "He's from the Lower District as well."

Kell glanced around the room and found some of the girls watching and whispering. "So, what's the deal with this place?" She nodded toward Mordecai's banded wrists. "Do they teach you how to control—"

She noticed the boys shift uncomfortably. Mordecai's eyes slipped to the classroom door. He leaned toward her and said, "We don't talk about that here."

Kell glanced at the other boys. "But I had heard they were going to teach us—"

"Sshh," Mason hissed. They all looked back at the door once more before Mordecai continued.

"No, not control it. Suppress it." He sat back. "Don't mention it, don't bring it up. And *don't* lose your temper," the boy said, his gaze meeting hers.

Heart starting to race, Kell whispered, "Why? What happens?"

"The Vault."

"What's the Vault—"

"Good morning," chimed Sister Lyla as she strode into the classroom wearing a light blue, button-down dress with a white collar and long sleeves.

Their conversation over, Kell hesitantly sat back, unease stirring in her gut.

She had never had a formal education, so it came as no surprise when she grew bored the moment Sister Lyla began writing words on the chalkboard at the front of the well-lit room and explaining their Latin and Greek origins. Tarquin had made sure Kell knew how to read and write and do basic math, but she had never had the patience for much else. Slumped beside Mordecai, she grew restless.

Fletcher, who was seated across from her, gently kicked her under the table to get her attention and then motioned for her to sit up. With a sigh, Kell straightened herself but began slouching again within two minutes.

"Kellick?" called Sister Lyla, her hand paused on the board. "Am I boring you?"

"Oh, I, uh, never did this school stuff. I guess I'm not used to it."

Sister Lyla relaxed and gave a pleasant smile. "I'm sure you'll grow accustomed to it. In the meantime, please show your classmates and this classroom respect and sit up."

"All right—Uh, yes ma'am."

Kell did her best to stay focused, but after an hour of listening to Sister Lyla lecture, she simply couldn't take it anymore. She needed to be moving; she had done manual labor all her life. Sitting for hours made her body stiff.

Two hours in, Kell stood quietly. Though Sister Lyla had her back to the classroom as she wrote mathematical equations, other students watched Kell, wide-eyed. Mordecai motioned fervently for her to sit; in response, Kell pointed to her aching back and made a face. She moved to the rear of the room and began to stretch.

"Now, when we see a letter in combination with numerals," said Sister Lyla, turning around, "we know that that letter is acting as a represent—Kell, what are you doing?"

"Don't mind me. I can't stay seated for so long," Kell replied nonchalantly. The students whipped back around to Sister Lyla to see how she would react. "Is that all right?"

The sister smiled. "Physical exercise is always encouraged here, however, it's best we do it within designated times and places." She gestured politely. "Please, take your seat."

Kell begrudgingly returned to her chair. "What time do classes end?"

"They end when they end," Sister Lyla replied with a sweet smile.

Kell raised a hand as she had seen others do but didn't wait for the sister to call upon her. "I'm sorry, but what's the point of all this? Just sittin' here, listenin'?"

Quiet gasps erupted around the classroom.

Sister Lyla set her book aside and leaned on her desk, the smile on her face never faltering. "To educate the next generation, to teach you discipline, and to expose you to the world."

"But what does all of this stuff have to do with the work we'll eventually be doin'? It's just numbers and letters and old stuff. Why do we need to know it?"

"So you can become well-rounded adults," the sister replied.

Kell glanced at Mordecai. "All right, sorry."

Sister Lyla gazed at her for a moment longer before returning to instructing. Both Mordecai and Fletcher shook their heads at her, wild smiles on their faces. Kell wondered what she had done.

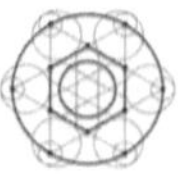

Panting, Simon glowered at Dockett. He was more than irritated; he was furious. Now that he knew the swarthy man planned to take him under his tutelage and train him for upcoming games, Simon felt he could unleash righteous anger upon his keeper. The only problem was that he couldn't land a single blow on the man.

Dockett nonchalantly twirled a Bo staff of unfinished rattan wood before resting it across his shoulders. "For some reason, I thought you'd be faster. What do you think they're gonna be doing, boy? Standing there, waiting for you to attack?"

Simon wheezed over his knees and then straightened himself. He was covered in a fine layer of sweat and dirt. More than once, Dockett had rolled him across the practice courtyard situated along the western side of Madam Parthemos' vast residence.

With a steadying breath, Simon began circling Dockett, hands bared in loose fists. If he could just slug the lanky man once, he could die happy. Dockett wasn't an abjectly evil individual, but the humbling beatings he dispensed enraged Simon. For two days now, Simon had been trying to land a hit on him. Yet Dockett had fended him off in every instance. Already Simon had tried to goad him into dropping the Bo staff, but Dockett had dismissed his banter.

"Come on," chided Dockett. "The crowd's getting bored. You take this long in the real thing, they're going to turn against you."

Simon darted toward Dockett. The man swung with his staff, but Simon evaded it by ducking. He made it one step closer before the Bo staff came spinning from the other side and whacked him along the side of his head.

Simon crumpled to the dirt, purple and black stars flashing in his vision. He woke a second later but kept his eyes closed. He heard Dockett sigh and then start to walk toward him, the sound of his boots crunching on the hot dirt. Head still spinning but determination swelling, Simon readied himself.

Dockett stopped beside him, waited a moment, and then gave him a solid kick to the hip. "Come on, kid. Wake it up."

Muscles coiling within him, Simon rolled onto his back, intertwined his feet with Dockett's knees, and kicked. Dockett went down, but not before smacking Simon across the face with the staff. The burning sensation that accompanied the blow was the last thing he remembered.

He woke up shortly thereafter to water being poured on his face. With a gasp, he sat up—and then rolled over and vomited into the dirt. When he finished wiping his mouth, he found his hand covered in blood. His nose was broken.

Dockett stood over him, a wide smile on his tan face. "You good?"

Simon gingerly touched the bridge of his nose and then grimaced. "Y-you broke it."

Dockett shrugged. "Come on. Let's get you to the doctor."

The lanky man led Simon into a neighboring building and up a flight of stairs. At the end of a long hallway were enormous glass windows that revealed a woman dressed in a blue dress and a white apron organizing medical tools in a polished cabinet.

Upon entering, Dockett passed her a flirtatious wave. The woman's eyes fell on Simon and her frown deepened. "What have you done to him? He's just a kid."

"Smacked him in the face for being a smartass," Dockett replied. "A little discipline."

The woman hurried to Simon. With soft hands, she turned his face this way and that. "It looks broken."

"It *is* broken," Simon corrected as she passed him some cloths to keep the blood from further running down his chin.

"I'm Eevie. I'm Dr. Gray's nurse. I tend to Dockett's pro-fighters." Although her wavy, blond hair pinned away from her face gave her the appearance of someone in her mid-twenties, Eevie's blue eyes were old. Simon recognized the look and respected her for it. "Let's get you sorted out, shall we?"

She led Simon to a private exam room and had him sit on the side of a bed. As she washed her hands and prepared examination tools, she said over her shoulder, "I wish you'd not get them so young, Ellis. What fun can it be to work with kids?"

"You start them young and train them up—"

"And then you just have them killed in the ring," interrupted Eevie with vehemence.

"He's not fighting this fall. He's too young," Dockett replied, leaning in the doorway.

This was news to Simon. "I'm not?"

Dockett shook his head. "No, you're too valuable to use as fodder."

Eevie started cleaning the blood from Simon's face. "So magnanimous of you."

Simon glanced at Dockett. He hadn't heard anyone talk to the tall man like that before. Most everyone approached the Lanista in deference, politely agreeing to his comments and readily following his requests. But here was a lowly nurse snapping at him.

"It's true. Simon here's not fighting in *this* fall's Munera."

Eevie stopped what she was doing and looked at him. "What do you mean *this* fall? Are there to be more?"

Dockett shrugged, folding his muscled arms over his lean, bare torso. "It's not been announced officially, but the Munera is set to become a yearly event."

Eevie scoffed in anger. "I was wondering why we were starting to see an influx of fighters."

"It's going to be… every year?" murmured Simon, his heart dropping. "Why?"

Dockett regarded him. "The User population's gotten out of control. Even with the Culling, they're spreading like fleas. Government can't keep up with them all."

Eevie glanced at Simon's wrists. "He's not a User, Ellis. So why is this child in my infirmary?"

"His Majesty enjoys some sport in the ring. If we just let the Users kill each other, where's the fun in that?" He motioned to Simon. "Mix in some normal people and *now* you've got a game!"

"I'm going to fight Users?" whimpered Simon, eyes wide.

"Well, not this year, but in the future, yeah."

Eevie tilted Simon's head back and looked up his nose. "Like I said, what's the fun in having children fight?"

"When he fights, he's not going to be a child anymore. Come on, Eevie. Finish him up. We got work to do."

Eevie turned on Dockett. "Get *out*."

Hands raised in surrender, Dockett stepped out of the exam room, leaving Simon with Eevie.

"Honestly, they get younger and younger," said Eevie, gently examining the length of Simon's nose with two fingers. She steadied Simon's face with the other hand. After a moment, she pressed hard along the left side of Simon's nose, causing him to cry out in pain; a crunch resounded in his head. Eevie held the cloth to his nose to stop the excess bleeding and then leveled with Simon. "I've treated several of Ellis' fighters, all of them young, but not like you. Pay attention, watch the interactions happening around you, keep your mouth shut."

Simon nodded.

She pursed her lips and caressed his face. "I'm sorry you've ended up here." Simon couldn't help but lean into her warm touch. She lowered her voice. "Get stronger, find sponsors, and win."

Simon glanced at the door. "How do I get out?"

"By winning all the events."

"What are the events?"

Eevie gave him a sad smile. "You'll learn soon enough. Come back and visit me when you've begun to earn free time." She stepped back and examined her work. "Don't get smacked in the face again. It'll be beyond repair. Keep cold compresses on it for the next day if you can. The area under your eyes is going to turn purple. That's normal."

Simon slid off the table, a little unsteady. "Is there… anything I need to know about Dockett?"

Eevie glanced at the door. "He's one of Madam Parthemos' Lanistas, a trainer of fighters. She has three Lanistas in total—one for the pro-fighters, one for the Users, and one for the normal fighters. Lanistas usually have one or two fighters they proclaim as their champion." She met Simon's gaze. "You're Dockett's Champion."

"Champion?" Simon thought.

"Ellis—He usually goes by his last name, Dockett—has legally taken you on; I'm sure he already signed the papers with Madam Parthemos. He must feed, clothe, and take care of you." She grinned. "Of course, Dockett doesn't want you to know that because, well, that's less money in his pocket." She began washing her hands. "But he's got the funds. So, remind him of his legal obligations."

"Thank you," Simon said. He met her gaze and then dropped his eyes to the floor. "Um… do you… do you think I could hug you?"

Eevie smiled sadly and gathered him into her arms. "Any time you need a hug, come find me."

Careful of his nose, Simon embraced her tightly, allowing his fears to surface and tears to spring to his eyes. "Thanks…" he murmured, clenching her skirts.

6

Isolation

"KELLICK."

Kell looked back at Father Legotis who stood in the doorway of the small cafeteria.

"Could I borrow you for a moment?"

The thirty or so students who had been cleaning the cafeteria tables and throwing away refuse paused in their work; a hush came over the room. Unsure of what to make of the sudden silence, Kell glanced at Mordecai to find his eyes wide. She saw him shake his head ever so slightly.

"Kellick."

"Uh, sure—Yes, sir." With a parting glance to Mordecai, she followed the father out of the room. The moment she was in the hallway, she heard everyone in the cafeteria burst into whispers. Determined to head off whatever encounter she was about to face, Kell asked, "Can I help you with something, Father?"

"Yes, actually." Father Legotis led her down a hallway and through the long breezeway that connected the church to the other buildings. "I heard from Sister Lyla that you don't care for education."

"I don't see the point of sittin' for hours and listenin' to old stuff when I could be learnin' on the job." Kell trotted to keep up with the father. "That's how I learned most everything. You know, I was told how to do it and then I had to put it to practice."

"Ah, I couldn't agree more," the father replied evenly.

They passed through the lobby and stepped into a cavernous room. Kell gawked as she looked up at the vaulted ceiling. Rows and rows of maple pews crowded the opulent space; nooks showcasing various images adorned the surrounding walls. At the front of the enormous room was a three-tier dais that boasted two magnificent chairs set on either side of the stairs, a large table decorated with a purple runner, and various golden symbols, chalices, tools, and decorations. An enormous golden tree with spiraling branches clung to the wall behind the table and stretched upward to the glass windows along the rafters.

"Whoa," was all Kell managed.

"'Whoa,' indeed." Father Legotis ushered her to the front of the room and then went to a closet hidden behind one of the enormous chairs. He slid the door open and withdrew a broom, a mop, a bucket, rags, and several bottles of what Kell could only assume were cleaning agents. "We have service tomorrow morning. This entire room needs to be cleaned."

Kell gaped at him. "The whole thing?"

"The whole thing. The floors need to be swept and mopped. The pews need to be polished." He turned to her. "You said students need to learn on the job, right?"

Kell frowned. "Is this because I was asking Sister Lyla questions in class?"

"It is the duty of a student to listen and learn just as it is the duty of a teacher to teach."

"So, we can't ask questions?" Kell asked incredulously.

"No."

"But how do we—"

"Kellick." Father Legotis regarded her solemnly. Kell defiantly held his gaze. After a moment, he nodded and gestured to the church. "Get to work. No one else is to assist you, am I understood?"

"Yeah."

"The next time you respond to anyone in that manner, you will receive discipline. Yes?"

"Yes, Father Legotis."

He nodded, said, "Get to work," and then left.

Kell turned to study the enormous space. It was going to take hours of work to complete her assignment. Deciding that she'd rather be cleaning than sitting in a stuffy classroom, she collected the broom and pan and wandered to the front of the room to discern how she should begin. She tested the weight of the pews; they were heavy, but she could move them. She had hauled crab cages out of the sea many times. A couple of benches wouldn't be too difficult.

With that in mind, she got to work. It took two hours to sweep the whole room. Though it wasn't exceptionally dirty, she found pleasure in clearing it of the small debris parishioners left behind. Once she filled her bucket with water from the outside spigot she had spotted the day before, she started mopping, humming a common shanty she and Simon used to sing.

Her singing was quickly hushed as she realized the mop she had been given was worn and filthy and seemed to be making the wood floors dirtier. She took soap outside to the spigot and thoroughly scrubbed the mop, sudsing the loose and fibrous tendrils until they started to lose their grime. Only when she was sure they were clean did she return to her work.

Some two and a half hours later, she finished mopping. Standing at the back of the church, mop in hand, she proudly regarded her work. The room's floors glistened in the late afternoon sunlight. She washed out the bucket, laid the mop out to dry outside the exterior door, returned the remaining supplies to the closet, and then got to polishing every wooden surface.

With polishing rub on her rags, she ran up and down sections of the pews, picking up trash, crumbs, and little bits of hair that she found along the way. By the time the dinner bell rang, she was finished. Happy with the hard work she had completed, she skipped off to eat.

Mordecai spotted her and eagerly waved her over. He wrinkled his nose as she joined them. "You stink."

"Oh, sorry."

"What'd he have you do?" he whispered.

Kell shrugged. "Sweep, mop, and polish the church space. Not a big deal."

Mordecai exchanged looks with the others. "And you finished it?" he asked.

Kell looked between them. "Yeah, why wouldn't I?"

"You were only gone for the afternoon. You did it all in just one afternoon?"

"It's not hard work…" Kell sat back. "Did I do somethin' wrong? Why are you lookin' at me like that?"

"So you did *everything*? You swept the *entire* church and mopped it?" prompted Fletcher.

"And polished *all* the pews and the front table?" continued Mordecai.

"Yeah. Was there more that I missed?"

The boys shook their heads. With another shrug, Kell ate.

She expected to see Father Legotis that evening; she was sure he would want to thank her for the good job she had done, but he never showed up. Just before bed, Kell hurried out of the dorm, down the breezeway, and back into the church to make sure she hadn't missed anything. Mordecai's reaction irked her.

When she arrived, she found a few acolytes dressed in burgundy robes loitering near the front of the cavernous space. At first, it appeared as though they were talking, but the longer she looked, the more she discerned.

"Hey!" she shouted, marching down the side aisle. The acolytes, four in total, turned in surprise. "What the hell are you doing?" She noted the uneven pews, dried footprints on the floor leading to the front, and cleaning supplies thrown haphazardly in a pile near the storage closet.

"You shouldn't be here," said one of the men, striding down the dais. He met her at the end of the aisle.

"I just cleaned all this up!" Kell raged, gesturing to the floors.

"Users are not allowed in the church," the bearded man replied, urging her away with arrogant hand waves. "Leave."

Kell planted herself beside a pew.

The acolyte nearly ran into her. "You shouldn't be in here—"

"Aris."

Kell and the man named Aris looked back at Father Legotis as he strode into the church. "Father!" called Kell, hurrying to him. "I cleaned the entire church and they came in and trashed it."

The father looked over the acolytes, regarded the church, and then sighed. "Kellick, I told them to come here."

Kell's shoulders dropped. "What? Why?"

"Because after I explicitly told you to complete this task by yourself, you went and asked others to help you."

Kell gawped.

"This was your punishment for disrespecting Sister Lyla, but you asked others to assist you. Now, that's not fair. Frankly, I'm surprised the others would even agree to help you. They know the penalty—"

"What are you talkin' about?" Kell interrupted, rage mounting. "I was here for five and a half hours, cleanin' this stupid place."

"There's no way you were able to complete it in such a short amount of time by yourself."

Kell glowered at him. "Why not?"

"No one's ever been able to get it done in such a short amount of time. Dozens of other students have had the same punishment and it's taken them easily eight to nine hours."

She looked back at the acolytes and then at Father Legotis, incredulous. "Why would I lie? What reason do I have to lie?" When the father opened his mouth to reply, she kept going. "Why would I want to go back and sit for hours when I can be workin' and doin' somethin'? I would rather be in here than that dusty classroom! So why would I lie?"

A sharp look entered Father Legotis' eyes. "Calm yourself, User."

The derogatory name tethered Kell to the earth, reminding her of the precarious situation she was in. She tried to regain control of her demeanor, but the misaligned pews and the dried footprints on the polished wooden floor to her right further aggravated her.

Tears blurring her eyes, she glanced at the acolytes, who had retreated to the dais, and then at Father Legotis. "Why would I lie?"

Father Legotis stepped back, his face dark with emotions Kell couldn't identify. "Go back to the dorm, Kellick. You'll reclean the church tomorrow morning before service."

Kell felt a burning sensation along her fingertips; it made her skin itch. Struggling to put into words her anger and hurt, she started and stopped several times. "Is this why… This is why… Why would you…" She rubbed her fingers along her thumb to stave off the uncomfortable sensation. "I don't—I don't understand…"

Father Legotis took several steps back and then made a small gesture to the acolytes. In the meantime, he said, "Kellick, I'm sorry this has upset you. It's a lesson that all students here at the abbey must learn."

"What lesson—"

Kellick sensed someone behind her but didn't have the time or wherewithal to move. Aris' arms wound around her and wrapped upward so that his palms pressed along the back of her neck, placing her in a submissive hold. As Kellick kicked backward in an attempt to free herself, another acolyte took hold of her middle; yet another grabbed her feet. Together, they lifted her from the ground.

Panicked, Kell struggled momentarily before, in the back of her mind, she felt that same click, that same release of energy that she had experienced on Donahue Street. Heat gathered around her fingertips and hands as she fought to regain control of the situation. Before she understood what had happened, a glorious burst of orange flames erupted around her.

She hit the ground hard, dazed. Though she could hear Father Legotis disseminating commands, she could make no sense of them. She felt hot, angry, confused. Blinking to clear her vision, she clambered to her feet and leaned on a pew. When she felt it give, she turned to see the wood beneath her palm crumbling in smoldering flames and smoke.

With a cry of surprise and horror, she staggered backward into the wall.

It was true.

She was a User.

Panic and fear taking full control, she looked to the father for guidance, reassurance. He was there to help her, after all. Instead, she found Father Legotis some pews away, his face folded in murderous intent. "Please…" she whispered, afraid. "What do I do?"

Kell felt a sharp pinch along the back of her shoulder, and then she slumped down the wall to the floor. Her vision began to tunnel and the rush of emotions that had been swirling around her faded. Her eyes closed, and the world around her darkened into oblivion.

When she woke, she remained motionless. It was black. Even as she strained to peer through the abyss, she questioned whether she was awake. After a moment, she touched her eyes and felt her eyelashes flutter against her fingertips. She took a few breaths to wake herself up and then slid her hand across the floor. The texture was cold and rough like cement.

Kell rolled onto her back and opened her eyes wide in an attempt to take in light. But it was impossibly black. She cleared the gunk in the back of her throat that had formed and then pushed herself upright.

It was silent; there was no sound of any kind. Beyond disoriented, she placed both hands on the floor and felt around to ground herself. As her rekindled panic began to eat at the lingering effects of whatever drug the acolytes had administered her, Kell fought to keep herself from screaming. The intimate darkness made her think of the long nights out at sea that she had experienced. Except here, there were no stars, no waves lapping along the hull of a boat, no fresh sea breeze to keep her tethered.

On hands and knees, she shakily swept the floor around her. When she met no obstacles, she shuffled off in one direction. Within a few paces, she found a wall. With a frantic smile, she stood. Keeping the rough wall on her left, she carefully stepped forward one, two, three—She immediately ran into another wall.

Kell groped the second wall and then followed it, constructing a mental image of her prison as she went. After another three paces, she found the corner of another wall. "It's a room," she murmured to herself, always keeping her left shoulder against the solid surface.

Upon locating the fourth wall and running her fingers over it, she felt a difference in the textures. It was smoother than the others and felt like metal. Kell dropped to the floor and traced the edges of the door with her fingers, trying to figure out where the bottom seal was. Perhaps she could let some light in. Her efforts were in vain, however. Only when she had run her hands over every inch of it did she sit with a sigh.

How long had she been in there? How long were they going to keep her in there?

Then Mordecai's words rang in her ears—the Vault.

So, *this* was the Vault, the thing that he had fearfully spoken of just that morning. Kell grimly marveled at her ability to have received the most severe punishment available at the abbey after just two days. Would Tarquin be proud or angry? After thinking on it, she decided that he would be proud of her for speaking her mind. He had always encouraged that in her. She had been brought up as male, after all. Boys were allowed to speak their minds, interrupt, and argue.

Perhaps that was why everyone was so upset. Girls weren't supposed to do that, even ones who looked like boys.

Kell lay back on the cold floor and mulled over all that had happened. She grew annoyed when her heartbeat became so loud that she couldn't think anymore. She kept her eyes closed to prevent herself from further hallucinating. She had heard from Tarquin about new fishermen who hallucinated out at sea on moonless nights because they had nothing to look at.

A thought occurred to her. She had made fire; couldn't she make fire again? Just a little bit? She rubbed her fingers against her thumbs. They didn't feel hot and itchy anymore.

She remembered the anger and frustration and injustice she had felt arguing with Father Legotis but couldn't bring forth a single spark.

Folding her arms behind her head and closing her eyes, she thought of being on *Polaris*, rocking back and forth. Somewhere nearby, she could hear the sea's waves. Though there was no wind, she envisioned the stars overhead and, in her mind's eye, looked out at the darkened sea. She couldn't see anything, but that was fine. Often the waters appeared as inky swirling eddies around the boat. Eventually, she slept.

The cranking of a lock woke Kell some hours later. She sat up, bleary-eyed, and squinted as cracks of light began filtering in. When the door finally opened, she had her eyes covered. Squinting, she looked up at Father Legotis' silhouette.

"Good morning," the father said calmly. "How are we this morning?"

Kell thought to reply with some snarky response but decided she needed to use the bathroom more. "Fine, Father Legotis. Thank you."

He nodded and stepped aside. "Classes begin in an hour. Please get cleaned up and eat breakfast."

Covering her eyes, she left the Vault which, she discovered, was behind a rolling bookshelf in the father's office. Ignoring Father Legotis' steely gaze, Kell left.

7

Users

DRESSED IN CLEAN CUTOFFS AND a faded shirt, Kell carefully painted ink on her wrists to mimic the bondage tattoos of a User. Although Tori had gone to breakfast ten minutes earlier, she nevertheless needed to do it fast and precisely. Her linework had to look like the bands the other students wore even under intense scrutiny, especially today. She was low on clean clothes and had to wear short-sleeved or sleeveless shirts for the next day or two until she could find other long-sleeved tops.

Once the ink dried, she stashed her supplies and then headed for breakfast. When she entered the cafeteria, everyone turned to look at her. She collected a tray of eggs, potatoes, toast, and fruit and hurried to where Mordecai and the other boys sat. They glanced around the room for Sister Lyla, Father Legotis, or any of the acolytes before talking.

"What'd they do to you?" asked Mason, leaning across the table.

"I cleaned up the entire church yesterday afternoon and then the acolytes came in and trashed it. Father Legotis said there's no way I did the whole thing by myself and that I would need to do it all over again." Kell glanced again at the doorway. "So, I got angry."

The looks on the boys' faces reflected the same emotion—dread. "What happened?" urged Mordecai.

Kell bit into her toast which, despite her ordeal, tasted delicious. "They knocked me out and put me in the Vault."

"See? I knew that's what they had done," Fletcher told the others. "Everyone knew you didn't come back to the dorm last night."

Kell shrugged and continued to eat.

Mordecai regarded her. "You don't, uh, seem too choked up about it."

Kell made it through her first slice of toast before she calmly replied, "If that's the game Father Legotis wants to play, I'll play it." She cut her eyes to Mordecai. "For now."

Mordecai leaned into her. "They are cold, ruthless. He once left a girl in the Vault for three days straight. They had to send her away because she went crazy."

"Like I said, I'll play Father Legotis' game—until I won't."

The rest of breakfast was eaten in an uncomfortable silence.

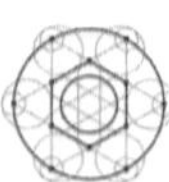

It was a glorious morning in late September. Though it most certainly wasn't autumn, there was a coolness in the air that foretold of the season's impending arrival. Swinging a Bo staff aimlessly, Simon watched Dockett speak with another fighter who looked to be fifteen or sixteen. The boy, dressed in pants and nothing else, was large for his age and bulky with hard muscles and broad shoulders. He also wore the wrist tattoos of a User.

While Simon couldn't hear Dockett's instructions, he could see the lanky man gesturing toward him as he spoke with the teen.

Already it had been a few weeks since his arrival at Madam Parthemos' Ludus Magnus, School of Munera Games. Though it had been a staple of the Upper District for decades, the public's support of such an institute had increased ten-fold, especially since the implementation of the Culling all those years ago. Aside from actually being forced to participate, Simon agreed with the games, as the Munera gave Users a purpose. Otherwise, they were inclined to cause trouble for law-abiding citizens of Eclat.

Dockett gave the signal to Simon who rested his staff across his shoulders as he had seen his instructor do many times. "This is Kent. He's a User," said Dockett. "He's been training here for two years. So, he was a little older than you when he arrived." The Lanista approached Simon. "His first arena fight is this fall."

"And?" prompted Simon. What was Dockett wanting?

"I want you to knock him out."

Simon gaped. "I can't do that. He's huge. And a User. How am I supposed to fight him?" He shook his staff. "I got a stick!"

Dockett shrugged. "That's for you to figure out." He nodded to Kent.

Kent spread his feet out to establish a wide base and then settled into a fighting stance. The air crackled as two rings of crimson materialized around his wrists. Simon gawked, his eyes drawn to the energy. To Dockett, he said, "I've never seen a User do... that stuff. What can he do?"

The Lanista again shrugged and then leaned against a nearby retaining wall to watch.

Simon turned to further study the User but had to abruptly end his observance as Kent lunged at him. With a gasp, Simon staggered aside, painfully aware of their size differences. Kent was enormous! But more than that, he was a User. Simon didn't have the faintest idea what that entailed.

As Simon fought to regain his footing, Kent dove after him. Simon felt whirling, hot air scorch his skin as the teen's fist passed inches from his face. Panting and caught off guard, he turned and ran, causing Dockett to belch out raucous laughter.

"What are you doing, boy? Don't think Users can run?"

When Simon turned to face Kent again, he found the teen far too close to use his Bo staff. Kent went to grab him, but Simon, using their extreme height difference, managed to lean out of the way and then duck under his subsequent attack. As Kent regained his composure, Simon took the time to put distance between them again. He needed to know what a User was capable of before he allowed Kent to get that close again.

"Let's go, kid," Dockett chided. "You're losing the crowd's interest. Your goal is to get in there and incapacitate him as quickly as possible. No dancin' or movin'. Just get in, get out."

Simon held his staff out to the side as he had seen Dockett do and watched Kent. The teenager grinned; he seemed to be enjoying the lesson. Simon was sure it was because he probably viewed it as a for-sure victory and a confidence booster.

Kent stretched his neck from side to side and then raised his fists once more. He was fast for his size, Simon had determined. But the discrepancy in their heights caused him to punch downward instead of straight forward. With a plan forming, Simon decided it was time to give it a try.

Slowly, they circled one another. Kent was light on his feet; his dark eyes were eager and intense.

Simon feigned left then right before darting forward, his staff drawn to his body. Though Kent had fallen for the first feint, he had paid the second one no attention and seemed ready for Simon's attack. The moment Simon was in range, Kent threw a fist. The air around Simon's head sizzled as he side-stepped the assault. With a cry, he raised his staff to deliver the final blow, but Kent turned and caught it. With his free hand, the teen smashed a fist into the side of Simon's head.

Simon was unconscious before he hit the ground.

When Simon opened his eyes, Dockett was kneeling beside him. "You good?" asked the Lanista.

Simon blinked to clear his vision and then grimaced as a killer headache roared to life in his skull. "Yeah." When he looked around, he found Kent was gone. "Where's... what's-his-name?"

"Went back to the barracks. I don't like Users to be outside for too long." Dockett examined Simon's head and then chuckled. "I thought you had him there for a minute."

"Yeah, me too."

"But that was good. You spotted what he was doing and went after it. Now, we just gotta get you faster and stronger." He patted Simon's shoulder. "Come on. Get some water and then we'll keep strength training."

As Simon drew himself to his feet, he asked, "Are all Users the same?"

"What do you mean?"

"Do they all fight like Kent?"

"No," replied Dockett. "Each of 'em is different. Actually, Kent's skills as a User are pretty poor. That's why I brought him out here in the first place. He can't hardly conjure fire."

"What were those glowing bands on his wrists? I thought he was Bound."

"Oh, he's definitely Bound. If he weren't, you'd be dead right now. Those red rings appear when they *use* energy. Some of the stronger Users can conjure two rings, like, two glowing bands will appear on their wrists. Obviously, they're exceptionally dangerous. So, we keep a close eye on them."

"So, the more glowing band things they've got, the more dangerous they are?"

"If they are an Unbound, then yeah. But all Users are Bound when they're young. It keeps them under control. The most rings you'll see anyone around here conjure is two."

"Have *you* seen someone with more?" asked Simon before drinking heavily from a bucket of water.

"Nope. Even our strongest, most resilient, and formidable Users can't get past two. So, don't worry." Dockett grinned. "I mean, they can kill you, but your body will still be around to bury."

Simon leaned against the retaining wall. "So, I've gotta fight Users like Kent?"

"Well, there will be others fighting too, but yeah. I see real potential in you, kid. Who knows, maybe one day you'll be sending Kent to the arena dirt."

Simon liked the sound of that.

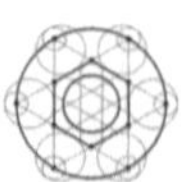

"What are you doing?" asked Tori.

Kell startled over her desk. "I was just playin' around," she replied, quickly hiding the paintbrush she had been using to paint the bands on her wrists. Tori closed the door to their shared room, eyeing her. "What are you doing back?"

"Sister Lyla and I finished early." Tori regarded her suspiciously and then let her gaze drift over to the desk where Kell's paintbrush had left smudges of ink on the oak wood finish. Kell followed her gaze and grimaced. "Are you... painting your cuffs?"

Thinking quickly, Kell sighed. "Yeah, they're old; the ink's faded. They look blue-black now. It bothers me. So I paint them."

"You're not supposed to mar or otherwise deface the tattoos," chided Tori. "It's the law."

"Oh, I'm not?" Kell looked at her wrists which she had mostly finished. She kept the unfinished side facing away from Tori. "But if I don't, then they look faded." She pretended to strain to see Tori's hands. "Don't yours look faded?"

Tori didn't appear as though she fully believed her. "Yes, so?"

Kell shrugged. "In Eclat, they like to see the cuffs plainly. If they're faded, it's difficult for us to be, uh, identified. You know?"

"I've never heard that."

"Well, you're from the Middle District, right? It's like that for us in Drayburns Harbor." Kell tidied up and attempted to wipe the ink off her desk with a towel, which she immediately regretted as the towel became permanently stained. With a sad frown, she looked at Tori. "Do you think... they'll give me another one?"

Tori scoffed, sat at her desk, and began reading.

Realizing she had just missed a close call, Kell grabbed a book she had borrowed from Sister Lyla, clambered into bed, and also began to read. She wasn't especially good at it, but it kept her mind busy. Unfortunately, the book was a retelling of ancient stories in modern prose, and within minutes, Kell was asleep.

The following day, like all the other days, she rose, did chores, ate breakfast, and then attended classes until lunchtime. She ate with the boys and then cleaned the cafeteria. Afterward, she went to special tutoring with a handful of other girls who were behind in their studies, including some eight- and nine-year-olds.

She was the perfect student. She never asked questions; she diligently studied and completed all the assignments and was always on time. Although she often grew drowsy in class, she forced herself to stay awake, if only to stare at the opposite wall. Occasionally, she would answer an easy question to make it seem as though she were paying attention.

By October, the northern winds had swept in, chilling the abbey. Fires roared in the cafeteria and common room, but other rooms remained cold. The students were given extra blankets as well as jackets that had been measured and made for them.

The days grew shorter as did Father Legotis' patience. Though all of the students were trying their hardest not to upset him, the smallest infraction often caused his stately composure to fracture. Kell got the sneaking suspicion that he did not like them, not because they were kids, but because they were Users. He avoided them often; any interactions he had with students were disciplinary.

Since he couldn't stuff all thirty or so students in the Vault, he brought them in shifts, Kell included. For the transgressions of one, all suffered. He ruled the abbey with an iron fist, always adamant that he was doing it for their well-being.

Of course, Sister Lyla was exceedingly sweet, but she was a tattletale. Any ill word she overheard, she reported to Father Legotis. Kell was certain that behind her smile was an insecure and weak-willed person.

When they were not following the rigid schedule set for them or suffering one of the father's punishments, the students at the abbey got along well and played outside behind the church on its expansive grounds. They had leather balls they tossed or kicked and often held races and other short games that could be completed in the amount of outdoor time they were allotted.

Older teenagers looked after the younger ones and helped them in their studies. But Kell didn't like interacting with them. The handful of teens who had been at the abbey for years were no longer human; they were soulless creatures bent on pleasing Sister Lyla, Father Legotis, and the burgundy-robed acolytes whom they saw daily.

One October evening as Kell turned the water off in one of the three communal showers, she realized she had forgotten her nightgown, which Sister Lyla had gifted her, in her room. Wrapped in only a towel, she peered out from behind the cloth curtain. One of the other showers was running, but it was late and most of the others had retired to their rooms.

Making a quick decision, she ripped open the curtain, towel wrapped around her like a thick slip, and started to step out. But as she brought her foot forward, it caught the hem of the curtain. Suddenly off balance, she fell forward out of the high-lipped bathtub and crashed onto the floor with a squeal.

She heard the other shower curtain open so its occupant could peek out. Groaning, Kell started to get up only to realize her cover had come undone. With a gasp, she snatched at the towel—still stained black with ink—and looked at the other shower's occupant. It was Mordecai. Eyes wide, he ogled her before hurriedly snapping his curtain closed.

Burning with embarrassment, Kell scrambled out of the bathroom and sprinted back to her room. She slammed the door closed behind her, startling Tori who, as usual, was bent over her desk reading. "What's wrong?" the girl demanded.

"I fell out of the shower," panted Kell, leaning against the door. "And Mordecai saw me. He *saw* me."

Tori's gaze slipped to Kell's wrists but she asked, "What did he say?"

"Nothing," Kell replied, going to her bunk where she had left her nightgown. "He just looked at me and then went back to showering."

"Then it's not a big deal, right?"

"I guess. Still, I don't think he knows I'm a girl. I mean, he knows, but I think this might change some things." Kell pulled her nightgown, an ugly pink floral piece, over her head and then began toweling off her chin-length hair. "I just don't want him to treat me any differently."

"Hm," was all Tori said.

Accustomed to her roommate's cold and brief responses, Kell sat at her desk, retrieved her inkwell, and with her back to Tori, began repainting her cuffs. Shortly before lights out, Tori left the room, presumably to go to the restroom as she did every night. Kell rolled over in bed and was asleep before she came back.

It wasn't the morning bell that woke her but the sound of heavy footsteps in the hallway. Kell squinted at the clock on the wall across the room and could make out that it was three-something in the morning. She buried her head under her pillow.

When the footsteps stopped outside her door, however, she rolled over, alarmed. "Tori," she whispered. When Tori didn't reply, Kell rolled out of bed and looked up in the top bunk. Tori's bed was empty.

Dread spread through Kell like a wildfire. At that moment the door to her dorm room opened to reveal several men—some whose figures she recognized, others she didn't—gathered in her doorway.

"What's going on?" asked Kell, backing toward the rear wall.

"We have been told," said Father Legotis, flipping on the light in her room, "that you are not Bound."

Too shocked to reply, Kell just squinted at them.

As the father's acolytes entered the room, Kell's fear swelled. She had grown up as a boy; she had spent her entire life working with and alongside men. But something about the situation set off alarm bells in her head. These men were large in comparison to her thirteen-year-old self and towered over her.

"I am Bound!" she shouted, bracing against the window.

Aris, Father Legotis' most prominent acolyte, grabbed hold of her. As she struggled fiercely, another acolyte took hold of her arms and held them out. Realizing they were going to check her painted cuffs, Kell began to fight harder. But she was no competition for the four acolytes who now restrained her.

Father Legotis approached her with a white cloth which, Kell discerned, was wet. The father placed the washcloth on her left wrist and rubbed vigorously. Though her skin burned, Kell didn't utter a peep. When Father Legotis stopped, he turned it over to reveal blue-black smudges of ink all over the cloth.

Without a word, the acolytes ushered her through the doorway into the hallway. Kell hollered and screeched; she fought and struggled until she felt the familiar pinch of a needle along her thigh. "No!" she screamed. Reaching deep within herself, she sought that flicker of energy that she had come to recognize as her talent as a User. Though the hallway was getting darker, she knew she could still do damage.

She focused on that word—damage. Maiming, injuring, hurting.

Goosebumps rose along her spine as her fingertips began to itch and burn. Though she felt tendrils of darkness licking at her consciousness, she could still hear and sense everyone. Rubbing her fingers together, she fixated on that burning sensation.

Only when she was suddenly jarred and her knees gave out beneath her did that release erupt around her. Gloriously brilliant flames poured from her palms as she crawled on the floor in an attempt to free herself. With that unlocking came a renewed vigor to fight and a fresh wave of energy. She could see a little better now.

As she set the hallway aflame, she scrambled in the other direction, suddenly unhindered. Panting, she staggered to the staircase. When she tried to go down the stairs, she stumbled and toppled down to the first-floor landing. Wheezing and groaning, she urged herself to get up. If she sat for too long, the drug would overtake her, even in her heightened state.

She lurched for the nearest door and leaned against it, willing her hands to locate the lock. She heard a click and the door suddenly gave. Kell collapsed on the bricks outside. She could see nothing.

Suddenly, hands were on her.

"Get off!" she screeched.

"It's me, it's me," came a voice.

"Mordecai?"

Mordecai drew her up, struggling with her weight. "You have to go. Now."

Kell leaned heavily on him as he started leading her across the lawn's cold grass. "They… drugged me… again."

"I figured," he replied. "You need to hide until it wears off."

"Where?" she whispered, losing consciousness fast. "Morde—"

"Come on, Kell." He jostled her and groaned when more of her weight rested on him. "Stay with me. Kellick, come on…"

She managed to fight off unconsciousness long enough for him to lead her to the enormous privacy bushes that surrounded the rear garden of the abbey. Kell fell into the cold, dew-heavy grass, her mind a moment away from sinking into the sweet release of unconsciousness.

8

On the Run

SHE WAS MOVING THROUGH THE market, drifting through it as if she were on a boat. At her side was Simon, his blond hair thrown back and bright eyes eager. Somehow, he knew she was a girl but he didn't act as though it bothered him. On the contrary, he seemed pleased to have her company.

They paused at a fruit vendor. Simon excitedly pointed out the bright red strawberries piled in small baskets along a cart that they could never afford. As he haggled with the vendor, Kell watched him. She was content to just take him in, to observe him in his natural environment. He was so handsome, even though he had become gangly with age.

A sound prompted Kell to glance down Donahue Street. When she couldn't determine what it was, she returned her attention to Simon but found him already jogging away. "Wait, Simon!" she called, running after him.

He turned and pulled her into an alley. Heart hammering and face flushed, Kell relished the touch of his arms around her and the softness of his skin. He was warm and smelled good. As Simon held her, she snuggled closer. Though they were about the same height, she somehow found a way to rest her cheek on his shoulder. With a contented sigh, she sunk deeper into her dreams.

Twittering house sparrows burrowed into her consciousness before the cold did. Kell listened to the birds for a long time before stirring, nestling closer to the warmth beside her. It took her a minute to realize that Simon was there beside her. Bleary-eyed, she bolted upright, smacking her face into a limb. "Sim—"

Mordecai lay beside her, his face a shade of pink. Utterly confused and disoriented, Kell looked about. She blinked several times to clear her vision and then gazed down at the black coat that covered them.

"Where are we?" she asked.

Mordecai lost his embarrassment quickly and dragged her back to their bed of old mulch and damp leaves. They were in a hollow of sorts among the privacy shrubbery. Behind them was a black, wrought-iron fence as well as a dense line of bay laurel shrubs. Beyond that was the residential street that ran along the backside of the abbey's property.

"You set the abbey on fire last night," Mordecai explained, staying prone.

"I…" It all came back to her. She leaned over Mordecai and carefully pried apart a set of thick branches. The dorm was a veritable disaster zone. Although the church appeared untouched, the middle of the dorm and the clergy apartments were gone. As the wind shifted, smoke and debris lifted into the air, giving the illusion that the building still burned.

Mordecai sat up beside her and looked as well. "The fire brigade fought the fire for several hours before going home a bit ago."

"What about everyone else?" asked Kell. "Did I—"

"The others got out and stood on the lawn just after I got you hidden. I couldn't move you after you knocked out." He leaned back on his elbows. "So, we've been here ever since."

Kell sat back in the hollow, stunned. "I did that."

"Yeah, you did." Mordecai reached between them and took her hand. Kell felt a wave of heat wash over her, a reminder of her unusual dreams, before she realized he was looking at the smudged ink along her wrist. "So, they *are* fake."

She yanked her hand away.

Mordecai stared at her in awe. "You're Unbound. How? Everyone gets the mark when they're born."

"It's a long story."

"Is that why you've been dressing like a boy?"

"Well, no. It's just how I was raised."

"Are you a criminal? On the run?" Mordecai pressed.

"Uh, kind of."

He thought for a long moment. "So, what are you going to do now?"

Kell fell silent. She hadn't thought that far ahead. What *was* she going to do? She had just set the only place that would take her on fire.

"I'm sure Father Legotis has notified the Containment Office. They'll be looking for you… us."

Kell glanced at him. "Us?"

Mordecai shrugged. "Wherever you're going, I'm going."

"What about Fletcher and Mason?"

"Everyone at the abbey was sent there because no one knew what to do with us. Our own families didn't know what to do with us. We were there because we had nowhere else to go. Mason and Fletcher will either figure out their own paths or stay there for the rest of their lives." Mordecai passed her a charming smile. "I'd rather see where you go than live in the abbey any longer." He drew a long breath and peered past the iron fence. "Besides, you're going to need someone who's familiar with the area."

Kell considered him and then looked down at her tattered and dirty floral nightgown whose hem was scorched. "Where would we go?"

"Northeast of the city? At least make the Containment Office work to find us."

There were so many unanswered questions. How far would they have to travel? If the Containment Office was anything like the regulators in Eclat, they had eyes and ears everywhere, all in an effort to keep Users under control.

Kell's eyes fell to the smeared ink along her wrists.

"What are you thinking?" prompted Mordecai.

"That Tori turned me into Father Legotis. She saw me darkening the lines a few times. I managed to make up excuses, but I think she figured it out last night when I got back from the… showers." Remembering that Mordecai had seen her mishap in the communal showers, she blushed and fidgeted with a nearby twig. "I hadn't darkened the bands in a day or so and they had faded."

Mordecai cleared his throat uncomfortably. "That would make sense. Tori hates everyone, especially people from the Lower District in Eclat." He looked out at the wrought-iron fence behind them. "There's a bent bar back here. We rescued a stray dog last year and wrenched the bar aside so it could slip out before Father Legotis could kill it. I bet we could fit through." He ran an appraising eye over her, frowning. "We're going to have a hard time hiding you right now though."

Kell grimaced at the ugly nightgown in agreement.

Mordecai thought, his blue eyes darting from the abbey to the ground and to the street behind them. "Stay here. I'll be back in a while."

"Wait, where are you going?" hissed Kell as he gathered his black coat.

"To find you clothes."

"Mordecai." She grabbed his arm and pulled him back. She didn't know what she wanted to say to him. She just didn't want to be left alone.

Mordecai passed her a smile. "I'll be back." And with that, he crawled through the bushes to the bent iron bar, wriggled through the fence, and pushed through the laurel shrubs on the other side.

Kell craned to see him but the vegetation was too thick. The confidence she had felt with him nearby crumbled. Suddenly alone and with no idea where to go or what to do, she felt trapped. Government officials were undoubtedly looking for her. She didn't know anyone in the city. Even the necessities of life had become abruptly unassured. She sincerely hoped Mordecai would return.

The morning though bright was chilly, and Kell worked to keep herself warm in the hidden hollow. She withdrew her arms and legs into the body of the garment and tucked her knees to her chest. Feeling the cold skin of her legs pressed against her bare chest, Kell was reminded how vulnerable she was.

She eventually dozed and found some relief from the pervading chill as the sun rose. Though throngs of people walked past on the sidewalks just behind her, she droned them out. It wasn't until a certain voice caught her attention that Kell awoke in alarm. Motionless, she lay in the dead leaves, listening. Yes, she was sure of it; that was Father Legotis.

Heart pounding, she peered out from under the edge of the bushes and spotted several sets of feet walking in her direction along the line of shrubbery. Careful to remain quiet, she drew back toward the wrought-iron fence, glancing at the bent bar through which Mordecai had left.

"We spotted a trail in the dew shortly after dawn," said Father Legotis, drawing near. "We think it's from them but can't be certain. Of course, we haven't seen them since."

"I'm sure they're long gone," came a silky response. Kell shifted to get a better look at the speaker. It was a forty-something-year-old woman dressed in a predominantly red suit that was marked with a golden tree whose branches spiraled outward along her left breast. Her almond-colored hair was pulled back in a neat bun decorated with braids. Her brown eyes were inquisitive, sharp, and extremely intelligent. The composure with which she moved bothered Kell. Father Legotis was a person to be wary of; this woman was dangerous. "So, it was a boy and a girl, is that correct?"

"Yes, but the girl was raised as a boy, so she prefers to wear boys' clothes. I'm sure you'll find her dressed as such," explained Father Legotis. He stopped just beside Kell's hiding place. "See here? The dirt is disturbed like someone was dragged."

When Kell heard the shuffling of someone kneeling, she decided it was time to leave and hurriedly turned on her knees and began crawling away.

"There's someone in there!" Father Legotis cried. "Kellick! Mordecai!"

The branches just behind Kell suddenly caught fire, flaring in a frightening blaze. With a gasp, Kell scrambled faster to the bent fence.

"Madam Nicolea, what *are* you doing?" the father asked. "You'll kill them!"

"You said one of them is Unbound. We can't be too careful," the woman replied coldly as another wave of fire caught the branches.

Kell withheld a cry of pain as she felt flames lick her legs and feet. She hauled herself through the bent bar and tumbled out onto the sidewalk.

"They're on the other side!" called the woman named Madam Nicolea. "You three, go that way. The rest come with me."

Panting, Kell wildly looked about. She hadn't seen which direction Mordecai had gone. Making a quick decision, she took off north down the neat brick street. Holding her nightgown above her knees, she dodged well-off men hurrying to work and women dressed in long, stylish gowns and enormous fancy hats strolling arm-in-arm.

Determined to lose her chasers, she took a right at the next intersection, bypassed an outdoor café, and sprinted northeast. Only once she entered a manicured park with gravel horseback riding trails did she chance a look behind her. No one was following. Wheezing, she slowed, eventually coming to a stop along a grove of enormous trees to observe her surroundings.

As she leaned against one of the giant elms, she sensed a presence. Before she could turn around, a force like a train careened into her, knocking what little air she had from her lungs. With a stunned cry, she plowed into the ground, scraping her face along the gravel path. Her arms were twisted behind her with a power that reminded her of Tarquin.

Turning her head, she found a single young man dressed in a burgundy suit kneeling atop her. He, too, was panting. Kell realized that he was probably the only one who had been able to catch her because of his age and physical prowess.

"Please, please," she gasped, struggling against his grip. She kicked and tried to roll her hips, but she didn't have the power to unseat his weight.

"Quiet," the man grunted, tightening his hold on her and looking behind him for backup. With a snort of disdain, he sat aside and, maneuvering her arms into a submissive hold, pulled her to her feet. Kell struggled, but the twist he had her wrists in provided exquisite pain.

Still breathing hard, the man, an associate of Madam Nicolae judging by his attire, escorted Kell toward the park's entrance, his head on a swivel. Kell frantically searched for a way to escape, but the park was mostly deserted, save a couple strolling along a path some distance away.

"I didn't mean to," Kell feverishly explained. "It was an accident."

"And that's why you're Unbound?" the man replied.

"No, I... I couldn't—I wasn't..."

Kell heard the pounding of footsteps before she saw Mordecai emerge from the intersecting street to their right. Without stopping, he charged them.

As the older boy lunged for the man, Kell's captor threw her, knocking her knee forward to break her run before turning to engage Mordecai. Kell caught herself barely but her knee grinded against the bricks. Whirling around, she saw Mordecai level a punch at the man. His opponent easily dodged him but hissed as if he had been struck. Kell saw the air shimmering with heat around Mordecai's fists as the older boy turned to attack again.

Spurred by the revelation that Mordecai was, in truth, a User like her, Kell launched herself at their opponent. Though she didn't feel a snap of energy like she hoped, her sudden entrance into the battle caught the man off guard. Mordecai's fist connected with the man's face, toppling him with a loud sizzle. Mordecai leaped onto their downed opponent and struck him two more times, both times leaving vivid burns and blood.

"Mordecai, Mordecai," called Kell, dragging him away. "Come on."

"This way." Mordecai led her into the park and down the gravel trails at a sprint. They passed a man on horseback, but neither party bothered the other. Beyond exhausted, Kell eventually collapsed to her knees in the grass along a shaded trail.

Panting loudly, his hands on his hips, Mordecai ran his eyes over her. "You're pretty hurt."

Kell gingerly touched her face, winced, and then looked at her fingers which had come away bloody. "He got me good," she replied. "How'd you find me?"

Mordecai chuckled. "You ran right past me."

"I did?"

"Yeah, the both of you."

"Did…" Kell swallowed, her mouth dry. "Did you see anyone else?"

He shook his head. "No." He wiped the sweat along his forehead. "You're fast and have good endurance. Why'd you leave? I was coming back."

"Father Legotis and some people found me."

The look on Mordecai's face changed. "The Containment Office. The guy who caught you is from it."

"There was a woman in a red suit with Father Legotis," Kell added. "Madam Nicolee, Nicola, something like that."

"Nicolea." Mordecai folded his hands on top of his head. "I know of her. She heads the Containment Office. I've heard she's ruthless, goes after Users like a dog tracking a fox. Doesn't matter how far you get, she's always right behind you. She's a User herself."

Both Mordecai and Kell glanced warily around the wooded area.

"Can we get out of the city by nightfall?" asked Kell, standing. She took the long hem of her nightgown and tied it into a knot along her left thigh.

"Not before nightfall, but maybe by midnight. If you're willing to keep traveling after dark."

Kell touched her injuries again and then sighed. "Lead the way."

9

The Munera

"WHAT'S THAT?" SIMON EYED THE metal contraption in Dockett's hand.

"An iron collar."

Simon backed away to the opposite side of his small, private quarters, which wasn't far. "What's it for?"

Dockett leaned in the doorway, unfazed. "We're going to the Munera today to watch the games."

"Yeah, I know. What's the collar for?"

"For you."

Simon tried to make himself bigger. "No, absolutely not. I am not your slave!"

The Lanista nodded. "It's true. You're not a slave."

"So, I'm not wearing it."

"You *are* going to wear it, and you're *not* going to put up a fight about it. Got it?"

Simon gazed at it, his confidence leaking from him. "I'm just going with you to watch. Why do I have to wear it?"

"Because you're going to run."

"I swear it—I won't run."

Dockett shook his head. "Nope. Put it on. You're not a slave, but you are property. *My* property. It comes off after the games. But so long as you're outside the training grounds, you will wear it."

Knowing he had no other choice, Simon approached the man with disdain. He stood still as Dockett latched it around his neck and secured it in place with a mechanism Simon could not locate. The collar was heavy and uncomfortable; he was sure he was going to grow weary of wearing it. In addition, he felt self-conscious and humiliated. He hated Dockett more than ever at that moment.

But Dockett didn't seem to notice or care. Without a word, he led Simon along the first floor where the other pro-fighters roomed, through a practice courtyard, and into the adjoining building. Simon kept his head down, utterly defeated. The collar was heavy and bruised his pride.

They left through the side door into the wide alleyway where several automobiles waited. Dockett motioned him into a black one as he clambered into the front seat next to the driver. After a polite exchange, the driver pulled out of the alleyway, alongside several other vehicles, and turned left onto the main avenue.

Simon hadn't left Ludus Magnus since his arrival three months prior and had forgotten just how magnificent the streets and surrounding buildings were in the Upper District. Though it was October, clusters of pink and white hydrangea crowded the flowerbeds in the median. Sweet potato vines, the last of the season, cascaded down dangling flowerpots of every building.

The buildings themselves towered over the clean streets, leaving Simon to wonder what everyone did for work to be able to afford such luxurious flats and offices. While horses were common in the Lower District of Eclat, especially by farmers, Simon saw no evidence of the creatures along the main avenue.

Far ahead, an open-air stadium built of concrete, marble, and steel and decorated with polished cream-colored travertine stood against the landscape of ornate brick buildings. The closer they drew, the larger the magnificent edifice appeared until it blotted out the sun. Their transport pulled up to what appeared to be an entrance used by staff.

Simon thanked the driver, to Dockett's amusement, and followed the Lanista to a pair of doors. On either side were regulators armed with side pistols and rifles. Simon eyed them but, as they approached, the men there grinned and stepped aside. While Dockett exchanged small talk, Simon inched closer to the lanky man. The irony that he sought reassurance and protection from his property owner rather than the officials sworn to protect the public did not escape Simon.

Although the regulators were glad to talk and joke with Dockett as they unlocked the doors, when their gazes turned onto Simon, their eyes hardened into something akin to malevolent pleasure. Simon looked at the floor and hurried after the Lanista.

Together, they strode down a long, cold hallway that gradually sloped upward and was illuminated by fluorescent lighting that periodically flickered.

Countless steel doors with locks on them lined the cement walls. A shiver rose through Simon.

As they came to a larger space that intersected with other corridors, Simon's mouth fell open. They were underneath the stadium seating and were level with the arena floor. Enormous glass windows reinforced with steel surrounded the entirety of the stadium's ground floor. The arena itself appeared to be coated in a layer of thick sand that had been meticulously combed into concentric circles. For some reason, six-foot-tall sections of palisades, tall fence-like structures, littered the arena, creating a maze. Simon noted that each palisade was lined with rows of white sachets.

As Dockett turned to speak with a man bearing a clipboard, Simon approached the large window, gaping. The arena was bigger than anything he had ever seen. People seated on the opposite side of the stadium appeared as faceless, ambiguous humanoid figures.

"What do you think?" asked Docket, joining him at the window.

"It's huge."

The Lanista knocked on the glass. Its sound was muted. "It's treated against heat." He nudged him. "Come on. I want to show you where the pro-fighters gather and introduce you to some people."

Dockett led him along the outer ring of the arena kept safe behind the reinforced glass. When it grew crowded with affluent patrons, Dockett directed Simon to a door that led to another sloping hallway.

Although the corridor was wide, the pro-fighters lined up along the opposite wall made Simon feel claustrophobic. The air was cool but tense; the smell of bodies was strong. Dockett's hands fell on his shoulders as he bent to speak with Simon. He turned the boy's head. "You see all these fighters?"

Simon nodded, taking in the odd demographic of people gathered there. He had expected to see enormous men wearing nothing but breechclouts and brandishing battle axes. Instead, he found a variety of people, including a handful of women, along the wall. While most of the fighters were lean and muscled, some were overweight or small. Although the majority of the fighters boasted bronze skin in varying shades, Simon was surprised to see others with darker and lighter complexions. There didn't seem to be a rhyme or reason for the assortment of people gathered. All carried naked swords either in hand or strapped to their waists.

"The pro-fighters prepare here, away from the regular fighters."

"What's the difference?" Simon murmured.

Dockett motioned to the people lined up. "They've been trained and know how to fight. The regular fighters are just thrown in there to add some entertainment, give the Users something to kill." Dockett sighed wistfully. "After your eighteenth, you'll be here, waiting to enter the arena."

Simon wilted under the gazes of the fighters nearest them. It wasn't that they frightened him but that he felt ashamed to be in their presence.

"These fighters have been training for months, years." As if to the men and women there, Dockett added, "If they survive all five rounds, they earn their freedom."

The Lanista led Simon to an enormous man near the front of the line. The fighter smiled congenially and approached them.

"This is Thiago Cazallo, my current Champion."

Simon frowned. "Your current Champion?"

"Well, I intend to turn you into something like Thiago. Every Lanista handpicks a fighter to represent them in future battles." Dockett grinned. "Thiago's been representing me for a few years now in showcases and demonstrations. This is his first Munera."

Simon looked the tall man over. Thiago, who couldn't have been more than twenty-two, wore loose cream-colored pants that bunched around his ankles. Like the other fighters, he was barefoot and sported a bare sword on a belt situated high on one hip. He was a handsome man with a short crop of black curls and glistening black eyes. He looked like an approachable person, not a killer.

"Who do you have here, Dockett?" Thiago asked.

"This is Simon."

"Yeah, I've seen you in the yards." Thiago winked at Simon. "Gotta feed him more. He's scrawny. Gotta grow big, kid, to become a winner."

Dockett offered Thiago a hand. "Just like you." Their hands met, and Dockett hugged the man. "I'm wishing you the best of luck today."

"If only to fill your purse," countered Thiago quickly.

Dockett laughed, looked over the other pro-fighters, waved to a few, and then turned Simon around. "Never conquered!"

"Always feared!" chorused the reply.

Dockett clapped Simon on the shoulder and escorted him out of the tunnel. Overwhelmed, Simon didn't pay attention to where the Lanista took him until Dockett began guiding him up a flight of stairs that opened into the elevated stadium seating. They sat at the ring's edge alongside the lip of marble that rose up before them. With the arena below, it was now more evident that the palisades set up were less a strategically placed maze and more a series of barricades behind which fighters could hide.

Dockett greeted a few other people before leaning into Simon. "There are five events a fighter must make it through to earn his freedom. The first—"

"If Thiago's won, why hasn't he been freed?"

The Lanista whacked the back of his head for interrupting but answered anyway. "He hasn't won the Munera, only showcases and the like. Even still, many who have spent years training don't leave the school. They can earn good money by continuing to represent a Lanista or train incoming fighters." Dockett sat back. "Now, the first event is," he pointed at the arena, "the Proving Trial. See those fence things?"

"What are the packets hanging on them?"

Dockett chuckled. "It's called APEX, acetone peroxide. Comes in little crystally bricks. Super explosive, doesn't like heat." Simon turned his head in thought. "Most Users aren't in control of their abilities. Any stray flames, and they blow themselves—and sometimes their opponents—up."

"A-and... they do this at every Munera?" whimpered Simon, heart hammering.

"Usually. It's a good way to get everyone excited. The second event is Weapon Combat, self-explanatory. The third is Tether Play, groups are shackled together. The fourth is Hand-to-Hand Combat, again self-explanatory. And the last one is Single Combat, that's the one you wanna make it to, yeah?"

Simon nodded numbly. The enormity of the games, the number of people, the inherent danger... After a moment, he asked, "Dockett? Can you come out alive even if you don't win?" Trying to put a spin on it to make it sound less like he was worried for his own safety, Simon continued. "I mean, if you sacrifice all those well-trained fighters in one game then you've run out of fighters. You gotta train a whole 'nother batch. Right?"

Dockett scoffed in mild amusement. "Not bad, kid. Yeah, if they're really hurt, then we withdraw them—save them for another day. If the injuries aren't bad, they keep battling. You gotta make it through all five, Simon," the Lanista said, wrapping an arm around him.

"But I'm... fourteen. I can't... What am I supposed to..." Simon felt tears welling up in his eyes and looked at the floor.

"Stay focused," Dockett said. "Train hard. The Users that come out of those doors over there," he pointed across the arena at the ornate gates, "are what's standing between you and freedom. So, study them. Watch them. Learn from them. The stuff I've been telling you is the same stuff they've been told. If they make it through all five rounds and best a fighter in Single Combat, they also get their freedom. Do *not* let them win. Ever."

Simon knew he was trying to cheer him up, to encourage him, but in that moment, he felt nothing but utter despair.

Dockett left him to his thoughts to chat with a neighbor. With the noise around him, it was easy for Simon to block out the conversation.

How had he ended up there? How had he forgotten that he was to fight, to win, and to make money for his Lanista and the Ludas Magnus? What had happened to the others he had been imprisoned with? Where had they been taken? Why hadn't his parents come looking for him? Why had he ended up alone in that jail cell? Why hadn't Kell been in there with him? Why had his best friend abandoned him with the regulators?

His vision swimming, Simon did his best to hide his tears, but he couldn't help the fat droplets that slid down his cheeks. He knew Dockett saw him, but the Lanista kept jovially talking.

A sudden boom like a cannon startled him from his thoughts. Men standing before enormous drums along the northeastern side of the stadium began playing, pounding in unison a steady beat. Simon wiped his eyes and tried to focus his attention on them and their dramatic movements that were visible even from a distance.

As the tempo quickened and the rhythm grew in fervor, Simon spotted a collection of affluent-looking people appear along the eastern side. Dockett whacked Simon's shoulder as he stood; Simon copied him alongside the audience. "That's the royal family," the Lanista murmured. "Madam Parthemos is also over there."

Simon couldn't make out any defining features of the royal family except that there were perhaps five or six of them—four males and one female? He couldn't tell.

Speakers around the stadium buzzed to life.

"I welcome you all," came a woman's voice.

"That's Madam Parthemos," Dockett explained as the thought occurred to Simon.

"I am Madam Parthemos, President of Ludas Magnus, School of Munera Games." Her voice across the stadium speakers had a slight delay but not enough to be obnoxious. In fact, it seemed to add to the general anticipation in the air. "I am exceptionally pleased to bring forth for your entertainment the Fourteenth Munera in honor of His Majesty's fiftieth birthday."

Raucous applause erupted from the stadium as Simon looked about in utter confusion. There were people who *liked* the monarchy?

Madam Parthemos continued. "We have prepared the very best fighters and Users to do battle today. They come to thrill, to surprise, and to delight—but above all, to earn the lofty title of Fighter Supreme. Now, let's meet our challengers!"

The gates on the opposite side of the arena opened to admit a steady stream of Users. Simon leaned on the arena wall, hatred stirring in his heart. Even from a distance, he could discern the black tattoos on their wrists.

Unlike the fighters he had met, the people entering the arena carried no weapons. They were dressed in various garb conducive to battle, though most of the men were bare-chested. Simon noticed that there were more women in the group than allied with the fighters.

The stadium swelled with boos, jeers, and hateful shouts as the Users lined up on the sand just outside the gate and turned to face the royal family.

Madam Parthemos waited for the derisions to calm before saying, "And now, I present your fighters!"

The noise around Simon was deafening. It almost made him forget that one day he would be down in that ring. With Thiago in the lead, the fighters trotted out from the gates below. Simon watched over the railing, his hands cold and heart pounding. He desperately wondered how Thiago remained unfazed by the clamor. If anything, the enormous man appeared focused, intent, his gaze set on some distant point on the other side of the arena.

"Now, His Majesty, Godfrey Trevarthen II, King of Berceau, will bestow a blessing of good fortune on today's Munera and her fighters."

A gravelly voice pealed through the speakers. "Best of luck to you, my fighters. Remember," King Godfrey took a steadying breath, "Never conquered…"

"Always feared!" shouted the fighters below in unison as the audience applauded.

Simon glanced across the arena at the Users who were fidgeting in their line. He was pleased to see that they didn't appear as confident, unified, or organized.

"Thank you, Your Majesty," said Madam Parthemos, commandeering the microphone with an attractive purr. "Our first event is the Proving Trial. Users and fighters must face each other in an arena equipped with volatiles. Those standing at the end of fifteen minutes may move on to the next event. Users and fighters, you may take the field. Await my signal to begin."

Simon saw the line of Users, of which there were about thirty, run along the northern side of the arena before spreading out to hide behind the countless palisades. Similarly, the fighters positioned themselves throughout the arena. Some of the fighters in the arena could see the Users, but others remained visible only to the audience.

"Begin!" commanded Madam Parthemos, her voice accompanied by a loud boom of the drums.

The entire arena erupted into chaos as two explosions set a collection of palisades aflame. Simon jumped and then leaned on the marble railing again, eagerly searching for Thiago. He didn't know anyone else on that field, so he was rooting for Thiago, Dockett's Champion. As flames spread to another palisade and another explosion reverberated throughout the arena, the fighters and Users clashed.

Temporarily forgetting his dread and horror, Simon studied the Users, watching how they moved as they attempted to hit the fighters charging toward them. Most Users' attacks were short-lived bursts of orange flames that made the air around them shimmer, but there was a group of them stationed in close proximity to one another who appeared able to draw forth more energy. Their assault on the encroaching fighters was more organized and controlled.

While other Users' flames careened carelessly into the explosive-ladened palisades, the unified group of Users took turns intentionally setting fire to the wooden barriers and shielding themselves from the subsequent explosions. Their attacks, although brief, were controlled and purposeful. Simon thought he understood their strategy.

"They're trying to create a bare battlefield," explained Dockett, leaning forward to speak to Simon. "If they get rid of all the barricades, the fighters have nowhere to hide. They must fight head-on against the Users; it gives the Users the advantage."

Simon nodded, his eyes locked onto Thiago. The enormous man was running along the southeastern side of the arena, weaving between the palisades, a naked sword in his hand. Two other fighters were with him, following his lead and working together. When a fiery plume vented from a nearby User, a fighter left Thiago's side and disappeared behind an already smoldering palisade. Although smoke coated the arena, the audience could clearly see where Thiago's comrade was going.

Roars of applause and encouraging shouts followed him as he darted out from behind the burning barricade, wrenched his arm back, and launched his sword. The weapon buried itself in the User's chest, the force of the blow carrying the victim back several steps; the User teetered to one side and then collapsed in the sand.

Thiago's comrade retrieved his weapon with cold brutality and then hurried back to Thiago. Elsewhere in the arena, Users began to burn two fighters alive, allowing their screams to momentarily tear through the stadium.

"Look, look at Thiago," urged Dockett, also leaning on the railing to point. Simon found Thiago doing battle alone with two Users who were frantically trying to keep him at bay. But Thiago dodged, lunged, rolled, and theatrically evaded their constant stream of flaming assaults. Even from such a distance, Simon could see the Users tiring as their movements began to grow sluggish and their shoulders slumped.

At that moment, Thiago darted in, his sword a magnificent sweep of silver. The first User fell to his attack as if he were relieved. The second's defense grew feverish as she realized that Thiago was closing in on her. A momentary feeling of pity visited Simon as he watched the young woman fight for her life, throwing fire with such ferocity that it scorched the sand black. But Thiago was an unstoppable force.

When the woman faltered, the large man slid in beside her and cut her down with a swift upward slash. Simon saw blood spill onto the sand as the woman staggered and then crumpled in a pile, dead. Thiago and his accomplices hurried onward, slaying as many Users as they could, until Madam Parthemos' voice stopped the event. All movement ceased on the field. Applause rose from the audience.

Simon saw Dockett silently count the remaining fighters and then smile. "We lost twelve; the Users lost seventeen." The Lanista sat back with a sigh. "Damn, that was too close. They've gotten better. That's worrying."

"Who's gotten better?" asked Simon.

"The Users. Usually, they lose around twenty or so. Nearly two-thirds of their ranks." Dockett began thinking. "Did you see that team of Users, the ones purposefully setting the palisades to explode? We gotta watch that in the future. That was an effective strategy."

Simon saw the remaining thirteen Users drag themselves to the other side of the arena, weary. The surviving eighteen fighters lined up just below Simon and Dockett.

"Let's go, Thia-*go!*" Dockett shouted down at his Champion who was panting. The charming man raised his sword at the Lanista and the audience called to him, clapping and whistling.

After the arena was cleared, which took roughly half an hour and was completed by dozens of staff, the second event—Weapon's Combat—began under the watchful eye of two referees bearing long poles.

"Why would they start with two games that give Users an advantage?" asked Simon. "That's not fair."

"The second round isn't to their advantage," Dockett replied.

Simon frowned. "But in the last round, they were trying to clear the arena of the barricades. That would give them an advantage. With nothing to hide behind, they could take on the fighters."

"Yeah. But that was the first round. This is the second." Dockett grinned. "The Users are tired. Drawing energy requires endurance. Many of them don't have that. The second event is usually a good one for us."

Dockett's assessment was accurate, of course. The second round, which lasted all of five minutes, ended with half a dozen more Users dead. The fighters lost only five.

Once more, the arena was cleared of refuse, bodies, and blood before the third event began. In Tether Play, both teams were shackled together in varying combinations and made to work together to fight. Because the Users had only seven remaining, they were shackled together in one threesome and two pairs. The fighters, whose team was nearly double that number, were given more flexible combinations—one group of four, two groups of three, and a pair.

By the end of the third event, Simon could clearly discern the exhaustion on the Users' faces. Their skin had taken on a gray pallor; they wheezed and struggled to remain standing, often leaning and bracing on one another. Both teams only lost two in the third round.

"The Users are getting' tired," remarked Simon, watching them. "What's their problem? Didn't they train like us?"

"They did, but I'm led to believe that doing so is hard work. Those remaining," Dockett motioned to the Users staggering off the field, "are tougher than even our fighters. That shit they use is hard on the body. They have to be strong to channel it."

Simon considered recommending that they get a handicap of some sort but stopped himself. Give the Users a handicap? That was laughable!

An hour's intermission was announced at which time Dockett took Simon to get cinnamon-sugar buns, strawberries, and wine. Lost in thought regarding the matches, Simon didn't bother to consider escaping into the crowds. He knew it was impossible, especially since he wore the heavy collar which garnered him looks of interest. Instead, he thought about how he would have bested the Users in the arena.

The fourth event—Hand-to-Hand Combat—was a livelier affair as everyone had had a break. The Users were semi-refreshed and appeared enthused like the fighters. The free-for-all gave the Users a distinct advantage; however, they ended up losing three more by the end of the event. But they managed to take four fighters down with them.

Going into the final round, the odds were against the Users, for which Simon was grateful. He didn't know if he would be able to bare it if the Users bested Thiago and his fighters. Madam Parthemos quickly explained the situation as it was.

"With only two Users available to fight, the final event, Single-Hand Combat, will be altered to accommodate their numbers. There will be three battles. Among the Users," explained Madam Parthemos, "a decision will be made as to who will fight twice. Best two out of three wins the Munera!"

Applause followed as the two referees from before reentered the arena, saluted the royal family, and then separated to visit with each of the teams.

Madam Parthemos announced, "Fighting for the Users in this first battle is Kidane Tsehay!"

Boos erupted as a dark-skinned man in his late-twenties moved to the center of the arena. Dressed in nothing but cutoffs, the man gleamed in the sun. He did not acknowledge the crowd, and Simon wondered what he was thinking. Kidane was muscled, lean, and appeared sure-footed. If he weren't a User, Simon would have cheered for him as the man was fast, light on feet, and lithe.

Kidane's opponent was a thirty-year-old woman named Sadie who carried a sword. She was the most muscular woman Simon had ever seen; he was certain she outweighed even Kidane with her bulky muscles and broad physique. Her blond hair was braided and tied back to reveal strong shoulders and a square face. She wore pants and a bandeau, which seemed to be what women were allowed. With practiced ease, she flourished her sword as she approached the referees and Kidane.

With a jerk, Kidane forced glowing red rings to materialize around his wrists and took a fighting stance.

To Simon's utter astonishment, the fight was over in less than thirty seconds. In an awe-inspiring show of talent, strength, and cunning, Kidane drew Sadie in before setting the entire space around him on fire. Sadie was a smoking and blackened corpse before the one-minute mark. Silence filled the stadium. It was no wonder Kidane had survived to the final event. He was even-tempered, watched his opponents, and was purposeful when he attacked.

As Madam Parthemos urged him to the sidelines, the second User approached the center of the arena but waited several paces back as staff collected Sadie's charred remains.

The second round was a drag to watch as the User, Cesar, was far too fatigued to stand much less compete in Single-Hand Combat. He was quickly cut down.

The final round brought Kidane to Thiago, two individuals with vastly different combat styles.

"Let's go, Thia-*go*!" shouted Dockett, encouraging a large portion of the surrounding crowd to pick up the chant. Even Simon was muttering it, his eyes fixed on Dockett's champion. The stadium hummed with excitement before settling into a tense hush the moment Madam Parthemos called for the battle to begin. Unlike the other events, this one was done in absolute silence. Only the sounds of combat and the men fighting could be heard.

Thiago was quick to throw Kidane on the defense, swinging his sword with graceful arcs and quick thrusts. Unable to get a motion in edgewise, Kidane dodged and evaded, frequently barely missing the sword's tip.

Kidane tried to attack, but the flames he created were brief and not nearly as powerful as earlier. He was tired. But Thiago appeared fresh, eager, and intent on winning.

Simon hissed as he saw Kidane take a thrust to the side of his arm as he dodged, but the umber-skinned man managed to stay ahead of Thiago's blade—barely. As the referees circled the two, their poles ready to separate them should the need arise, Thiago began mixing in martial arts, drawing Kidane closer.

Simon saw Thiago grimace as he passed through shimmering air that could only be heated fumes. But the man was relentless. He didn't stop. In fact, Thiago's attacks grew faster, more precise, more intentional, forcing Kidane to constantly move away until he finally tripped on his foot and rolled backward.

Covered in sand, the dark-skinned man spun to his knees, panting, and glowered at Thiago. Spurred by the hushed calls from audience members who ventured to say anything, Thiago brandished his weapon, which was adorned with blood, and approached Kidane.

"Come on, Thiago," Dockett muttered, standing and pacing, his eyes glued to the arena. No one in the audience dared to utter a word to the Lanista blocking their view. "Come on."

When Thiago was a few paces from Kidane, he raised his sword to deliver the final blow, a triumphant grin on his face. Simon nodded. There was no way for Kidane to defend himself. He was beyond tired, weak, and without his supernatural abilities.

As Thiago moved forward in two great strides, Simon saw Kidane swiftly draw a circle in the sand around him and then raise a trembling hand to meet Thiago's descending sword. A funnel of fire flared from Kidane's outstretched palm to engulf Thiago's upper half.

"No!" screamed Dockett, nearly leaping over the railing. Several patrons grabbed him to keep him from falling into the arena.

The torrential storm of fire around Thiago lasted for longer than any other, scorching the sand and turning it black. Flailing, Thiago fought to rid himself of the ravenous flames, but he took the fire with him as he dropped to the arena floor and began rolling. After a minute, he fell still, his body charred and unmoving.

The stadium erupted in an uproar of boos and cries of dissent. Simon watched as Kidane, panting, rested his head on the sand in relief and weariness. The two referees waited for him to rise to his feet. Once Kidane stood, the referees raised the User's hands. Madam Parthemos announced him as the Supreme Champion of the Munera, causing the crowds to seethe. A User had won.

Limping and bleeding, Kidane was led from the arena, his back to the hisses and cries of derision that followed him. Simon felt conflicted, moved, but above all else, determined. If a User could win freedom, then Simon could too.

10

Conflagration

ONCE THE SUN SET, TEMPERATURES dropped. Barefoot and wearing nothing but sleepwear, Kell was miserable. Her feet hurt from the cold and she shivered violently. But she didn't dare complain or bring Mordecai's attention to her discomfort. She didn't want to be a burden or make him think that she couldn't handle the cold. But as the evening wore on and her pace slowed, Mordecai took notice and drew them down a dirt road to a farm along the outskirts of town.

Realizing that he intended to walk straight up to the farmhouse's low-set porch, she pulled him to a halt. "What are you doing?" she whispered.

"Asking for help. I know them."

Kell kept her grip on his arm as it reassured her. Also, he was warm, despite no longer wearing his black, abbey-issued coat. "But they'll know we're on the run. The Containment Office would have put out a broadcast or something, right?"

Mordecai smiled. "They don't have a radio."

Although she didn't believe him, she wanted badly to get warm. Nervous, she held onto him as they walked up the porch steps; Mordecai rapped in a friendly rhythm on the tattered wooden door. From within, the sound of footsteps reverberated. Momentarily, an elderly man dressed in faded, thread-bare pants and a worn plaid jacket answered.

The man squinted at Mordecai and then at Kell.

"Good evening, Mr. Wooding." Mordecai's voice had taken on a different tone, a more proper one. "I hope we haven't disturbed you."

"Who is it, Eli?" came the voice of a woman from the next room.

"It's Mordecai. And he's got a friend." Eli Wooding stepped aside and motioned them in. Although bent with age, Eli appeared strong with broad shoulders and a stubborn expression on his weathered and wrinkled face. He closed the door behind them with a gnarled hand and looked them over. "What happened to you two?"

Kell glanced at Mordecai, hoping he had thought this out.

"I was out for a walk and found Lillian here wandering in the cold." Mordecai wrapped a protective arm around her. "She was kidnapped but managed to escape. I'd take her to my residence, but I'm afraid we're quite a walk from the estate, and with her in the condition that she is… I was hoping that we could perhaps rest here for the night."

An elderly woman shuffled out from the kitchen of the three-bedroom farmhouse. "Oh, my goodness, you poor girl. Look at your face! And wearing nothing but that raggedy thing."

"Stop fussing, Flossie," Eli chided, returning to the plush chair next to the hearth across the sitting room. He picked up the book he had folded over the armrest. "She'll make it."

Like Eli, Flossie was also slightly bent forward, but she walked with an altered gait. Her white hair curled around her wrinkled face and emphasized the enormity of her thick glasses. Dressed in an ankle-length dress and an apron, she appeared comely.

Flossie gestured Kell to her with a pitiful smile. "Come here, dear. Let's get you cleaned up. Such a good young man you are, Mordecai."

Mordecai passed her a grateful smile. "Ms. Flossie was a part of the Kingston Agricultural Society. She used to take care of sick and hurt animals. You're in good hands, Lillian."

Kell nodded and allowed the old woman to lead her to the couple's bedroom. As Flossie fawned over Kell, the old woman prepared a hot bath. After Kell washed and reveled in the glorious warmth, Flossie helped her dry off and then dressed her in worn pants, an old but very comfortable long-sleeved shirt, a rough sweater that had seen better days, and thick socks. The old woman then tended to Kell's torn-up face.

"I don't think you'll need sutures, but some of these cuts are nasty," Flossie murmured, gently dabbing antiseptic on the wounds. Kell grimaced. "Please have Lord Othonos bring you to a doctor."

"Who?" asked Kell.

"Othonos, Mordecai's family." Flossie took a comb to her and began combing her damp hair. "You poor dear. I can't believe those brutes, going after such a young girl. And they even cut off your hair. Tsk, tsk."

"Thank you for your kindness," Kell replied.

"Mordecai was smart to stop by."

"Why?"

"We heard just this afternoon that there's an Unbound loose in the city." Flossie shook her head in dismay. "I can't bear to imagine the poor souls who have the misfortune of running into him."

Heart thrumming in her ears, Kell stayed quiet. She had just scrubbed the remnants of the ink on her wrists off in the bath.

"Come on, dear. Let's see what the menfolk are up to." Flossie wrapped Kell's hand around her thin arm and escorted her to the sitting room where Mordecai and Eli talked.

"See?" said Eli, motioning to her. "Nothing to fuss about. Right, young lady?"

Kell flashed him a smile. "Nothing at all."

Mordecai beamed, his relief obvious. Kell looked down at the bedding that Eli and Mordecai had put together on the floor before a fire. "We've got that electric stuff, but nothing warms a room like a hearth," said Flossie. "I hope it's to your satisfaction. We don't have the spare bed anymore since we hardly get visitors."

"You're more than generous," Mordecai assured them. "We're so thankful you took us in. We will find a way to repay your kindness."

"Nonsense, we're glad to have visitors. Right, Eli?"

Eli grunted as he gathered his book and headed for their bedroom. "There's more wood on the back porch if the fire gets too low. But you shouldn't need it."

Flossie imparted them a sweet smile before shuffling after her husband and closing the door behind them.

Mordecai started turning off lights in the sitting room as Kell burrowed into the strange-smelling quilts on the floor. Once the sitting room lights were out, Mordecai joined her, pulling the shared quilt over him with a shiver. "Before I got sent to the abbey, I helped them often. Their kids moved away a long time ago and have forgotten them. I haven't been back in over a year, but…" He smiled to himself. "I knew they'd take care of us."

Kell glanced back at the closed bedroom door and then whispered, "They know about me."

"Why?" Mordecai's voice was just as quiet.

"Ms. Flossie mentioned something about being frightened of the Unbound User wandering the city."

"I hope not to reveal that to them." Mordecai studied her face and then grinned. "You are all sorts of chewed up."

"What's this about an estate?" Kell murmured, rolling over to face him and yawning. She noted the slight frown that crossed Mordecai's face. "You don't have to talk about it if you don't want."

"You're from Eclat, so I'm sure you've never heard of the Othonos family. They're big here, a wealthy family. They funded the automobile industry when it first got going. And before that, they supported military contractors. High rollers."

"And you're one of these high rollers?" queried Kell quietly.

"*Was.* Turns out they don't like Users. I was the first in the family, for whatever reason, and…" He drew a long breath. "I've spent the last year and a half at Abbey of the Sacred Tree for it."

"Why only the past year and a half? They knew when you were born, right? You're marked."

"They found out when I was a month or two old. Got me marked and then forgot about it, thinking it was all under control. Then about a year and a half ago, I melted my father's very expensive armchair. It just… caught fire under my hand in his study." Mordecai's gaze became distant. "They dropped me off at the abbey with no explanation, no goodbye, nothing." He pursed his lips. "I'm sure it was a relief for them to be rid of me."

Kell gently kicked him under the covers. "Don't say that. I'm sure if they knew how much you've helped me—"

"An Unbound," Mordecai interjected. Kell fell quiet. "Get some sleep. We'll head out in the morning."

As Mordecai snuggled in, Kell watched him, his face becoming ever more familiar. Although he didn't look as rough as she did, he appeared worn. She was sure he would have liked to bathe because he still smelled faintly of smoke from the abbey fire, but he hadn't wanted to cause any suspicion by asking.

Feeling the comradery and safety of friendship, Kell burrowed under the blankets and slept.

The smell of breakfast cooking woke her sometime early the next morning. Though they had planned to strike out just after dawn, Mordecai was still asleep. Kell stretched and then sat up, feeling refreshed but hungry. She hoped Flossie and Eli would be willing to feed them. By the looks of it though, they didn't have much and felt conflicted asking for food.

As Kell stared into the smoldering fire, a chill ran through her, forcing her to collect her sweater which she had discarded the night before. Her movements woke Mordecai. She saw the ravenous look in his eyes as he smelled breakfast.

Together, they folded the blankets into neat stacks and then wandered into the kitchen where Flossie was busy in front of a three-burner stove. "Good morning, Flossie," hummed Mordecai.

The old woman startled and then smiled. "Oh goodness, good morning, you two. Were you able to sleep? I'm sure the floor was quite hard."

"No, no," Mordecai assured her with a congenial smile. "We were so tired that we could have slept anywhere!"

Flossie motioned Kell over and examined her face. "Much better. Looks much better. Try to keep it clean, yes?"

"Yes, ma'am."

"Good. My skills are for animals, not humans." Flossie gestured to Mordecai. "Make sure she's taken care of. She's a young lady."

Mordecai grinned as Kell turned away with a frown. "Of course."

They gratefully accepted a meager breakfast of chicken broth soup, toasted bread with butter, and potatoes before profusely thanking the elderly couple.

"Please stop by whenever you can," Flossie said, nudging Eli beside her.

Eli grunted and leaned on the porch support beam. "Yeah, come by whenever."

Mordecai nodded, thanked them again, and then jumped off the porch with Kell in tow. Where the dirt road intersected with the Woodings' driveway, he turned left to go northeast.

"Mordecai!" hollered Eli.

They looked back at the farmhouse.

"The other way!" the old man shouted, motioning southward.

Realizing that they had nearly been caught, Mordecai feigned confusion, looking both ways before throwing them a smile and a wave and starting down the road toward the city. Once they were out of sight from the farmhouse, they deviated from the dirt road and headed north again. Only when they were sure the elderly couple couldn't see them did they venture back onto the dirt road that led into the sprawling wooded hills outside Avives.

"So, where exactly are we going?" asked Kell after a while. She kicked a rock along the road that went tumbling off into the surrounding vegetation. Flossie's old boots were a little large for her thirteen-year-old feet, but she had managed to cinch them down enough that they didn't rub her heels.

Mordecai shrugged. "To find somewhere safe to lie low, I guess."

"You guess?"

"Look, I'm playing all of this by ear." He folded his hands atop his head. "If we don't find anything then… we'll just have to keep traveling."

"To where?"

Mordecai stopped in the middle of the desolate road lined with enormous ash trees and looked back at her.

"I'm completely behind you on this, but I also want a plan," Kell explained. "We can't just strike off into the forest and hope to survive. We don't have supplies, food, water, tools."

Mordecai regarded her thoughtfully.

"We have no weapons, no map, nothing."

"I know there's another city out there," Mordecai argued.

"Right, and how far away is it? Two days' journey? A week? And how are we supposed to do all of that and not be sidelined by the Containment Office?"

"I don't know, Kell! All right? I don't know!" Mordecai paced the road. "I'm making this up as we go. I thought we could just head out and that everything would fall in place, but I don't know. I've never been outside the city."

Kell gazed at him. "You've never been outside Avives?"

He shook his head. "Flossie and Eli's house is as far as I've gone."

Realizing that she had been depending on Mordecai's perceived mental map that didn't actually exist, she felt panic start to rise in her chest. "How far are the docks from here?"

Mordecai shrugged. "The other side of the city. We can't go to the docks. Besides, who would give us passage for free?"

Although Kell would feel more comfortable near the sea and was certain she could work something out with the local fishermen, Mordecai was right. They couldn't make it through all of Avives without being caught. They were on the Containment Office's most-wanted list. "Are there any streams that run through the area?"

"I don't know where they are but yes. They run through Avives as well. What do streams have to do with anything?"

"Streams provide water and sometimes food. If we find the right one, we can follow it north and have some sense of security."

Mordecai weighed her suggestion and then nodded. "Fine. Let's do that then. Not like we have any other plans."

For the next several hours, they headed in a northeasterly fashion, keeping to the dirt road and hiding when vehicles or horses passed. Once the dust cleared, they emerged from the thick vegetation and continued. Eventually, Kell recommended that they leave the road and search farther in the forest for signs of water, to which Mordecai hesitantly agreed.

Conversation that had been light along the road turned to silence as they forged a trail through the forest of holm oaks, evergreen shrubs, coniferous trees, and tall grasses. Kell took the lead, her head on a swivel for signs of movement. She noticed that Mordecai seemed uncomfortable and glanced back at him frequently to make sure he was keeping up.

As the afternoon sun heated the forest and streams of sunlight filtered through the canopy of broad-leaf trees, Kell suggested that they rest in the glade ahead. She had long since taken off her sweater and tied it around her waist and had pushed her sleeves over her elbows. Once they were in the clearing of low, rocky outcroppings and thin grasses, she rolled her pants legs.

As Kell watched Mordecai, she noted the way that he studied the rocks and picked at the surrounding grasses. A shuffling of leaves across the glade garnered his intense attention before he realized it was a brown squirrel. "So, you've really not been outside the city?" Kell asked.

She wasn't accustomed to hiking through woodlands, but striking out into unknown territory was similar to sailing. One used nature, flora and fauna, and the stars to navigate and learn about the surrounding area.

"No," replied Mordecai tensely. He looked at her. "You?"

She shook her head.

Mordecai scoffed. "I hate being out here. It's awful. There aren't any roads or signs; there's no food or water. I have no idea where we're going. And you're just," he waved a hand in her general direction, "you're just going off, having no idea where we are. No maps, nothing."

Kell glanced up at the position of the sun. "I mean, I have a general idea of where we're going."

"How? There's literally nothing here! Just a bunch of trees and rocks! And why are you smiling?"

"We were heading northeast until about two o'clock. Then I moved us to the east because the tree species changed. I figured that has to mean something."

Mordecai gaped at her. "How did you—How do you know that?"

Kell shrugged. "I just... do."

"Wait, how do you know what time it is?"

Kell pointed at the sun.

A smile broke across Mordecai's face. "You're joking. All right, I get it. I'll lighten up. Just say that next time instead of—"

"I'm not joking. It's a little after three o'clock right now. If we keep heading this way, I think we'll hit a river or stream or something. Look." She pointed to the surrounding grass. "These are also different than what we were passing through earlier. They're wider."

"Oh," was all Mordecai murmured.

After resting for a while longer, Kell started east again with Mordecai close behind. They startled a group of red deer and even glimpsed a lynx from a distance. Nuthatches, goldfinches, and warblers twittered about in the expansive treetops as lizards skittered under logs and rocks to escape the encroaching humans. Kell spotted something akin to a gerbil or a small rodent but couldn't properly make it out as it quickly vanished through the underbrush. Occasionally, a large shadow overhead announced the passing of a raptor or vulture.

Kell reveled in the abundant wildlife and allowed her gut to guide her. When they had left the dirt road, they had spotted very few animals. Now though, the forest teemed. Water had to be nearby. It was evening when Kell caught the scent of something. She paused in step and breathed deeply. Mordecai stopped beside her.

"What is it?" he asked, cautiously sniffing the air as well.

"I think I smell water. Come on."

Mordecai hurried after her. "What?"

After a minute of jogging, Kell grinned as the sound of running water reached her ears. With a whoop, she slid down a shallow embankment and jumped up and down along a river's edge. "Yes! Yes!" she squealed, delighted with herself.

The river was probably thirty feet across and, although shallow, moved swiftly. The water was clear, save the deeper segments near the middle, and revealed smooth river rocks of varying sizes as well as trout and carp that drifted with the current.

Mordecai watched her from the top of the embankment, a puzzled expression on his face. "How did you do that?"

Kell looked back at him, beaming. "Do what?"

"How did you know there was a river over here?"

Kell shrugged. "You just have to look for the signs."

He joined her, and together they drank heavily, satiating their thirst. Mordecai sat back on the damp dirt and gazed at the river. "Was it obvious? Or am I just that… inept?"

Kell plopped down beside him. "You know how when we were in Avives and I didn't know where to go? I didn't understand how the city streets intersected or where to turn or anything? But *you* did?" Mordecai nodded thoughtfully. "It's the same out here."

"But you told me earlier you had never been outside Eclat."

"Not in forests, no." She gazed happily at the river. "But I grew up on boats, sailin' for days with no land in sight. You have to look at the world around you and understand that everything's got a purpose and a reason. Reading nature and the signs it gives you is important in knowin' where you're goin'."

Mordecai grinned, which warmed Kell immensely, and then eyed the water. "So, what are the chances—oh, fisherman—of catching me a fish?"

Kell had been wondering the same thing. She could create a makeshift fishing pole out of a sturdy stick, but the problem remained the same. They didn't have anything they could fashion into a hook. She looked Mordecai's clothes over. "Let me see your beltline," she demanded. Flushing slightly, Mordecai lifted his shirt. "Do you have clasps or buttons?"

"Buttons."

"Mine has buttons too."

"What are you looking for?"

"Something to make a hook from."

Mordecai lurched toward her, scaring her. He pulled at Flossie's sweater tied around her waist. "Clasps! Your sweater has clasps!"

Once she determined it was possible to unknot the metal clasps from the sweater and bend the delicate metal to join together, she began unwinding the hem of Flossie's old sweater and pulling the weaving apart in great strands of strong cotton. In the meantime, Mordecai wandered along the riverbed to look for frogs and insects.

Within the hour, Kell was fishing. She caught three bream, two trout, and, to their surprise, a large catfish. Overjoyed, she admired the half a dozen fish before realizing they had forgotten one crucial thing—they had no way to make a fire. Mordecai also noticed the problem.

"Couldn't we just start one on our own?" He smiled. "We're Users."

"Can you conjure fire?" asked Kell.

"Well, no. Not yet. But *you* can."

"I don't think that's a good idea."

"Why not?"

Kell scoffed. "Because I tend to *set* things on fire."

"Yeah! That's the point."

She lowered her gaze to the fish between them. "No, I mean, I catch everything on fire. That's the reason we—I mean, I—had to leave Eclat. I, uh, caught half the Lower District on fire." She drew a long breath. "And then I set the abbey aflame."

"Oh." Mordecai frowned in thought. "Well, I can give it a try, I guess. Can you get the fish ready to be cooked? I'll collect wood and work on getting a fire started."

Kell looked around. "Is this where we're staying tonight?"

"Might as well be," Mordecai replied, already picking up dried driftwood and thin branches and sticks.

Kell brutally gutted the fish with her hands and ran straight, green sticks through them to be roasted over an open flame. She clambered to the top of the embankment to see how the construction of Mordecai's fireplace was going and found a random assortment of sticks, branches, and logs thrown haphazardly in a pile with no gulley or ring of rocks to define a fire pit. An amused look spreading across her face, she watched as Mordecai traipsed through the forest, dragging with him more kindling. He seemed content with the work.

"Whatcha doin'?" Kell asked.

Seeing the look on her face, he frowned. "Why?"

"You've got a good stockpile there. Do you want help building the fire?"

Mordecai dropped his additions onto the growing precarious pile. "This *is* the fireplace. Why are you looking at me like that? Fire needs wood; I got the wood."

Kell cleared her throat and tempered her amusement. "You need to clear the surrounding area and build a ring with stone or dirt first."

Mordecai stared at the pile and then sighed. "To keep the fire from escaping."

"Yeah."

"Well, look, how was I supposed to know that? All the fires I've been around have been in hearths." Disheartened, he began clearing the surrounding ground of grass and leaves that could easily catch. Kell helped him.

Once they had surrounded the branches and assortment of sticks with what rocks they could find, they paused to catch their breaths. Kell glanced at her skewered fish which waited on a nearby rock and then said, "Now, we need fire. You can do this."

Mordecai shook his hands out, flexed his fingers several times, and then concentrated. Kell saw the air around his palms shimmer in the light of the setting sun. The swelling heat that accompanied the glimmering brought her hope.

Mordecai touched the sticks, going so far as to even hold thin branches in each hand. Though the wood between his fingers smoked, it didn't catch. With a sigh, he slumped to a crouch. "I can't do anything right."

"It takes practice," encouraged Kell. "You can do it. Try again with this one." She passed him a dry stick with dead leaves still clinging to it. "Come on, you can do it."

Staying low, Mordecai tried again, the effort drawing perspiration along his forehead and causing his hands to tremble. The dry leaves started to curl, and then nothing happened. He shook his hands again and then continued. Kell grew excited when she saw a spark, but it was a fluke. For the next ten or fifteen minutes, Mordecai worked to evoke fire, but only heat ever left his palms.

Panting, he eventually flopped back onto the cold earth. "This is so dumb. We'll just eat the fish raw."

Kell glanced down at her wrists which were now clean of all traces of ink. Perhaps she was in better control of the energy now that she was familiar with how it felt. Maybe she could better channel it. "I'll try." She positioned herself in front of the pile of wood.

Mordecai sat up. "You sure?"

"No," she replied matter-of-factly. "But I'm hungry and want another win. Feel like I haven't gotten many of those recently." She waved him back and then turned her attention to the kindling pile.

The air was chilly with the setting of the sun, and shadows overtook the forest. It was dusk, that time when natural lighting converged with shadows to create illusions, tricks of the mind. As Kell steadied herself before the mound of wood, she thought she saw movement within it, as if something were burrowing through, pushing aside sticks and twigs. She blinked to clear her vision and then, palms out, searched for that switch, that sensation of release that she often felt when the mysterious energy left her body.

Her fingertips began to itch, and she rubbed them against her palms, noticing that her skin was hot.

"You're doing it!" said Mordecai excitedly, drawing closer.

The moment confidence solidified within her, fire erupted from her palms. Startled by the abruptness and heat of it, she staggered backward, spraying brilliant orange flames not only on the wood pile but on the ground around her. Suddenly panicked, she shook her hands to rid them of the flames, but all the motion did was spread fire all around them.

"Stop!" Mordecai cried, stumbling out of the way.

"I don't know how!" Kell shook her hands again and then balled them into fists. When even that didn't work, she buried her burning fists into her armpits. She felt the energy ebb and then stop. But the damage was done.

Eyes wide, she gaped at the enormous flames that engulfed the pile of deadwood and licked the trunks of neighboring trees. Already, the forest was catching fire, the dry underbrush from summer and early autumn exacerbating the situation and engorging the conflagration within seconds. As the fire leaped with ease up the trunks of trees and spread, its heat rose into the sky, causing cooler air to rush in behind it.

Kell squinted against the wind and heat, horrified—not for the first time—by the destruction of her ability. Mordecai snarled a hand around her arm and pulled. "Let's go!" he shouted.

They ran blindly along the river, tripping over roots, brush, and hidden vegetation and dragging each other along. Despite the distance they kept between them and the fire, the flames seemed to be alive, trailing after them with ease and spreading upward and outward in every direction.

From her periphery, Kell caught sight of flickering orange and yellow fingers fifty feet or so from their position. It was as if the fire were trying to head off their escape.

"We gotta cross the river," Mordecai panted, coughing from the smoke that now drifted through the forest. In the light of the flames, birds and animals alike swarmed past them, paying them no heed.

Together, they slid down the embankment and crashed into the icy water. Kell gasped as she stormed through the river, kicking water around her until suddenly the riverbed gave way. She toppled in over her head. Foregoing her panic, she began swimming, despite the immense drag that her winter clothes created.

"Kell!" shouted Mordecai, his voice muffled and panic-stricken.

She turned mid-stroke to find him struggling to keep his head above the water. With the light of the fire growing ever brighter, she could discern the fright in his eyes. Wanting to drop her boots but afraid that she would come to regret the decision later, she powered back toward Mordecai, swimming hard.

His mouth and nose were just above the waterline and the whites of his eyes gleamed. As she neared, she saw his face go underwater. With a deep breath, she dove, streamlining under the water the final foot or two. She tangled her fingers in his shirt, but when she tried to pull, she felt no upward movement. Mordecai wrapped his arms around Kell as he struggled ineffectively to reach the surface.

Realizing that he was going to drown them both, Kell stopped trying to swim for the surface and instead swam downward. Immediately, Mordecai released her. Eyes wide open, she was still unable to see the bottom of the river, even when she suddenly scraped her chin on it.

Steeling herself, she gathered her body under her, placing her feet on the bottom and angling upward. She pushed off as hard as she could, using the river's current for an extra boost. She saw a rush of white that was Mordecai's shirt and snarled her fingers in it. Kicking hard, she swam upward, and they broke the surface together.

Mordecai turned in her grasp to climb her to keep his head above the surface, but Kell ducked underwater again, leaving her friend to flail. Kell came up behind him. She clamped an arm over his right shoulder, looping it across his chest.

"Stop!" she screamed, struggling to keep them buoyant. "Stop moving! Lay back, lay back! I got you!" Mordecai fought her a moment longer and then did as he was told.

Her breathing coming in rasps, she lay on her side and began swimming to the nearest shoreline, which happened to be the side opposite the fire. The moment her boot touched the rocky bottom, she dug in and began hauling Mordecai out of the river. When the water was to their knees, she urged him to move on his own.

Wheezing, Mordecai dragged himself out of the river and collapsed on the muddy and rock-encrusted embankment. Kell lay beside him, shivering. Across the river, fire continued to spread, devouring everything in its path and moving swiftly as if it were a living creature.

For several long minutes, they were still, panting.

"Thanks," Mordecai eventually murmured.

"Yeah." Kell felt as though she had tumbled down a ravine and been dragged along a river bottom. The teenage boy beside her weighed more, and both wore winter clothes—pants, long-sleeved shirts, boots, and sweaters. She reflected on the fact that she had very nearly just drowned and wholeheartedly thanked Tarquin for his many years of swimming, diving, and water rescue lessons.

Weakly, Kell rolled over and began stripping out of her boots. Realizing what she was doing, Mordecai followed suit. Together, they squeezed their soaked clothes. Though Kell didn't care at the moment whether he saw her, she nevertheless turned her back to him as she pulled off her sopping shirt and began wringing it out. Mordecai also kept his back to her to give the appearance of privacy.

"What now?" Kell asked with a shiver once she was dressed again in her still-wet clothes. She refused to put the sweater back on.

"That fire's going to find a way to cross soon," Mordecai said. "We need to be gone by then." Kell began climbing the embankment. In silence, they staggered onward through the forest.

11

Respite

IT WAS WELL PAST MIDNIGHT when Mordecai found an outcropping of rocks nestled between the trunks of large broad-leaf trees. Using a stick, Kell swept out the dead leaves and refuse from under the ledge, prodded the darkened space to ensure nothing living remained, and then shakily sat. Mordecai didn't ask what she was doing. They had been running for far too long on little food.

Stressed, tired, and cold, Kell wanted nothing more than to curl up and sleep. As she lay down under the rocky ledge, her back to the wall, she tugged on Mordecai's shirt, urging him to join her. With a shiver, he lay down beside her. Their clothes were still damp and the air, which smelled faintly of smoke and dew-damp vegetation, was cold.

Shivering, Kell scooted closer to Mordecai, forcing him to lift his chin so she could burrow closer to his chest and then spread the now-tattered sweater over their arms. They shivered into each other until Mordecai sighed and drew her against him, allowing her to curl her legs against his abdomen.

The cold seemed to disperse quickly afterward. Eyes staring at the creases of Mordecai's shirt in the heavy shadows, she considered all that had happened since they left the abbey and how, without Mordecai, she wouldn't have made it out of the city. Not for the first time, she flushed with gratitude and nestled into his chest. "Thank you," she whispered.

He cleared his throat. "For what?"

Kell barely heard him as the warmth between them lulled her to sleep. Her rest was deep, but not deep enough to distract her mind from the sudden silence of the forest that crept into her sleep.

With a startled yelp, Kell woke an hour or so later. For as far as her eyes could see in every direction the forest pulsed with an orange and red glow.

Though she couldn't hear the fire's incessant crackling and popping yet, she knew it was coming. They needed to move.

"Mordecai, wake up. Come on, wake up." She climbed over him and stood with a grimace. "Shit…" she murmured, searching the forest for a darkened section that wasn't yet on fire. "Shit, shit…"

"Whaz wrong?" Mordecai grunted, joining her.

"The fire," she breathed, heart rate skyrocketing.

Mordecai whirled around. "How did it… We ran for—How could it have… What do we do?"

Spurred to action, Kell took off running east with Mordecai on her heels. Although their path ahead glowed orange, she hoped it was a trick of the terrain, that perhaps the fire was on a hillside or knoll beyond what was immediately in front of them. Maybe there was still an escape route.

They ran through thick, dry vegetation, tripped over logs, and stumbled as old tree branches snarled their pants legs. They climbed a ridge and only realized it once they crested it, which was elevated above all else by way of a gradual incline. Panting, Kell surveyed the land around them. The fire was everywhere, making its way to the top of the elongated ridge where they had found refuge.

"What do we do?" wheezed Kell, turning to look at Mordecai. He was filthy, like her, and the fear in his eyes reflected the horror in hers.

He shook his head, turning to observe the barren trees around them before searching for a path. "Maybe there?" he offered, pointing northward at a sliver of black that jutted out along the land against the glow of the fire. "But we have to hurry."

They broke into an all-out sprint, hardly noticing the obstacles they encountered along the way. Kell could hear the fire now; even above her panting, she could hear the popping, hissing, and general roar of the inferno.

"Come on!" panted Mordecai, surging past her with his long legs. "Come on!" Kell ran as hard as she could but she was worn. Rescuing Mordecai hours earlier had forced her to use every ounce of strength at her disposal. She was exhausted and weak. But she didn't call to Mordecai as he began to put distance between them. Instead, she urged herself, cajoling herself to dig deep and fight.

Her fingers itched and burned, but she wrote it off as her body telling her that danger was near. Even as her adrenaline began to ebb, she pushed on, ignoring her legs that threatened to give out beneath her every pounding step. They could make it! One hundred yards away was a stretch of forest that had yet to incur the wildfire's wrath. Beyond it was a clear swath that led directly north.

Wind gushed around them as the surrounding flames gathered strength and sucked in the cold nighttime air to spur their rampage. Kell could feel the heat starting to lick her skin. Though the fire didn't seem immediately close, its roar and power were undeniable. Staring at Mordecai's back, she realized that she was slowing—dramatically. Already he was thirty or forty feet ahead of her. She tried to call him, but her voice was gobbled up by the wind.

Kell urged her legs to keep going, but the more she focused on them, the clumsier they grew. Upon her next step, her boot caught the entangled branches of a downed limb. With a gasp, she flew forward, the incline of the ridge further accelerating her fall. She toppled head over heels through dead leaves and underbrush before a white-hot pain knocked her senseless.

Moaning, she woke seconds later and rolled over. The sky and the stark tree boughs within her field of vision whirled sickeningly overhead. She clenched her eyes shut as she sat up. The moment she was upright, the earth tilted to the left and then reached up to claim her.

Kell thought she heard Mordecai but couldn't be sure. Her head ached fiercely, and every time she opened her eyes, she couldn't keep the world around her from spinning. Wheezing, she clutched the leaves around her, wondering what had happened. It took her a moment to recall the sudden blossoming of pain and the cause—a rock. She had smashed her head into a rock.

Gingerly and without exactness, Kell tried to probe for injuries, but the simple movement of her arms made her feel as if a yawning chasm had just opened beneath her.

A shadow passed in her periphery, but she chalked it up to the flickering shadows drawing ever closer. There was distant shouting and… discussion? Kell struggled to maintain consciousness, forcing her eyes open and lifting her head. When her vision briefly steadied, she gaped in confusion.

A woman stood several feet uphill, her body silhouetted by the great flames racing toward them. Kell could discern nothing about her except the amber-tinged rings of energy that glowed around her wrists. Starting to feel her head loll, Kell grasped at Mordecai who had come to kneel beside her.

They watched as the woman made full-body gestures at the encroaching flames, her movements purposeful but enigmatic. She pointed and then moved her hands downward and outward several times, stepping back and then rotating on the spot. The following motions she made were too complex for Kell to keep up with as a spell of dizziness struck her. With a whimper, she leaned against Mordecai who protectively wrapped his arms around her, his eyes never leaving the newcomer.

Grimacing, Kell fought to keep herself upright, but it felt as if she were sliding down the ridge. Mordecai's hands barely kept her tethered to reality. "Come on, Kell," he murmured, jostling her. "Stay awake."

"My… head," she whispered, but it didn't seem like he heard her. "My…" The world around her faded as she crumpled against him.

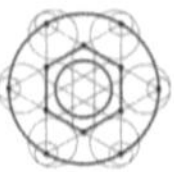

Dockett's laugh broke Simon's concentration. "Lookie here, you didn't run away."

Simon frowned at the ground before he continued his third set of pushups.

"Thought you might make a break for it last night," Dockett said, circling him.

With a sigh, Simon sat back in the courtyard dirt. "I did."

Dockett paused mid-step. "Did you now?"

Simon looked at him. "Made it to the door that leads to the alley we normally go through."

"But?"

"I ran into Eevie." He wiped the sweat along his brow.

"Hm," was all Dockett said, his gaze drifting elsewhere.

Simon lay back in the dirt and began to do sit-ups. "So, here I am."

"You like her, don't you?" Dockett remarked.

"You're one to talk," Simon retorted with a grunt.

The Lanista paced the courtyard for a minute before saying, "If you got past the sentries and made it that far, you could have run. So? What'd she say? What made you turn around?"

Simon stopped, his sweaty back gathering dirt from the earth. "My parents are probably dead. They didn't come to get me at the jail. No one did. Not even…" Kell's name was on his lips, but he couldn't speak it aloud. "I don't think anyone I know made it out of the market that day. There's literally nothing left for me in Lower Eclat." He considered the low-hanging gray clouds overhead, the conclusions he had formed the previous night solidifying within him. "So, I'll get stronger and wipe out every User I cross paths with. I'll train and fight in the Munera so I can make every single one of them suffer like we did." He sat up and looked back at Dockett. "I'll be your Champion. You won't find another like me."

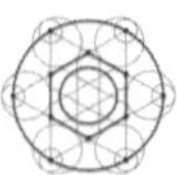

Perplexed, Kellick studied the ceiling in the dim light of morning. It was wood, but it was… wavy—like roots! The ceiling, walls, and floor resembled the underside of a tree, knotted and gnarled but flowing from one side of the large room to the other to create a relatively flat surface. She brushed the wall to her immediate right, picking at it with her nails so that chips of what appeared to be bark peeled off.

Certain she was still loopy, she closed her eyes. The light filtering through the enormous lattice windows along the front of the room illuminated the inside of her eyelids.

She could hardly remember the previous night; it was a blur. How she had made it into the narrow but very comfortable bed in which she currently lay, she didn't know. The whole place smelled faintly of lemongrass, an earthy but sweet and refreshing scent. Outside birds greeted the sun despite the chill in the air.

Kell pulled the quilts up to her nose and breathed deeply, content for the first time in several days. Though she was still dizzy, especially if she moved her head too fast, she felt—for some reason—safe. With a deep sigh, she went back to sleep.

She woke mid-morning to the sound of pots and pans clattering elsewhere in the home. As she stirred, she heard someone cross the room. Cracking her eyes open, she looked up at Mordecai who was smiling at her. "Hey," he croaked.

"Hey," she whispered.

"How are you feeling?"

Kell turned her head and saw the room swirl. She grimaced and closed her eyes. "My head hurts."

"You smashed it into a rock or something," Mordecai said, resting on the side of her bed. "There was blood everywhere. I didn't even realize it until we started carrying you—Oh yeah, there's someone here you should meet. Terin?"

There was no answer.

"Terin?"

"She's out back," came the gravelly voice of an elderly woman from across the room. Kell started to roll her head back to look at the speaker but thought better of it and waited until the senior moved into her field of vision.

The woman was short, far shorter than most other women, and ample around the middle. Her frizzled, gray hair was loosely pulled into a large bun at the back of her head and gave her a wayward appearance. The senior looked Kell over with dull, silver eyes, glancing at her wrists twice before meeting her gaze. The wrinkled skin that hung on the woman's face was loose around her jowls and made her thin mouth appear sterner. She wore a button-down calico cotton dress of sage green whose sleeves had been rolled to her elbows to reveal strong hands and forearms; only the tops of her socks were visible.

Mordecai stood politely. "Kellick, this is…" He eyed her apprehensively. "Ms. Re—"

"Nope," the old woman interrupted.

Mordecai shifted uncomfortably. "This is Renata."

"Kellick, huh? That's a weird name," Renata remarked, crossing her arms. "Never heard that name before."

"My… uncle named me after the first thing he saw."

Renata gazed at her, her head cocked. "Which is what?"

Kell glanced at Mordecai before murmuring, "A kellick anchor."

"You're named for an anchor? Wow, your parents must have hated that."

Kell attempted to sit up. She made it halfway before being forced to hold her throbbing head.

"I imagine you are still dizzy." Renata started back across the room. "I'm making tea that'll help with that. Lie down. Don't need you collapsing and bleeding all over my house."

Kell did as she was told. The moment her head rested on the small pillow, the pain disappeared. Confused, she looked at Mordecai who, seeing the expression on her face, shrugged. He kneeled beside her and chuckled, "I'm relieved."

"Why?" Kell breathed.

"Because I thought she didn't like me." He grinned. "Turns out she's just mean to everyone."

"Where are we?"

Mordecai sat on the floor next to the bed. "We're in the middle of nowhere; that's all I can say. Terin helped carry you last night. We got here a few hours ago." He scrutinized the room and said lowly, "I think it's just Renata and Terin here."

"Out in the middle of the forest?"

Mordecai glanced warily over his shoulder and then scooted closer so he could whisper into her ear. "There's something else you should know—Terin's Unbound."

12

Friends and Enemies

"SIMON, I WANT YOU IN line with the others today," said Dockett, shedding his jacket to reveal his toned torso despite the chilly morning air. He motioned to the dozen or so fighters milling about near the barrel of wooden swords situated in the middle of the barren practice yard.

Steeling himself, Simon hurried over. He was the youngest there and the smallest by far. The others, eleven men and two women, all of whom were at least in their early twenties, muttered in amusement to one another and gestured toward Simon. Remembering what he had declared to Dockett, Simon lifted his chin and hardened his face.

"Weapons!" Dockett called, waving to his assistant, Arden, across the practice yard. While the fighters dove for the wooden swords in the barrel, Simon watched Arden open a metal gate and call someone beyond the doorway.

A moment later, a line of Users, their tattoo bindings apparent in the morning sun, marched into the practice yard. They appeared anxious, jumpy, and unprepared. Though Simon scowled, he couldn't help but note the handful of women among their ranks.

"This is an assessment," announced Dockett, striding into the vast expanse between the two groups, a large Bo staff slung over his shoulder.

Simon retrieved one of the last wooden swords available, standing on his tiptoes to grab its hilt over the lip of the barrel. The wooden sword was heavy, a lot heavier than he expected. Worry bloomed in him as he turned to evaluate the opposing group.

"You can maim, injure, whatever—but no killing. I didn't pay good money for you chicken-hearted unlicked cubs to be offin' each other without an audience. Got it?"

The fighters chorused a loud, "Yes, sir!" startling Simon horribly. Dockett looked at the Users who, even to Simon's untrained eyes, appeared utterly horrified by what the Lanista had just said. Where did they think they were? Had Dockett told them? They had to know, right?

"Users," Dockett said, "You may use whatever meager abilities you have so long as you do not kill anyone. I understand you can't always control it. That's fine. We have precautions in place." Dockett looked back at the fighters. "If I call rest, you are to stop fighting. Am I understood?"

"Yes, sir!" This time Simon joined in the coordinated response. He watched with some pleasure as some of the Users backed toward the door through which they had come.

"If myself or Arden or Tomas call you out, you retreat to the sidelines over here." Docket pointed to the benches on the eastern side of the yard. "The group with the most remaining members gets extra portions tonight at dinner." He looked between the two groups and then sighed and strode to the side of the yard, saying more to himself than to anyone else, "All right, let's get this over with."

Simon tried to calm himself, to steady his hands, but no matter how much he tried to force his wooden sword still, it trembled. He could feel the gaze of the enormous dark-skinned man, whose name he knew was Ferrik, beside him. Stubborn, he settled his eyes on the Users. Hadn't he told Dockett that he would make them pay? That he would make them suffer like they had him?

Feeling that familiar sense of injustice and rage, Simon gripped his weapon tighter.

Dockett loosed a sharp whistle. Encouraged by the more experienced fighters' confidence and their uniform movement forward, Simon made sure to stay in step with them. He smirked as he saw the Users, who were more a collection of fidgeting bodies rather than a purpose-filled group of combatants, back up until they couldn't.

This was going to be easy. Simon smiled, bearing his sword.

As the dozen fighters circled the Users and began berating them with curses and degrading insults, they shook their swords at them and bluffed attacks. Though some of the more honorable men had taken up defensive positions around the female Users, it was evident that all were going to have to fight or risk being brutally injured.

Egged on by their meekness and their inability to make a stand, Simon drew closer, too close. A young teen User with long, tangled sandy-blond hair lashed out. A rolling wave of fire streamed from a fist, instantly transforming the chilly October air into a stovetop surface. A mighty kick from Ferrik, the dark-skinned man to his left, sent Simon toppling into the dirt, saving him from the worst of the fiery assault.

Embarrassed, Simon scrambled to his feet but ended up just watching. In the seconds that he had been down, all-out fighting had erupted. He staggered aside as another belch of fire roared past him.

He didn't want to be there. He didn't want to be so close to fire. It scared him too much. He had only barely made it off Donahue Street that disastrous morning three months ago. His family and friends hadn't been so lucky.

Panicked, he inched away from the fighting, his breathing coming in rasps. He was a fisherman's son, not a fighter! He should have escaped when he had the chance. Why had he let Eevie distract him?

The blond-haired teenager who had initially attacked him took a brutal lateral strike from Ferrik's sword and then crumpled to the ground near Simon, wheezing and coughing. Simon's mature ally met his gaze and motioned to the blond User before turning away to fend off another's attack.

Simon approached the teenage User cautiously, his sword before him. He knew he was to strike the boy unconscious or to otherwise incapacitate him but… he was down. He was already injur—

The blond suddenly looked up to meet Simon's eyes, his face full of rage, injustice, and pain, the scar on his left eyebrow brilliant against his tan and sweaty face. The sounds of the battle around them faded as Simon suddenly recognized Ambrose, Hugh's son.

Ambrose's hair was longer and his face gaunt with stress and fatigue, but there was no denying it. Everyone on the docks was familiar with the vertical scar that cut through Ambrose's brow. He had received it by walking up behind his father who reared back with a cleaving knife to butcher the day's catch.

Recognition tinged Ambrose's hazel gaze. "Simon?"

"You're… a User?" was all Simon could say.

Holding his injury, Ambrose glanced over his shoulder at the fighting and then rose. "What are… you doing here?"

"You're a User," Simon muttered. "Were you always a User?"

Ambrose nodded weakly, his brows folding upward. "What are you doing he—"

"Did I say stop?" roared Dockett who had somehow made it over to them without being seen or heard. He whipped his Bo staff over his shoulder and smacked Simon along the shoulders, sending him sprawling into the dirt beside Ambrose. He turned to assault Ambrose, but the teenager held up a fist, his knuckles already flaming. "I've fought more Users than you've seen, boy. Get movin'!"

Ambrose passed Simon a look before turning and running back into the melee.

Dockett snarled a hand around Simon's pants hem and yanked him up. "Where the fuck is my champion, the one you were speaking of? 'Cause I don't see him!"

"I just—I know—That's Ambrose. He's a—"

"I don't care what the hell he is! Your comrades are over there fighting and you've left them!" He kicked Simon in the butt with his booted foot. "Get over there and help!"

Forgetting his sword in the dirt, Simon scrambled into the battle. His lack of a weapon and general disorientation immediately sewed confusion among the participants, causing fighters to sidestep him and Users to momentarily stop their attacks as the innocent child flinched at their nearness.

The next minute, Arden took hold of Simon and led him out of battle. He shoved him onto the bench along the eastern side of the yard and then jogged back into the chaos. Defeated, humiliated, and completely in shock, Simon hung his head.

The fight ended a few minutes later. It looked as though it was a draw, gauging by the number of people who had joined him on the benches and those who remained. Ashamed, he kept his gaze turned down at the dirt. He didn't hear Dockett call his name until someone whacked his shoulder.

Simon found the Lanista's blue gaze and immediately dreaded what was to come.

"Here, now," Dockett called.

Aware that every person there was watching him, Simon rose and shuffled to the lanky man.

"You too."

Simon glanced up to see Ambrose hesitantly join. A cut along the left side of his face oozed blood and his arms were scuffed up and bruised.

"Since there's been a draw, Simon and Ambrose here will be the deciding match," Dockett announced. Simon shook his head in desperation. "Winner not only gets extra portions tonight but the day off tomorrow."

"Dockett—" Simon hadn't even gotten his plea out of his mouth before the Lanista turned on him and snarled his fingers in Simon's hair, effectively shutting him up.

"You win this, or you're sleeping in a cell tonight. Got it?"

Dockett released him and stalked to the benches, giving Simon time to look at Ambrose who also appeared frightened. There was no way he could win against the eighteen-year-old, especially since Ambrose was a User. Simon searched for his sword but remembered he had seen Arden pick it up with the other wooden weapons.

"Let's go, boys!" Dockett called, brandishing his Bo staff.

With an apologetic shrug and a worried grimace, Ambrose stepped forward, his fists positioned in front of him. Simon shakily took the fighting stance that Dockett had taught him—left foot forward, knees bent, hands open and positioned in front of his face, elbows down. Even still, as Ambrose shuffled forward, Simon inched backward.

Dockett left the benches with his staff, prompting Ambrose to send a spiraling flare of fire at Simon. Its heat and momentum, Simon realized, were greatly reduced and he understood that Ambrose was not coming at him with aggressive purpose like he had earlier. Simon dodged the attack and started to move forward but halted as he saw Dockett stalk over to Ambrose.

Ambrose blanched and turned his fists, which had erupted in orange flames, toward Dockett. With speed Simon didn't know Dockett possessed, the Lanista feigned a blow to the back of Ambrose's head. Ambrose turned to meet it, a plume of blistering fire venting in a single motion. But Dockett was much too fast for the inexperienced teenager and whirled away at the last second to land a nasty blow across his gut with the broadside of the staff.

Ambrose doubled over and then collapsed, audibly gasping for air. "You dare turn those cuffed hands on me, you piece of alley shit?" Dockett snarled. The Lanista jerked Ambrose semi-upright and then looked at Simon. "Get over here and hit him."

Simon's feet felt like lead weights, but with Dockett's threats looming over him, he joined them. The lanky man held Ambrose still before slapping Simon across the face. Tears gathering in his eyes, Simon finally met Ambrose's gaze.

Having finally caught his breath, Ambrose steeled himself and gave a small, indiscernible nod. A tear tracked down Simon's dirty cheek as he reared back and delivered a blow to Ambrose. Dockett let the teen crumple to the earth, unconscious.

"The fighters win today," the Lanista announced. "Everyone gets extra portions and a free day tomorrow." He turned on Simon. "Except you."

Simon cried, his gaze on Ambrose.

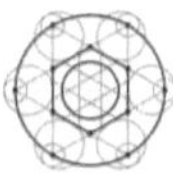

It was late afternoon before Kell felt steady enough to stand. Though Mordecai had stayed with her most of the day, she was relieved to be independent and coherent once more. Renata's teas had helped tremendously.

She had finally met Terin, a tall, nineteen-year-old young woman with black, kinky hair so thick that she seemed to struggle wrangling it every time it broke free of its bonds. Terin was lithe and had an athletic build. Unlike the majority of women that Kell saw in the city or even along the docks, Terin refused to wear dresses, instead opting for pants, boots, and various men's shirts. She was a rebellious spirit with a sparkling smile and bronze skin that gleamed in the October sunlight. Her dull teak wood-colored eyes, however, belied her generally cheerful outward appearance and hinted at past hardships.

"Hey, you're up," Terin called as she appeared around the side of the house, her stride comfortable and long. Mordecai followed carrying firewood.

Kell, who had been standing in the doorway of the living house marveling at its design and creation, grinned. "Yeah, the world's not spinning anymore."

Terin ran an appraising eye over her. "Without the old lady clothes, you'd pass as a boy." She nodded to her chest. "Except for them breasts poking through."

Kell frowned, blushing against Mordecai's sudden searching gaze. She had taken the bandages off at the abbey prior to bed and had not given her budding breasts a second thought. Still dressed in the worn long-sleeve blouse and pants the elderly woman had gifted her, Kell self-consciously folded her arms across her chest. "The clothes aren't mine."

Terin chuckled. "I can tell."

Kell stepped aside so she and Mordecai could enter the unique home.

"Let's get you bathed and see if any of Renata's clothes fit you."

"She's old too," Kell muttered.

Terin laughed. "They're better than what you're wearing."

Kell watched Mordecai deposit wood next to a stone-encrusted hearth on the other side of the sitting room. She noticed that he was devoid of dirt and filth. Though he wore the same clothes, his garb also appeared clean and washed.

"I'll draw a bath and then see if Renata's got anything you can wear." Terin disappeared into the kitchen, leaving Kell alone with Mordecai.

Kell joined him in the middle of the room. "Who are these people?"

He shrugged, keeping his eyes off her. "Terin's an Unbound User. That's all I know."

"Are they connected with anyone? Like Eclat or Avives or... I don't know." She sighed. "I'm just so..."

"Tired?" offered Mordecai.

Kell met his gaze. He looked exhausted; his eyes were heavy and his face taut with stress. They had been going since the fire at the abbey a few days prior. "Yeah," she admitted.

"Kellick?" called Terin from the room beyond the kitchen. "Come on."

She imparted Mordecai a look and then crossed the sitting room. At the kitchen's threshold, she peered in, ogling the clay stove and oven with confusion. They were made of earth; that much she could discern. But they appeared like nothing she had seen before.

The stove was at waist-height and had two "burners" upon which pots could be placed. The opening directly beneath those burners was free of charred wood, ash, or fire refuse. The oven, which was directly adjacent to the stove, was of similar build but boasted a dome shape and a chimney that rose through the ceiling of intertangled branches and roots. Black soot colored its entrance.

Various dried herbs hung from the ceiling—Kell frowned in confusion as she scrutinized the bundles. Where she expected to see ribbons or twine holding them together were spindles of new tree growth and vines that neatly wrapped around the herbs to keep them tight against the ceiling. As Kell gawked, she became aware of Terin leaning in the opposite doorway, an amused smile on her face.

"What are we looking at?" the young woman asked.

"How did... It looks like the ceiling is holding these herbs. How did you make it do that?"

Terin chuckled. "Viterra." She ushered Kell into the next room which was far smaller. It had a large open-air bay window that overlooked the rest of the forest and the narrow river that ran behind the house. Under the window was an impressive clay bathtub with deep, steaming water.

Seeing no faucets, Kell looked about the small room. "Where'd you get the water? How is it hot?"

Again, Terin laughed. "Viterra." When Kell only stared at her, bemused, the young woman grew solemn. "You don't... know what that is, do you?" Kell shook her head. Terin cocked her head in interest. "But you... You're Unbound, right?"

Kell glanced around, unsure if she should be answering such a sensitive question aloud.

"Oh." Terin thought for a moment and then said, "Um, so, everything around us... No... Uh, Unbound draw Viterra from the Earth. We *use* the planet's energy as our own. For people who are cuffed, like Mordecai, they can only access small amounts of that energy. They've been blocking from drawing more."

"But not us..." breathed Kell, her eyes steady on Terin.

"Yeah, not us. Once we learn to, we can use that energy and control it. But energy comes in different forms—fire, water, air, rocks and dirt, organic materials like plants. So it's—"

"There's more than just fire?" Kell interrupted, eyes wide.

"Of course. Why would there only be fire?"

Kell glanced out the enormous window and then at the bathwater. "I've only ever seen fire."

"That's because it's the easiest form of Viterra to access," said Renata, appearing in the doorway of the washroom. "Doesn't matter if you're cuffed or not, fire is easy to channel. But if you can't control fire, you can't control anything else." The old woman gestured to the tub. "Get 'er washed, Terin. We'll talk later." Renata passed old eyes over Kell and then left.

After a bath, Kell felt refreshed but more confused than ever. Users could evoke more than just fire. What an extraordinary revelation! All her life, she had only ever heard the other boys and those along the docks mention Users' inability to control the fire within them. Never before had Kell heard of instances where water had been turned onto fishermen or trees had come to life. Grinning, she dressed in the clothes Terin had found for her—gray slacks, a pale yellow long-sleeved, collared shirt, socks, and a small bandeau.

After slipping the bandeau on, Kell scrutinized herself, hiking it up and adjusting it until it felt kind of comfortable. With a frown, she finished dressing. It would take time to grow accustomed to the restraint around her torso. Ruffling her short hair into place, she left the washroom and entered the kitchen where she found Terin reading a rather lengthy paperback book at the small gnarled and knotted table of roots that jutted from the wall.

"Everything fit well enough?" the young woman asked.

"For the most part," Kell replied, pulling at the bandeau.

"You'll get used to it. When they get bigger, you'll want one. It keeps them from flopping everywhere."

Blushing, Kell sat on the strategically bent roots across from Terin. Drawing a slow breath, she said, "I want to know everything. All of it."

Terin laughed. "I expected as much—"

All laughter faded from her face quite suddenly.

"What?" asked Kell, glancing around before looking back at Terin. "What's wrong?"

With her middle finger, the young woman quickly drew a circle on the table of roots and then pressed her palm atop it. An amber ring materialized around her wrist.

Fascinated, Kell waited a moment before asking again, "What is it?"

Terin's brown eyes flashed a frightening shade of murder as she stood brusquely and headed for the front doorway. Startled by the abrupt change in the young woman, Kell hesitated before following her.

"Stay here," Terin told Mordecai who had just returned, carrying more wood.

Mordecai exchanged looks with Kell before dumping the kindling near the hearth. "What's going on?" he whispered, alarmed.

"I don't know. We were talking and she just—" Kell gestured toward the doorway.

Mordecai tugged her across the sitting room to peer out the window, carefully keeping the majority of his head hidden. Kell joined him.

Terin stalked out beyond the treehouse into the expansive glade, her gait stiff, body squared, and gaze set to the southwest. Kell was about to say something but movement in the forest stopped her. Momentarily, a horde of people on horseback left the tree line. Mordecai hissed in anger as a woman dressed in crimson maneuvered ahead to lead the group.

"That's her," Kell whispered. "That's the woman who tried to burn me."

Mordecai whirled around, searching the house. "Where's Renata?"

"I thought she was with you."

He looked back at the approaching group. Of the nine riders, most were dressed for the weather with long pants and light uniform jackets of brown. But Madam Nicolea wore a red riding suit with polished black boots, her brown hair pulled back in a severe bun at the back of her head.

"This isn't good," Mordecai hissed.

Kell watched the group approach Terin. Staying hidden, she and Mordecai listened, their faces barely visible above the window edge.

"Good day," greeted Madam Nicolea. "Might you be the owner of this," she scrutinized the enormous treehouse, "residence?"

Terin's response was curt. "What do you want?"

Madam Nicolea swung out of the saddle and landed gracefully beside her bay gelding. She passed the reins to the mounted man beside her and then, taking her riding gloves off, strode toward Terin. "I apologize if I've offended you. That was not my intention. My name is Elpida Nicolea. I'm Deputy of the Containment Office in Avives." She held her hand out to Terin. "And you are?"

"I know who you are." Terin didn't move. "What do you want?"

Madam Nicolea cocked her head in mild interest before rescinding her handshake. "You know of me, hm? Very well, then you know I'm not here for pleasure. We've been pursuing two fugitives, two Users. Dangerous kids. They set Abbey of the Sacred Tree in Avives on fire. From what I gather, they torched much of the surrounding forest as well." The woman eyed Terin. "They wouldn't have passed through here, would they?"

Given Terin's generally threatening demeanor, Kell didn't think the young woman would respond.

"They did," said Terin. "We gave them food and water, and they left yesterday afternoon."

Madam Nicolea's gaze passed sharply over the organic abode, causing Kell and Mordecai to duck out of sight. "Yesterday afternoon, you say? They're moving surprisingly fast." She sighed. "Could we trouble you for some water? We exhausted our supply dealing with the fires."

"There's a river that way," Terin replied, jerking her thumb in the direction.

Madam Nicolea held her gaze before her eyes flickered back to the tree-hewn house. "Do you live here alone?" the deputy asked.

Terin blocked her. "My living situation is not relevant."

"I was just wondering—"

"Hold on, Terin. Hold on," called Renata, shuffling out from behind the treehouse. Where she had been, Kell didn't know. "What's all this ruckus about?"

"I beg your pardon," said Madam Nicolea with sincerity that would have tricked anyone. "I'm Deputy of the Containment Office in Avives. We're pursuing two fugitives, two Users. They burned an abbey in town. Your… *granddaughter* said they passed through here yesterday and that you rendered aid? Could you describe them?"

"Two boys," Renata said, her gait becoming more halting. She cleared her throat obnoxiously. "One older, one younger. Said they were traveling. We gave them some roast pheasant and water; they were off before the sun set."

"Did they appear injured?"

Renata thought. "No, they seemed to be in good spirits."

"What were they wearing?"

Renata looked at Terin. "Do you remember?"

Terin mustered a shrug. "Nothing out of the ordinary—just pants and shirts, some boots."

"Oh, one of them was wearing a hat," Renata added convincingly and then she gave a hacking cough.

"Oh, thank you. I'm sure we'll be able to catch up. They've got to rest sometime." Madam Nicolea studied the vast trees that intertwined to form the two-story residence. "My, this is an unusual home. How did you construct it *and* keep the trees alive?"

"It took many years," replied Renata. "My late husband was an artist and was eager to see if he could force plants to grow in a certain manner." She gestured weakly toward the house. "This is the result."

"What a magnificent experiment!" exclaimed Madam Nicolea. "May I see inside?"

Kell looked at Mordecai with wide eyes. Surely the old woman wouldn't oblige!

"But of course," replied Renata, turning for the house.

Kell and Mordecai scrambled away from the window. Kell knew they shouldn't haven't trusted Renata and Terin! The two women had probably been on the fence about housing Kell and Mordecai and the damning report of how she had burned the abbey to the ground had just tipped them over the edge.

Kell searched the relatively bare room for somewhere to hide. Aside from a sofa made from the skins of some short-furred animal and the end tables of neatly organized roots, the room was empty. She turned to follow Mordecai to the kitchen but felt a spark of something, a brief fluttering of energy. Mordecai must have felt it too because he paused mid-step, bewildered.

Kell lurched as the roots beneath her feet suddenly bucked and slithered backward; together, she and Mordecai toppled into a black abyss.

13

New Beginnings

HISSING IN PAIN, KELL FIDGETED against Mordecai and looked up at the roots snaking closed. It was black, horribly dark; no light penetrated the organic weave of intertwined roots. Mordecai breathed hard beside her as he attempted to right himself. Groping for one another, they remained quiet as footsteps reverberated overhead.

"Oh my, how lovely," she heard Madam Nicolea breathe. "Amazing. And you and your husband did all of this by hand?"

"We did," replied Renata, standing directly over their heads. "It took many, many years as you can imagine."

"What do you do for food?" the deputy asked, striding across the sitting room to the kitchen. "I beg your pardon, but living so primitively at your age must be quite difficult."

"I'm lucky my granddaughter is here," Renata replied, her voice gravelly. "She hunts, and I keep a small herb and vegetable garden out back. We also have a herd of sheep. It's hard work living out here, but I wouldn't have it any other way."

"Mh-hm…" Madam Nicolea's voice was distant. When she next spoke, the warmth in her voice was gone. "You keep a fastidious home."

"Thank you."

"Could I see the upstairs?"

"Certainly."

The deputy's booted footsteps echoed overhead as she and Renata crossed the sitting room to the narrow staircase along the eastern wall.

Kell leaned into Mordecai, gripping his arm for comfort. If they were found, there would be no escape. They could only trust that Renata and Terin knew what they were doing.

Eventually, Madam Nicolea's voice filtered through the roots as they returned to the sitting room. "When did you say the two fugitives left your residence?"

"Yesterday afternoon, close to sunset," Renata replied.

"I see."

"Please feel free to use the river for water," Renata graciously continued. "I would offer food, but we hardly have enough to satiate ourselves, much less a sizeable group such as yours."

Kell didn't hear Madam Nicolea respond, so she assumed she had left. With a deep sigh, she released Mordecai and began feeling for the walls. If the danger had passed, she wanted to leave the black prison. It reminded her far too much of the Vault at the abbey.

Suddenly there was a flash of orange light that broke through the intricately intertwined flooring. Kell staggered backward as she felt the accompanying heat.

"They set it on fire," she whispered, groping for Mordecai. She accidentally hit him along the side of his head.

Mordecai held her, his grip trembling. "Hold on, hold on. Maybe it's not that."

"No, she set the place on fire." Kell could feel the panic rising in her throat. "Mordecai, the fire. The fire."

"Calm dow—"

Another flair of light thinned the organic spindles above them, and smoke began drifting into their makeshift prison. Unable to control her terror, Kell braced against the roots with a whimper as light began penetrating the mesh overhead. The tangle of coarse roots was at just a level that she couldn't push with the backs of her shoulders nor could she fully extend her arms; she couldn't exert the necessary strength. "Mordecai!" she cried and then coughed against the invading smoke.

"Don't give up! Come on!" he shouted, the crackling of fire turning into a steady roar beyond their cell.

Together, they continued to search, pulling and pushing, tugging and jerking, constantly testing the roots. All the while, the smoke grew denser and their coughing intensified until, growing dizzy and unable to catch her breath, Kell slumped into the bottom of the pit. Momentarily, Mordecai joined her, wheezing.

Forgoing crying because she could no longer properly breathe, Kell buried her face in her shirt and urged Mordecai to do the same. Just as she turned to lie lower in the pit, there came pounding footsteps overhead. Someone dropped to the floor above their heads.

Kell felt that familiar fluttering in her chest and squinted up as the roots overhead pulled apart to reveal Terin who appeared generally disheveled. Flames roared around her but none touched her. As she reached into the pit, her wrists adorned with two golden bands of energy, a gust of fresh air engulfed them, and Kell took a deep breath.

"Come on!" Terin called. "Let's go!"

Kell took her arm and clambered out of the prison.

"Wait right beside me," the young woman instructed, reaching for Mordecai.

Kell gaped at the roaring inferno around them. The ceiling was on fire. The walls crackled and popped and roiled with water as it boiled from the living roots. The kitchen was nothing but a hellish oven.

"Let's go, let's go!" Terin called, once she drew Mordecai upward. She charged toward the back of the house that was ablaze. She made a series of complex signs within the span of a few seconds, and the wall opened.

Together, they escaped, running through flames that somehow didn't touch them before careening into the creek. The iciness of the clear water tore a gasp from Kell's throat, but she reveled in its familiarity.

Terin didn't let them stay there for long. Plunging across the shallow tributary, she urged them to follow.

"What about Renata?" called Mordecai as they ran on.

Terin didn't answer.

She led them deep into the forest, up and over a ridge, and to a glen north of the ruined home. When they finally came to a spot upriver, the young woman let them rest.

Lying across a downed tree next to the river's embankment, Mordecai worked to catch his breath. Kell sat beside him, panting, her gaze on Terin who was angrily pacing the embankment. Eventually, Kell exchanged looks with Mordecai and then pushed herself to her feet and cautiously joined Terin.

"Thanks for coming for us," Kell said.

Terin grunted as she continued to stare out at the passing river.

After a moment, Kell ventured, "What happened?"

"Bitch set our house on fire," seethed Terin. "She knew you were there; she just couldn't find you." Terin kneeled, picked up a collection of pebbles, and began chucking them into the river. "So she set the whole thing on fire."

Kell swallowed. "And Renata?"

Terin threw two more stones and then, with a snarl, lifted an enormous rock from its resting place deep within the damp soil. The amber rings around her wrists flared as she pulverized the rock between her palms, allowing its dust to slip through her fingers. "I told her," Terin snarled, "that *I* would handle them. I told her that I… This was *my* chance—"

"Wait, is Renata… Did they kill Renata?"

Terin released the remaining dust and gravel and wiped her hands on her pants, scoffing. "What? No. Renata's Unbound. They can't do shit to her."

Kell relaxed, looking back at Mordecai who also appeared relieved. "I'm glad."

"But I should have been the one to duel that bitch. It should have been *me*! After everything she did…" Terin kicked the water in frustration and then stormed off down the shoreline.

Mordecai joined Kell, his gaze set on Terin.

"What was that about?" Kell asked, confused by Terin's outburst.

"I'm going to guess that she's had some run-ins with the Containment Office," Mordecai mused.

Kell squeegeed her clothes, watching Terin as the young woman disappeared around the river's bend. "What now?" she asked.

Mordecai pulled off his shirt and squeezed the water from it. "I think you and I should move on." He lowered his voice. "I don't want to cause more trouble."

Kell frowned. "But where are we going to go? We can't survive out here, Mordecai." She looked out at the river. "If we were on the ocean, we could, but not here."

"Are you crazy? The ocean would kill us even quicker."

Kell didn't feel like arguing, so she took to pacing the river's edge. They couldn't go back to Avives—for obvious reasons—and returning to Eclat was out of the question. Eventually, she sat on a rock in the sunshine to dry off.

She wasn't a planner, never had been. Tarquin had never really talked much about ambition or purpose or direction. Although he planned, it had only been about when and where they would fish that day. Preparing meals, scheduling maintenance or cleaning days, or going to the market had never been a part of Kell and Tarquin's lives. They ate what they caught and whatever someone else shared; maintenance and cleaning were done whenever; and if it was time for the market, well, then maybe they'd go or maybe they'd sleep in.

Kell sighed. Now she wished she knew what it meant to plan. No matter how she tried to focus on the future or assign a goal to herself, she couldn't see it in her mind's eye. Where were they going? What did she hope to achieve? How were they going to survive?

"What are you thinking?" asked Mordecai, kicking a rock beside her.

Kell leaned back on her hands and squinted up at the autumn trees and their vibrant hues so vivid in the glorious sun. "What's north of here?"

Mordecai stopped his fidgeting. "I… have no idea."

"Would Terin know?"

"If she grew up in Avives like me, then no—"

The sound of rushing water caused both of them to look downriver. Kell's mouth fell open. Surfing up the river was Renata, who appeared to be standing upon the rapids themselves, bracing on the outline of a circle that glowed a pleasant shade of moss green. Her forearms each bore two green rings that remained in place as she balanced on the transparent circle. The plain dress she wore flapped around her boots.

Kell and Mordecai watched as she calmly surfed up to them, stepped onto the dry shoreline, and shook her hands. The circle under her feet disappeared as did the bands around her wrists. Her hair was disheveled, but Kell speculated that it was more as a result of her surfing rather than battle. Otherwise, the old woman was remarkably unscathed.

With a heavy sigh, Renata resettled a bulky satchel over her shoulder and looked between them. "Where's Terin?"

Mordecai, who was just as speechless, pointed over his shoulder.

"Yeah, well, I'm sure she is pissed. All right, let's get situated and then I'll have her go find the damn sheep."

"What about Madam Nicolea?" asked Mordecai.

Renata smirked. "Oh, her. We came to an… understanding."

"But…" Kell exchanged looks with Mordecai. "Your… house."

Renata settled her gaze on a point in the distance. "Well, it's gone. But not to worry, I've got another." Her beady gaze suddenly turned on them. "So, you two burned down an abbey?" Mordecai pointed at Kell who swatted his hand away. "Which one was it? Ashwood Abbey?"

"Abbey of the Sacred Tree," Kell muttered, glancing at the water.

Renata grimaced. "Yeah, that would explain why they've chased you out this far. Did'ja do it on purpose?"

"What? No!" sputtered Kell. "They… found out I'm Unbound. I made a run for it… and accidentally set everything on fire."

Renata gestured at Mordecai. "And where do you come into the picture?"

Mordecai's shoulders slumped. "I helped her escape."

"But you're Bound, I see." Renata shifted her weight back and forth in thought. "Real fast, you two—What do you know about Arcane Circles?" Both shook their heads. "Well, that explains a lot."

She stepped a few paces away so she was on the damp dirt near the waterline and then drew a surprisingly precise circle around her with the tip of her boot. In a quick jerk she struck her forearms together, as if spreading a drop of perfumed oil, igniting a band of green around both wrists. A glowing circle materialized under her feet. Now that she was closer, Kell could discern cryptic symbols that scrolled around the circle's edge. Delicate intersecting lines fanned out beneath Renata to form perfectly aligned decussate squares, triangles, and circles.

The old woman studied Kell and Mordecai, gauging their reactions, and then said, "A mighty river can go wherever it wants. It is as ancient as the Earth itself and is wild, unpredictable, and seemingly unstoppable. But over time, humans have come to know how to control its strength through the use of different types of dams. With dams, we can stop or change a river's course, control its flow, and utilize its power. Viterra is like a river, and Arcane Circles are like dams."

Renata passed an appraising eye over Mordecai. "You're Bound. You've been given a cement wall through which very little Viterra can pass. What you are able to conjure will be through training and willpower. You will not be able to access the full Flow, ever. And for that, I am sorry." She looked at Kell. "But you… You're a torrent of Viterra careening down a mountain pass without hindrance. You are dangerous and powerful."

The old woman adjusted the satchel across her shoulder and then motioned to them. "Spread out, the both of you. Draw a circle in the dirt. Any time you are going to access the Flow, define yourself to the Universe. Strongly and confidently announce yourself."

Kell stepped away from Mordecai and clumsily drew a crooked oval in the dirt. Mordecai's wasn't much better.

"Again. Better this time."

It took several tries before each was able to draw a relatively even circle.

"Good," Renata instructed, shuffling around them to examine their work. "Much better. You've defined yourself to the Flow, but the Arcane Circle will not come into being unless it's activated." The old woman touched the underside of her wrists together, nodding for them to copy her. "We've defined the Self, now we activate the first Field. It's a fast, sharp movement. Wait, wait!"

Kell and Mordecai looked at her abruptly as both were about to do as she had instructed.

Renata pointed to Mordecai. "You first. Remember, it doesn't have to be hard, just fast."

Kell stepped back as Mordecai spread his legs within his drawn circle and, with a determined look on his face, struck his arms downward as if he were trying to start a fire using flint and steel. Nothing happened.

"Try again," Renata urged.

Mordecai did so and was rewarded with a red glow that briefly flickered into existence and then vanished.

"Once more."

Kell could discern the discouragement on his face but knew better than to interrupt his concentration.

Mordecai studied his wrists for a long moment, his eyes tracing the faded tattoo that marked him as Bound. After a long moment, he drew a steadying breath and struck his wrists. The Arcane Circle beneath his feet again flashed; no glowing bands formed on his wrists.

Before Renata could say anything, Mordecai struck his wrists again. The circle under him flickered before returning to its mundane state. He did it again and again and again. Each time, the circle flared to life but stayed illuminated for only a second before sputtering out.

"I know he can do it," said Kell suddenly, certain that she needed to convince Renata before the old woman decided to distance herself from the Bound boy. "I saw him, well, I didn't see him with those glowing bands, but I know he can access the, uh—what's it called?—the Flow."

Renata's gray eyes searched them both before she said, "We'll keep working on it. Now, you. Mordecai, come over here beside me." With Mordecai behind her, Renata gestured to Kell. "Let's see what you can do, kid."

Standing in her circle, Kell envisioned what she had to do. Fists clenched, she quickly struck her wrists together in a downward movement just as Renata had shown them. The circle under her flared to life. Kell gasped as she felt that familiar snap within her followed by a dizziness that rocked her body. Blinking, she fought to keep herself upright, her legs swaying under her as though she were rocking back and forth on *Polaris* in rough weather.

"Easy, Kellick." Renata's voice was steady and tethering like an anchor. "You're channeling a lot of Viterra right now. In time, you'll be able to control how much you draw from the Flow. But for now, take it easy."

Kell looked at Renata and Mordecai, her heart thrumming in her ears. Slowly, her world steadied.

Renata scrutinized her, nodding in thought. "Water, huh? Interesting. Look at your hands."

Kell did as she was told and found ethereal bracelets humming around her wrists, their weight unfamiliar but satisfying. They were the color of a summer sky, deep bright blue. The Arcane Circle under her was also blue. The scrawling symbols that rimmed the circle appeared different than the ones that adorned Renata's circle. "W-water?" Kell asked, her voice hoarse. "What do you mean?"

"There are six elements—fire, water, earth, flora, air, and metal. Most Unbound with no training will gravitate toward only one. Your element is water. Terin's is fire. Mine is flora." She looked at Mordecai. "Even you will eventually be drawn to a specific element." Renata approached Kell, studying the Arcane Circle. "Because you are drawn to the element of water doesn't mean you can't access the others. It simply means that that's what you are most comfortable with."

Kell frowned. "But all the Users I've ever seen have red bands. And none of them use circles."

"Red is the color of imprisonment. It reveals activation of the Flow through bondage." Renata shook her hands to rid herself of the Viterra she had conjured; the bands and her circle vanished. "And of course, no one's using Arcane Circles. They've been all but forgotten. Avives, Eclat, and other cities have been systematically wiping out our people for decades, targeting elders to stop the spread of information."

Kell looked at her, alarmed. "Is that why you live out here?"

Renata smirked. "No, I just hate everyone." She drew a deep breath. "When you need to stop channeling Viterra, break your circle or purposefully shake your hands like this." The old woman showed her, and Kell mimicked the technique. "Only you can break your circle, no one else. If your concentration wavers, if you become mentally or physically spent and can no longer channel the Flow, it will break." She sighed. "I don't want to go too long without the both of you studying."

Grinning triumphantly, Kell looked at Mordecai, pleased with herself. When she saw his tempered smile, she scolded herself for causing him to feel shame. With ease, she had just accomplished something that was a struggle for him. Of course he was disappointed.

"Come on, you two. Let's find Terin, make sure she's not destroyed the ridge." Renata started down the shoreline. Kell and Mordecai followed silently.

They found Terin seated on an enormous boulder near the river's embankment, burning twigs between her fingers. Two amber bands of Viterra glowed around her wrists; the rock upon which she sat was adorned with an amber Arcane Circle. Spotting them, she knocked aside her pile of kindling and stood. "Well?" she called to Renata.

"They're gone." Renata joined her. Terin slid off and landed gracefully on the bank, her mane of thick hair following her. The young woman opened her mouth to argue, but Renata stopped her. "It's over, done. She's gone. We won't speak of it anymore, understood?"

Disappointment darkened Terin's face but she nodded.

"Good. Now, go find our stupid sheep and bring them to the house in the glen. We'll meet you there."

Terin passed Kell and Mordecai an indiscernible look and then headed southwest back over the ridge.

They watched her pick her way through the underbrush. "Terin requires patience," Renata admitted, her arms folded behind her. "She's had a hard life and, understandably, holds a lot of grudges."

"One of those grudges wouldn't be against Madam Nicolea, would it?" Mordecai asked.

"Yeah, Madam Nicolea's at the top of her kill list." Renata cleared her throat and continued north along the river. Mordecai and Kell kept up to better hear her. "I will not let her further tarnish the good name of our people by setting out on some revenge plot. She's worked too hard for that."

"So…" Kell glanced at Mordecai who motioned silently for her to ask what they had both been wondering. "What happened between Terin and the Containment Office?"

Renata thought before saying, "That's not really for me to share. Suffice it to say that she's been gunning for Nicolea's death for a few years now. I'm sure if she got the chance, she'd go for it." The old woman's mouth pulled into a firm line. "And I've got to make sure that never happens."

"You said that you and Madam Nicolea had come to an understanding? What… does that mean?"

Renata snorted. "I sent her and her men running into the forest, of course." She glanced back at them, a wolfish look in her gray eyes. "If you fight, make sure your opponent knows who they're up against. Nobody wants to face off with an Unbound." The old woman grinned. "I imagine they'll be warning others before sunset not to venture into these woods."

"Aren't you worried they're going to come after you?" asked Mordecai.

"And do what?" Renata cawed gleefully. "I can turn this whole forest against them. And they know it."

They were quiet for a while as they picked over the talus field that had appeared at the base of the next ridge. It was nearing supper and Kell was hungry, but she didn't dare say anything to Renata for fear of appearing ungrateful.

The clouds that she had spotted on the horizon a few hours ago eventually made their way overhead to blot out the warmth of the sun. With her clothes still damp from their brief swim in the tributary next to the house, Kell grew chilled. She knew Mordecai was also cold because of the visible goosepimples that materialized on his bare arms.

It wasn't long before thick drops of rain began to plop unpleasantly atop Kell's bare head. As a steady rain broke over the hilly region, Kell folded her arms to herself and bowed her head in an attempt to stay warm. Mordecai chattered quietly beside her as shivers wracked his body.

Renata led them over the adjacent ridge, whose trees were shedding their colorful leaves, to a glen on the other side. Nestled between several large oaks was a single-story home consisting of intertwined tree roots and branches and hardened earth. Unlike the previous home, this residence had no windows and appeared more like a prison rather than a place to live. Nevertheless, Kell gratefully followed Renata to the side of the structure to escape the pouring rain. When she saw no door or place of entry, she exchanged weary looks with Mordecai who was shivering violently.

Renata made a swift, perfectly even circle in the wet dirt at her feet, conjured Viterra, and then placed her hand on the earth wall. A beautiful arched doorway materialized under her palm. Kell trailed after the shuffling old woman.

The home smelled heavily of dry earth and basil and was completely dark. After a moment, Renata set her satchel down in the light of her Arcane Circle and then masterfully constructed several windows to permit the fading daylight to enter. Tree branches pulled together along the outside of the structure and formed eaves to safeguard against the rain.

Now that there was light, Kell could clearly discern the home. It was a large, single room with a small table and accompanying chairs and two beds replete with folded blankets; all the furniture was made of living roots that rose from the earth. The floor was dry, hardened earth that had been cleared of all dust. An open hearth occupied the rear wall and appeared ready for use as it was already supplied with kindling. Renata lit the wood there with a flick of her wrist and began shaking out her clothes. Kell and Mordecai huddled next to the growing fire until Renata passed surprisingly gentle fingers over them. Water seeped from their clothes into her palm, leaving their ragged wardrobe completely dry. Casually, she threw the water outside and went about her business.

The old woman spent the next hour opening up the house and reshaping it to accommodate her new guests. She widened the room and created two more beds; the table near the hearth grew in length as well. A bench rose from the ground on the table's opposite side.

Dried herbs hung from the ceiling just as they had in the previous home. As she went about her work, Renata periodically muttered to herself, supplying both questions and answers as she toyed with ideas. Outside, the rain droned on and thunder grumbled in the distance.

By the time Renata decided she was finished, Kell was nearly asleep in front of the fire and Mordecai had stripped out of his shirt and was lying on his back staring at the ceiling. The old woman passed them an approving look and then began to empty her satchel, placing smaller leather pouches on the table as well as a few plants.

Kell rolled her head back to watch her, hoping she bore food. When she saw nothing edible, she sighed heavily.

"I heard that," Renata said, her back turned to them.

"Sorry," murmured Kell.

The old woman finished what she was doing and then left the home, disappearing into the rain. Kell sat up and looked at Mordecai who shrugged. Renata returned a few minutes later with a large urn braced on her hip and a pot in her hand, both made of clay. Realizing there might be food after all, Kell jumped up and offered to help.

After several visits to the cellar behind the home which was dug straight into the earth and covered with tightly woven roots, the home began to take on life. That evening, they sat to eat a simple meal of pickled vegetables, dried meat, and a starchy soup of wild grains. It was the best food Kell had ever had.

Terin joined them late, dry but in a bad mood. How the young woman had managed to escape the rain with it pouring as hard as it was, Kell could only speculate. But Terin came bearing gifts—a bag of smoky clothes, another satchel that contained seeds, and a variety of personal effects from the other home. After stripping down to her bandeau and flustering Mordecai, she unceremoniously lay down on a bed and slept.

Since it seemed the rain was there to stay, Kell settled into one of the new beds alongside the inner wall. When she rolled over and met Mordecai's gaze, she smiled warmly. She liked having him nearby; it made the place feel more familiar.

She dreamed that night of Simon. She was back on Donahue Street at the Saturday market, weaving through crowds of people. Tarquin was there but he was a distant figure that hung in the background like a haze. As she danced between carts and darted between well-to-do merchants, she glimpsed Simon sprinting ahead of her.

Just when she caught up to him at a merchant's stand, which was selling strawberry-flavored fish, she suddenly felt a cool breeze on her bare skin. She looked down and found herself naked before him. Simon gawked at her, his bold eyes making her face to turn crimson. Kell tried to explain herself, but already the expression on his face had changed to one of hurt and anger—the same look he had imparted her as he was being hauled off by the regulators.

In the next instant, the regulators were there, dragging Simon down the street. Still nude, Kell tried to go after him but felt something holding her. She screamed for Simon until hands began dragging her backward. A potent blend of fury and panic bloomed in her. Caring only that she hurt whoever dared to contain her, Kell tapped into the secret pool of energy within her.

That familiar click resonated within her and her fingers grew itchy and warm. Heat erupted around her palms as she lurched forward, extracting herself from the grip of her captors.

A sudden pain seared the side of her face, knocking her from her nightmare. Panting, Kell blinked to clear her vision which was flecked with rolling purple stars. The walls around her were unfamiliar and, for a moment, she thought she had been captured by the regulators alongside Simon.

Someone snapped their fingers impatiently next to her face, startling her. Shakily, she turned to look at Renata who stood beside her bed, a glowing green Arcane Circle under her feet and two fields activated along her arms. Becoming aware of the situation, Kell sat up in alarm. Renata met her gaze. "You awake?"

Kell glanced at Terin, who sat in her bed, tussle-haired, and nodded. She heard movement near the entryway and turned to find Mordecai peering into the home from outside. "What happened?" Kell managed, her voice a rasp.

Renata motioned her out of bed. Dressed only in her pants and a bandeau, Kell shivered but obeyed. The old woman backed away and then pointed to the wall against which the head of her bed rested. From the bed to the ceiling, the roots were scorched black. At that moment, Kell smelled the smoke that hung in a thick haze around them. Wide-eyed, she looked at Mordecai who appeared shaken.

"Come on," Renata said, going to grab her spare coat, the Arcane Circle following under her feet. "Get dressed."

Kell whirled on Mordecai. "I'm so sorry. Did I—Are you hurt?"

Mordecai shook his head but didn't offer anything else.

"Get dressed," Renata urged, striding with more authority than Kell had seen her exude since their meeting.

Dread filling her, Kell dressed and followed Renata out of the home.

14

Lessons

SHIVERING MORE FROM ANXIETY THAN the cold, Kell stumbled after Renata through the glen. Although it had finally stopped raining, the ground was waterlogged and squelched under her feet. Some clouds remained, but it was light enough that Kell could discern Renata's posture. Years seemed to have dropped from her shoulders, allowing her to move with the ease of a middle-aged woman. Kell glanced back at the home and saw a fire flicker to life within.

Renata led her farther through the glen, her pace quick, until they reached an expansive area without trees. No longer carrying two fields of Viterra with her, Renata turned to her.

"Now," the old woman said, "right now, we're going to put a stop to this. You lack discipline. We're going to fix that." She drew an invisible circle in the pale grass with her boot, struck her wrists, and pulled bands of Viterra to her. "Do the same," she instructed.

Kell looked down at the water-worn grass and the puddles of rainwater that had collected along the uneven earth. Clumsily, she drew half a circle and then turned to complete it.

"Again," Renata demanded, pointing to another spot directly adjacent to Kell.

Still upset, Kell drew a similar shape of failure. When she looked back at Renata, she saw the woman sigh and then peer about the glade in thought, her face gently illuminated by the glowing bands along her wrists. "Over here." Renata guided her to a large pool of rainwater. "Take your boots off."

Recognizing the no-nonsense tone of an irritated adult, Kell jerked off her boots and socks, set them somewhere dry, and rolled up her pants legs.

Grimacing, she treaded lightly into the puddle; a shiver ran up her spine. The water was icy.

"Feet apart, arms relaxed." Renata began pacing around her. "Draw a circle in the water."

Not sure how having numb toes would help in the terribly difficult task of drawing a perfect circle, Kell pointed her foot and began outlining a circle around her position. The moment she reached the point where she had begun, Renata ordered, "Again."

Kell did it once more, and again Renata demanded that she perform the circle. Shivering and growing cross, Kell worked to keep her mouth shut. She didn't like being told what to do, much less while standing barefoot in water in the middle of October.

"Faster."

Kell threw an annoyed glance over her shoulder at the old woman.

Renata's response was immediate. "Uh, no." With a flick of her wrist, she commanded water from the puddle to strike Kell's leg with surprising force. The cold bit into her skin.

Kell yelped and danced out of the way. "What are you doing?"

"Your lack of discipline is the reason you're out here in the first place," Renata replied, shadows from her Arcane Circle darkening her eyes.

"You haven't told me what we're doing!" Kell argued. "We're just out here spinning around! For what? I can't see anything, my feet are freezing, and I don't know what I'm doing!"

Kell didn't have a chance to cry out as the earth beneath her feet suddenly shifted and rotated ninety degrees. She staggered and then crashed to the ground, her knees sinking into muddy grass. Fury rising within her like an ocean swell, she forced herself to hear Tarquin's calming voice in her head.

Renata didn't seem to care. "Get up." Kell pushed herself to her feet, shivering. She turned to meet the old woman's gaze. "Get in the water." Kell bit her tongue and did as she was told. "Now, draw a circle."

Kell pointed a foot and traced three-quarters of a circle around herself; she came back around and completed the circle with the other.

"Again. Faster."

Kell did so, continuing to struggle to complete it in less time.

The command came again, and again, and again.

Eventually, Kell stopped feeling the cold water or the chilly nighttime air on her skin. Her mind settled. Though she was still irritated with Renata, the focus the action required restrained her frustration and kept her pliable.

Sometime later, Renata finally said, "Now, strike," as Kell completed her umpteenth circle. Without a moment's hesitation to think or ponder on the act, Kell struck her wrists together in a downward movement. Blue light blazed to life in the glade and glistened on the water around her. The radiant bands of blue that hummed around her wrists were warm and pleasantly heavy. The Arcane Circle that glowed under her feet beneath the water felt comfortingly rough, like standing on sand.

The sensation that welled within her was different than before which caught Kell off guard. Accessing the Flow had always felt like a switch, like a jarring click deep behind her navel. But this time, the warmth that she felt from the Viterra suddenly flooding her was familiar, soothing, and gentle. There was no mighty and sudden leap into its current.

Annoyance forgotten, Kell looked at Renata. Perhaps the old woman *did* know what she was doing.

Renata approached her. Kell took a step back as she sensed the woman's larger far more impressive presence shift the Flow around them. Like two magnets pushing and pulling each other, Kell felt the Viterra in her respond to Renata's, straining at first to join it before drawing Kell another step away.

Renata hummed and then said, "Shake it off and do it again. Draw a circle and strike." She relinquished the Viterra she held, dousing her figure into darkness, and started back toward the house.

"Wait," Kell called. "How many times should I… do it?"

"Until I come back for you."

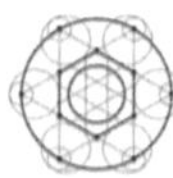

It was cold. Still, Simon made a conscious effort not to show the extent of his discomfort to the older, more mature fighters. The days of November were short, chilly, and intermittently cloudy and rainy. But the weather never derailed training. So, there he stood at attention in the early frosty air of the practice courtyard, dressed in pants and nothing else, a sword just as naked as him in his hand.

The dark-skinned man, Ferrik, who had become his mentor, nudged him. Simon glanced at him. The man nodded his chin upward in silent encouragement. Hands aching from the cold and joints tight, Simon worked to keep his body from shivering.

Across the courtyard, Dockett spoke enthusiastically with Tomas, the Lanista in charge of Users. Simon watched his owner, hoping his anger and hatred toward Dockett and Users would keep him warm. After a few minutes, Dockett clapped the Users' Lanista on the shoulder and stalked back to the line of fighters as the man disappeared through the doorway through which Users were housed.

"Simon, Buck, Kouza, and Curio," Dockett called, motioning them from the line.

Unsure what this was about, Simon left the other fighters, sword in hand, and joined Dockett in the middle of the enormous courtyard. The others beside him, he noticed, were all relatively new or young. Despite being in the Lanista's care for several months now, Simon had yet to grow accustomed to Dockett's barbaric and often traumatizing tests. His gut warned him that yet another was coming.

As Dockett looked over their swords, Tomas reappeared with an armed guard and a handful of Users in iron cuffs. Simon was relieved to see Ambrose was not among them. The cognitive dissonance his acquaintance created within him always confused Simon to the point of frustration.

Dockett motioned for the Users to line up across from Simon and the others who had been called and then said, "These Users were recently arrested for crimes. They were to be put to death, but Madam Parthemos graciously stepped in and volunteered them for a higher purpose." Dockett paced in front of them. "Instead of wasting their deaths, we're going to use them to inspire."

Simon felt a tremor run through his body.

"Today is the day of your Bleeding," continued Dockett, his keen blue eyes falling on Simon. "A warrior is not a warrior until they've killed. There are five Users here who have been deemed no longer necessary for society. Each of you will kill one. I will decide who executes the spare. If you do not follow through, the entire corps will face discipline. Am I understood?"

"Yes, sir!" the boys chorused. Simon's voice cracked.

"Good." Dockett pointed to Simon. "Let's go."

Simon shakily stepped forward, his grip weak on his sword. An armed guard separated a middle-aged woman from the prisoners and pushed her toward Simon.

The woman, a short, stocky individual, met his gaze, her brown eyes mournful and tear-filled. Her dark brown hair stood out against her pale skin. Her beige dress was tattered and her face oily and dirty. Simon couldn't see the tattoos that marked her as a User because they were hidden by heavy, iron cuffs.

"Please…" she whispered, her plea a puff of hot air that crystalized in the morning light.

Simon heard his sword thud onto the earth before he realized he had dropped it. Struggling with the horror of the situation, he clumsily reached for the blade and dragged it back into place.

"Simon…" warned Dockett nearby.

Trying to steel himself, Simon took a few deep breaths, but all that did was make tears well in the corners of his eyes. Uncaring that the Lanista saw it, Simon looked back at Ferrik. The wise, older man passed a hand over his own face, silently reminding Simon to block all emotion. Simon took another breath and then set his face into a stoic expression.

"Please, please, young man," the woman begged, falling to her knees. "I've got children, younger than you…"

"Do it," Dockett demanded. "Do it now."

Simon tightened his fingers around the sword's hilt, a silent sob escaping him, and reared back as he had been taught, sword perpendicular to his body. His stance was wide, solid. He only distantly noticed his arms trembling as the woman's weeping flooded his senses. With a hoarse cry, Simon swung.

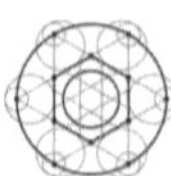

"Do it, do it now," Renata patiently instructed.

Apprehensive, Kell hesitated further. She looked down at the Arcane Circle humming beneath her boots and then at the glowing blue cuffs around her wrists. It was mid-November; she knew it would be beneficial to have someone else at the home who could use fire, but the idea of causing untoward damage to, well, everything greatly worried her.

She sensed a slight fluctuation in the Flow. Knowing instinctively what was coming, she pointed at the eddy that lapped at the rocks beside her and jerked a flat hand up in a sharp and practiced motion. A sheet of water with tremendous momentum and power abruptly shot up and blocked the dirt clod that Renata had sent her way. "I'm working on it!" Kell told her teacher.

"Nothing's going to happen," Renata continued, striding toward her, her own Viterra and Arcane Circle a verdant glow. "We're near the river; I'm here. You're safe. Come on. It's just you and me."

Kell steadied herself, her feet spread in a wide, solid stance, her hands positioned before her, one slightly higher than the other. As she drew a deep breath, she felt the Viterra shift within her. Her fingertips grew warm and itchy—and trembled. She was afraid. Terribly afraid.

The old woman surveyed her. "Focus on the wood pile. That's the only place the flames are going to go. Come on."

Eyes fixed on the pile of kindling they had collected, she finally pointed at the wood and, with both hands extended palms down, rotated them upward, as if coaxing flames to rise from her fingers. Small, blue flames bloomed in her palms. Spurred by their sudden appearance, she encouraged more Viterra there; the flames increased in size and then promptly changed to red-orange. When the heat became almost unbearable, Kell moved her right hand toward the wood pile, palm out.

"Ah—faster!" corrected Renata the exact moment the fire erupted in an alarming blaze, no longer restrained. Kell staggered back into the water to escape the inferno. As Renata easily smothered the fire with a single gesture, she explained, "It has to be faster. We've talked about this. Fire is quick, powerful. You must be like fire—decisive, strong, and fast. Now, again."

Kell collected herself and tried once more.

The month of November brought much-needed structure to Kell's life, providing her with both instruction and purpose. She quickly learned that although Renata was a naturally terse and unsociable person, the woman was a masterful teacher. While she taught Kell to better control her access to the Flow, Terin worked with Mordecai to build a strong foundation of necessary actions, movements, and gestures that would be used once he was able to conjure Viterra.

Of course, they had chores to complete such as chopping wood, cleaning out the hearth, organizing the cellar, and scrubbing the clay pots and pans, but both Kell and Mordecai spent large chunks of the day learning about their gifts and how to use them.

"Viterra is all around you," Terin told them one afternoon. "There's a reason it's called Viterra; it's alive. It's in the earth, the ground beneath your feet. It's in the river, the grass and trees, the fire in our hearth, the clouds, the sky. And how useful it is comes down to whether you can channel and control it."

In a swift, clean movement, she pointed the toe of her boot and drew a complete circle around herself in the moist dirt alongside the river without picking up her foot. She ended in what appeared to be a martial arts position with her left leg slightly bent and supple and her right leg, which was angled behind her nearly perpendicular to it, straight and steady. Her hands remained open, her palms forward with one in front of the other, ready.

"How'd—Renata never showed us that," Mordecai said in awe.

"Renata's not young any more. Look here, you use your standing leg like a... Oh, what's that thing called? The thing you use to draw circles on maps and stuff?"

"Scribe compass?" Kell offered.

"Yeah! A scribe compass. Use your standing leg like the needle; your free leg is the pencil." Terin straightened herself and motioned to Mordecai. "The positions we've been working on? That's why they're so important. They allow you to conjure in differ situations. Learn the base traits and then learn their derivatives for each element. Once you've mastered those, you can mix and match."

"Every element has its own set of traits?" asked Mordecai, aghast. "How many is that?"

Terin shrugged. "I don't know. Dozens?"

So, they set off learning the base traits of each of the elements. Because Kell was water and Mordecai had yet to show an affinity for any particular element, Terin and Renata began teaching water traits, each focusing on a single student.

Unsurprisingly, Kell picked up the basics within the week with glee. She loved being able to conjure water and control the world around her. Although they mostly practiced by the river, Renata periodically asked that she evoke water within the home to fill a pot or do laundry.

Conjuring water felt different than evoking fire. Kell found that, while fire was quick to form, water was not. She was accustomed now to pulling Viterra from the Flow, like dipping a cup into a rushing river, but bending its power to her will was an ongoing struggle. Fire rushed to her command easily; Renata had said that it would. But water was reserved, placid, patient. Kell observed that she was most successful in controlling and conjuring water when she was calm, collected.

In the mornings, Mordecai and Kell underwent physical conditioning to tone their bodies. According to Terin, it was important that they be fit and strong to better channel the Flow. When Kell pointed out that Renata could hardly run from the house to the river let alone complete daily conditioning, she was awarded three more laps around the glen while carrying water buckets.

Renata taught traits in the afternoons, instructing them on how to move their bodies and hands. Although Terin provided advice and suggestions, it was the old woman who tirelessly showed them traits and their derivative forms.

Water traits were easy for Kell as the movements resonated with her sense of being on the open sea. Smooth sweeps of the arms, low and then high like the crests and troughs of waves. Bent knees to help stay balanced. Light elbows and flexible shoulders. Strong fingers that moved like the surf coming ashore. Soft steps upon the balls of the feet. Turns within the Arcane Circle to redefine the Self to the Flow and to strengthen the Viterra's power. Kell reveled in both the familiarity and newness of it all.

Unfortunately, Mordecai did not find water traits as rewarding and often grew angry with his inability to conjure anything. He stormed off on several occasions, only to come back once Terin had spoken with him at length. Though Kell wanted to share her excitement with him, she kept quiet. He seemed like he was always in a bad mood.

After that, Renata began teaching them separately. Although they practiced the traits together every morning during conditioning to cement them into muscle memory, they took turns receiving instruction from Renata.

After water traits, they moved to fire traits. Kell immediately found herself inexplicably angry and moody, which helped her better understand Mordecai's state of mind. Through the end of the year, she worked on fire traits, struggling to overcome the well-earned fear of fire that she had developed over the past year.

"What's wrong with me?" Kell huffed at Terin one frosty morning. Despite the light crunch of snow that blanketed the glen, she was sweating. She angrily pushed her ear-length hair away from her face and once again contemplated cutting it all off in annoyance.

Together, they watched as Mordecai went through the fire traits, his movements sharp, decisive, and controlled. Fire demanded power and directness. Though the fingers and hands were used to command direction, forming the Viterra into fire required palm thrusts, punches, and powerful lateral and vertical strikes. Even from her position a good distance away, Kell could discern the air around Mordecai's fists shimmering with heat in the cold, morning light.

"Nothing's wrong with you," Terin replied.

"I've been working on fire traits for three months. It took me a few weeks to master water." Kell watched Mordecai enviously. He wasn't as fluid as Terin but he had his own type of power. Had Kell not been so distraught by her own ineptitude, she would have been admiring his charm and growing physique. As it was, however, she was miserable and hated that he was so far ahead of her.

"Mordecai barely knows water," Terin said. "Watch him next time. He's halting and stiff. If or when he ever becomes capable of conjuring water, he's not going to be able to control it well." She nudged Kell. "Don't compare yourselves."

But that didn't stop Kell from watching Mordecai in all that they did and envying him. He appeared so adept, so skilled. He was a quick study and asked many questions to ensure that he understood how to complete a form first before attempting it. Even when she watched him through their water traits, Kell could discern no difference in his steps from hers.

January and February were cold months with several bouts of snow. But that didn't seem to bother Renata and Terin who, when they needed to, melted paths to the river, cellar, and other crucial areas, like the woodpile. Near the middle of February, Renata ended up creating a new room adjoined to the main home. Although some tools and supplies were moved there to clear up space, the supplemental room was deemed for training.

"If you mess this up, you burn the house down," Renata said, her voice gravelly. Her gray eyes studied the newly formed wall of roots and the open windows she had just created before settling on Kell. "Now, draw the circle, strike, and go through the traits."

Chilled because the old woman had opened the new room up to prevent disaster that afternoon as they practice, Kell shivered, drew a breath, and then drew a circle as Terin had shown them to do months ago. With her right foot still braced along the rim of the circle, Kell struck her wrists together, igniting the first field. She was pleased to see the iridescent form of a second ring, a sign of her growing mastery, starting to materialize along her forearms.

Remembering that she was dealing with fire, not water, and that she needed to move with purpose, Kell started the fire traits. The first form settled her Self with a downward motion of her hands. She stepped forward, raised her forearm perpendicular to her body as if to block something and sunk her other elbow backward.

As she completed the next several traits, all of which were similar in movement and style, she felt her fingers begin to itch. Determined not to let the sensation overpower her inner calm, Kell let the burning swell. She closed her eyes and pushed through the next trait—a knee jab that extended forward.

"Faster," Renata instructed suddenly, breaking Kell's concentration.

Irritated, Kell looked at her. The moment she did, however, the fire that had begun to collect around her fists flared. Startled but knowing what to do now, Kell pressed her palms together, enclosing the base of the flames. When the fire went out, she shook the Viterra from her hands. "I almost had it," Kell snarled.

"Did you?" Renata pointed to the ceiling overhead which was charred.

Kell howled in fury and stormed out of the house past Terin and Mordecai who had been watching from the adjacent room. She couldn't go far because snow still blanketed the ground, so she followed the path to the river on the other side of the glen. How was she going to get it right if everyone kept interrupting her? She just needed to—Kell kicked a rock with her boot, but it didn't move, leading her to stub her toes.

With another feral snarl, she smashed her boot into the ice-encrusted rock several times until it was free and then chucked it as far as she could. Panting and enraged, she stalked off to the river.

She hadn't walked along the river's edge for very long before she began regretting having left the house without a coat. When she turned to go back, she found Mordecai picking his way over the snow-covered rocks to her, a coat in hand. Suddenly embarrassed by her outburst, she redirected her attention to the river.

"Figured you'd be cold," he said, passing the coat to her.

"Thanks," Kell muttered as she gratefully slipped into it.

They watched the ice flow for a long moment before Mordecai said, "I think it's in your head. Why you can't do fire."

Knowing that he was right but unwilling to admit it, Kell stayed silent.

"Fire hurts people, destroys things," Mordecai continued. "You're scared of it."

"I'm not scared of it."

"I'm scared of water."

Kell looked at him.

"I... hate water. I hate rivers," he motioned to the moving water and ice in front of them, "I hate the ocean..." He fidgeted. "When I watch you go through the water traits, I get so... frustrated. And angry. You're so good. You look natural. It comes to you so easily. I want to be like you."

Kell felt some of her annoyance melt away. "Yeah?"

Mordecai nodded. "Every time I go through the water traits, I just think about how much I don't want to be anywhere near water. I mean, you know we have to channel the element and take on its, uh, traits, but I... I hate water so much." With a smile, he touched her comfortingly. "You can do fire. Your forms are good. You just get inside your head and remember the bad stuff."

The weight of his hand and the warm smile he imparted her made weird feelings blossom inside Kell. Blushing, she grinned and looked out at the river. "Thanks for saying so, Mordecai."

To her surprise, he slipped his hand down her arm and wrapped his palm around her icy fingers. Kell's face blazed crimson. When she looked at him, she was surprised to find him also blushing. Mordecai cleared his throat. "We're in this together, yeah? You and me."

Kell squeezed his hand and smiled. "Yeah."

That afternoon, Kell successfully went through the fire traits and conjured flames.

15

Newcomers

Simon turned fifteen in March and began to train in earnest, undergoing conditioning that Dockett deemed acceptable for someone of his size and age. Of course, Simon didn't agree, as it seemed he was unable to do anything the lanky man demanded. He remained last in all exercises, including distance running and weight training, and consistently brought punishment to the group for his inability to keep up. He got the feeling that if he weren't Dockett's Champion-in-training, the others would have made him mysteriously disappear.

But as Simon picked up fencing and swordplay, he discovered he had a knack for it. Though he lacked the power the other fighters had, he was fast and a quick learner. Ferrik rarely had to show him a skill more than once before he could replicate it with speed. It was his lack of strength that was his enduring downfall and cost him nearly every mock battle. Still, Dockett must have been impressed because he kept a sharp eye on Simon and encouraged him on occasion.

As the weather began to warm, he started learning combat scenarios and forms with Ferrik. It was during these one-on-one practices in the smaller courtyard adjacent to the main school that he caught snippets of conversation drifting on the wind as passing high-ranking officials and nobles strolled through.

"Why is everyone so upset?" Simon asked Ferrik one evening over supper.

"What do you mean?" the tall man asked, his mouth full.

"Lords Graham and Reseigh were talking about the, uh, ministers of something." Simion struggled to remember what the two men had spoken about. "They were saying that the ministers need to be reined in soon?"

"Oh, that." Ferrik sat back with his bowl of starchy soup and thought through a long drink. "So, from what I understand, there's the king and then under him is something called the Council of Ministers, which he is actually a part of. They bring stuff up for the king to approve and then, once he says yes, they oversee it." Ferrik shrugged. "I can't say for sure, but it sounds like the council isn't agreeing with what the king is and isn't approving." He continued to eat before saying, "Honestly, keep your nose—and ears—out of it. It's got nothing to do with us. Now, eat."

Simon obeyed, mostly because he was hungry, but still mused on all that he had heard. The lords' passing conversation wasn't the first he had heard in regard to the discontentment within the imperial palace. If the hearsay was spilling into the streets, undoubtedly the situation within had to be dire. Though Ferrik said it didn't concern them, Simon questioned that. Not because he understood politics, but because he had learned early on that everything came from the top down. And when large sums of money, like those being passed around at the Munera, were involved, things got nasty.

That night, he dreamed about home and about his life on his family's boat. He dreamed about fish and azure seas and about the music his father used to play on the concertina. He saw warm but smelly docks that reeked of fish waste and refuse as well as flocks of seagulls and pelicans that frequented the area. A voice called out to him in his dreams.

"Simon!"

With a grin, he whirled around to find Kellick waving to him from the street. Simon was overjoyed and ran with a skip to greet him. He gave his best friend a tight hug, and arm-in-arm they started down the docks, laughing about nonsensical jokes. A nostalgic sense of security overcame him and he sank into his longtime friend's presence with relief.

But the sensation was short-lived as the sunset in the west suddenly flared into a raging conflagration. Simon groped for Kell, but his hands met emptiness. Panting and coughing from the smoke, he spun around in search of his friend, but Kell was nowhere to be seen. He turned to start running, but someone grabbed him, and he was whirled around to face a gaggle of regulators. As he was led away, he heard Kell screaming his name, his voice registering in an octave Simon hadn't noticed before.

Simon woke to find his bedding soaked with sweat. With a groan, he rolled over to brace against the cold, stone wall and stared into the dim light of his quarters. He replayed the traumatic moment once more, trying desperately to remember everything as it had happened. The regulators, his parents begging, the shouting... Simon focused on that. The longer he thought about it, the more convinced he was that Kell had been calling for him, but that his voice had sounded... strange. High-pitched and pinched.

True, Kell hadn't become a man yet. Simon himself had only just started growing hair at the time, but that register… Maybe it *hadn't* been Kell. Maybe it had been his mother, but in the chaos of the moment, he had been unable to discern it.

And then, of course, the shattered windows and flames had come. A User had been at the market that morning.

Simon fell still, a thought forming in his mind. The fire hadn't begun until he had been arrested. And even as his parents had begged for his release, there had been no flames. It was only after it was decided that he was to be jailed and was being dragged off did percussive explosions of glass rain upon the street. Was Kell somehow involved? But that didn't make sense. He wasn't a User. It had to have been someone else there.

Still, the timing of the events irked Simon. That coupled with Kell's literal abandonment in his greatest time of need bothered him tremendously and, though he missed his longtime friend, the bitterness that swelled within him because of Kell's desertion fed his increasingly pessimistic perception of the world and fueled his hatred for Users, the people who had killed his family and upended his life.

Once more, he swore to himself in the dark of the night that he would be a part of their annihilation—there in the arena or elsewhere. He would see to it that every last one was destroyed.

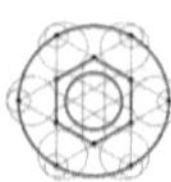

Spring came in a glorious burst of green, ushering in warm winds, high blue skies, and blankets of new verdant leaves. The glen erupted in brilliant shades of purple and yellow as spring beauties, trout lilies, and common bluebells emerged during the great awakening. Having never seen such an expansive space of flowers, Kell reveled in it and spent much of those chilly days admiring the flowers.

Mordecai turned fifteen in April and, to Kell's amazement, began growing as fast as the flora. Each week, it appeared as though he had gained another half inch. It wasn't long before he was significantly taller than all three females. He complained of his knees bothering him frequently from the rapid growth. His body began hardening and showing definition although his limbs remained disproportionately long. In addition, his facial hair started to come in quicker, prompting him to ask Terin to purchase a razor next time she traveled into Avives for supplies.

Kell grew also but, to her chagrin, not fast enough. Being surrounded by such mature friends made her feel insignificant and silly, as though whatever she said or did held no merit or weight. She still hated her monthly moon time but had grown bitterly accustomed to it and the pains it brought. Terin helped her take care of herself during those times, and Mordecai was taught early on—alongside Kell—about female anatomy and physiology from Renata.

As if to further emphasize the growing distance between them, Kell began to notice how much attention Mordecai gave Terin, who had turned twenty in January. At first Kell had thought nothing of it, especially since Mordecai had expressed some interest in her, but after a while, she grew jealous of how often he made Terin laugh or how close they were when she taught him. Kell tried not to let it bother her and focus solely on her training.

By May, she was able to masterfully wield water and conjure and control fire comfortably. Renata began teaching them flora traits to help with food production and maintenance as only she and Terin had been contributing to the garden and surrounding crops that supported the house.

Although Kell didn't dislike flora traits, she didn't like the forms either. Manipulation of the Viterra in such a manner required far too much precision and exact skill, something which Kell didn't have the patience for. Water traits made sense; fire traits too had a certain feel to them that felt right. But flora traits were off-putting and forced Kell to spend enormous amounts of time taking Viterra and returning it to the vegetation around her.

Though Mordecai had yet been able to conjure much less control any elements in the past months, Kell was pleased to know that he also did not find flora traits agreeable and struggled to stay focused and patient. Nevertheless, they continued conditioning and training, often practicing throws, evasions, and blocks that imitated trait movements on each other.

Their routines carried them deep into the following year.

"Wait, what?" Kell asked one June day shortly after her fifteenth birthday. "You wanna fight me?"

"Not fight, spar," Terin corrected as she churned butter with the small handset they had. "Renata wants me to test you."

Kell glanced at Mordecai. "With what element?"

"Why don't we just start with what you're most comfortable with, hm?" Terin continued to spin the mixer's handle. "Water?"

"What are the rules?" Mordecai interrupted with interest.

Terin looked at Renata who was squinting at a needle and thread in the sunlight of the open window. "Don't maim or kill each other," Renata replied without missing a beat. "Anything else goes."

Kell shrugged. "Yeah, I guess we can." She added with a smug grin, "Is it fair though?"

Terin frowned. "What's that mean?"

"Just that your specialty isn't water. Will it be a fair fight?"

Terin chuckled. "Oh, sweet summer child, worry about yourself."

Kell didn't like being called a child and the older girl's chiding pricked her. "Fine, yeah. I'll spar with you."

"Kellick," Renata said, her tone a warning.

Knowing what she had done, Kell softened her reply. "Yes, Terin. Sparring sounds like fun." Renata looked up from her needlework, her stern eyes fixing on Kell. "What?" Kell asked. "I was nice!"

Renata glanced at Terin and then returned her attention to the thread. "Terin's your teacher."

Kell held her tongue as she had been taught, turned to Terin, and politely said, "I'm sorry, Terin."

"It's fine," Terin replied with a smile to Mordecai. The simple gesture infuriated Kell.

"Kellick, take a walk," Renata evenly instructed without looking up from her work.

Gladly, Kell thought, leaving the table and striding outside. Dressed in a pair of cutoffs, a loose, cream-colored blouse that had once belonged to Terin, and no shoes, she followed their worn path to the river that ran around the ridge to the east.

Since their arrival, Terin and Renata had purposefully changed some of the landscape to bring the water closer to their abode. Instead of tracking straight southwest, a small tributary now wrapped around the base of the ridge to swing past the treehouse before rejoining the rest of the river.

Overhead, the cloudless, azure sky promised another warm afternoon. Teetering out onto the smooth river rocks, Kell watched the cool water churn around her ankles, its trickling and swirling soothing. Minnows came to greet her and pick at her skin, their nibbles like little kisses.

She wasn't sure why Terin got under her skin. The young woman was easy to get along with, a patient teacher, and a knowledgeable individual with seemingly vast amounts of life experience. Despite their having been together for nearly a year and a half, Kell knew less about Terin than even Renata, the most tight-lipped old woman she had ever met.

All that she had gathered from Terin was that she had grown up in a suburb of Avives and that she had been in trouble with the Containment Office. Any time Kell or Mordecai had asked further questions, she had grimaced dramatically and said with a chuckle, "I'd rather not talk about it."

All Kellick knew was that she didn't like it when Terin laughed with Mordecai or shared knowing expressions.

Deciding that she was done just looking at the water, Kell ripped her shirt and bandeau over her head and slid out of her cutoffs. Wearing nothing, she took a few steps into the deepening water and then plunged headfirst into the tributary's swirling eddies. All of her worries vanished, her heartrate slowed, and her mind calmed. Eyes wide open, she swam frog stroke along the bottom, which was no deeper than about five or six feet, and then gracefully pushed off. She broke the surface, took a breath, and then dove again.

She examined silt and touched the algae that had finally begun to accumulate on the rocks that had been there prior to Renata rerouting the river. Fish scattered as she passed but returned once she surfaced. Kell lay on her back and let the gentle current draw her downriver as she stared up at the azure sky. With her ears underwater, it was quiet, peaceful. She could hear her heart beating, strong and steady. She could feel the heat of the sun on her face and chest and the nibbling of curious fish on her legs. And for a moment, she was free, her mind unshackled.

She was part of the river, carelessly meandering between ridges, gliding under low-lying tree boughs, sneaking between rocks, passing through reeds, and wholly one with the world around her. And for a moment, she thought she glimpsed something within her mind's eye, a kind of epiphany that almost permitted her an unhindered, divine view of the Flow of Viterra.

But a passing collection of leaves grazed her side, startling her from her pensive thoughts. She turned and realized that she had drifted farther than she meant to. Annoyed that her time of introspection had been interrupted, she began swimming upriver, her arms wheeling out of the water with power and legs kicking.

When she returned to the bank where she had left her clothes, she found Terin sitting on the rocks, waiting. "I came to chat but when I got here, all I found were your clothes." The older woman smiled. "I thought you had finally gone back to live with the other mermaids."

Panting, Kell found her footing. "What's there to talk about?"

Terin regarded her for a moment before she started picking at a plant. "Why don't you like me?"

Kell hadn't been expecting that. "I don't *not* like you."

Terin frowned and stretched out her legs. "You throw me dirty looks all the time. I can feel you watching me. Did I do or say something?"

Kell studied Terin. "You… spend too much time with, uh, Mordecai."

"What?"

Feeling stupid, Kell picked her feet up to tread water for a minute and work off some of her stress. "I don't know. You just… you give a lot of attention to Mordecai." When she looked back at Terin, she saw something akin to realization on her face.

Terin leaned forward, resting her arms on her legs. "Mordecai can't access the Flow, Kell. How do you think that makes him feel? How do you think he feels when he sees you successfully mastering every set of traits and he still can't conjure fire?" She sat up with a sigh. "He needs encouragement, support, understanding. I give him those things because Renata… and you… can't."

Kell rested on the silty bottom and gazed at Terin. The young woman's bronze skin glistened in the afternoon sunlight; her puffy crown of curled, black hair shadowed her eyes and added age to the expression on her face.

"I'm not interested in Mordecai, yeah?" Terin said. "And I'm not looking to start anything."

"Does he know that?" Kell asked impulsively.

"Probably not." Terin grinned. "Should I make that more apparent to him?"

Kell didn't think it was funny but she nodded nonetheless.

Terin stood. "Fine, yeah. I'll let him know." She planted her hands on her hips. "Now, are you going to stay a fish this afternoon or are we going to spar?"

Deciding she would let everything go for the time being, Kell trudged out of the river, dried off, dressed, and followed Terin to the practice field just north of the treehouse where the sheep meandered. Once Mordecai and Renata spotted their return, they joined them to watch, scattering the herd.

"You all right?" asked Mordecai as Kell continued to vigorously shake water from her shoulder-length hair.

"Yeah, I'm fine." Kell stopped and met his gaze. "Sorry."

Mordecai smiled, bemused. "For what?"

"For worrying you," she replied.

Mordecai glanced at Terin and Renata who were a few dozen paces away. "What traits are you going to use?"

"What I'm best at, I guess."

Kell stepped away, drew a quick but precise circle around herself, and struck her wrists. She could do it now in a single, fluid movement. She stretched her neck and rolled her shoulders, her eyes flicking down first to the Arcane Circle humming under her feet and then to the single set of blue bands that encircled her wrists and the ghost of a second pair.

Terin left Renata and did the same. Kell couldn't help but compare her movements to the older girl's. She was further displeased when she saw Terin's double rings which indicated her mastery of the Physical.

"Use whatever you want," Terin said. "First one to hit the ground loses."

Kell knew she was going to lose; the disparity between their skill levels was painfully obvious to all present. But she wanted to show Terin that, maybe in time, she too would be just as powerful—Kell stopped, her head cocked in confusion. Her Arcane Circle shivered in response to a disturbance in the Flow. She thought it was to Terin's more powerful draw of Viterra, but when Terin, too, appeared bewildered, Kell grew concerned.

"Renata?" asked Terin, turning to their teacher.

As Renata ignited her own circle, Kell turned to Mordecai who had joined her. "What is it?" he asked.

Kell shrugged. "It feels weird. Like someone's touching the Flow or… something. I can't explain it—"

Renata let out a coarse laugh and looked northward. All followed her gaze. "We've got visitors."

"It's… not the Containment Office," Terin supplied, confused. "Who is it?"

The old woman shook her hands to release the Viterra she had conjured and started back to the treehouse. "Come on, you three. We need to tidy up."

Kell exchanged looks with Terin who shrugged.

After two hours of cleaning, sweeping the trails around the home, tidying the outhouse, organizing the cellar, chopping wood, and caring for the sheep, Kell was worn out. When she had asked who was coming, Renata had cryptically answered, "Friends," and then returned to widening the firepit along the western side of the home.

"Hey, Kell?" called Mordecai from out front.

Kell, who had been stacking wood, wiped her forehead with the back of her arm and looked at him. Mordecai nodded north, down the glen. Kell bristled when she spotted what appeared to be a group of people along the bottom of the ridge. She felt Mordecai tense beside her. After a moment of watching them, Kell whispered, "Who are they?"

Mordecai's response was hushed. "I don't know."

"Renata?" shouted Kell over her shoulder. "Someone's here."

Renata shuffled out of the treehouse, her hands folded behind her back. "They've taken their time."

Kell and Mordecai joined her, positioning themselves behind their teacher. It didn't matter that she was an old woman; she had seen off the Containment Office without breaking a sweat. They were confident in Renata's ability to defend them should the need arise. Dressed in a knee-length calico cotton dress of slate gray that matched her frizzy hair, her pale feet bare on the earth, Renata gave a broad wave overhead. It was returned by a single person.

"Who are they?" asked Terin, jogging down the river trail, her gait jostling water from the enormous clay jug she had balanced on her hip.

"Nomads," the old woman replied with a grin. "We accidentally ran into each other decades ago, and since then, they've made it a point to swing by for a visit every few years."

"I've been here longer than that," Terin replied, setting down the jug. "I've never met them."

"Last time, you were in Avives getting supplies. Before that, you were sick with summer fever and were delirious."

"Wait, nomads?" Mordecai thought for a moment. "The First Whispered? They're real?" Renata smirked.

"Who are the First Whispered?" asked Kell, turning her wide eyes back on the approaching group of people.

"I heard they were the first ones hundreds of years ago to discover how to access the Flow." Mordecai looked at Renata. "Right?"

The old woman nodded, her gaze distant. "Yes, they are the original Unbound."

"And they're… here?" Terin fidgeted. "Why are they here?"

"I told you, we're friends." Renata started down the glen, her gait a little faster than usual. It seemed to Kell that she was eager. Terin hurried after the old woman, leaving Kell and Mordecai alone to finish the chores.

Eventually Renata led the newcomers back, a pleased expression on her usually stern face. Kell, who had had time to make herself more presentable, warily watched the group. There were two dozen in total, most of them young and middle-aged men, although Kell spotted two young women in their midst.

All of the guests had fine, platinum blond hair that glowed a warm silver under the blue turbans most wore. The First Whispered were tan and boasted varying shades of blue eyes. Their clothes were foreign and showcased vibrant embroidery on lightweight blue, black, and silver jackets with long sleeves that fluttered in the summer breeze. Kell was surprised to find swords tucked into the sashes at their waists. Some even carried bows and quivers of arrows.

The distance in their gazes irked Kell who slunk closer to Mordecai. They were tall and spoke quietly to Renata who grinned wolfishly and motioned Kell and Mordecai over. "This is Denez Jullou. He's leader of the Tribe. He's taking the hunting party east back home. Denez, this is Kellick Fisk and Mordecai Othonos, my other students."

Denez nodded to them both. Kell returned a slight smile but otherwise said nothing to the tall, imposing man. Though willowy, Denez was large and had keen blue eyes that seemed to catch everything all at once. The manner in which he moved gave the illusion of an ethereal being passing through their plane of existence; he was fluid and intentional.

Renata finally drew the man's attention back to herself as she spoke at length. With finality, the old woman turned and showed them to the large area which she had arranged and tidied up a few hours earlier. Kell noted that, among the twenty or so nomads, two didn't appear to belong.

The first was a young man with black, shoulder-length hair pulled into a messy bun at the back of his head. Though he couldn't have been more than eighteen, his amber eyes were old. He was dressed like the other men in the group, wearing a belted, lightweight tunic with long, flowing sleeves and carrying a sword at his waist. He sported some scruff along his jaw and upper lip.

The man who remained no more than a pace behind the older teen glanced at Mordecai and Kell and then, seemingly deciding that they weren't threats, returned his attention to Renata and Terin. He was scruffy, grizzled, with a topknot of brown hair gathered in a loose queue that emphasized the shaved sides of his head. He was muscular, more so than any of the men in the group, and carried a sword at his waist. A quiver of arrows was slung over his right shoulder; he carried an artfully-crafted bow alongside it.

Kell returned her gaze to the teenager. She studied the side of his face as he listened to Renata speak.

"What's wrong?" asked Mordecai under his breath, following her eyes.

"I… feel like I've seen him somewhere before." Kell maneuvered around Mordecai and edged closer to the western side of the house to get a better view of the black-haired teenager.

"Of course, you may use whatever space you feel fit," Renata was saying to Denez who nodded amicably, a slight smile pulling on his finely sculpted face.

Kell peered around a First Whispered to continue to examine the young man. He was like an image from a dream, something she knew intimately but could hardly picture in reality. The teenager leaned into the middle-aged man and murmured something, a smirk drawing the corner of his mouth upward.

In that instant, Kell knew. Righteous anger swelled within her. Forgoing the months of disciplined training she had completed, she sidestepped the man near her and launched herself at the teenager with a savage snarl. Her heart nearly exploded from the ensuing justice as her prey stumbled and fell backward with her on top. Fingers knotted in his tunic, Kell reared back and punched as hard as she could. She got one good strike in before he blocked his face, gathered a leg under him, and kicked her hard in the chest.

She landed in the dirt, wheezing, but the adrenaline surging through her body burned off the pain. Suddenly remembering her training, she scrambled to her feet and completed an Arcane Circle in a single, fluid motion and struck her wrists. By then, her target had managed to get to his knees and withdrawn his sword.

Kell didn't know what she was doing; her body was moving through muscle memory. Hands extended, palms down, she jerked upward, drawing water from the soil around her. It came to her with such momentum that it forced her hands upward. Nevertheless, she remained balanced and threw it at her opponent, flourishing it with strong but pliable fingers.

The moment the water left her hands, she grabbed at the Viterra circulating through her and conjured more water. With glee, she saw that the speed and power of her first assault, a snapping jet of water, had caused the black-haired teenager to stagger back several paces, off-balance and in obvious pain. More water materialized and circled her, remaining effortlessly within the boundaries of her Arcane Circle.

Unwilling to give her target a chance to counter, Kell attacked, tapping into the water traits that she had committed to muscle memory. She slid her foot forward and then, directing with willowy fingers, swooped downward, allowing her opposite arm to swing up behind her. Her front leg bent to accommodate the quick motion before snapping upward and stepping strongly toward her opponent. The band of raging water around her crystallized with a loud crack before she let out multiple palm strikes.

Ice shards erupted into the space between them—and then melted into harmless water a few feet from the amber-eyed teenager, dropping to the ground like raindrops.

The middle-aged man with a topknot darted between them as Renata stepped in front of Kell, her gray eyes steely and unyielding and her Arcane Circle of green humming. Panting, Kell glanced at her target and then back at her teacher. She could hardly comprehend herself much less her the old woman's sudden presence.

"Kellick," Renata warned, her voice low.

Kell shook her hands to release the Viterra gathered there. The ice circulating around her dropped to the ground with a heavy thud. Infuriated, she stalked off.

16

First Whispered

KELL PACED THE RIVER'S EDGE, tears of anger and frustration streaking down her face. She let out a few enraged sobs and then petulantly kicked the water. The intense focus she had felt while conjuring was broken; now she felt drained and unbelievably hurt. It was him—the teenager from the Saturday market in Eclat, the one who had fraudulently reported her and Simon to the regulators and gotten Simon arrested.

A fresh wave of sobs erupted, and she squatted in the low-lying vegetation to bury her face in her arms.

It was *his* fault!

Why had Renata stopped her?

In time, Kell calmed and began reviewing all that she had done while overcome with rage. She was both pleased and horrified by the power she had drawn and the speed with which she had commanded it. She had not thought about the movements or gestures; she had wanted only to exact revenge on her opponent.

A short time before supper, Kell eventually gathered herself and wandered back to the treehouse. The air was different there with so many people gathered; even from a distance, she could discern the light of multiple fire pits. The smell of food drifted on the wind, and her stomach growled. She loitered on the trail under the trees for a long while, staking out the area and locating her target. She saw the teenager standing away from one of the fires speaking lowly to the willowy group leader, Denez.

Kell compared him to what she remembered from that day in the market. Perhaps he was taller, his hair was longer most certainly, but the way he held himself—she mused—*was* different. He appeared pensive as Denez spoke at length with the middle-aged man who sported a top-knot and responded at length when the First Whispered leader asked him a question. Denez obviously held him in high regard because the leader gave a curt but acknowledging nod before striding off.

Kell spotted Mordecai climb out of the cellar along the southern side of the treehouse and met him at the side entrance of the home. He caught her gaze before hurrying in without a word.

"What have they been doing?" she asked, following him to the hearth.

"I'm not… supposed to be talking to you right now," he replied, glancing over his shoulder in search of Renata.

Kell frowned. "What? Why?"

Mordecai shrugged, passed her an apologetic glance, and then scampered back out. Kell stood alone in the house, a heavy sadness resting upon her shoulders. She knew at once this was her punishment. Steeling herself, she gathered a quarter loaf of bread, dried venison, valuu cheese—a spicy cheese they made from ewe's milk—and a canteen. She also grabbed the top blanket from her bed. With it wadded under her arm and the food safely stashed in a satchel, Kell struck out from the house toward the river.

Once along the river's edge, she laid her blanket and satchel on a sloping rock and began collecting kindling. Although it was June, it still grew chilly at night. The light of a fire would also make her feel less lonely. By the time the sun was hidden behind the ridge and much of the land was in shadow, she sat beside a nicely roaring fire.

Eating her dry sandwich, Kell stared at the swirling eddies in thought. She felt calmer now, not as frenzied. If she had—

A stone clattered nearby and she looked to find the black-haired teenager standing along the trail's end atop the embankment. Kell leaped to her feet, body tense like a coil. She prepared to draw an Arcane Circle.

"Wait, wait!" the young man commanded. "Hold on."

Kell stepped to keep the fire pit between her and the newcomer. If she needed to, she could easily use the fire before her. Behind him, she spotted the man with the top-knot leaning against a tree in the shadows, watching.

The amber-eyed teen approached the fire pit so he was well illuminated by its glow.

"What?" Kell snapped.

"I—Why did you attack me?"

She fell still, caught off guard by his innocence.

"I asked you a question. Why did you attack me?"

The authority in his voice made her bristle. "I'd have killed you had Renata not stopped me."

"Why?"

Kell scrutinized him. Was he playing dumb to escape her wrath? "You don't remember?"

"No, clearly. I've been traveling with the First Whispered for nearly seven months now. I would remember seeing someone—"

"And where were you before that?" interrupted Kell.

The young man passed an appraising eye over her. "Traveling."

"And before that?"

"Why?"

"Where were you two years ago?" Kell demanded.

The teenager was quiet for a long moment, his brows furrowing as if he were trying to remember. "The capital… Why?"

Kell glared at him over the fire. "Go back to the others. You're not safe here."

"Please, tell me!" He sounded earnest.

"All of this… All of it is your fault!" Kell exploded. "Simon, the-the fire, everything—it's *your* fault!"

"What are you talking about?"

Outraged, Kell struggled to keep herself from leaping over the fire at him. She could no longer speak coherently. She wanted to throttle him, to unleash her rage upon him. But his guilelessness kept her from attacking. "You—I—How could—" With a frustrated scream, Kell turned on heel and stormed off.

She still dreamed of Simon frequently and often relived that day at the market. The expression on his face when he had spotted her hiding behind the cart haunted her. She had no idea what had happened to him and assured herself regularly that he was safe, that his parents had picked him up at the Lower District jail and that he was back working aboard the family boat. She couldn't bear to consider the alternative.

Seeing a face that was so integrally tied to that traumatic day triggered her. She could hardly cope with the slew of emotions that threatened to overwhelm her once more.

Well into the evening she wandered along the river, periodically considering returning to her camp. But the solitude gave her time to reflect— and second guess herself. Sometime around midnight, she returned to her smoldering fire, shook out her bedding and reset the kindling, and then snuggled in, her gaze set on the orange, red, and amber flames. Eventually, she slept.

The following morning, she woke at dawn with a crick in her neck. Massaging herself, she considered her next course of action—return to the treehouse or stay by the river for another day. Drawing a long breath, she gazed up at the purple and pink sky and listened to the birds twittering in the treetops and riverside bushes. The bubbling of the water soothed her frayed nerves and now encouraged her. After splashing her face and attempting to set her untidy hair, she gathered her satchel and bedding and solemnly headed back.

She was unsurprised to find most everyone awake. Some sort of sizzling meat cooked on charred fire-top pans as the First Whispered milled about and sipped steaming liquid from carved bone bowls and short mugs. Their conversation was low, hushed.

Kell watched them from the river trail, her bedding wadded under her arm. The way they moved was odd. She had thought it was just Denez, their leader. But the longer she observed them, the more she realized that they all moved in a peculiar willowy way. Their movements were minute; individuals maintained tight but strict bubbles of space between one another. If anyone rose to collect food or drink or to simply accommodate a neighbor, they moved without superfluous motion.

Renata appeared in the doorway of the home, her eyes set on Kell. Knowing that she owed the old woman an apology for something, Kell dragged herself to the treehouse. Standing before her like a disobedient puppy, Kell said, "I'm sorry, teacher."

"For what?" came the cold reply.

Despite the minutes she had been thinking on it, Kell could not come up with an answer. She didn't know what she had done wrong other than attack someone who had set off a chain of events that had changed the course of her life.

Renata's frown deepened. "You haven't learned anything."

"No, you don't understand, teacher," Kell pleaded. "Please, let me explain."

"My singular goal since your arrival has been to teach you discipline—"

"Please, listen."

"Kellick, your assault on our honored guests reflects—"

"I know him!" Kell blurted out. Renata fell quiet. "I know him. Please, believe me. I would never just attack someone like that. Please, Renata."

Renata thought for a moment and then drew her into the home. Mordecai was there, tending to a pot hanging over the hearth. Renata made a motion, and he quickly left. Alone, the old woman planted her hands on her hips. "Talk."

Kell explained all that had occurred, detailing her relationship with Simon and Tarquin's occupation to the schedule of the Saturday markets and rescuing the girls from the untoward behaviors of the older teens.

"You're saying he was the one who turned you and Simon in?" Renata asked, now seated at the table.

"I *know* he was."

"Did you see him?"

"He was with the regulators when they grabbed hold of me and Simon. He accused us right there, calling us thieves." Kell's voice grew quiet. "Do you know what they do to thieves in the Lower District?" The old woman nodded, her gaze set on the wall across the room. Feeling exhausted from her rehashing, Kell collapsed in the chair across from her teacher. "I shamed you in front of your guests, but he… he is the cause of *everything*." She looked at the old woman. "He is the reason Simon was arrested that day, the reason I," she drew a sharp breath, "set flame to the market, the reason Tarquin hauled me to Avives… I'm here sitting before you because of him."

There was a long silence between them before Renata stood. "Come on."

Kell followed her teacher outside. The relaxed atmosphere vanished as it was apparent that a conversation of great importance had transpired between Renata and Kell.

Terin, who was seated next to an older woman, looked on, curious. The teenage boy with black hair and his constant middle-aged companion stopped their discussion to lay wary eyes on them.

"My pupil informs me that though her behavior was sudden and troubling, she had a reason—she knows him." Renata motioned to the teen.

"Is this true, Bellamy?" asked Denez, standing from his seat by the fire. "Do you know this girl?"

The eighteen-year-old shook his head. "No, I've never seen her in my life."

"I wasn't a girl—" Kell exclaimed before she could stop herself. When all eyes fell on her, she shied. "I didn't look like a girl then. I looked like a boy…" She pushed her hair away to reveal her forehead, ears, and jawline and then met Bellamy's gaze. "Two years ago, you were at the Saturday market in the Lower District in Eclat. My friend and I caught you cornering two girls in an alley. You didn't like that." Seeing the sudden recognition in the teen's gaze, Kell released her hair. "So, you lied to the regulators, saying we had stolen." She leveled a malevolent glare at him. "Simon was arrested. I've not heard from him since."

Bellamy's face reddened as he fumbled for a response. "I didn't know you were Unbound. I wouldn't have done that—"

"It shouldn't have mattered who I was!" Kell seethed. "You took *everything* from me. My home, my family and friends, my life."

"Bellamy, does Renata's pupil speak the truth?" asked Denez, alarm tinting his voice for the first time.

Bellamy licked his lips, glancing at the First Whispered around him before meeting Kell's gaze. "Yes. She speaks the truth. But that was a long time ago and I—" He appeared as though to be wrestling with what he wanted to say. "I shouldn't have done that. I was a-angry with what had happened and there was a lot going on and…" He drew a calming breath, and the color in his face faded.

Bellamy left his position by the fire. Realizing his intention, Kell backed away, but Renata stopped her with a firm hand. Up close, Bellamy was tall, far taller than even Mordecai, and Kell was once more reminded that although she had been the same size—sometimes taller—as the boys while growing up, beyond puberty, she was painfully female. His black hair, which she remembered as being cut short, was thick and pulled into a bun at the back of his head. His amber eyes were sharp and… guilt-ridden?

This revelation shook Kell who had fantasized of killing the nameless merchant's son who had set her on her cruel path.

Bellamy drew himself before her. "I am sincerely sorry for any pain that I have caused you and your friend. Were he here, I would apologize to him as well."

"Well, he's not," Kell snapped. She felt Renata's hand twist into her back and grimaced. "But, uh, thanks for saying so."

"We are aware," began Denez, "that Bellamy has transgressions for which he still needs to atone." The First Whispered leader looked between Kell and Renata. "We knew this when we agreed to take him into our company. What might he do as atonement?"

"Uh…" Kell glanced at Bellamy uncomfortably. Other than killing him, she wanted nothing to do with him. "I don't… know." She turned to Renata.

"You're staying with us until the end of the week?" asked Renata. Denez nodded. "Kell will have an answer then."

Bellamy met her gaze and bowed his head. "I will do what must be done to atone for the trouble I have caused you and your friend. Please, excuse me." With quiet dignity, he returned to his companion, keeping his back to everyone.

"Thank you for bringing this to our attention," said Denez with a slight nod, his flaxen hair spilling over his shoulder. "With this out in the open, I'm certain we will be able to reestablish your *satt.*" And with that, he returned to the other First Whispered.

Kell turned to Renata. "My what?"

The old woman patted her arm. "I'll tell you later. Go help Mordecai finish cooking."

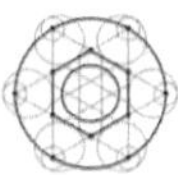

Sitting in Eevie's exam room, a stiff switch of birchwood bandaged tightly to his fractured arm, Simon strained to hear Dr. Gray through the walls.

"—absolutely preposterous. I can't believe that…" The doctor's voice faded as he turned away from their shared wall. Simon glanced at the open exam room doorway and then leaned closer to the wall. "Obviously, he's got to stomp out these uprisings *now*."

"But with His Majesty being so gung-ho about the Munera, I doubt he'll take such drastic measures," replied the gray-haired noble who frequented Dr. Gray's office at Madam Parthemos' school. Simon had seen him around often but didn't know what his job was. "He needs the Users. The Munera brings in billions of galets every game; it's easy, easy money. He can't afford to implement scorched earth policies, no matter what those animals are doing."

"At some point though, he's going to be forced to make a decision," Dr. Gray mused. "We can't allow Users to keep getting away with this shit, pardon my language."

"No, I agree, I agree."

There was a momentary lull before Dr. Gray added, "I'm sure you've heard—the games will start occurring yearly beginning this fall."

"I heard."

"They've had to ramp up training to get seasoned fighters ready. The only good news to come from the rebellions is the massive influx of Users we've managed to get a hold of." Dr. Gray sighed. "But that does mean that I have to treat more of those scum."

"I'm terribly sorry to hear that. And you've talked to the madam about hiring a few more assistants?"

"Oh yes. Actually, my new team is to arrive in three weeks. Once they're fully trained, there'll be about a dozen of us."

"That many?" exclaimed the graying man.

Dr. Gray chuckled. "I don't think you realize how many fighters and Users we have housed here. Eevie and I are struggling to maintain any type of standards. Our office is a revolving door of patients."

"How about I send out for some—"

Eevie entered the room, startling Simon from his eavesdropping. He grinned at her. Eevie regarded him with an amused but suspicious expression. "What were you doing?"

"Nothing," Simon replied. He turned the conversation back to her. "Did you find what you needed?"

"Yes." She pushed back a blond tendril that had escaped her coiffure. "It was buried in the bottom of a box. We're constantly getting new shipments. With all the patients coming in, I just don't have the time to restock the supply room."

"I could do that for you," Simon offered without thinking. He passed her a flirtatious grin.

Eevie smiled. "I'm sure you could, but I suspect Dockett won't like you missing training to do so."

"I can do it after supper."

Eevie handed him a dusty bottle of a mysterious liquid. "Take a teaspoon every six hours. If you don't, you're going to have a hard time staying in training."

Simon stood. At sixteen, he was now slightly taller than her. "Thanks, Eevie."

The young woman with old eyes smiled at him sadly. "Please don't use your injured arm. I know it's just a fracture, but don't fall on it, block with it, or use it to hold a sword." Simon frowned. "If you reinjure yourself, that arm isn't going to heal properly. You're setting yourself up for more pain later on."

"I'll try."

Eevie kissed his cheek. "Good, now go."

His face warm, Simon left the nurse's company. He glanced back at the closed door behind which Dr. Gray and his visitor discussed interesting matters.

Dockett groaned when he saw Simon's bandaged arm and paced the yard for a moment. "What'd they say?" he eventually sighed.

"It's broken."

"Goddamn it." Dockett planted his hands on his hips. "I told you stop rolling like that. Gonna snap your little chicken arm. And now look!" He gestured vehemently at Simon's limb.

"It's a fracture," Simon offered, glancing at Ferrik and Georgie who were watching as they continued their exercises. "Eevie said I can use my other arm to hold—"

"Do you know how long it's taken you to hold a sword the *correct* way? And now she wants you to hold it with your shit hand?" Dockett stomped around the yard for a minute.

"Does it hurt?" asked Georgie, panting.

Simon shrugged noncommittally though, in truth, it hurt pretty bad.

Georgie grinned wolfishly at him. "That'a boy."

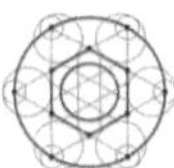

Kell nudged Mordecai playfully. "They're weird, right?"

Mordecai glanced at the First Whispered, a collection of whom had taken off into the forest to go hunting. "Yeah, weird."

Seeing the look on his face, Kell drew his eyes to her. "What's wrong?"

He shrugged and continued to scrub the clay pot in the basin. "Nothing. Just thinking."

Kell sat at the table beside him. "About what?"

"Just stuff."

Realizing that he wasn't wanting to visit with her, she snagged a strawberry and then headed out with the intent to learn more about their visitors. Bellamy had gone with the hunting party, so she had free reign of the area.

Through the trees, she spied Renata strolling along the forest trails with Denez, talking and nodding. She wondered what they discussed that made her teacher appear so grim.

Wandering through the remaining dozen men and women, Kell found the air to once again be tranquil and without tension. She was pleased when one of the young women waved her over.

"We're going to the river," she said. Her pale locks were adorned with small decorative cuffs and hooks intertwined into a single long plait that was drawn back to reveal a sharp jawline. Her eyes were an astonishing shade of sky blue. She was the most handsome woman Kell had ever laid eyes on. "Did you want to join us?"

"Yeah!"

"My name is Gytha." She gestured to the twenty-year-old beside her. "This is Aethel."

Kell passed them slight smiles. "Kellick."

"That's an intriguing name. Where are you from, Kellick?"

"Call me Kell… Uh, Eclat, the Lower District."

Gytha's blue eyes grew wide and she and Aethel exchanged looks of alarm. "So it's true? You *are* from Eclat?"

"How are you not Bound?" asked Aethel, searching her wrists once more.

"I grew up on a fishing boat." They started down the familiar trails toward the river.

"I can imagine it's been hard adjusting to living so far inland," Gytha offered kindly. They walked on in silence for a moment before she continued, "We can tell that you've been through a lot. You and your friend Mordecai."

"And Terin," added Aethel.

Figuring they were referring to her outburst from earlier that morning, Kell ignored the comment. "Are you two Users?"

The two young women grinned at one another before Gytha said, "Our people were the first, uh, *Users*."

Seeing her discomfort, Kell asked, "What's wrong?"

"We do not call ourselves Users. That is the derogatory word that was given to us by people who cannot access the Flow."

"Oh." Kell considered this, remembering how she had never heard Renata or Terin call themselves Users. "What do you call yourselves then? Just First Whispered?"

"But that gets far too cumbersome," Aethel replied good-naturedly.

"Renata's called us Unbound before." Kell looked at Gytha. "Is that name acceptable?"

Gytha nodded enthusiastically and grinned. "That's a wonderful name. Our people do not call ourselves that, but we do like that name a lot. We call ourselves Tribe. It's not as descriptive as Renata's name, but it is old."

"What about Bellamy?" Kell suddenly queried. "Is he Tribe?"

"No, he is a guest," replied Aethel with a knowing smile. "We recognize that you dislike him, but we believe in second chances, especially for people who were once our enemies."

Kell stopped. "Wait, what?"

The two women looked back at her. "He is third in line for the throne in Eclat."

Kell gaped.

"Yes, we do not usually flaunt his title, but given your history with him, we will share that information with you."

"His father is… the king?" Kell whispered.

"Oh no. His uncle is." Aethel looked to Gytha. "His mother's brother, correct?"

Gytha nodded.

"Why is he out here?" was all Kell could think to ask.

"That is something he must tell you. But for the time being, just know that we are aware of his past transgressions and are helping him on his journey of atonement." Gytha started for the river again. "We noticed you have a proclivity for water traits." She chuckled softly, a huffed whisper. "That makes sense now seeing as how you grew up on a fishing boat. Perhaps you'd be willing to give us a demonstration?"

"Sure!"

Once at the river, Kell eagerly showed off her skills, creating wide whirlpools, dancing atop rapids, and parting the river with ease to reveal the algae-ridden plants along the silty bottom. Gytha and Aethel clapped and marveled at her talent before asking, "Can you freeze large sections of the river yet?"

Kell frowned and shook her head. "No, I don't think so. Not yet. I can just do the spots closest to me."

"Oh, that'll come in time," Aethel assured her.

"You're a User—Unbound." Kell strode across the water's surface, balancing atop her Arcane Circle. "Can you show me what you can do?" She paused. "Or is your affinity not water?"

Gytha chortled. "All of the elements belong to us." And with that, she stepped onto the water—without the use of an Arcane Circle—and lightly tiptoed to the middle of the river.

Kell gaped, aghast. "How-how did you do that? Where are your fields? Your circle?"

Aethel grew somber. "Renata only knows and teaches what she was taught."

Gytha strode back to them and gracefully stepped back onto the shoreline. "In the beginning, our method of accessing the Flow was the only method known. It was knowledge that we inherited from the generations before us. We were formidable, well-respected. Did you know the Tribe commanded a spot on the Council of Ministers in the capital?"

Kell shook her head.

"But all of that changed when Leon IV came into power over a century ago. He saw how much influence we wielded and decided it superseded that of even the crown. So, he reached out to Chantis, the country to the east of Berceau, who gladly agreed to assist him, and they began a full-blown genocide." Gytha's gaze grew distant. "We were able to fight back and many escaped, but the Crown had people working for it who knew how to block access to the Flow."

"That's possible?"

"Of course. That talent is reserved for only a select few Users within the government. But that is a different story for another time… They used that form of arcana to control our people. The older generations were purposefully targeted to prevent knowledge from being passed down. Even now, the countries of Berceau and Chantis continue their battle against us. But we're the First Whispered, the people who first harnessed Viterra. We went into seclusion in the mountains to the north."

"Is that where you're from?" asked Kell, fascinated.

"The mountains are cold. To reach them is several weeks' journey across wild lands. The coasts are relatively urban and the weather is mild, but farther inland, it's pure nature." Gytha smiled. "So, what Renata knows is the new style that was invented by those without the knowledge of Old. The First Whispered's methodology remains unchanged."

"So, you don't use Arcane Circles?"

"No."

Kell studied the ground. "What about fields? The bands on your wrists? You have to master each field, right?"

"That's remains true. We still have to master each field—the Self, the Physical, and the Mental—before we achieve Synchrony."

"What's Synchrony?"

"Wielding all fields in unison."

"But why can't I see your fields?"

"Because it is not how you perceive them," replied Aethel.

Kell looked between them, lost.

Gytha thought for a long moment and then asked, "When was the first time you saw someone with red fields, shackles?"

"Maybe… five or six years ago," Kell replied. "I don't remember much, only that the man was very upset and that… there was a glowing set of red bands on his wrists."

"And you asked others about that, right?"

Kell nodded.

"And they told you—what? That those red, glowing bracelets form only on *Users*?" Gytha explained. "Do you see where I'm going with this?"

"Uh, no," whispered Kell.

"From that moment on, you knew that glowing red cuffs meant User; those bands represented something arcane, something unfamiliar, something mystical. It was how you learned of the existence of something supernatural—Viterra. Now, you didn't call it that because you didn't know that name, but you understood that *something* made Users different."

"So, the red bands appear because I think they should be there?" clarified Kell.

"Not just you. Everyone in Berceau. It's what marks a User, after all," Aethel replied. "Everyone knows a Bound User reveals red fields. It is what is expected. Therefore, it is."

Kell thought, her mind whirring. "But there have to be other Unbound. It's not just you, right?"

"The monarchy has been proactive in keeping the Bound population in check." Gytha rolled a rock underfoot. "When Leon IV established the first Culling, they specifically went after the elders." She peered sadly at Kell. "If everyone who knows the Knowledge of Old is no longer around, it can't be taught. All documents, books, scrolls—everything was destroyed. I'm sure somewhere someone has an old scrawled book or something detailing pieces of the Old Knowledge, but without a teacher, the information is useless. It can't be passed around. So, new ways to access the Flow had to be created."

"They've had two other Cullings since then," said Aethel. "One seventy-five years ago and then another—"

"Sixteen years," Kell grimly supplied, remembering what Tarquin had told her about how she had come into his possession.

Aethel nodded. "Such horrible acts decrease the population, but we just keep coming back. We're resilient."

Gytha sighed. "At any rate, methods and techniques had to be reinvented to give the art form."

"Renata is a master in her own right," interjected Aethel. "She is disciplined in nature and precise in her control of Viterra, but she can't access the Flow using our methods."

"We've tried teaching her," Gytha continued. "She's too ingrained in the New Knowledge, which is unfortunate." She looked at her friend. "With the structure she has maintained in the elemental traits, if she could learn the Old, she would be unstoppable."

"You're saying Renata can't do what you do?" concluded Kell.

Both nodded.

"Could I do it? Could I learn the Knowledge of Old?"

Gytha smiled kindly. "It might be possible, Kell, but we're not going to be here long enough to teach you."

"Then, I'll go with you. I'll leave with you!" Kell blurted.

Gytha leaned close, her platinum blond plait slipping over her shoulder. "Your place is here, Kellick. You are not Tribe."

"I thought... I thought everyone who could access the Flow was Tribe?"

"No, not usually. Although there have been exceptions," explained Aethel. "But that is why we will continue to call you Unbound." She grinned. "I like it better than Tribe anyway, don't you?"

Kell glanced at a small flock of starlings as they passed overhead. "You let Bellamy travel with you."

Gytha backed away with a thoughtful sigh. "True. We're letting someone who is not a First Whispered—and not even Unbound—travel with us, but his case is different."

"But you could pass knowledge to me!" Kell pleaded.

"Bellamy is in a position to possibly instigate real change throughout Berceau," Gytha said solemnly. "He came to us, humble, and we accepted him. He will not live with the Tribe indefinitely; his time is limited. So, we will teach him all that we know…"

"That's not fair."

"Well, I suppose we could teach you some things." Gytha stepped out onto the water once more, her boots never once sinking below their soles. "We haven't much time."

Kell swallowed her disappointment and nodded gratefully.

17

Growing Up

KELL LISTENED TO GYTHA'S INSTRUCTION for the rest of the day, returning to the treehouse only to eat. Renata didn't seem concerned with her absence and Mordecai only glanced at her in passing.

Well into the evening Kell tried to grasp the complicated way with which First Whispered viewed life, Viterra, and the Flow. Sometimes it made sense; other times, Kell grew frustrated as she strained to comprehend the new ways of thinking.

The First Whispered believed in the existence of *satt*—harmony within the self—which helped them foster stronger ties to the Flow. Denez's words from earlier in the day regarding Bellamy disturbing her *satt* now made more sense. His presence had caused her distress and disrupted her *satt*, and for that, he had apologized. Even as she struggled to understand it, the concept intrigued Kell and kept her constantly studying Gytha for ways to achieve *satt*.

That night, Kell returned with Gytha to where the other First Whispered camped. The hunting party had returned with two bucks and three rabbits which Renata and Terin had helped skin and prepare for supper. As she listened to one of the Tribe members play a small flute, Kell bounced her foot against the base of her root-woven bench and watched the others.

"Hey," Terin greeted, joining her. "You've been gone all day." The young woman sat beside Kell and passed her a bowl of rabbit stew, root vegetables, and spices.

Kell inhaled deeply and grinned. "Yeah, I've been with Gytha. She's been teaching me." She began slurping the soup. "Oh, this is good."

Terin swirled her soup thoughtfully. "Is it hard?"

"What?"

"The stuff she's teaching you? Their way of, uh, thinking?"

Kell mused over a bite of tender rabbit. "Yes and no. Everything is so foreign. Strange. I don't get a lot of it. But sometimes, I feel like I'm on the brink of, you know, understanding. It's really hard to explain."

"Oh, yeah."

"I'm sure if you asked, she'd teach you too," Kell offered.

Terin chuckled uncomfortably. "Eh, probably not. They wouldn't want someone like me."

Kell glanced at her beneath her lashes. Terin was staring at the ground, oddly pensive and melancholy. She sensed there was more to Terin's response than what she understood. "You all right?"

The young woman passed her a weary smile. "Of course. It's just been a long day." She stood. "I'd better go see if Renata needs help." And she hurried off.

Kell watched her flit back into the treehouse. Something felt off about Terin, but she couldn't discern what it was.

When the venison was ready, Kell happily partook in the feast but eventually began to feel lonely. Terin didn't return; Renata was visiting with Denez and the other First Whispered; Gytha was busy helping the others cook; and Mordecai was nowhere to be seen. Kell caught Bellamy's gaze briefly across two firepits but quickly returned her attention to her clay plate.

After she finished eating, she retreated to the treehouse in search of Mordecai. When she didn't find him but noticed that one of the large pots was missing, she headed to the river. Though it was dark, she knew the trail by heart and felt at peace strolling along its worn edge. As she drew near, she heard a cry of anguish and frustration. Kell paused mid-step. That was Mordecai.

Deciding that he didn't sound as though he were in trouble, she hesitantly continued until she reached the elevated embankment. Below along the river's rocky shoreline, Mordecai was practicing water traits. In the moonlight, she could discern for the first time the stiffness in his movements. His hands, though bent correctly, moved with jerks and his arms and legs lurched from one stance to the next. Water was not his affinity.

Kell squatted and watched, feeling both pity and frustration. He spun to create an Arcane Circle, struck his wrists, and then growled as red rings sputtered briefly to life. With no Arcane Circle ignited and no fields illuminated around his arms, he moved into the next set of water traits, forcefully trying to draw water from the river. The river water never deviated from its course. Mordecai kicked the swirling eddies angrily and stomped around it for a moment before calming himself and settling down to try once more.

Had they not been practicing water traits for months? How could he still be so bad at them? A thought occurred to Kell, causing her to fall still. Gytha had indicated that once drawn from the Flow, Viterra was what one perceived it to be. That's how the Knowledge of Old worked, more or less. That coupled with Mordecai's innate fear of water...

Kell slid down the embankment to join him. He was so involved with his training that he didn't notice her until she was within a few feet of him.

"God, Kell," he wheezed, bending over his knees. "Don't sneak up on me like that!"

"Sorry..." Kell scrutinized him in the moonlight. "I've been watching you."

Mordecai straightened himself and peered out at the river. "Yeah? So?" he asked bitterly.

Setting aside her realization from a moment ago, Kell asked, "What's wrong? You've been avoiding me all day."

Panting, Mordecai planted his hands on his hips and just shook his head.

"No, you've not been able to look at me all day." Kell marched around him to meet his gaze once more. "What's going on?"

"It's nothing. Nothing, Kell." Mordecai slumped and started back to the trailhead.

"You're... not doing it right. The water traits," Kell called after him.

"You think?" he snarled, whirling on her. "But I'm doing it exactly like Terin and Renata taught us."

"You're too stiff. Not like water."

"Let's be real here," Mordecai replied, "I'm never going to conjure anything. We've been at this for two years and I've not once been able to create an Arcane Circle. And then you—" He gestured to her angrily, "You just whip it out perfectly and-and..."

Kell approached him. "And what?"

Mordecai shook his head. "Nothing."

"No, tell me!" She grabbed his arm when he turned to leave. "Mordecai, tell me."

"Kell, you almost killed that guy. You just... you used the traits effortlessly and, I don't know, it was..." He shrugged. "It was frightening. And-and it just made me so worried and angry and frustrated."

"I... scared you?" Kell gazed at him, stunned. He nodded, avoiding her gaze. "I'm sorry."

Mordecai shrugged. "I mean, it's over, done. But what am I supposed to do after that? I can't ignite a circle; I can't conjure anything. I'm older than you but still can't do anything. I'm failing in every sense of the word."

Not knowing what else to say or do, Kell gently punched his shoulder. "You'll figure it out. We have good teachers—Terin and Renata. You'll get it. I know it."

"I don't feel that way," Mordecai murmured.

There was silence between them before Kell said, "Can I make a suggestion?"

"Hm?"

"I think you should let me teach you how to swim."

Instead of immediately disregarding the idea, Mordecai looked at her in ardent consideration. He fidgeted uncomfortably and then nodded. "Yeah."

Briefly, Kell got the strange desire to hug him, to wrap her arms around him, but she tamped that down. "Come on. Let's head back."

With a sigh, Mordecai agreed.

Over the next few days, Mordecai began interacting with Kell more but remained clearly depressed. Kell didn't invite him to her private lessons with Gytha for fear that he would disrupt the relationship they had formed, but she did spend most of the other time with him. Though they agreed he needed to learn to swim, Kell thought it wise to wait until the First Whispered were gone before teaching him.

For the rest of the week, Kell sat with Gytha every morning and listened to her detailed explanations of how the First Whispered perceived world. In the afternoons, she attempted to access the Flow without igniting an Arcane Circle but never created so much as a spark. Every meal she ate with Mordecai. On occasion, she caught Bellamy watching them, but he looked elsewhere when she noticed his gaze. Never did the young man say anything to anyone other than the First Whispered.

Before Kell knew it, it was time for their guests to leave. Though deeply disappointed that she had been unable to access the Flow using the Old Knowledge and that her new teacher was departing, Kell was relieved knowing that their lives were about to return to the old and familiar.

As Renata stood off to the side with Denez and several other First Whispered, Kell, Terin, and Mordecai watched from the side of the treehouse. Terin was joking about the kindness one of the hunters had shown an animal during a hunt when she was interrupted by Bellamy. She fell silent, and Kell stiffened.

Bellamy passed Terin and Mordecai polite nods before setting his gaze on Kell. "I'm pleased to have met you, Kellick. I hope our paths cross again."

"They won't. Don't worry," she replied, perhaps a little too tersely.

Despite the remark, Bellamy held out his hand. "I swear to make things right."

Kell considered him and then firmly took his hand. "You'd better."

A flicker of a smile crossed his face as he released her hand. "Terin, Mordecai—take care."

"Yeah," was all Mordecai uttered. Terin remained, her gaze darker than usual.

Bellamy rejoined the middle-aged, grizzled man to await their departure.

"Kellick, a moment?" called Gytha from a group of Tribe members. Kellick followed her away from the others. "Keep practicing. You're young. You can learn it—the Old ways. Find your *satt*. Remember, the Flow resides in everything. Find peace within yourself and the rest will follow." Gytha tapped her cheek affectionately. Kell grinned at her.

The First Whispered and Bellamy and his cohort left shortly thereafter.

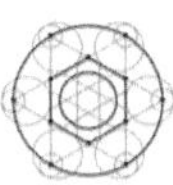

Eevie glowered, her arms folded across her chest and hip thrown to the side. Simon grinned through a grimace. "Sorry…" he wheezed. He couldn't quite make it sound as though he weren't in pain.

"I *told* you," she seethed. The nurse fidgeted in thought and then stormed from the exam room.

Simon was left sitting on the exam table, his injured arm throbbing and trembling. The horrible ache that penetrated his core kept him on the verge of sobs. He had tried to listen to Eevie and give his broken arm time to heal, but Dockett had had other ideas. Simon glanced down at his shaking fingers, disgusted with how weak he was. All it had taken was another bad fall, and his arm had snapped again.

Tears slipped down his cheeks, but he quickly wiped them away. He listened for Dr. Gray or Eevie. When he heard nothing, he allowed more tears to well in his eyes. Not for the first time, he cursed his existence and the life he found himself trapped in.

Some ten minutes later, Simon finally heard footsteps and cleaned his face and eyes to hide all evidence of pain. A moment passed before Eevie dragged Dockett into the exam room and threw him into the counter with surprising force for her petite frame.

"Look at him!" she snarled.

"Eevie, come on," Dockett muttered, glancing at Simon.

Eevie shoved him again and pointed at Simon. "You swore to me you wouldn't hurt this boy. What happened?"

"He fell wrong," the Lanista replied. "That's not my fault."

"He rebroke it, Ellis." Eevie sighed. "It snapped. He might not ever be able to properly use it again."

Dockett ran a grubby, tense hand over his face. "I don't know, Eevie. What do you want me to do?"

"Put him on rest. You've been pushing him for over two years now. I'm surprised it didn't happen sooner." She began rummaging through the drawers of the wheeled cart stationed near the exam table. "Make him rest."

Dockett sighed. "For how long?"

"At least two months."

"Two months! Come on, Eevie. That's not possible."

The nurse whirled on the Lanista so fast that Simon thought she was going to slap him. He had never seen Eevie so fired up. Similarly, he had never witnessed Dockett take a verbal lashing without so much as a retort. "You've crossed a line, Ellis," Eevie fumed. Her anger would have encouraged others to back away, but Dockett didn't move as she spoke into his face. "If you hurt this boy one more time, *one* more time, Ellis, I'll-I'll…" She shook with rage.

Dockett put a surprisingly gentle hand on her shoulder. "I know, Eevie. He can rest. For now. Do your best to fix him up. Yeah?"

Simon glimpsed tears slide down her cheeks before she nodded, wiped them away, and then returned to withdrawing tools and bandages from the cart.

Dockett drew a long breath and then passed an appraising eye over Simon. "Get some rest, kid." And he left.

Stunned by the exchange, Simon looked between them. He had never seen that side of Dockett before. He had seen the man's rage, disappointment, and fierceness, but never had he witnessed Dockett yield, much less to a woman. Everything Simon suspected had just been confirmed.

Eevie sniffed and then turned to Simon. "All right, let's get you feeling better, shall we?"

"Am… I really going to have a break for two months?"

The nurse's lips pursed. "If I have anything to say of it."

Simon winced as she began unwinding his bandages and splints. After a moment, he said, "Thank you, Eevie."

Eevie leaned in and kissed his cheek. Her voice was warm. "You're welcome, Simon."

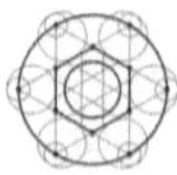

"This is so dumb!" sputtered Mordecai as he thrashed through the water, obviously panicked that he was going to go under.

"You're standing," Kell argued. "You're literally standing. Calm down!" When he started to stomp back to shore, Kell waded after him. She grabbed his arm and jerked him to a stop. "Mordecai, stop panicking. Look, look!" She pointed to the water that swirled around their shins. "How are you going to drown in that?"

"This was a stupid idea." Mordecai ripped his arm from her grip and started for the shoreline. "Come on."

Kell could feel his fear. She understood it; she had felt the same about fire. He needed to relax, to lower his guard. "Look, just come sit in the water with me," she called. "Right here. Just come sit here." And she did just that. Dressed in a bandeau and shorts that had once been pants, she settled herself comfortably in the shallow water and looked back at him. "Come on. Right here," she said, patting the water beside her.

Mordecai kept walking.

"You're never going to be able to conjure water if you don't at least try to understand it."

That made him stop. With a heavy sigh, he returned and sat beside her, tense and uncomfortable. Kell tried to remember all that Tarquin had taught her over the years. Synthesizing so much information was going to be a challenge.

"Swimming isn't a fight," she explained. "If you find yourself fighting water or struggling, you're doing something wrong. Water is fluid, so you also have to be fluid."

"What does that even mean?" grumbled Mordecai.

"Don't fight the water. Don't struggle with it. The harder you fight it, the quicker you lose." Kell slipped farther into the river, leaving Mordecai where he was seated. "Like the current here. Watch, I'm going to fight the current."

Taking a breath, she lifted her feet and began stroking hard upriver. She swam arm over arm, her face in the water, until she was gasping for air. She stood up some feet from where she had started. Panting, she swiped her hair from her face.

"See?" she asked Mordecai. "I'm tired and I didn't really go anywhere even though I tried really hard. When you fight water, you always lose." She waded back to him and held out her hand. "So don't fight it. Learn to work with it."

Mordecai reluctantly took her hand, and she pulled him up. She led him a few paces in and then kneeled so the water passed around her chest. He stiffly joined her.

"Get used to water being near your face, to it moving around you."

Mordecai shifted and looked down at the bottom.

"See the fish?" Kell whispered, pointing to the minnows gathering around them.

For several long minutes, they stayed in that position or in variations of it until Mordecai was more relaxed. Eventually, Kell began asking him to put his face in the water, assuring him that he could bring it up at any time. After a few panicked tries, he finally managed to hold his breath for longer than a few seconds.

Grinning, Kell watched as Mordecai's ears dipped under the water. Immediately, he came back up with a gasp. "Yeah!" she squealed, splashing water at him.

Mordecai smiled, exhilarated. "I saw fish! I saw them move underwater!"

"I know!"

They practiced well into the afternoon. By the time the sun began to fade below the opposite ridge, Kell had Mordecai in deeper water—though he could still stand if he needed to—stroking upriver.

"All right, last time!" she called from several paces away from him. "You can do it! Swim to me!"

Mordecai shook out his arms, took a breath, and began swimming hard against the current. Though his form was clumsy and effortful and the timing of his breaths was unnatural, he slowly made progress. As he drew closer to Kell, she stepped back. He continued swimming. When he had nearly reached her, she swam laterally into deeper water until she could no longer touch the ground.

Mordecai followed her, his wheezing audible. Exceptionally pleased, Kell stopped treading water and let the current carry her to him. She grasped his arms and shouted at the water, "Roll over!"

Having already practiced lying the technique, Mordecai stopped stroking and rolled, awkwardly, onto his back. She helped him find his balance, gently touching the middle of his back to remind him to keep his chest pointed upward. As he caught his breath, she pulled him to shallower water. When she stood, she tapped his shoulder.

Mordecai tiredly drew his legs under him.

Elated, Kell hugged him. "You did it! Did you see yourself? You swam! Mordecai, you swam!"

To her delight, Mordecai embraced her with similar enthusiasm. "Thank you," he panted.

It took but a moment for her excitement of his success to turn into something else, something that made her feel warm and flustered. Suddenly aware of their bare skin touching, Kell pulled away and met Mordecai's gaze. He was still grinning, but a strange look had entered his eyes.

Kell cleared her throat and backed away. "I knew you could do it."

Mordecai appeared pleased. "You'll… keep working with me, right?"

Kell made to shove him playfully. "Of course—"

He caught her hand and held it between them. Mordecai's gaze searched hers before dropping to her lips. Bemused, Kell fidgeted under his scrutiny and then gently pulled away. She apologized—for something—and then left the water.

That evening as they ate dinner and Renata explained the hierarchy of their nomadic guests, Kell avoided Mordecai's gaze. Not because she didn't like the way he made her feel, but because she liked it too much. She often felt his eyes on her but pretended not to notice. If she spoke to him or looked at him, it was briefly.

She had grown up as a boy and had spent all of her time with boys. She was most comfortable around boys because she was one of them. But now, a boy was treating her differently, and that stirred feelings in her.

She knew she loved Simon; that was easy. He was the old and familiar, he was comfort, friendship, and family. He was her partner in adventures and her opponent in roughhousing and wrestling matches. But… Simon had only ever known her as a boy.

The way Mordecai had begun to look at her made her feel like a giant spotlight had been turned onto her. His attention made her jittery. When he accidentally bumped her while cleaning up dishes, she nearly jolted from her skin. Any time he neared her, she grew flustered and warm. She was torn between sprinting down the trail to the river to cool off and jumping enthusiastically into his arms.

"Kell? Help me get more water?" asked Terin, leaving the treehouse.

Kell gratefully hurried after her. "Yep!"

Once they were a safe distance from the house with their buckets, Terin said, "I talked to Mordecai the other day—like you asked."

Kell opened her mouth as the puzzle pieces started to fall into place but could think of nothing to say.

Terin stopped and looked at her in the darkness, the light of the treehouse illuminating parts of her face to reveal a smirk. "Let's you and me have a little chat about… things."

18

The Coming Seasons

AUTUMN CAME FAST AND UNEXPECTEDLY to the glen. One day Kell, Mordecai, and Terin were swimming gleefully downriver, and the next, they were huddled around the hearth in the treehouse. As they continued their training and moved into learning air traits—Renata wanted to start teaching earth and metal in the spring—Kell reveled in her newfound relationship with Mordecai.

He was sensitive, thoughtful, intelligent, and gentle. Having grown up with Simon's teasing and roughhousing, Kell didn't know that little touches could be so powerful until she found herself obsessed with the way Mordecai grazed his fingertips over her arm when he passed a bowl to Terin. Or the way he brushed past her to retrieve firewood. Or the way he nudged her foot under the table. Though she got better at hiding her embarrassment and excitement, his every touch set her heart hammering. Only when Renata finally called them out did they stop openly flirting.

Kell began learning to hunt with Terin, using new skills to better locate, trap, and slaughter prey. Terin was a good teacher, and Kell quickly came to appreciate the young woman's strength, instruction, and nuance. While Renata used Viterra like an extension of herself, manipulating the world around her to suit her needs, Terin utilized it in a much more direct manner. The young woman didn't have any qualms about disrupting nature to get to what she needed.

If a boar was hiding beyond a stand of trees, Terin would cause the earth beneath it to give way to ensnare it. Once trapped in the pit, she would kill it with the sharpened root of a nearby tree and then command the earth to return the boar to even land. Terin felled pheasants with gusts of air that broke their wings or slammed them into trees or to the ground. Catching fish was simple as she brought blobs of water containing her prey to land. Terin even used harsh methods of corralling on their small herd of sheep. She seemed to relish the control and power she had over the creatures.

One afternoon, Kell watched Terin maim a wild turkey with ice shards. The older woman chuckled as the creature flailed violently in the underbrush, spewing blood everywhere. Supremely uncomfortable with the scene, Kell put the creature to death with a quick, razor-sharp ice wedge. "I'm a fisherman," she explained to Terin who appeared disappointed that Kell had intervened. "We make clean, fast kills."

Terrin scoffed. "They die so we can eat. Why does it matter how we kill them?"

Unsure of how to reply and wholly distressed by Terin's response, Kell collected their kill and they returned to the treehouse.

As winter creeped in, Terin and Renata began teaching Kell and Mordecai how to stay warm using Viterra to manipulate the air temperature around them. Though Mordecai still had not been able to conjure an Arcane Circle, he continued to learn the traits to the best of his ability, practicing with Kell often when they had nothing else to do during the long winter evenings.

Sometime in March, when purple crocuses and yellow irises began to bloom, Renata turned to teaching earth traits. The movements were different from those Kell had previously studied. The stances were wide and stiff and made her legs sore for days on end. The motions Renata showed them were quick but square, utilizing their forearms and palms rather than their fingertips. Like the other traits, every part of the body was used to express commands and to further manipulate Viterra, but Kell had a hard time feeling comfortable with it.

Mordecai, however, appeared to rejoice in the style and quickly picked it up. Kell was humbled and tried to remember that Mordecai had felt the same when she had so aptly learned water traits.

From there, they began learning metal traits which, according to Renata, were a kind of extension of earth techniques. One late April day, she grabbed a small satchel from the cellar and unceremoniously scattered its contents— an array of pins, rings, clasps, buttons, pen nibs, and halter ringlets—onto the ground in front of the treehouse. The items bounced and flipped, glittering in the morning sunlight.

"Pick them up and put them back in the satchel," the old woman instructed. Kell and Mordecai waited for the catch. "Using only metal traits." Renata opened the satchel and set on the ground near her feet several paces away.

Mordecai looked at Kell as they both knew she was going to be doing the majority of the work.

Kell drew a quick Arcane Circle, ignited her fields, and considered how best to go about completing the task. In the meantime, Mordecai circled the area, looking at the items with unusual interest. Having grown quite aware of Mordecai and his body language, Kell hesitated to act, glancing at Renata and Terin to see if they had also picked up on his behavior. Her old teacher gave a single nod, signaling for Kell to wait.

Mordecai crouched beside a pen nib, his brows furrowed. Seeming to have forgotten the rule Renata had just set, he picked it up and studied it. Kell could see something akin to recognition light his blue eyes. He stood, his gaze intense on the nib, and ran a thumb over it.

After a moment, he looked down at the ground and then, with practiced ease, traced a circle around himself with a foot and then struck his wrists in a single motion. Two red bands of Viterra erupted around his wrists as a black Arcane Circle ignited under his feet. Mouth agape, Mordecai stepped back several paces, the circle staying underfoot. A manic smile spread across his face as he looked at the others.

"I…" He laughed in disbelief. "I did it! Look, I did it!"

Still astounded but drawing on Mordecai's infectious mirth, Kell whooped and ran to him. "You did it! You really did it!" She stopped short of leaping on him and studied his Arcane Circle with amazement. "Look, look, it's black! Mordecai!" She tagged his arm and danced around him in glee. "Look!"

Renata and Terin joined them, both wearing broad smiles. "It looks like you just needed to be with your affinity to first channel access to the Flow," explained Renata with a sigh. "I should have known your affinity was metal."

Mordecai didn't seem to hear her as he was still marveling at the glowing bands on his arms and the Arcane Circle that followed his every step. Beaming, he held the pen nib out on his palm and then, using the new movements he had learned the previous week, forced Viterra into the metal. The pen nib leaped into the air above his palm and twirled in the sunlight. Mordecai let out an exuberant burst of laughter and then swung around, widening his stance as he pointed to the other metal objects scattered about. Although only three or four items closest to him obeyed his commands, he didn't seem to care. With pure delight, he slung them easily into the waiting satchel and then began leaping around the practice yard. Kell's heart felt like it was going to burst with pride.

But as Mordecai scampered about picking up the metal bits and ends that their teacher had thrown, Kell fell still, confused—and she wasn't the only one. Several of the items outside of his range were springing from the ground as if of their own accord.

"Mordecai?" called Terin over his mirth.

Panting from the effort, Mordecai paused in his work.

Renata pointed at him. "Stop using your hands for a second."

Mordecai's face folded into worry. "Did I do something wrong?"

Their old teacher shook her head. "No, just… stop flitting about for a moment. Put down what you've got and be still." Mordecai obeyed, his fields and the Arcane Circle still ignited around him. Renata thought for a curious amount of time and then said, "Focus on the piece nearest you and, when you're ready, ask it to come to you—but only with your feet."

"What? Why?"

"Humor me," Renata replied.

Mordecai exchanged looks with Kell before settling into a wide-set stance, his hands clenched in fists and situated before him as though he were going to attack someone. He collected himself and then settled his gaze on the halter ring a few feet from him.

"It's not going to take much," added Renata. "I don't think…"

Mordecai adjusted his right foot and then slid it a mere two inches to the side. The metal ring lost its shape and whirred through the air as a hot flash of metal, nearly impaling Mordecai. With a yelp, he ducked aside at the last second to allow the ballistic to fly across the glen and hit a tree with a distant thwack!

Everyone was silent except Renata who began chuckling, and then snickering, and then cackling.

"What… just happened?" asked Mordecai.

Renata grinned wolfishly. "Your hands are Bound, but your feet aren't."

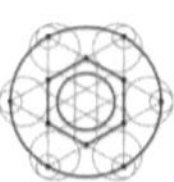

"Madam Parthemos, it's a pleasure," said Dockett, bowing courteously to the glamorous woman in the floor-length gown. Simon copied the Lanista, struggling to muster half the charm and elegance that Dockett somehow managed to whip out every time they met with nobles.

"Lord Dockett, I was wondering when—" Madam Parthemos glimpsed Simon and let out a breathy smile. "Ah, Simon Ashway. It certainly *is* a pleasure. My, you've grown since I last saw you. What a fine young man." Madam Parthemos fanned herself lightly with her lace fan. "You'll have to bring him around more often, Lord Dockett. I would love to see what he's capable of these days."

Dockett laughed. "He'll be as tall as me next year. I'm sure young Simon here would not be opposed to demonstrating his strength."

Madam Parthemos' hazel eyes languorously swept over Simon, but Simon had long since learned to bear any discomfort. Instead, he remained distant and observant, not allowing the woman's lusty gaze to influence him. "Hm, your intuition was right," Madam Parthemos eventually said. "I think he's the one. He'll make you money."

Dockett grinned. "I think so too."

"Please, enjoy yourselves." Madam Parthemos gestured to the innumerable people milling about the grand hall. "Supper will be announced soon."

Dockett and Simon bowed once more and then headed off to a table boasting crystal flutes of champagne and sparkling glasses of wines. "See? I told you," said Dockett, fondly clapping Simon on the shoulder. "You got a handsome face. Just gotta get it in front of everybody. Let people know you exist."

"I thought that's what next week is for," Simon muttered, politely refusing a flute of alcohol as he was not permitted to have it as a pro-fighter.

Dockett snarled his fingers around a delicate flute and downed its contents. He was presented another by a servant and happily took it. "It is," he finally said. "This is just preliminary. Mill about, meet people, let them look at you."

Simon glanced down at the three-piece suit of navy that he wore. He felt ridiculous, but if it was going to earn Dockett support and money, then he was all for it. "Sure…"

Dockett introduced him to a number of people whose names Simon immediately forgot, but at every meeting, Simon was the perfect gentleman. He acknowledged the ladies on men's arms who were often overlooked, asked after the health of older gentlemen he knew, and exchanged polite remarks with those elite he had never met.

After supper, which was a gluttonous affair that Simon hardly partook of, the men separated themselves to go smoke and visit in the adjacent lounge. Upon returning from the washroom, Simon found the lounge doorway congested with elegantly dressed guests. As he politely waited for the traffic to the lounge to clear, he listened.

"… absolutely agree with you," a middle-aged man with a well-kempt mustache was saying. "We must do what we can to keep the population of Users under control. If another Culling is what it takes, then so be it."

The noble who replied spoke lowly, "I hate that *some* don't understand this issue."

"Let us not forget the Dirty Dawn incident," another quickly interjected. "We overlooked one—only one—Unbound and suffered the consequences."

"My father's deputy was there that morning," another man chimed in. "It was a woman. She swallowed half of the Middle District in vegetation. It took the city two whole years to clean it all up." He leaned into the group. "She set the Munera training school afire, tore down a handful of government buildings, and killed hundreds of people. She was an absolute menace."

"That's exactly my point! We *cannot* allow such dangerous people loose. If we do not curtail their population now and enact stricter birthing laws, such refuse will spread. I'm, of course, speaking of sterilization."

Simon spotted a gap in the crowd and headed for it.

Over his shoulder, he heard, "Remind me, did they ever catch her—that Unbound?"

Simon didn't hear the answer as the response was spoken in a whisper for only those privy to the conversation. Catching sight of Dockett, he hurried across the lounge to the Lanista who was visiting with a young man who boasted the most unique amber eyes.

"Simon Ashway, I would like for you to meet Bellamy Trevarthen, Prince of Berceau, third in line for the crown," said Dockett with a polite bow.

Recognizing that he was meeting not a noble but royalty, Simon bowed deeply to the young man who appeared to be in his early twenties. "It's an honor to meet a son of the Crown."

The royal's response was muted, unenthusiastic. "It's a pleasure."

Simon straightened himself and adjusted his jacket, as Dockett had showed him, and then dared to meet Bellamy's gaze. The young man's eyes were intelligent but distant and cold. Not knowing how to approach the situation, Simon glanced at Dockett who intervened.

"Simon has been training for the past several years as my Champion. He intends to compete in the Munera a year from now."

"Ah, I see. How nice." Bellamy's gaze slipped across the room to a group of ornately dressed older gentlemen gathered near an enormous hearth. "I'm sure you've been working hard."

"Uh, yes…" Simon exchanged furtive looks with Dockett who eagerly tried to draw the prince's attention back to them.

"Simon here will be doing a showcase next week to unveil his skills and abilities in the… arena—Sire? I can't help but feel as though you are preoccupied. Perhaps we could visit with you at a different time so as not to interfere with your duties?"

Bellamy's brows furrowed and he nodded. "Yes, thank you." And with that, he strode across the room to the group of men.

"What… was that about?" murmured Simon.

"Those men are part of the Council of Ministers," Dockett explained under his breath. "As I understand it, the young prince has been gone for nearly a year and now he's trying to get back into the good graces of the Council."

"Where'd he go?" asked Simon, intrigued. "Was he sick?"

"I thought he was staying with family in Avives. Eevie heard from other medical professionals that when he came back, he was tanner, larger, stronger…" Dockett shrugged. "Don't know." He pointed with his jaw at the middle-aged man standing watchfully on the other side of the room. "That's Marko, his bodyguard. Goes wherever he goes."

Simon glanced at the man, noting his muscular physique and closely-trimmed graying hair. He was different from the others there in the room; he was dangerous.

"Eh, come on. I see someone we haven't met yet. Let's try to rustle up some money."

As Dockett led him across the enormous room, Simon glanced back at Bellamy, bothered. He felt as though this wasn't his first time meeting the prince.

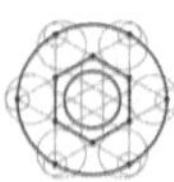

Kell watched Mordecai from outside the treehouse as he used Viterra to stir the stew cooking in the pot hanging in the hearth. A grin pulled at his lips. The Arcane Circle beneath his feet illuminated his boots with a dim black light; the glowing red bands around his arms stood out from the fire light. Kell smiled as she realized the silliness of the action—stirring a pot of stew normally would require less effort. But Mordecai was beyond enthralled and pleased.

Smiling, she carried in the pile of firewood. "You're a natural."

"It's… it's so easy." Mordecai looked at her. "Is this how it feels when you work with water?"

Kell brushed her hands on her pants and sat at the table. "I guess so."

The house seemed smaller, emptier since Terin and Renata had left for Avives that morning to collect their monthly supplies. And Kell was painfully aware that she was alone with Mordecai. Renata had assured her that they would be back in four days, but whenever Terin ventured into town, she often got sidetracked and didn't come home on her assigned date of return.

With the two powerful Unbound traveling, Kell wondered how she and Mordecai would get along. Renata had predicted bad spring weather in the coming days.

As Mordecai continued to gleefully cook—he had learned much from Renata—Kell watched him. "Do you ever miss home?"

"What home?"

"You know… your family."

The smile on his face faded, and he sat at the table with her. "Sometimes. I wonder how they're doing, but… I know they've not thought of me once since they dumped me at Sacred Tree." He tried to touch the red bracelets around his arms, but his fingers passed through them. "You?"

"I miss Tarquin. But other than that…" Kell sat back to lean against the wall. "There's nothing left for me there."

"What about that Simon person you always talk about?"

Kell picked at a knobby root. "Honestly… I don't know if he's… uh, alive."

Mordecai grew still. "Why do you think that?"

"Regulators grabbed him—they would have caught me too, but I ran. I abandoned him. And then… I got scared and that's when I, uh, set the Saturday market on fire." She remembered the enormous plumes of brackish smoke pouring into the sky and the wild flames that had engulfed the surrounding flats. "I burnt down half of the Lower District that day. I don't know if Simon escaped the regulators, much less made it out of the fire…"

Mordecai shook his hands to dispel the Viterra and then reached across the table to her. "You can't blame yourself for that."

"Then who do I blame?" Kell squeezed his fingers. "I can't even blame that guy, Bellamy, because he begged forgiveness. It's unfair."

Mordecai shifted. "No, you can definitely blame him. What's he gonna do? He's not around."

Kell slouched, resting her knee against the table, something that Renata regularly scolded her for. "You think he's still with the First Whispered?"

"Who cares." Mordecai stood and returned to the pot of bubbling stew to see if it had finished simmering. "You're too hard on yourself."

Kell watched his form fondly, taking in how tall he had grown and how well he had filled out. He was lean and toned from the hours they spent training and just existing in the wilderness. Though they were always well-fed, living on the land was hard work and required teamwork, strength, and discipline.

He wore a long-sleeved shirt with its sleeves rolled up to his elbows, a light vest, and a pair of slacks tucked into mud-spattered boots. His black hair, which had lightened to reflect faint hues of brown and red, was pulled back in a messy bun at the back of his head. When he grew sweaty or the humidity was too high, wisps of it escaped its confines.

"Hey, Mordecai?" asked Kell, running her eyes over him.

As he ladled out stew, he glanced at her with a smile. "Hm?"

"Where are you going to go after we leave here?"

He frowned. "Leave here?"

"We can't stay here forever…"

He passed her a bowl and then began collecting food for himself. "I… don't know. I've been avoiding thinking about it." Mordecai sat across from her. "This is paradise, Kell. We don't answer to anyone, except Renata, and we do *what* we want *when* we want. Do you know how rare that is these days?"

Kell stirred the contents of her bowl, watching as potatoes and chunks of venison mingled. "Gytha told me that the stuff Renata's been teaching us is the Knowledge of New."

"Not what the First Whispered practice?"

"Yeah…" Kell sipped a spoonful of the hearty broth. "Mhhm, that's good. You did good."

Mordecai flashed a charming smile. "I'm glad."

From there, conversation dropped off. The only sound between them was the crackling of the fire to ward off the chill of the encroaching night and the forest insects. After supper, they worked together to store the food and then carried the pot to the river to wash it.

As Kell scrubbed it with sand, she took solace in the sound of the running water. Once finished, she set the pot aside and sat back on the rocks. Mordecai, who had been perusing the shoreline, returned. "Ready?" He offered her a hand.

Kell took it, and he pulled her up, drawing her to him in the darkness. A quiet gasp escaped her throat as she found herself enwrapped in his arms. The sounds of nature seemed to pulse louder around her. She could feel the heat rolling off of Mordecai; she was certain he could hear her heart hammering against her ribs. Kell's fingers snarled into the back of his shirt as she hugged him tightly, relishing the intimacy.

Mordecai shifted against her so that his bristly chin brushed the side of her face. Though they had touched often, they had rarely been afforded the opportunity to be close for so long. After a moment, Mordecai leaned forward and gently pulled aside her hair, which had grown to hang just above her shoulders, to reveal her neck. Kell shivered; her knees threatened to buckle. His hot breath scorched her as he kissed the delicate flesh along her neck.

An involuntary whimper, a wholly unfamiliar sound, escaped Kell's throat as she melted against him. That seemed to amuse Mordecai because she felt his lips turn upward into a smile against her skin. Knowing now what she wanted, she eagerly drew away so they were even and then leaned in with the intention of kissing him.

Instead, she miscalculated the distance and smashed her forehead into his nose, causing them both to step apart in pain.

"Sorry! Sorry…" she muttered, fiercely rubbing her head. "Sorry."

"Why, Kellick?" Mordecai groaned, holding his nose.

Burning with excitement and embarrassment, Kell grabbed his vest and drew him back to her. "Sorry." She pulled his hand from his face in an attempt to scrutinize his injury, but it was dark and she could hardly find his eyes.

Mordecai drew a long breath, as if to calm himself, and then whispered, "Don't move." He cradled her face in both hands and then leaned in and touched his lips to hers. That was it. A simple kiss.

As he pulled away, Kell followed, leaving his grasp to return the kiss. They were bumbling, awkward. Kell had thought Mordecai might have had experience dealing with the opposite sex, but his inability to kiss was much like hers. They were excited, keen, and fully focused on one another.

After a few minutes of playing, kissing, and touching, they grew more comfortable with each other's movements and with the idea of being intimate. Kell found that though she didn't like how weak Mordecai made her legs feel, she greatly enjoyed the feverish sensation that spread through her body as he caressed her.

Still, Terin's solemn warnings regarding pregnancy echoed in her ears, so Kell worked to tamp down her lust. Mordecai, however, pushed his limits, excitedly reaching to touch where he had previously not been permitted to. Kell gently pushed away his hands or otherwise held them as they continued to kiss. He was persistent though, and she eventually yielded to him, allowing him to discover her breasts. But when a wayward hand slipped downward, she stopped him firmly.

"Sorry," Mordecai panted into the space between them.

Kell wound her fingers with his. "Not yet, all right?"

Mordecai nodded, already leaning back to continue kissing her. "All right," he breathed into her mouth.

Hours later, hand-in-hand, hair askew, and silly grins on their faces, they somehow found their way back to the treehouse where the fire had burned to coals and the oil in the lamps was nearly gone. They finished tidying the kitchen space and then got ready for bed.

Kell wanted desperately to sleep with Mordecai, just to lie beside another warm body, but didn't dare chance it. Mordecai had nothing to lose;

Kell did. It was just as Terin had said—Kell's self-discipline was the only thing keeping them apart.

That night, Kell slept horribly. Amped up on the new sensations and feelings Mordecai elicited in her and worried about her future, she tossed and turned until in the early morning hours she realized she had started menstruating. Recognizing the crampy feeling in her lower belly, she swung out of bed with a moody growl, retrieved her toiletries, lit a small lamp, and left for the outhouse.

The wind had picked up and the air was warm and humid. To the northwest, lightning illuminated the sky beyond the ridges. After taking care of everything, Kell hurried back to the treehouse just as thunder rumbled in the distance.

She threw her stuff onto her bed, blew out the lamp, and then stood in the open doorway to watch the encroaching storm. For some reason, she got a bad feeling in her gut—and it wasn't because of her monthly.

"What is it?" asked Mordecai, appearing behind her to look out.

"Storm," she replied. "It's been lightning a lot over there. See?"

"Mh-hm…" Mordecai leaned around her to peer down the glen. "Should we try to get the sheep into cover?"

Kell had also been considering that. Though she didn't feel like battling poor weather while cramping, she also didn't like the prospect of going without sheep milk and butter as it was their only source of dairy. With a groan, she turned and began dragging on clothes.

A few minutes later, she and Mordecai were jogging down the glen, searching for dots of white huddled under trees. Though the sheep were domesticated, they were mountain sheep which meant they had some wilderness smarts and knew to hang around the glen or else become a predator's meal. Unfortunately, the near constant lightning disrupted Kell's night vision, making it difficult to spot the herd. The moment she and Mordecai could once again discern the landscape, another streak of lightning erupted overhead followed by an earsplitting crack of thunder. Thick raindrops began plopping around them.

"There!" shouted Mordecai, pointing halfway up the eastern ridge.

"Why are they there?" Kell cried as a strong gust of wind swept through the glen. The sound it made was ungodly loud and took her curse with it.

They started for the sheep but didn't make it far before Kell felt her hair rise along the nape of her neck and arms. All too familiar with the warning signs, she screamed at Mordecai. Although confused, he allowed her to drag him to the ground.

Face pressed into the grass, Kell drew a circle in the dirt and then planted her palm in the middle of it. Gathering Viterra under her hand, she pushed. The earth beneath them gave, folding them into the ground as a purple-green bolt of lightning streaked a few dozen yards away to attack an enormous pine tree. Mordecai and Kell cowered in their shallow ditch, the power of nature compelling them to curl around one another and cover their heads.

Sheets of rain spilled across the glen; wind roared between the ridges, its howl ominous. Glimpsing an orange glow, Kell peeked over the lip of raw earth to find the mangled pine tree and the surrounding dry winter underbrush on fire.

No longer sensing static electricity in the air, she scrambled off of Mordecai and got to her feet. In a quick movement, she created a circle, ignited her fields, and began trying to control the fire. The glen was their home; if they let the winds grab the flames, they wouldn't win.

Kell felt a disturbance in the Flow as Mordecai also began drawing from it. Though he had never actually controlled or handled fire, he had all the knowledge and skills. Using identical movements, they commanded the growing fire back to the decimated pine tree and then, once it was contained there, stifled it.

As Kell switched to water traits and doused the tree with the collecting rainwater, she yelled at Mordecai to go after the sheep which had scattered farther up the ridge to escape the lightning strike. Only when she saw no more embers did Kell sprint after Mordecai, her Arcane Circle underfoot.

Using flora traits, they created root tethers for the nine sheep and led the flock back to the glen. Stumbling over fallen boughs and sliding on pockets of slick dead leaves, they eventually made it back to the treehouse, drenched and panting. Kell raised a small, low-to-the-ground shelter out of earth and roots and Mordecai guided the sheep into it.

Wheezing, they hurried back into the treehouse where they collapsed at the table, the storm still raging around them. They exchanged looks of disbelief, incredulous of the events that had just unfolded. The treehouse rattled but otherwise remained watertight. With the usually open doorways and windows sealed off, the house was stuffy and dark.

Kell lit a fire and began wringing out her clothes, still shocked at how close they had come to the lightning strike. Absentmindedly, she jerked off her shirt, wrung it out on the hot stones near the fire, and hung it near the hearth. As she adjusted her wet bandeau, she said, "So, how did it feel doing fire—"

She stopped as she spotted Mordecai's gaze on her chest. His bold eyes popped back up to her face and then he turned away, embarrassed.

For the first time, Kell felt self-conscious being so nearly nude in front of him. She was dressed in nothing but a bandeau and shorts often while they swam. Why was now any different? Burning with embarrassment but too stubborn to find something dry, she began pulling off her boots and continued her question, "How did it feel doing fire traits?"

"Oh, it was… strange. I don't think I actually helped. Using my hands, I don't think much gets past the, uh, cuffs." His back to her, he pulled his sopping shirt off, squeezed it out near the fire, and then flapped it open. When he turned to hang it next to the hearth, he caught her gaze again. The firelight gave his body an alluring glow.

Feeling desire rise within her, Kell cleared her throat and placed her soaked boots near the fire. "We can't keep this going once Terin and Renata get back."

"We could build our own house nearby," Mordecai offered.

Kell looked at him. She wanted so badly to bed Mordecai that the idea was appealing. "We can't," she whispered with a sad smile. "And you know that."

Mordecai grinned. "Yeah, but you just considered it, didn't you?"

"Yeah, of course. I want to—" She clamped her mouth shut, her gaze fixing on him.

A curious expression spread across his face. "Go on. You want to what?"

Kell shook her head and began ruffling the water from her hair. "Nothing. We can't do that."

"No." Mordecai crossed the space between them. "No, what were you going to say?"

"I was going to say, yeah, of course, I want to build a house—"

"No, no. That's not what you were going to say." He slithered a hand around her bare back and reeled her closer. "Say it." His eyes were crescents of smug mirth. "Say it, Kellick."

Annoyed, Kell pushed out of his grip. "Yeah, fine. I want to sleep with you. There? Happy?"

He chuckled.

"What?" she growled, continuing to shake the water from her limp hair.

"Just… I went to bed earlier thinking you didn't like me or… you know…"

Kell frowned at him. "We spent hours down by the river. Why would you think that I don't—"

"Because you kept pushing me away," Mordecai interrupted with an uncomfortable smile. "I thought maybe you were having second thoughts."

Kell gazed at him. So, boys *were* as dense as Terin described them to be. "Did Terin or Renata, uh, talk with you?"

"About what?"

"About," and she motioned between them.

"Us?"

Kell nodded.

"No, why would they? Wait, did they talk to you?"

Understanding now, Kell tied the top half of her hair into a knot and then, to avoid Mordecai's eyes, dried her feet by the fire. "Yeah, Terin talked with me before she left."

Mordecai joined her barefooted. "And?"

"I, uh…" Kell felt her voice shrinking. "Don't… wanna…uh, get…"

"What?"

"I don't wanna get pregnant." She glanced at him. He was staring at the fire. "If we—uh, you and me—if we, um, lie together, I'll get pregnant."

"Oh."

Kell nodded awkwardly.

A long stretch of silence spread between them before she managed, "I like being with you, spending time with you. When I've needed help, you've been there. I really like what we have and, um, I think… I think I love you." Before she let him respond, she quickly added, "You know, I just—uh… We make a good team." Not daring to look at him, she sighed. "So, there."

Thunder clapped overhead, startling them both. Wind whistled around the edges of the house.

Reminded that they had just escaped death, calmed a raging fire, and saved the sheep—together—Kell smiled. "Yeah, I think we make a good team." When she finally chanced a look at Mordecai, he was staring into the fire in apparent thought. Pleased that she had finally said what had been on her heart for months, she left the hearth for bed.

19

The Showcase

THE FOLLOWING MORNING, THEY WOKE at the same time they usually did, despite the night's events, and began their everyday routines. Mordecai's mood was strange, so Kell left him to cook breakfast alone. She retrieved firewood and water, released the sheep, and surveyed the glen for further damage. Even from the treehouse she could discern the blackened tree and scorched earth. Undoubtedly, Renata would want to know what had happened. Kell considered covering up the black marks but decided that was going to take more effort than she was willing to dispense at the moment and so turned her attention to the storm debris.

The poor oak trees had taken the most damage and had lost a number of limbs, some quite large in size, in the high winds. Kell got to clearing the area, dragging the heavy boughs with grunts and groans to a pile. Once the limbs eventually died and dried, they could be used as kindling.

Sometime later, Mordecai called her in to eat. It was cool out, but her work in the morning sun had made her hot and sweaty. Panting slightly, she returned to the house; Mordecai passed her an amused smile before depositing a cup of warm broth, bread, dried venison, apricots, and tea on the table.

Kell conjured Viterra and opened the windows of the house to let in cooling breezes as they ate. Aside from pleasantries, they didn't venture discussion. She was perfectly comfortable as they ate in silence but could tell that much was on Mordecai's mind.

"I wonder how Terin and Renata are faring," she finally said as they dried their now clean dishes. Though she didn't expect a response from Mordecai, she was still disappointed when he didn't engage in conversation. Unwilling to play games, Kell turned on him, blocking him from carrying the broth jar to the cellar. "You haven't said anything all morning. What's wrong?"

Mordecai chuckled. "I'm just thinking." He bypassed her.

Normally, she would have let him be, but they were alone. When he returned from the cellar, she barred him again. Mordecai tried to step around her, but she stopped him with a grin.

"Kellick," he growled.

Kell leveled an expectant look at him, and he folded.

"I feel bad, that's it."

That's not what she had thought he would say. "About what?"

Mordecai shrugged. "I'm older and I… put you in a situation—in an uncomfortable situation that…" He grimaced and looked away. "I'm sorry. I shouldn't have pushed so much. I was just…" He glanced at her through his brows. "I've wanted you for a long time and then I had you and… I was just so excited… I'm sorry."

Kell studied his face, grinning fondly. He was so handsome, so sensitive and thoughtful. In a single movement, she crashed into him, wrapped her arms around him, and squeezed him hard. "Thanks, Mordecai."

To her delight, Mordecai hugged her back, his arms strong around her back. Kell felt utter joy. "I love you," he muttered into her hair.

He had hardly finished saying it before she was kissing him.

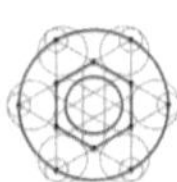

"You got this." Dockett shook Simon's shoulders. "Just like in the practice fights, don't let the noise distract you. They're going to be loud, yeah?"

Simon, dressed in a sleeveless tunic of blue and loose pants that afforded his knees ample movement, nodded. The weight of the sword at his waist gave him confidence. Recently, he had had his blond hair cut so it could no longer fall into his eyes and be a source of distraction.

Dockett paced nearby before glancing down the hallway at the other fighters lining up alongside him. "Doesn't matter what they send out, give them a show. Got it?" the Lanista continued. "Make them wanna bet on you next fall."

"Yeah," replied Simon, rhythmically clenching his fists to calm his nerves.

"Remember, you've got fighters versus Users here in a free-for-all. No winners, no losers—except those who die." Dockett met his gaze. "Don't you *dare* die."

"Yeah."

The enormous and ornate door to their left opened, and a man waved them out. Dockett gave Simon another squeeze and then stepped aside. With the other fighters behind him, Simon led the way into the exhibition arena, a small, indoor stadium located near the imperial palace. Although it was regularly used for other events such as auctions, animal baiting, executions, and forums, Madam Parthemos had managed to bargain her way in so as to better showcase her school's students.

The arena was significantly smaller than where the official Munera was held but it had many of the same qualities, including high walls and stadium seating. There was no applause as the fighters filed onto the sands. Instead, a constant buzz of conversation filled the air. Simon tried to stay focused on the task. Though to most he appeared stoic, unhearing, he could hardly stand still. The atmosphere spurred him to action. He could only imagine what the Munera would be like the following year.

Users entered from the opposite side of the stadium to fill the northern quadrant of the arena. Simon was dismayed and confused to spot Kidane, the dark-skinned User who had bested Thiago.

So it was true.

Even successful Users stayed behind, rejecting their freedom, because the money was too good.

A blond User entered the arena, and Simon zeroed in on him, his heart pounding. It was Ambrose. He hadn't seen the User since their interaction well over two years ago. He had heard that Ambrose had long since recovered but, studying him from across the arena, Simon wondered if that were true. The blond was tall, lean, and appeared ill. Even from a distance, Simon could discern his heavy eyes, slender form, and slightly hunched posture. He had suspected that the Users were not treated as well as the pro-fighters; Ambrose's condition seemed to confirm that suspicion.

Madam Parthemos greeted everyone and then introduced twenty-two fighters and twenty Users. There was no applause, only hushed comments and inquisitive murmurs between business partners. When the first two fighters to engage in combat were announced, Simon breathed out in relief. He had hoped he wouldn't be made to go first. He wanted to take the time to feel out the arena and crowd and to figure out what he needed to do to make Dockett money.

From the sidelines, he surveyed the crowd rather than watch the fights. He made furtive sweeps of the audience in to better understand who was there. He recognized a few faces from the other nights' gathering but most remained a mystery. He spotted, to his surprise, Bellamy standing near the top of the stadium, his bodyguard, Marko, beside him. Simon watched him lean in, speak lowly to Marko, and then motion to the arena. It seemed to Simon that Bellamy was not pleased to be there; in fact, gauging by his body language, he was angry or perhaps disgusted.

"Simon, fuckin' focus!" shouted Dockett from the seating directly behind him. Simon would normally have thrown him a look but in front of so many important people, he did as he was told.

With the first two rounds finished, Simon's name was called alongside Ferrik, his mentor. Unsurprisingly, they were pitted against Ambrose and a female User named Yasmin. Although it was frowned upon for a fighter to be killed in the showcase, Users could be sacrificed if necessary. Simon withdrew his sword as Ferrik spread out and readied his own weapon.

Madam Parthemos' silky voice purred through the surrounding speakers, but Simon couldn't hear it. His eyes were on Ambrose. Unsurprisingly, Ambrose was as equally vigilant. Squared up, Simon noticed that his acquaintance no longer appeared sickly. On the contrary, Ambrose was strong and intimidating. His hazel eyes were shaded by the arena lighting which emphasized the scar along his eyebrow. His entire demeanor had changed from the sidelines. He was all threat.

"Simon…" warned Ferrik from several dozen paces away. "Watch him."

Simon knew the Users had been training as well. Even still, Ambrose's transformation was alarming. Gripping the hilt of his sword, Simon breathed to calm himself. It wasn't illegal to kill Users—in fact, it was encouraged—but the Users' Lanista had also been working with his charges; this fight wasn't going to be easy. Ambrose had been under the school's tutelage for slightly longer than Simon and he was older.

The moment the signal to begin was given, two red glowing bands appeared on Ambrose's arms. Simon prepared himself for what he knew was to come. The air in the arena grew oppressive as fire erupted from Ambrose's palms and swept across the sand toward Simon. In the meantime, Simon glimpsed Yasmin dart toward Ferrik.

Knowing Ferrik could take care of himself, Simon ignored her and danced away from the line of raging fire. He needed to bring Ambrose into close-quarters, close enough for a sword. Ambrose also seemed to know this as he coated the arena with fire. Simon felt the heat lick his heels but continued to dodge, roll, evade, and leap, all the while trying to decrease the distance between them.

At one point, he passed Ferrik who was also trying to escape a fiery attack from his opponent. Simon briefly caught his mentor's gaze and, understanding the general positioning of the man's lanky body, changed direction and darted toward Yasmin who was focused on pursuing Ferrik. By the time she spotted Simon, he was already within killing range.

He felt his sword arm hesitate for a fraction of a second before he heard Dockett's voice in his head. Allowing muscle memory to take over, he brought the sword down with as much force as he could muster. When his blade met nothing but air, he spun on heel and lashed out laterally, catching Yasmin through the navel. The woman cried out.

His mind went blank. He drove through her, ignoring the crunching and visceral ripping that accompanied his attack. Yasmin crumpled, her body dropping in two pieces onto the sand. Panting, Simon whirled in search of Ferrik.

Realizing that his mentor was still struggling to close the distance, Simon jogged toward the north side of the arena with the intention of coming in behind Ambrose. But Ambrose saw him and ignited a conflagration around him, scorching the sand black. Surrounded by a ring of roaring fire, Ambrose watched Ferrik and Simon as they circled like vultures.

Simon didn't want this to end in a draw; Dockett had specifically told him not to tie. They needed to get sponsors and garner bets for next year's Munera. Simon paced the fire, forcing Ambrose to continuously adjust his position so that his back was neither to Simon nor to Ferrik.

When he saw Ferrik act as though he were about to leap over the fire, Simon spotted his chance. The moment Ferrik started running toward the flaming barrier, Simon also charged. Ambrose had seen Ferrik first and so turned his attention to the fighter, but Ferrik pulled up short. Simon, however, did not. With Ambrose momentarily distracted, Simon soared over the flames. He rolled on his shoulder to dissipate his fall before springing to his feet with practiced grace.

Ambrose spun on him and loosed a stream of fire. Using his momentum to carry him, Simon dropped to his knees and slid in the sand. He came up directly under Ambrose, sword pointed at the User's throat. Ambrose froze. The fire around them disappeared and the glowing rings around Ambrose's wrists faded. Wheezing, Ambrose lifted his chin.

Simon wanted to end it, to get rid of Ambrose so he wouldn't have to face him again, but he knew he gained more by showing mercy.

"Do it," Ambrose panted, looking out at the hushed crowd.

Simon felt his muscles twitch at the command but regained control of himself and rose to his feet. "Now's not your time."

"But it was hers?" spat Ambrose, jerking his chin toward Yasmin.

Simon drew away from Ambrose, bowed in the royals' direction, and then strode back to the sidelines with Ferrik.

An hour later, the showcase was over and the fighters were allowed to leave the arena. Dockett crashed into Simon with raucous glee.

"Boy, I damn near didn't know who you were out there!" The Lanista shook him excitedly. "Money's pouring in. You've got more than half a dozen people wanting to sponsor you! We're rich, kid!"

Simon grinned wearily—now that he was out of the arena, he was exhausted—and nodded. Dockett pounded on him for a moment longer and then turned to congratulate others.

"Simon," called Ferrik. Simon hugged his mentor. Ferrik clapped his shoulders, his skin tacky with sweat. "Well done, well done. I don't know how you knew what I was up to, but you did." He ruffled Simon's short crop of blond hair. "I would have killed the kid, but that's me."

Simon drew away with a chuckle. "It's more sportsman-like to give him another chance."

"You sure you just didn't wanna kill him?" teased Ferrik, flashing a large white grin.

Too exhausted to come up with a quippy response, Simon rolled his eyes and followed the others back to the room they had been prepping in. Because it wasn't usually meant to house fighters, the room was unusually lavish with wall-hanging mirrors, beautiful tile floors, and polished benches.

Simon trudged in with the others but stopped as he caught a glimpse of himself in one of the mirrors to his left. His clothes, skin, and hair were blood-spattered, his face worn, and sand was caked to some of the drying blood along his elbows, knees, and shins. The naked sword at his waist was coated in a film of congealing crimson. The look in his distant blue eyes was old, unrecognizable.

The longer he studied the person he had become, the more he didn't recognize himself, the expression on his face, or the way he stood.

Ferrik passed him with a chuckle. "Got a little something in your hair."

Simon slipped a hand through his hair, watching himself in the mirror. When he pulled his hand away, smears of blood wetted his fingers. In that moment, he felt bile rise in the back of his throat. Determined not to be sick, he hurriedly took water from a tray being offered by an in-house servant.

The water didn't help.

He passed a casual smile to one of the other fighters, Georgie, and then, unhurried, moseyed to the water closet across the room. He closed the door, looked at the toilet, and then threw up.

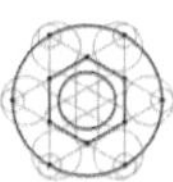

Renata returned on horseback two days later, agitated and without Terin. Alongside the supplies she had picked up, she escorted three horses, which bewildered Kell and Mordecai.

"Where's…. Terin?" asked Mordecai, searching the forest in case their friend was bringing up the rear.

"Things are getting heated in Avives," Renata explained, dismounting from her palomino gelding. "Reactionary groups of Bound are starting to mount protests along the coasts. Terin and I were separated."

Kell exchanged furtive looks with Mordecai as neither believed the old woman. Undoubtedly, Terin had purposefully gotten herself involved. Both knew how passionate she was about the rights of their people. If it brought her closer to dispatching officials of the Containment Office, she would be there.

"And the horses?" Kell asked.

Renata drew a long breath and looked at them. "We're leaving for a while."

Mordecai petted the bay mare nearest him. "And… going where?"

Renata, who usually had everything figured out, hesitated. "We need to leave the region, get as far away from the coast as possible. Probably go north." Kell lit up, something the old woman didn't miss. "I need to bring news to Denez. We'll head out at the end of the week."

Kell shied away from the horse Mordecai was handling; she did not care for horses. "What about Terin?"

A grim expression set across Renata's wrinkled face, and suddenly, she appeared exceptionally weary and stressed. "She'll catch up," was all Renata said. The old woman took the three horses, all three of whom only wore bridles, and headed toward the area where they usually created pens for the sheep.

"What do you think happened?" Kell whispered to Mordecai.

Mordecai shrugged. "Nothing good. I've never seen her so morose."

They watched Renata before Kell said, "Do you think she tried to keep Terin from joining the protests?"

"Yeah, of course. I wanna know what she meant by 'things got heated.'"

Kell looked around; the surrounding forest was home. It had been for years now. What would happen to it? To the sheep? To their home and personal effects? Suddenly sad and anxious, she took Mordecai's arm. Another great change was coming to their lives.

True to her word, three days later, Renata led the way from the glen atop her palomino. Mordecai and Kell followed riding double on the bay mare as the third horse carried significant packs and bags. Initially, Kell had begun riding in front as she was shorter and Mordecai could see over her, however, after a few paces, Mordecai had adamantly stopped the horse and forced them to switch. Kell didn't fully understand why, but she got the general gist that them riding in such close contact with her in front was dangerous. But she didn't mind riding behind him. She got to rest her head on his back when she grew weary. Besides, Mordecai was far more comfortable with horses than she was.

Renata waved good-naturedly to the flock of sheep grazing along the western ridge. With the cellar hidden, their house turned into a shamble of what appeared to be gully backwash, and the majority of their personal effects stored in the cellar, they headed north Sunday morning.

They rode in relative silence for a long time, though Kell and Mordecai pointed out wildlife to one another in the budding forest. Renata, however, seemed preoccupied and paid them no attention. Only when their pack horse, which she led, paused to forage did she come out of her thoughts and demand he move on. Other than that, she kept to herself.

"I'm worried," Kell muttered to Mordecai sometime mid-afternoon that day. He cocked an ear over his shoulder to better hear her. "She's not said anything all day... I'm gonna ask."

"I don't think you should. It's none of our business," he replied.

"Renata?" Kell called, ignoring him. The old woman glanced back at them. Kell gestured for Mordecai to ride closer so they could talk as they entered a large glade. "What's going on? What happened with Terin?"

Kell didn't think she would respond; in most instances, when they asked prying questions, the old woman distracted them or simply didn't answer.

"I tried to stop her. But she... *made* me go." Renata said, looking straight ahead. "She saw how the Containment Office and local government were treating the protesters." She shook her head, obviously upset. "I *told* her... I've taught her for *years* to... And she's just..." Renata didn't sound worried or sad. On the contrary, she appeared to be seething. "I couldn't persuade her; I couldn't stop her. Her mind was made up." The old woman drew a long, steadying breath. "I last saw her setting fire to the barricades that had been set up along the main thoroughfare. Others were with her and they- they were excited she was with them." Renata gritted her teeth.

"What are they going to do?" Kell ventured after a moment. "What are they planning?"

"Don't know. But with Terin in their midst, we need to leave. We're too close to Avives and even Eclat."

"Maybe she'll change her mind and come back," Kell offered, peering around Mordecai. "Does she know the way to the Tribe? She could meet us there." Renata shook her head. "Oh..."

Silence settled over them, and Mordecai maneuvered his mare back into single-file line.

That night as they sat around a fire eating leftover soup, Mordecai said, "We're on horseback. Do you think we'll make it to the First Whispered in less than three weeks?"

"Perhaps," mused Renata, unenthused by the conversation.

Eventually, Mordecai went to curry the horses while Kell cleaned up from supper. As she conjured water to wash the single pot they had brought, Kell sensed Renata's gaze on her. Self-consciously, she glanced at the old woman, who observed her from across the fire, and then tipped the pot upside down near the firepit to dry.

"I was like Terin once," their teacher began suddenly. Kell glanced at Mordecai and then sat across the fire from Renata. "I hated everyone, but none more so than those who... than those who couldn't access the Flow. Mundane people."

Kell listened raptly. Renata had never, not once, mentioned anything about her past. Any attempts they had made to further learn about her had always been foiled.

"I *hated* them. And why shouldn't I? They killed my sisters. They imprisoned my mother and tortured my stepfather. I wanted to make them suffer," continued Renata emotionlessly. "To make them feel everything that myself and others had."

The old woman gathered her thoughts before continuing. "My stepfather was a wealthy merchant in the capital who sold jewelry to the upper classes; he was well-known for his fine craftsmanship. We lived in the Middle District. Although he couldn't access the Flow, he married our mother who could. But the fact that she was Bound never bothered him. My two older sisters and I were from another marriage. And all of us were Unbound. Mother had managed to hide us until we were of age." Renata smiled slightly. "She actually found us a teacher in the Lower District who taught us how to access the Flow.

"When Mother married our stepfather, I was nearly twelve. Although I had been learning for years, we still had to be careful because I was approaching puberty. So, I kept myself away from our stepfather often, trying to appear like a dedicated student. But really, I was in the Lower District learning how to better control my budding abilities."

Renata shifted uncomfortably.

"My teacher was a middle-aged woman named Elsie who had been passed the Knowledge of New from her mother. Elsie taught us for years at a farm on the outskirts of the Lower District... But regulators found the place and stormed it. My two sisters, who were there to pick me up, were caught off guard and… killed by a sword." Renata clasped her hands before her. "My teacher was also killed. I ran into the forest and never looked back. I couldn't face my mother. Had I been able to better control myself, I wouldn't have had to visit Elsie's so often and my sisters wouldn't have had to come get me. Their deaths were my fault.

"Years later, I learned that my mother had been arrested and thrown into prison. My stepfather had been tortured because… he had told them that it was his idea to train me and my sisters, to spare my mother. I was so, so angry. I was furious with the world, bitter. I wanted everyone to suffer, to witness the deaths of their loved ones like I had…

"Denez found me a few weeks later barely alive in the forests outside the capital. I traveled with the First Whispered until I was strong enough and then set off west looking for something, anything.

"Over the years, I grew stronger and more confident in my abilities. I built on the foundation Elsie gave me and added to it. Pieces that were missing, I created or made up. It was a painfully arduous process. No one was there to show me; I had to feel everything out. When I was twenty-two, I returned to Eclat—and scorched as much of the Middle District as I could. The rest I swallowed in great masses of vegetation. Vines, trees, thorny and poisonous plants…"

"Is that why all the government buildings there look newer?" gasped Kell.

Renata nodded. "I did my best to wreak as much destruction as possible. And then… I left. They called it the Dirty Dawn." She stared at the fire. "I wound up working at a textile factory in Avives, putting buttons on skirts to earn a little money for a year or two. After that, I couldn't take the tedium anymore. I worked at a bakery and then found my way into a local flower shop. By the time I was thirty, I wanted to torch the entire country… I was like Terin."

Kell glanced at Mordecai who was also gazing into the fire.

"When I met my husband—"

"You're married?" interrupted Kell.

"*Was* married," Renata softly corrected. "He died several years ago."

"Oh… I'm sorry."

Renata passed Kell an uncharacteristic smile. "Don't be. His name was Brynmore and he was the best thing to ever happen to me." She rubbed her hands absentmindedly. "He was an Avives native—had grown up there and knew the area better than anyone because he was a courier. He made regular deliveries to the flower shop, and that's how we met."

"Did he know?" asked Mordecai. "Did he know about you?"

"Not in the beginning, no. But when we started seriously courting, I knew I had to tell him. I fully expected him to report me to the Containment Office. I was Unbound and trained. I was the exact enemy he had been taught to hate." Renata drew a long breath. "And then I showed him, and he… thought it was the most wondrous thing he had ever seen. He adored my abilities and encouraged me to use them in private.

"Eventually, we married and moved to the northern side of Avives to escape the city traffic and Containment Office. I loved him so much. But he grew sick years later. I couldn't heal him, though I tried, and doctors couldn't explain his symptoms. They just threw medications at him, hoping that something would work. It never did. He died in his sleep.

"But those nineteen years we were together were the very best. All of the hatred and bitterness that I had kept bottled up inside, he soothed away. I eventually told him what had happened in the capital and what I had done, and he…" Renata paused. When she spoke next, her voice was shaky. "He told me that my reaction was understandable. That I had been hurting and that, on behalf of Eclat, he forgave me." She chuckled wetly. "It's silly, but it helped so much. I let it all go. I let my family go, I let my anger and hatred go, and I just… lived.

"After Brynmore died, I didn't want to stay in Avives. It was his city, not mine. I began experimenting with living off the land. It turned out I had a knack for it because of my connection with Viterra and my affinity for flora traits. So, I bought some supplies and hiked off into the wilderness. I explored and moved around, wound back up with the First Whispered, lived with them for a few years, and then kept roaming. I eventually settled down in the first house that Madam Nicolea graciously set fire to."

"And… how did you meet Terin?"

"I was traveling back from one of my in-town visits and felt a disturbance in Flow. I found her in a nearby alley trying to roast a rat using Viterra."

Mordecai grimaced as Kell nodded in understanding. She didn't know that kind of hunger, but she was familiar with food insecurity.

"When I asked her what she was doing, she became defensive and tried to run. I trapped her with a root around the ankle and then asked about her family." Renata grew grim. "Terin's family was captured in the capital; she suspects they were made to compete in the Munera, even though neither of them was Bound; they were just mundane folks. But the Munera is a death trap for anyone who is not trained to compete in it.

"I grabbed her up and headed home. It wasn't hard. She was hungry, and I had food. I offered her a safe place, one that was hidden from the world." The old woman collected her thoughts for a moment before continuing. "From the beginning, I knew Terin had seen too much. She came from abject poverty and had been malnourished most of her life. That's why I never took bowls or plates from her once given. That's also why I always kept the cellar stocked, so she knew she could eat whenever she wanted.

"But fixing her hunger was simple. It turns out that before I had found her, others within her community had discovered she was Unbound and had... *toyed* with her. Hurt her, abused her, did unspeakable things to her—because she was Unbound. I tried to talk her through her trauma like Brynmore had with me, but that method didn't work for her. I took a different approach. Maybe she just needed a safe place and a teacher, someone to provide a steady and disciplined force in her life. So, that's what I did.

"I taught her, I trained her. I helped her better understand herself and her abilities. And in time, I loved her. So much. But I never told her about my own past, about my own bitterness and rage. I was afraid that doing so would validate her feelings and confirm that what she believed about the world was right, that everyone who was not Unbound was... evil." Renata looked at Kell and Mordecai. "Terin has a right to feel the way she does. But I don't want her going down the same path I did. Now that she's with the reactionary group, she's going to be surrounded by people who will believe exactly what she wants them to believe—that Bound and Unbound should be on top and that everyone else should... not. If she lets it, her hate will take control of her and soon, that's all she'll be able to see."

Kell looked uncomfortably back at the fire as Renata wiped her eyes.

"I begged her..." The old woman sniffed. "I *begged* her not to go. But she did..."

"Do you know if she's staying in Avives?" asked Mordecai.

Renata shrugged. "For now. But if they've gained as much momentum as I think they have, I suspect they'll spread to the capital in no time."

"Could we... stop her?" Kell looked between Mordecai and Renata. "Could we go back and track her down?"

Renata's voice grew somber. "She's made up her mind. She's following a purpose. Us simply appearing isn't going to sway her. We literally have no way to stop her."

The crackling of the fire filled the silence between them.

"If you didn't tell Terin any of this," began Kell, "why are you telling us?"

"Not telling her was a mistake. I failed her. Hopefully, I won't fail my other two students as well."

20

His Grim Reality

As they continued their journey northward, the March weather grew more erratic until they were forced to build shelter. The thunderstorms were fierce, but the snow that followed them was worse. Even with the low shelters of earth they built and a clay hearth roaring, the early morning hours were bitterly cold. Although they could stay warm while awake and traveling because they used Viterra to ward off the cold, such effects did not extend to them while they slept.

Initially, Kell avoided being anywhere near Mordecai at night for fear of what would happen in the dark, especially with Renata sleeping not six paces away. But as the weather continued to deteriorate and spring winter storms marched across the budding land, she decided she would rather rest comfortably than travel without sleep.

Once Kell had spent time in her own sleeping roll, covered in layers of coats and blankets, and she was sure Renata was asleep, she dragged her bedding to where Mordecai slept. Shivering, she made sure the bed roll was pressed against his blankets so the cold of the ground couldn't seep between them. She was unsurprised to find him wide awake and opening his blankets to welcome her.

Shaking hard with cold, Kell slipped into the heat of his bed roll. She snuggled close, folding her arms between them. Mordecai adjusted himself so their pelvises were nowhere near one another but otherwise clung to her. Kell's cheeks, ears, and nose began to burn as blood and warmth returned to them.

In that moment, she realized just how much taller and larger he was. She had always thought she would be one of the guys, that she was as strong, as tall, as toned and muscled. But since living with Mordecai, she had discovered that no matter how much she wanted it, her physiology just wouldn't allow her to keep pace with the growth of her counterpart. Though she had reconciled with this disappointment, she was reminded of it often.

As her hands warmed, she caressed his shoulder, marveling at the muscle there, and then tilted her face upward to kiss his stubbly chin. Mordecai swallowed, an action that didn't go unnoticed by Kell, and then bent down and kissed her within the cocoon of their heat.

Kell immediately put a stop to that by tucking her chin inward so her mouth was inaccessible. Mordecai seemed to know why, gave a humored huff, and then relaxed beside her. Finally warm, she stretched out alongside him and went to sleep.

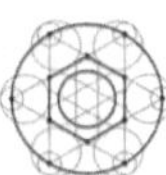

"Yee-haw!" shouted Dockett, joyfully grabbing Simon and swinging him around. "We just got our eighth offer!"

Simon laughed. "Yeah!"

Dockett shook him fondly and then, holding him by the shoulders, grinned. "The most offers of sponsorship I've gotten for a fighter is six. They must have seen something in your performance." Dockett gestured to Ferrik who was doing squats with yoked buckets on the other side of the training yard. "Actually, they're making offers for him too. People liked you working together. They're calling you two 'the Black and the Blond.' You made each other look good. Oh shit, son…" Dockett caught his breath but didn't lose his toothy smile. "I'm so proud of you."

"Thanks, Dockett," Simon replied.

"I knew when I saw you in that cell that you had the makings of a fighter. Now look at you. Eight offers? Simon!"

Simon cleared his throat. "So, I just have to win the Munera, right?"

The Lanista looked at him. "What do you mean?"

"Well, if I win… I can leave, right?"

Dockett chuckled uncomfortably. "Well, yeah. The king presents you with—You know, we can discuss that later. We still have a lot to do. Your Munera is still a year away. But money's going to start flowing in, kid. Just you wait." Dockett began leading him across the yard to Ferrik.

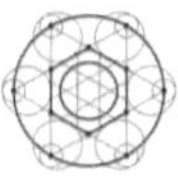

The winter weather eventually drifted east, leaving behind three feet of snow and ice. Renata led the way on her gelding, using Viterra to harden the snow to make travel easier for the horses. The pack horse followed and then Mordecai and Kell and their mare.

Although the temperatures remained below freezing, Renata's demeaner warmed considerably. She began smiling more, asking them questions about themselves, and riding alongside them when the terrain permitted. Although she had cautiously asked questions about their pasts over the years, she had not—in her words—wanted to pry. But now, more often than not, she was the one initiating conversation.

Something had awakened inside her. All the walls were coming down, and suddenly Renata was a relatively pleasant person to be around.

They reached the mountains a little more than three weeks after they began their journey. The terrain changed and the weather became mercifully mild, allowing them to shed layers daily.

Gorgeous, verdant meadows of rye grass dotted with fireweed, glacier lilies, arnica, and showy fleabane extended before them. Clear streams wound through the meadows to dump into a large river off to the east. Mounds of greening trees could be seen in the distance. Birds twittered and flitted as marmots and ground squirrels darted from their mounds.

Kell found herself speechless. She simply couldn't understand how such beauty could exist, especially after the weeks of horrible weather they had endured. "The First Whispered live here?" she asked Renata as they started across the sprawling fields.

"Around here, yeah," replied her teacher.

That evening, they walked their horses into the First Whispered village named Heim, which Renata explained meant home. Kell assumed they would be stared at or treated like awkward travelers. Instead, members of the Tribe called to Renata in greeting and came to meet them. Overwhelmed by the sudden noise when there had been none for months, Kell stayed close to Mordecai who, she could tell, also felt overstimulated.

Denez warmly welcomed Renata by making a sign to her and then pressing his forehead to hers. Renata returned the favor and motioned for Kell and Mordecai to join her.

"You remember my students, Kellick and Mordecai."

Denez passed an appraising eye over them both before a slight smile pulled at his tight lips. "How could I forget the girl who attacked our honored guest?"

Kell shrunk under the man's gaze, but Mordecai mimicked the gesture Renata had done, without the forehead touching, and greeted the old acquaintance. As Kell and Mordecai exchanged pleasantries with others they recognized, including Gytha, Renata took Denez aside to speak privately.

Eventually, Kell, Mordecai, and their teacher were shown to a smaller yurt which had been constructed upon their arrival. Although quainter than the others around it, their abode was large enough that they could each have a quadrant to themselves. Layered mats and hides were set atop low beams to create a warm floor. A cooking fire situated at the center of the yurt vented through a trapdoor in the roof. A lattice wall provided structure for the several subsequent layers of felt, cotton, and animal skins that kept the assembly warm.

Not wishing to be an inconvenience, Renata turned down food, forcing Mordecai and Kell to eat what rations they had left. Nonetheless, an hour later, warm soup and tea were delivered to their yurt. They took a sponge bath using hot water and then finally lay down to rest. Kell didn't remember closing her eyes.

The following several days were challenging as there was much around them where there had been none for months. Kell visited with Gytha but kept to herself and Mordecai for the most part. She was weary from traveling and didn't know what to say around the strange people.

Mordecai, on the other hand, consciously offered his help around the village, often leaving Kell for long spans of time that made her uncomfortable. She hadn't realized how steadfast Mordecai's presence had been in her life. It made her love him more.

Spring came into full bloom, bringing with it flowers, migrating herds, and continued training for Mordecai and Kell. Although Renata made exception for when Kell was receiving any type of instruction from Gytha, who had picked up teaching where she had left off, the old woman made sure their daily routines remained unaltered.

Within weeks, they were well settled within Heim, had chores and jobs, and actively participated in village life. Kell shared what she knew about fishing and net-making and showed the hunters the secure knots that were regularly used by fishermen out at sea. She also revealed to the First Whispered what she knew about navigation and about how to use the celestial skies—both of which they knew much about. Still, she was able to surprise them with new material.

In exchange, she learned a wide variety of talents and skills that relied not on the use of Viterra but on everyday knowledge. Navigation, medicine and herbology, trapping, and long-distance communication via whistles were taught to both her and Mordecai for several weeks extending into the summer.

Kell felt herself actively growing and maturing. She was being challenged, being forced to view the world in a way she had never before perceived it. To people of the Tribe, Viterra was in everything—not just in the elements she had learned about. Viterra and its Flow could be found in mundane actions such as washing clothes, fishing, or sitting by a fire. Viterra propagated everything and compelled the cycle of life and death onward. It's what brought autumn to the land and what ushered in the green of spring. Viterra and the Flow, the constant stream of cosmic energy from which it was drawn, acted as an intersection between the physical and mental. It was what bound every living creature on the planet to the inorganic.

In Heim, the First Whispered incorporated not only the physical manifestation of their gifts into their daily lives but the supernatural ones as well. Less familiar with the third field, the Mental, Kell scrutinized every observable occurrence of it. Whether it was someone freezing meat for storage using cryokinesis, a Tribe member petrifying materials to create a solid base for a new yurt, or someone accurately predicting incoming inclement weather, Kell remained on the lookout for any instance of the mystical and secretly hoped she would be able to access her third field soon.

Shortly after her sixteenth birthday and with Gytha's guidance, Kell managed to draw water from a stream without the use of an Arcane Circle. It was unbelievably difficult and made Kell wonder if she had even done it correctly. But gauging by Gytha's wide-eyed expression, Kell hadn't been hallucinating. A current of water had clearly left its place from the flow of the stream and deviated across the ground to her, seeping into the earth the moment she could no longer concentrate.

That summer was the best summer Kell had ever experienced. She felt fulfilled in every way. Not only was she learning her craft and new life skills, but she was coming into her own as a young woman. Gytha and a few of the other younger women in the village taught her how to better care for her hair and skin, how to apply light makeup, and about better methods to care for herself throughout menstruation. They also taught her about men since all knew that she and Mordecai were a couple.

They taught her how to please a man, how to please herself, and how to take care of herself afterward. Gytha gave her a tea mixture she could use after intercourse to ensure she would not get pregnant and better explained female and male anatomy, which eventually led to Kell's first lesson in pregnancy and childbirth.

Though initially awkward and embarrassed, Kell found the women's directness and lack of shame comforting and soon grew to trust their knowledge and expertise.

Although Mordecai continued to practice the elemental traits as Renata had taught him, he began working on footwork that would allow him to better utilize the full power of Viterra. By chance, Vidkunn, one of the most adroit hunters in the village, recognized what he was trying to do and offered to help. For hours, Vidkunn and Mordecai would work daily together by the stream, trying to come up with foot and leg gestures and movements that were precise enough to permit Mordecai to control Viterra.

Kell watched them infrequently as her own training and interests took her elsewhere. But she was greatly impressed by what she saw as, by midsummer, Mordecai had mastered metal and earth using a system of whirling kicks, knee jabs and leg extensions, specific feet movements, and ankle rotations. As he continued developing his system, Renata also helped.

When they finally had time to themselves—which wasn't often—Kell sneaked off from the village with Mordecai, following the stream into the forest two or three miles away. There they would play, share with each other their latest skills and talents, and of course, further explore the limits of their discipline.

Though Kell maintained a firm no-sex stance for fear of falling pregnant and Mordecai adamantly agreed for the same reasoning, that line regularly blurred. They kissed and touched, swam naked together often, and took every moment to learn more about each other's bodies. When they weren't training, working, or helping out in the village, they were fooling around; it was their favorite pastime. As the seasons changed, their relationship deepened.

In the heart of January, a wicked snow storm trapped the Tribe members in their yurts. Out of concern for Renata's aging body, Denez requested that the old woman stay in the elders' tent which had been constructed with heavier materials to keep the small collection of seniors warm. Renata reluctantly agreed, leaving Mordecai and Kell alone.

The wind howled and clawed at their yurt, making the wood creak. But the materials held. With a roaring fire going inside, an enormous stack of wood, and blankets everywhere, Kell and Mordecai were blissfully warm and comfortable. They had been in the yurt since that afternoon when the storm had first blown in off the mountains, but it felt as if it had been days.

Kell anxiously fidgeted as she practiced finger weaving yarn, using a technique that Aethel had taught her. But she hadn't mastered it yet and her mind was busy. She had been thinking about Mordecai the last few days and had been considering taking their relationship to the next level, but the very idea made her heart flutter in her chest. If they had sex, it wasn't an absolute that she would get pregnant, but there was a chance. Even if they were careful. Of course, she had the herbal tea Gytha had taught her to brew, but the possibility still frightened her.

She had been weighing the pros and cons for days, growing so frustrated that she had snapped at Mordecai several times.

Kell glanced across the yurt at him. He lay on his stomach near the fire, tracing a star map that she had made to teach the others. He must have sensed her gaze because he looked up at her and smiled.

With a frown, Kell returned to her work, tilting her head this way and then that as she struggled to remember which thread was supposed to fold under the next. After a few more minutes of tugging and pushing, she flopped back onto the warm mats and threw the work aside, untangling her fingers with disdain.

Sensing movement, Kell looked up to find Mordecai looming over her. "Giving up?" he asked.

Like her, he had grown. He was taller, broader. He had finally cut his deep brown-black hair so that it hung around his ears, something that he complained about every day that it was cold. His jaw was squarer now, and his voice had dropped to a rich timber. Though he was still gangly, he carried himself with purpose and power. When bundled up, he appeared like the other men in the village.

"It's dumb," muttered Kell. "It's pointless work. I'm not doing it."

Mordecai lay flat on his back beside her and stared at the ceiling. "Then don't."

Kell glanced at him from under her lashes, her heart suddenly racing. They had done nothing but explore each other's bodies all summer and fall; she had spent hours alone with him in the forest in varying degrees of naked.

Mordecai must have sensed something because he began conversation the moment Kell blurted out what was on her mind.

"How did you know that the stars—"

"I want sex."

He fell still, silent, his gaze still affixed to the ceiling.

Kell looked at him, uncertain if he had heard her.

Mordecai visibly swallowed. "You're... sure?"

She nodded, unable to say a word.

He sat up. "I'll get the beds ready. Will you fill the basin and warm it?"

Self-consciously, Kell drew snow using Viterra through a slit in the door and routed it in liquid form into the large basin situated near the fire. She tried to calm herself, but no amount of meditation or chiding could settle her nerves. Once finished, she placed her hands into the water and warmed it to a delightful temperature. With the water steaming, she looked at

Mordecai who was trying to tug one of the mats, which had gotten stuck under another, free to ensure the cold didn't get a chance to seep in.

"Can you—" he gestured to the low wooden desk pressing down on the other end of the mat. "It's stuck."

Kell pushed the desk aside, enabling him to quickly correct the mat. Unable to stop herself, she crossed the distance between them in two strides, grabbed hold of his shirt, and bore him to the floor. Mordecai enthusiastically kissed her back, his hands already searching for the bottom hem of her long-sleeved tunic.

Kell helped him, drawing the article over her head to reveal her long-sleeved undershirt. This Mordecai could handle himself. In a mad flailing, they threw their clothes off, hungry to get to one another's flesh. The moment her bare skin touched his, Kell sighed longingly and straddled him.

"You're… sure?" Mordecai panted into her mouth.

"Yeah. Just… be careful."

"I'll try, I'll try."

Wind rattled the yurt, which was already heavy with snow. The fire in the firepit crackled as logs settled and embers rolled over new kindling. The light scent of drying herbs, lavender, and wood smoke cloaked the warm abode, further drawing its inhabitants into the deep embrace of comfort and love.

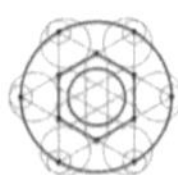

Simon paced his quarters, glancing out the window at the training yard cloaked in stark mid-February sunlight. The constant mist that had persisted all day had finally cleared off to reveal a setting sun among fiery clouds. He was weary, anxious, and lonely. Since Ferrik was training the new fighters in preparation for that fall's Munera, Simon had been left to his own devices. Dockett was busy handling his burgeoning finances, overseeing the new trainees and the veterans, and working to organize every aspect of the Munera alongside Madam Parthemos.

Hurting from something though he knew not what, he growled in frustration and headed downstairs to the infirmary. He meandered into the wing, which had been expanded earlier that winter, his gaze passing over the few fighters or Users who had incurred recent injuries. Nurses were tending them, but Simon didn't see the person he was there to visit. Dr. Gray strolled by, unhurried, dressed in a white smock.

"Uh, excuse me. Where's Eevie?" Simon asked.

The doctor didn't so much as look at him as he pointed over his shoulder.

"Thank you." Simon glanced at the others in the wing and, finding them distracted, hurried to the back where the old exam rooms were. He found Eevie seated at a desk in a narrow office, tapping her heel against her chair as she flipped through patient records. He politely knocked on the door.

Eevie didn't look up. "Hm?"

Simon grinned, taking in her tussled blond hair and slumped shoulders. "Got a minute?"

Eevie turned in her chair, her face lighting up. "Simon." A thought occurred to her, and she passed an appraising eye over him. "Why are you here? Please don't tell me you're hurt."

Simon leaned in the doorway. "No, I'm not."

Eevie stood. "Do we need to go to an exam room——"

"Actually," Simon entered the office and pulled the door ajar behind him, "I was hoping I could maybe talk to you here."

Eevie sat back, folding her legs to the side. "Certainly, is something wrong?" She frowned. "Is it Dockett? I swear, if he's——"

"No, no," interrupted Simon. "It's not Dockett. I actually haven't seen him recently. Um… I've been having, uh, chest pains. My heart starts hammering suddenly and I get really aware of, uh, of my breathing. I don't know what it is."

Eevie pushed the door closed with her foot. "Have you noticed if there's a pattern? Does it happen before or after certain events or actions?"

Leaning against the wall, he shook his head. "No, there doesn't seem to be any reason. Just sometimes, I'll be standing around or trying to rest and it'll come on."

"And how long has this been going on?"

Simon thought for a long moment. "A few months."

Eevie sighed. "Simon…"

"I know, I know—I should have come sooner, but the pressure of this stupid…" He drew a long breath and felt his heart suddenly pound in his chest.

"Did it just happen?" asked Eevie, standing. He nodded. "Does it happen when you're training or doing physical activity?"

"No. Just when I'm doing nothing. Like right now."

"Well, you're *not* doing nothing." She rested on the desk. "You're worrying. About the Munera. Has Dockett been putting a lot of pressure on you?" Simon gave a noncommittal shrug. "This ramped up after the second showcase last fall, didn't it?"

"How did you know that?"

"How many sponsors do you have now?"

"Last I heard, eleven."

"Eleven!" Eevie exclaimed in a hushed voice. She touched the door to ensure it was still closed. "*Eleven* sponsors?" Simon nodded. The nurse fidgeted for a long moment, her eyes darting about in thought. "Simon, that's more than any other fighter in the history of Munera."

"So I've been told." He watched her, a frown creeping over his face. "What are you thinking?"

"That there's something going on," the nurse mused.

"With the Munera?"

"Not just the Munera. I overheard…" She further lowered her voice, forcing Simon closer to hear her. "I overheard Dr. Gray talking the other day. The Council of Ministers is outraged."

Simon tilted his ear to her. "About what?"

"They're wanting stricter policies regarding Users, but the king is resisting."

"What's that got to do with my sponsors?"

"They're putting money into the pockets of people who can spearhead their cause and who can…" Eevie fell still, her mouth falling open slightly. She drew away and settled her eyes on Simon. The expression on her face alarmed him. Though she exuded worry, a calculating intelligence—one Simon was not familiar with—reflected in the depths of her blue gaze.

"What?" he whispered, suddenly worried. "What is it?"

"They need someone to be the face of strength and superiority against all Users." As if a switch had flipped, Eevie smiled kindly and then sat back with a casual shrug. "I think that's you…"

"And… what does that mean… for me?"

She reached through the distance between them and took his hand with a comforting grip. "Let's see what we can do to take some of the pressure off of you, yeah?"

21

The Fields

MORDECAI TURNED EIGHTEEN IN APRIL and was deemed a man by the First Whispered. He underwent the rite of passage that all men of the Tribe do by staying seated on a river overnight and rose the next morning fully welcomed into the village's hunting band.

Kell heard from Gytha who had been told by her friend's sister that Mordecai had asked Denez and Renata about Union, to which Kell gaped. Gytha grinned.

"But I'm sixteen!" Kell argued, shocked.

Gytha shrugged. "Ashild's sister made Union at fourteen. They grew up together. It's the same with you two, right?"

"But at sixteen? Not even in Eclat do we do that." Kell rocked back and forth soothingly. The concept of marriage had fleetingly crossed her mind on occasion, but she hadn't dwelled on it. She loved Mordecai more than any other person, but the idea of matrimony frightened her. Tarquin wasn't married; neither were most of the men she had known along the docks. Simon's family was a different story.

"But it's just hearsay," Gytha added quickly with a sly smile. "Would it be such a bad thing to make Union with Mordecai though? You already share a yurt. You've been in that yurt for months by yourselves. A proposal would make it official. Not much would change."

Kell thought on it, trying to find excuses. "We don't... intend to stay here for forever. What would people say if we went..."

"Returning to Eclat or Avives would endanger Mordecai," Gytha said, her tone suddenly low. Kell looked at her. "He's Bound. That can't be hidden. Avives, and especially the capital, are starting up another round of campaigns to round up Bound."

"How do you know that?" whispered Kell, horrified but unsurprised.

"We got word last week about a number of incidents in both areas that have warranted increased governmental responses."

Kell met Gytha's gaze. "Terin and her group?"

"In Avives, yes. Though it's said that they'll be moving east to Eclat soon." Gytha sat back. "Think it over, Kell. You two are safest here."

"That's not what you said two years ago."

Gytha began untying one of her braids. "What did I say?"

"That if we're not First Whispered, we can't stay with you. Remember? I was arguing with you about that guy from Eclat who was staying with you."

"Ah, Bellamy. Yes." She ran her fingers through her long, blond hair which was crimped from her plait. "Much has changed. Renata is an old acquaintance; she has always been welcomed here. Though Mordecai is Bound, he has proven that he has the flexibility to conceive of new ways to utilize Viterra. And you…" Gytha smiled. "I didn't think it possible for someone who was versed in the New to learn the Old, but here you are doing just that. All three of you are welcome here."

"Are we a part of the Tribe?"

Gytha paused, playing with her hair as she thought. "Allow me to talk to Denez about that. If you were to become full members of the Tribe, would you stay?"

"I… don't see why not," Kell hesitantly replied. She didn't like committing to something so readily.

Gytha nudged her fondly. "Think about it."

"What about Mordecai?"

"Do you love him?"

Kell frowned.

"Do you like spending time with him? Do you think you make a strong team? Are you good partners?"

"I don't know. Yeah?" Kell leaned back on her hands in thought. "Is that all it takes? Just being a good team?" She looked at Gytha. "You haven't made Union."

"And I don't intend to," she replied.

"What?"

Gytha grinned wolfishly. "It's too much fun being untied. I like my freedom. Besides, it's hard meeting people, you know?"

"Then why are you trying to get me to do it?"

"Because you two are meant for each other. Somehow, your paths crossed and," she shrugged, "fate tied you wrist-to-wrist."

Kell looked back at a collection of bushes within which a titmouse flitted from branch to branch. "If… we made Union, what would be the cons?"

"Well, you're promising to be tied to him for the rest of your life. So, there's that. If you had any dreams about sleeping with anyone else, then forget those. Here at Heim, home responsibilities are shared between mates, but I've heard it's not the same elsewhere." Gytha tapped her leg playfully. "Please don't make a decision based off what I'm telling you. You have to listen to your gut. Don't let my words disturb your *satt*."

Kell nodded, already consciously working to settle her ruffled demeanor.

"Come on. Let's head back. I think we've done enough today."

That night after bathing in the chilly river with Gytha, Aethel, and Inga, Kell returned to her yurt, shivering. The spring air was cold. Though she could have kept the chill at bay with Viterra, she chose not to, instead hurrying through the yurt's front door.

Mordecai, who had been examining a knife, glanced up as she entered but didn't say anything. Kell patted her hair with a cloth and then trotted over to the fire for warmth. She only wore one of the robes that had been gifted her the year prior. Shivering, she held her hands by the fire.

Mordecai cleared his throat and motioned to the other side of the fire. "I made tea."

"Yes," whispered Kell, snatching the steaming mug from the low table. "Thank you." Sipping the tea, which was a pleasant mixture of mint and chamomile, she considered Mordecai over the fire's flames. After a moment, she asked, "Do you think we make a good team?"

Amused, he looked at her, his black hair falling across his brow. "Yeah. Why do you ask?"

"You think we get along well?"

"Yeah?" A suspicious smile pulled at his lips. "What makes you ask?"

Kell shrugged. "I was just wondering if you thought so too. Because I think we do." She glanced between him and the fire. "And I don't think I'd mind… if our team was made permanent…"

Mordecai studied her for a long moment and then flopped back with a groan. "Ugh, I *knew* it was going to get out. You girls gossip too much."

"It's not gossip if it's true though." Kell got up and went to him. "It's… true, right?"

"Yes," he growled. "But I wasn't meaning for you to know about it for a while." He sat up. "I was just talking to Denez about it because I don't know anything about… well, anything. I don't know if there's requirements or rituals or if either of us has to be a certain age."

Kell sat beside him and ran her finger along the side of her mug. "And? What did he say?"

"In the Tribe, girls may marry as soon as they are women and boys when they have completed their rites." Mordecai looked at her. "But we aren't part of the Tribe. Denez said that city laws are different but that most agree you can't marry until you're eighteen… which I am, but you aren't."

Relieved, Kell smiled. "Then maybe we'll just be engaged for a while. Yeah?"

"You don't seem disappointed."

She gazed down into her tea. "I… got really scared when Gytha told me."

"What? Why?"

"Because I don't know anything about being a wife or a-a mother. A fisherman raised me." Kell took a long, cautious drink and then added, "Besides, I don't like doing the stuff that the women do around here, much less in the city. I don't wanna weave," she gestured to yet another sewing project she had discarded in frustration on the floor across the yurt, "or sew, or-or take care of kids and cook and make yurts and just sit around. I wanna go hunt and explore and roam and-and be back on a boat and swim and fish and just… do whatever I want."

Mordecai scooted closer and kissed her cheek. "Sounds good to me."

"Someone's got to take care of… wherever we end up, and I don't think that's something—"

"Then don't. Do whatever you want. I'll follow you wherever you go." He motioned toward the door. "You want to travel? Let's do it. You want to head back to Eclat? Let's go. You want to start your own fishing business or something? I can swim now. Not a problem."

Kell breathed a sigh of relief and happiness. "You're sure?"

"Yeah, I'm sure. If I follow you, life will be interesting." He spoke into her ear. "Why do you think I followed you out of Sacred Tree that night all those years ago?"

Chuckling, Kell pressed her forehead to his. "Thank you, Mordecai."

He kissed her lips and then sat back. "You're mine. And I'm yours."

The following month, Denez and a handful of others disappeared for several weeks. During their absence, Heim began packing. Kell learned that the Tribe was preparing to head east in search of new land and Denez and his group had gone ahead to scout for locations. Each day, Tribe members stowed more items or otherwise destroyed them. Earthenware such as clay pots, bowls, and cups were returned to the earth. The lattice walls of the yurts were slowly dismantled and laid into the soil. Areas that had accommodated heavy traffic within the village were resewn with grasses, bushes, and flowers.

By the time Denez and the others returned, the entire village was ready to go. The following morning, the First Whispered, Renata, Mordecai, and Kell set off east, walking in single-file line. Tribe members carried personal effects such as clothing and bedding on their backs using a backframe composed of roots that wound around items. The three horses that Renata had brought were each fitted with a travois, a type of A-frame structure with drag poles upon which heavier items like yurt canvases, precious metalwork, and the like could be carried. Renata had worked with the animals for a few weeks to familiarize them with the devices.

Everyone was excited; the atmosphere was energized and the younger members of the Tribe, who were unburdened with the responsibility of carrying supplies, ran ahead, chasing one another. Kell and Mordecai brought up the rear with Renata, who sat astride her palomino, to keep the horses under better control.

The journey along the southern side of the mountains was a lovely one. Vibrantly-colored wildflowers dotted rolling green meadows and provided a constantly changing selection of scents. The river, which they eventually met, rolled and churned, producing a nonstop rush that made Kell feel whole. Set against the picturesque backdrop of snow-capped mountains, the scene was stunning.

The First Whispered followed the river east, keeping it on their left until Denez froze the water and led the group across it northward. As the elevation rose, Kell found she had quite the vantage point and could make out a road in the distance that led south.

"What's that?" she asked Renata.

"The road from the capital to the country of Chantis," the old woman replied, squinting against the afternoon sun. "Can you see the train tracks alongside it?"

"Yeah. How long would it take to get from Eclat to Chantis?"

Renata shrugged. "Depends. If you take a train, several hours. I think I remember hearing fourteen hours or there about."

Kell stopped, her eyes set south. "And to the capital? How long would it take us to get to Eclat from here?"

Renata pulled her horse alongside Kell and Mordecai. "Are you feeling drawn there, Kellick?" Her teacher's words reverberated deep within her, and Kell fidgeted. Renata always knew.

"Hm? No," Kell lied.

Several weeks after Kell's seventeenth birthday on a hot July afternoon, the Tribe stopped to take a break, choosing an arm of the river to set up camp for a few days. Having practiced numerous times over the years, Kell and Mordecai constructed their yurt quickly and efficiently. A hunting party found a pair of elk, and an enormous pot of venison stew was made. Sitting by a communal fire, as it was too warm to light the firepit inside their yurt, Kell stared into the flames, disconcerted.

Since they had passed the road that Renata had identified as leading to Eclat, she had been restless, short-tempered even. Each day made her more agitated. That night, after Mordecai had lovingly teased her into having sex, she fell into a deep sleep.

In her dreams, she was back on the docks of the Lower District in Eclat. The smells, the sights, and the sounds—all of it felt so real, so familiar, so close.

Hands in her pockets, she studied the boats as she passed, taking in the details of each. When she came to a familiar slip, she paused, her brows furrowed. The Ashway family boat, *Merry Maiden*, was docked. A single light flickered from within.

Feeling compelled to continue, she made her way down to her boat *Polaris*. Her heart sang with joy at the sight of its rust-stained sides and chipped paint. Eager to see Tarquin, she leaped aboard and burst into the cabin. He wasn't there. Growing concerned, she climbed up to the wheelhouse. It was empty. As panic gripped her, she turned on heel and ran into town, stopping along the way at the places her adoptive father normally visited—the rope house, the port authority office, the port mechanic's, a bakery. There was no sign of him.

Thinking that perhaps he was at the market, Kell booked it up Miller Road to Donahue Street. There were no carts, stands, or marquees. She paced the sidewalk, ignoring the newly constructed flats around her. Where else could he be?

A strange sensation suddenly tugged at her, causing her to stop mid-step and set her gaze down the street. Though automobiles rolled by, their bright headlines jumping into her eyes, there was nothing else along the street. Frowning, Kell started back to the port but was once again stopped. Something was calling her, pulling her.

Deciding to heed the sensation, she broke into a run, moving to the northeast toward the Middle and Upper Districts. In a few magical strides, she found herself standing outside a large, magnificently opulent building. She tried to read the sign situated outside the main entrance but couldn't make out the words. All she knew was that something inside the building was calling her.

Kell blinked and suddenly she was in a strange corridor. Though not well lit, it wasn't unwelcoming. Soft lamps burned along the wallpaper-adorned walls; polished wood floors creaked under her. As she passed a window, she peered out to get a better idea of where she was.

It seemed she was on the second story as she could clearly discern a courtyard of trees, neatly pruned bushes, and lovely flowerbeds. Polished benches were positioned under the trees which, if she looked closely, appeared to be bearing lemons. Further confused, Kell trotted down the lengthy hallway, glancing periodically out the windows.

By the time she reached a door, the vantage point had changed to showcase a large dirt yard that extended to another building illuminated by exterior lighting. Her attention on the door, she tentatively touched it. The feeling was strongest here, she was sure of it! All of her instincts urged her to enter.

Drawn by curiosity and by the nagging feeling within her, she gave in to the impulse. She entered in a blink. It was a quaint room, not opulent like the building's exterior, but not ill-kept or ratty. A dying candle flickered faintly on a nearby desk. Though there wasn't much else in the room, Kell's pounding heart chided her to proceed with caution.

She focused on the sleeping form of a man whose bed was situated in the opposite corner of the room next to the window. Kell shuffled forward, craning her neck to see who it was. When she reached his bedside, she fell still, her gaze on Simon.

For years, he had remained fourteen in her mind. She had seen his impish smile and skinny body hundreds of times in her memories and dreams.

The man sleeping before her was not what she remembered. He was long and heavy with large shoulders and muscular arms. His hair was cut short along the sides, emphasizing the longer swath of blond that covered his forehead. It appeared he had broken his nose at some point as it was slightly crooked along the bridge. A faint scar decorated his cheek. His jaw was rough with honey-colored stubble.

"Simon," she breathed, looking him over. Though she couldn't make out much more of his body due to the blankets, she could tell that he had been through a lot.

"Kell."

Her name on his lips startled her.

"Where have you been? What happened? Are you all right?" she asked near tears. "Where are you?"

"Munera… school," he murmured in his sleep. "You?"

"It's a long story. How long have you been here?" She dreaded the answer.

Simon rolled away from her, revealing his bare muscled back. "Years."

Kell reached out to touch him. "I'm sorry. I'm so, so sorry." She sank to the floor beside his bed. "I should have gone after you, or I should have-have at least been arrested with you."

"You left," he sighed.

"I was so scared, Simon. I-I… I couldn't let myself be arrested. There's…" She touched his back with delicate fingers. "Please, forgive me."

Simon folded away from her and didn't say anything. "Simon, please. Look at me. *Simon.*" She stood and attempted to roll him back over, but her hands passed through him. Tears sliding down her face, she gazed at him. "I'm coming for you. I'm coming to get you. All right? So, you just wait."

"Don't... bother," came the response.

A sob erupted from Kell as she staggered backward. Trying to settle her *satt*, she forced calmness into her voice. "Fine. Be... as stubborn as you want. But I'm coming for you." She turned for the door.

"Tarquin..."

"What?" Kell's eyes fixed on his form. "What about Tarquin?"

"He's... here too. New... fighter."

"What? Why?"

"Don't know." Simon rolled onto his back and sighed in his sleep. "Just came... today."

Resolve settled in Kell's gut. "Yeah, tell him to hold on too. I'm coming for the both of you."

Simon made a sound like a scoff but didn't say anything else.

Kell backed through the door, passing through walls like a specter. She was drawn over the Middle District and then whisked north through cloudless skies. She jolted violently back into her body.

Panting, she opened her eyes to find Mordecai sitting beside her with a tiny lamp lit. His hand was on her leg and his eyes full of loving concern. "What... was that?" he whispered.

In the light, she could make out sweat on his brow. "I don't know." She could hardly talk. "I don't know, I don't know. It... It felt... Mordecai, I was there. I was there with..." She gasped. "Simon. I know where Simon is! And Tarquin!" She rolled out of bed, panic consuming her. "They're at the Munera school in Eclat!"

"What?"

"Yeah, Simon's been there..." Tears spilled down her face, and she fell still. "He's been there for years. Mordecai, he's been there for *years*."

"All right, all right—But it was a dream, right?"

Kell looked at him. "That wasn't a dream. That couldn't have been a dream."

"Has it happened any other time?"

"I mean, sometimes, but not like that—"

"Kellick? Mordecai?" called Denez from outside their yurt.

Kell's reply was shaky. "Y-yeah?"

Denez entered, carrying fire in the palm of his hand to light his way. His eyes fell on Kell. "Are you all right?"

"How did you know?" Kell whispered, wide-eyed.

"You disrupted the Flow. Most everyone in camp knows." Denez seated himself a short distance from them to run an appraising eye over her. "You look... like you've seen something."

"A dream. I was dreaming." Kell tried to find words to better explain herself but instead ended up just pleadingly gazing at Denez.

The Tribe's leader nodded thoughtfully. "But it wasn't a dream, was it?" She shook her head. He looked at Mordecai. "What did you see?"

"She was having a full conversation with, uh, a friend."

Kell turned on him. "You heard it all?"

Mordecai nodded. "Yeah, you were talking to Simon and... it wasn't going well." He was silent for a moment. The next time he spoke, it was with a grim sense of understanding. "We're... probably going to be leaving the Tribe... soon."

Denez rested his hands on his knees. "I see."

"What was that?" Kell asked softly.

"There are four fields. The Self, the Physical, the Mental, and Synchrony. To gain control of the first two fields, everyone follows either the Knowledge of Old or of New. The third field, the Mental, manifests differently for each person and cannot be easily taught. It depends upon an individual's mastery of the first two fields, their intentions, and their perception of their own abilities."

"What do you mean?" Mordecai queried.

"You are able to do because you believe you can. How you perceive Viterra and your own abilities influences how you are able to use them." Denez glanced at the lamp to his left in thought. "Kell, don't you find it remarkable that someone who is not from the Tribe has been able to start learning the Old Knowledge?"

"Gytha's a good teacher," Kell replied, not seeing the point of his question.

"Gytha is a good teacher because her manifestation of the third field is persuasion. She uses Viterra to set into motion thoughts, ideas, and ways of thinking." Denez held Kell's gaze. "She's been using it on you since you first met."

"Oh," was all Kell could say.

"This is not a bad thing. Gytha is extraordinarily sensitive about her skill and has asked for my permission a number of times to use it to help you be more pliable and receptive to the complexities of our culture and the Old Knowledge. Without it, you would not have been able to do what you can right now."

"I'm not a master of the Old," argued Kell. "I spent all winter just trying to unfreeze a block of ice. I think you're giving me more credit than I deserve."

"Nevertheless, the third field is manifesting for you."

"So," Kell considered how best to frame her bewilderment, "how did I find Simon? How did I… trace him hundreds of miles away and find his exact location? Denez, I was standing in his room, looking at him. How did I do that?"

"It is my understanding that you have a strong tie to this person, yes?" asked the Tribe's leader.

Kell nodded. "We grew up together. He was my best friend."

"And you've dreamed about him before?"

She frowned. "How did you… know?"

"Because astral projection requires that you have a strong focus. But this is the first time you've done this, right? Has anything changed recently that has made you focus more on him?"

Kell shifted uncomfortably. "We passed the road to the capital a while ago."

"Yes, roads, paths, and trails often act as guides because they can elicit different meanings. A road can be a road, or it can symbolize a journey, a direction, or even self-actualization. A path through a forest can be a path, or it can represent following through on a decision. That road must have been weighing on your mind and guided you directly to your focus."

Overwhelmed, Kell murmured, "They have Tarquin." She forced the tears welling in her eyes to stay put. "Simon told me that Tarquin had just arrived at the school."

Denez looked at Mordecai. "Who's… Tarquin?"

"Her adoptive father," explained Mordecai.

"In my dream, I was looking everywhere for him, but I couldn't find him. And then… I felt a tug, like someone was calling my name from a long way off. And I found Simon." Kell wiped her eye on her shoulder. "They took Simon. They can't have Tarquin too."

Denez sat back, his solemn gaze set on the floor. "There's more at play here that you need to be aware of, Kellick. Hallmund reported two weeks ago that the reactionary group she's embedded in is on the move. They've been clashing with the Containment Office for months in and around Avives but," he nodded, "they're moving to Eclat because it's hosting the Munera in the fall. I don't know if they're going to disrupt the games, but I suspect that it is their desire to wreak as much chaos as possible. Going back to Eclat is dangerous, especially for you." He looked pointedly at Mordecai. "To return while Terin's group is seeking vengeance would be unwise."

Kell could feel Denez's gaze on her as she considered her options. When she wavered in fear at the leader's words, that strong resolve that had visited her in her dream blossomed. And she knew she was being called.

Denez nodded as if he had heard her proclaim her path aloud. "When will you leave?"

"Tomorrow morning," Kell replied, glancing at Mordecai.

"May I suggest that you leave once you've arrived at our new camp location? You've already been traveling for weeks and are low on supplies. This will also give you time to flesh out your plans." He nodded toward Mordecai. "I assume you'll be leaving with her?

When Mordecai didn't answer, Kell asked, "How far out are we from the new camp?"

"About three days." When she grimaced, Denez continued, "Your friend has been in the care of the Munera school for years. He'll survive a few more weeks."

"What about Tarquin?" muttered Kell.

"If he's anything like you, he'll manage."

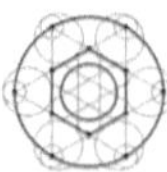

Simon sat at his desk, his gaze set on the hazy purple sky aglow with the coming dawn. He was convinced—that *hadn't* been a dream. It had felt too real. Kell's presence had been palpable. With a growl of frustration, he leaned on his elbow and slouched further in the chair.

But Kell… hadn't looked like Kell in his mind's eye. The person standing at his bedside had been a young woman with shoulder-length, brown hair and inquisitive hazel eyes that knew him intimately. The roundness of her once-familiar face had given way to a fine jawline, a thin chin, and rising cheekbones. The clothes she wore were foreign but nevertheless revealed the swell of breasts and lean shoulders. That had been Kell, but it hadn't.

Of course, this thoroughly confused him. However, the longer he dwelled on it, the more sense it made. He had already led himself to believe that Kell wasn't what she had said she was. So, the revelation was helpful but left him uncomfortable.

And just what did she think she was going to do? Barge into Madam Parthemos' school and whisk him and Tarquin away?

Tarquin!

Simon rose. He needed to find the man and get him into Dockett's good graces immediately. He hurriedly dressed and left his quarters on the third floor. Disgustingly familiar with the school by now, Simon strode down the flights of stairs, passing servants preparing the school for the day, and trotted to the northern end where the non-pro fighters who were not going to be trained were kept.

Guards, servants, nobles, clerks—everyone knew and respected him because of his status as Dockett's Champion and his proven prowess. With ease, he encouraged one of the armed guards to let him into the intake hold where he knew Tarquin would be.

Though Simon himself had never spent time in the clammy place, he had visited it a few times with Dockett. It was held below ground directly adjacent to the training yard. Prisoners deemed strong enough to fight but not worth the time and effort to train were kept there until the Munera so they could be slaughtered for sport by skilled Users. It gave the appearance of fairness.

Hands in his pockets to appear unbothered, he meandered down the cold, stone aisle that ran between metal cells. Though lamps illuminated his way, he still found it difficult to see. He was pleased that at least the air was well circulated now; the last time he had been down there, the fighters' hold had reeked.

He casually peered into each of the cells, searching for an enormous form that he could recognize anywhere. He eventually found Tarquin in a cell with two others. All three were still sleeping. Simon considered how best to help the man. Settling on a course of action, he crouched by the bars.

"Tarquin," he whispered. When the behemoth of a man didn't move, Simon hissed his name again.

Tarquin stirred and then rolled over to look at him. Simon was taken aback by the injuries he had incurred. Tarquin's left eye was swollen shut and his bearded face was lumpy; even still, Simon could discern the man's surprise. "What are you—" Tarquin sat up and then looked down the row of cells. Lowering his voice, he asked, "Simon?"

Simon smiled. "It's good to see you."

As Tarquin moved closer, he looked Simon over. "God, Simon Ashway. Look at you. You're... all grown up. How'd you know I was down here?"

"I saw them bring you in yesterday."

Tarquin glanced down the aisle again. "How long have you been here?"

Simon gave a grim smile. "Since the day the regulators took me from the market."

"Is it just you here? Anyone else?"

Not wanting to visit that topic just yet, Simon pivoted. "How'd you end up in here? They going after fishermen now?"

Tarquin groaned softly as he shifted. "No, my years of *forgettin'* to pay taxes brought me here. Regulators came for me day before yesterday. You know what they're gonna do with us?"

Simon swallowed. "Nothing good. I'm gonna see if I can get you out of the hold and into the pro-fighters' dorm. You'll have to start actually training, but—"

"Wait." Tarquin gazed at him. "Pro-fighters? What are you talking about?"

Simon wetted his lips. "You're at a training school for the Munera. Everyone in here is going to fight at the games… I'm going to be fighting as well."

Tarquin swallowed visibly in the lamplight and nodded.

"Let me see if I can get you into the trained fighters' dorm. It's better than here. You're going to have to actually train though. We have less than three months left." Simon stood. "If anyone comes to inspect you, act as strong and, I don't know, gung-ho as you can." He turned to leave.

"Simon," Tarquin softly called after him. Simon looked back. "You never asked…" The large man thought for a moment and then shook his head. "Never mind."

"I'll find you later." Simon started from the hold, struggling to keep his face stoic.

22

Revelations

THEY ARRIVED AT THE NEW camp two days later than planned as one of the elders in the Tribe had become too sick to travel. Although Kell and Mordecai had discussed their plans ad nauseum with each other and with Renata, Kell did not feel any closer to finalizing their course of action.

As she curried the horses in the fading light of the summer evening, she mused over the most enduring of their problems—how to get to Simon and Tarquin. No matter how she looked at it, there was no way for her to get *in* the school much less get *out* with Simon and Tarquin. Eclat was a four-week journey from their current location. If they left tomorrow, they would be arrive mid to late-August in the capital. There was no way to know how long it would take them to get into the school.

Mordecai joined her shortly after sunset to lead the horses into a pen they had formed out of roots. Leaning on the makeshift fence, he said, "You know how we've been told why we shouldn't leave?" Kell hung her arms over the fence and looked at him. "Well, Beiner just mentioned that the Council of Ministers in Eclat has passed anti-User legislation."

"What does that mean?"

"He said that anyone who is Bound is being rounded up and forced to live in designated neighborhoods and flats." He ran his fingers over the freshly-woven roots. "The regulators are… killing indiscriminately. They're using any excuse they can to kill any Bound individual they run into."

"So, it's happening again—another Culling," Kell muttered.

There was silence between them for a long moment before Mordecai said, "Kell, I'm going to say something that might anger you. I just need to— What are you and me, the two of us, going to be able to in Eclat? What can just the two of us do?"

Kell tried to appear level and even as she regarded him, but her thoughts raced. After years of wondering and fearing for him and being nearly strangled by guilt and shame, she had found Simon. No amount of rational thinking could dissuade her from what she knew she needed to do.

"We're going against a historically-entrenched system of oppression and persecution for the sake of one man."

"Two," Kell corrected.

"Right, Tarquin. *Two* men."

Kell pulled her arms taut on the fence to stretch her shoulders and said, "Well, how else can we get in there? We're on our own. We've got no one on the inside who'll be able—" Mordecai gasped, startling Kell. She looked at him, wide-eyed. "What?"

"Bellamy," he whispered. "Denez would know how to get in touch with him. He can help us."

Kell grimaced. "I don't know… If Bellamy is as high-ranking as they say he is, I can't see what excuse he could make to be anywhere near the school."

"That's speculation." He nudged her. "Let's ask Denez. Bellamy might not be able to show us in himself, but he would know the people who could get us in."

After considering the plan, Kell nodded, and they hurried off together in search of the Tribe's leader.

"And so… you're wanting Bellamy to help you enter the school to save your friends?" queried Denez once they had explained their plan to him. He paused in his work of fletching arrows to regard them.

"Yes," Kell replied. "I know he probably wouldn't be going to the school, but is it—"

"Bellamy rarely visits the school as he ardently disagrees with everything that it stands for," the Tribe leader replied. "His disdain for the place is well known."

"But could he get us *in*?" pressed Mordecai.

"But could you get yourselves *out*?" Denez countered. "This plan will… draw attention to Bellamy at a crucial time in his, uh, mission."

Kell frowned, her head cocking to the side. Not once had Denez ever stumbled over words or been left searching for what he wanted to say. "What do you mean?" she asked.

Denez drew a long breath. "Nothing, forget I said anything." He began rotating the shaft of the arrow for inspection, but Kell stopped him with a firm hand, an audaciously forward action. Denez kept his gaze steady on the ground, his body rigid.

"The lives of my friend and my father are at stake." She released the arrow and straightened herself. Recognizing the stiffness in the leader's shoulders, she bowed her head in deference. "Please, we're struggling to come up with a solution. If they were your people, your family, you would do anything to save them, wouldn't you?"

Denez sighed and, leaning on his knees, passed Kell a hardened look. "Bellamy is planning to overthrow the Council of Ministers. The crackdown on the Bound is being spearheaded by the Council despite the king refusing to support it. So, Bellamy's seeking to overthrow the Council."

Mordecai gaped. "How?"

"I do not know."

"Why was he traveling with you?" asked Kell. "How did he even know about you?"

"His younger sister, Hetty, who was Bound, was killed four years ago. It was made to look like an accident, but it was no accident. Shortly thereafter, his mother committed suicide." Denez regarded the arrow he had been working on. "Bellamy began looking into legislation concerning what they call Users. He didn't understand Bound persons and disdained them, even though his sister was one. According to Bellamy, the palace librarian led him to some old books that described not only our people but our presence within the Council. So, he came looking for us."

"He wanted answers," said Mordecai, "and you wanted a voice."

Denez nodded. "While with us, he concluded that the only way to reverse the course of history was to overthrow the Council of Ministers and insert his own men. He did not share how he was going to do that." The Tribe leader looked between them in the light of the nearby fire. "You're not First Whispered, so I can't tell you what to do, but I advise you not to interfere with Bellamy and his mission. For the good of our world, it *must* succeed. You two are outliers, the unplanned for. It is with great delicacy that I tell you—the lives of your friends are not worth the future of all Bound and Unbound."

Kell glowered at him, her mind racing. White fury coursed through her body, causing her face to flush and hands to tingle. "Fine," she managed. "We'll figure out another way." And with that, she strode off.

After raging for a robust half hour away from the camp so no one except Mordecai could hear her, Kell finally flopped onto the lush summer grass, panting. Tears came unexpectedly, and she turned away from Mordecai. She was so frustrated. Since her dream with Simon the previous week, she had been anxious and restless, feeling the urge to go but feeling restricted in her movement.

When she finally got control of her emotions and sat up, she found herself alone. Mordecai had returned to the village to give her privacy.

Knowing she needed to help him pack, Kell wiped her face, produced a small flame in her palm without the use of an Arcane Circle, and headed back.

After half-heartedly visiting with some of the women, she returned to the yurt she shared with Mordecai. Seeing movement next to a lantern near their residence and recognizing her fiancé's silhouette, she raised her hand and flared the flame to produce more light.

"What are you doing?" she asked, spotting backframes and supplies.

"We're leaving for Eclat in the morning. Gytha, Aethel, and Beiner gave us what they could for travel. We won't take the yurt since it's summer. But we need to pack blankets because the eve—"

Kell hugged him fiercely. "Thank you," she breathed, burying her face in his shoulder.

He held her, his arms strong and supportive. "We'll figure everything out when we get there."

The following morning, they rose before the sun and quietly finished packing. Kell dressed in a knee-length, sky-blue robe that boasted lightweight short sleeves. Thin pants and supple boots would protect her legs from insects. She braided the front half of her hair away from her face to keep it out of the way.

Already, Renata had given them what money she had stored, and they had agreed the night prior that it would be best to travel without the aid of the horses as Kell and Mordecai had no idea what they would do with the beasts once they arrived in Eclat.

Unsurprisingly, several First Whispered, including Denez, and Renata woke to send them off. Though still angry with him and his callous words, Kell politely thanked the Tribe leader, pressing her forehead against his.

As she drew away, he stopped her. Their faces a few inches apart, he said, "I hope you find what you're looking for, Kellick Fisk. You are always welcome here."

Humbled, Kell replied with some embarrassment, "I apologize for my behavior last night. I upset your *satt*. I hope you were able to resettle yourself after my outburst."

Denez reached between them and tapped her face fondly. "Where you're concerned, it's quite difficult."

"We'll be back," Kell said.

The leader nodded. Kell and Mordecai bid the others goodbye, trading sincere thanks and heartfelt gratitude, before turning to Renata.

"I'll see you off," Renata muttered, shuffling into the purpling dawn.

Kell and Mordecai waved to everyone and set off after her. Only once they were a good distance from the village did their old teacher stop to regard them. "Take care of each other. You're not wayward kids anymore." Renata looked at Kell. "Watch out for Terin. You're going to run into her in Eclat, I guarantee it. She's trained, Kellick, and has become empowered by all that's transpired in Avives. If you cross paths with her, I can't say that you will escape unscathed."

"Do you still love her, Renata?" asked Kell.

"I always will. Just like I love you two. But every person must decide their own path. Terin has chosen hers, and you two have decided yours." She nodded to Mordecai. "Remember discipline, patience, kindness, mercy. You might not be First Whispered, but you *are* my students." With unexpected tenderness, she ushered them both into a single embrace. Afterward, she cleared her throat and shooed them off.

"We'll be back," Mordecai said, his voice thick.

Renata nodded, her lips pursed. She looked old standing alone along the tree line.

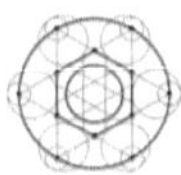

Simon glanced furtively at Dockett to gauge his reaction as Tarquin barreled through a practice dummy, his enormous mass easily driving the humanoid replica into the neighboring wall. The Lanista watched, his muscled arms folded over his chest. After a moment, he rubbed his stubbly jaw with a grimace. "I don't know, kid. He's... old."

"He's not that old," Simon replied, avoiding Tarquin's prying gaze. He kept his voice low. "He's hard-working, strong. He's a fisherman, been one all his life. Hauled everything in by himself. Do you know how much weight that is?"

"Yeah, but he can't fight for shit," Dockett argued.

Knowing now was the time for an impassioned appeal, Simon approached Tarquin. He passed the older man a pointed look before smashing his fist into Tarquin's beefy arm. Kell's father didn't move. Simon looked back at Dockett. "You're telling me we can't use this? Look at him! He's a bull! Imagine the power here. He just needs technique."

Dockett ran an appraising gaze over Tarquin before looking at Simon. "Fine, I'll take him. But you need to be focusing on your own work. A lot's riding on September. Pair off with Ferrik and do morning conditioning again." Simon grinned and then passed Tarquin an encouraging nod before hurrying off.

Throughout the morning, he kept an eye on Tarquin from across the training yard. He had vouched for his strength, but he didn't know what kind of endurance the bearded man had. It quickly became evident that he didn't have much. Dockett yelled at him and tested him repeatedly to determine what aspects needed to be improved upon. But it was evident that Tarquin was out of shape.

"Friend of yours?" asked Ferrik, forgoing a Bo staff attack to relax.

"Yeah." Simon took a long breath to calm his breathing, his eyes on Tarquin. "He came in yesterday. I convinced Dockett to take him on. But I'm not sure how long that's going to last."

"He's a big guy. I wouldn't want to be on the receiving end of one of his blows. But if he can't even make it halfway across the arena…"

Simon nodded, trying to think of ways to inspire Kell's father. If he didn't want to be slaughtered by Users in the arena or in a halftime event, then he needed to be training with the other pro-fighters. Even a few months' practice gave him a greater chance of survival in the Munera."

"Hey, Simon."

Simon looked back at his partner and mentor. Ferrik drew closer. "Don't… put much stock into him, yeah? The older guys don't last very long."

"Yeah, I know."

Simon spent much of the rest of the day watching Tarquin from a distance. Tarquin was ungodly strong and could lift barbells and cement blocks with ease. But when it came to aerobics, he grew winded within seconds. By the end of the afternoon, the bearded man was bent over vomiting along the side of the training yard from the effort he had exerted.

Simon finally got a chance to talk with Tarquin at supper that evening in the fighters' mess hall. Since Tarquin was new, everyone avoided him— except Simon. A small, hardened loaf of bread in his mouth and an enormous bowl of rice, stewed meat, and vegetables in his hands, Simon made his way to Tarquin and sat beside him on the chipped and splintered benches.

"You finished your first day," Simon said with a slight smile. He noticed Tarquin poking at his rice. "It'll get easier. The first few weeks are the toughest. At least you're not getting beat."

Tarquin glanced at him. "You should have just left me with the others. I'm fifty-six. My back is messed up from pulling in nets for years. I can't—" He licked his lips; his voice was raw. "I can't keep up with you."

Simon glanced at the other fighters with whom he was familiar, his gaze catching Ferrik's. After a moment, he lowered his voice and leaned closer to Tarquin. "I… heard from Kell."

Tarquin looked at him, startled. The worry, fear, and hope that shone in the bearded man's eyes shamed Simon. "When? Is she all right? Where is she—" He stopped, realizing his mistake. "I mean… he."

Simon pursed his lips. "I thought so. Uh, so it's going to sound strange," he winced, "maybe like I'm lying, but she came to me in a dream."

Tarquin sat back and continued to pick at his food. "Oh. That's what you mean."

With a quick look around at the others again, Simon nudged his leg. "No, this was different," he said lowly. "He… She… This wasn't a normal dream. The point is she told me that she was coming for us—the *both* of us."

Tarquin shook his head. "You've been in here too long. Even if your dream could see the future or whatever, you do her a disservice. She's not dumb enough to return to Eclat."

"So, she's not in the city?" Simon whispered.

"No, I took her to Avives years ago." His throat closed around his words. "Haven't heard from her since."

Simon mulled over this new information as he ate. "Why… did you take her to Avives? What's in Avives?"

Tarquin met his gaze. "She's a User, Simon. She's the one who set the Lower District on fire."

"What?" Simon felt his body grow cold, his limbs limp.

His eyes still on Simon, Kell's father added, "She's Unbound."

Simon set his bowl on his leg, his gaze on the ground.

"She's… not even my real daughter. I found her near the docks. I didn't know she was an Unbound but I… suspected."

"Why didn't you say anything—" Simon cut himself off as he realized the answer. To protect Kell.

"She accidentally set the market on fire because of you. Your arrest triggered her." Tarquin shook his head. "I couldn't… I couldn't… People saw her. I couldn't let the regulators get her; they'd kill her. I grabbed her and ran."

Several minutes of silence expanded between them as Tarquin half-heartedly ate and Simon attempted to process all that had just been divulged.

Simon eventually asked, "So? What's in Avives?"

"I left her with an abbey for Bound children. Taught her how to draw fake cuffs on her wrists." Tarquin scoffed. "I doubt she's still there. I'll be surprised if she even made it a full year there. She pushes too many buttons, doesn't like being told what to do."

"She's… Unbound." Simon picked at his food. An array of emotions vied for prominence within him. She was a User; worse, she was an Unbound. She was dangerous, volatile, unhinged. She was the very thing he had been training to kill.

An image of the young woman who had visited him in his dreams the night prior flickered through his mind. She hadn't looked dangerous, murderous. She had looked… normal.

But she had left him to be arrested by the regulators. She had forsaken him by hiding because—

Simon drew a long breath.

She couldn't be caught. She couldn't let the regulators get a hold of her. She wouldn't have been imprisoned; she would have been killed.

"If…" He cleared his throat. "If she's not at the abbey anymore, where would she be?"

Tarquin shook his head. "Like I said, I haven't heard from her in years."

Considering his dream, Simon went on. "Do you think… she found someone to teach her?

"What?"

"The dream…" Simon met Tarquin's dark gaze. "It wasn't a dream. She was there, standing next to me. I could see her clearly."

Hope once again sparked in Tarquin's eyes. "What did she look like? Did she look good?"

"Yeah, she, uh, looked older. Obviously. Her hair was longer and she was taller. She, uh, looked like a young woman."

Tarquin looked away, his eyes glistening. "Shit…" He sniffed. "And you're sure? It wasn't a dream?"

Simon shook his head. "I could feel her touch me. She was talking to me. I told her you were here. She said she was coming for us."

Seeming to believe his story now, Tarquin nodded. "She didn't say where she was?"

"No."

Tarquin drew a long breath, his enormous shoulders rising as he did. "All right."

"All right?" Simon studied him.

"If Kell says she's coming, then… I guess I should hold on until then."

Guilt bloomed in Simon at the false hope he had just instilled in the bearded man. What if it *had* been just a dream?

Tarquin turned on his food with more enthusiasm and ate heartily. Nonetheless glad that he was able to inspire the older man, Simon followed suit.

23

The Capital

KELL DUCKED UNDER THE SHELTER she had just put the finishing touches on and shook out her hair next to Mordecai. He grimaced and then looked out at the pouring rain. Their journey had been a slow one. According to the map Denez had drawn for them, they were hardly a quarter of the way to Eclat despite having traveled for nearly a week and a half.

"I'm glad it's not cold," Kell muttered, pulling off her travel robe. She easily withdrew the water from it, a trick she had recently learned. As she turned to do the same for Mordecai's clothes, she continued, "When me and Tarquin fish in the winter, it often rains and it's miserable work. I can deal with being wet and I can deal with being cold but not wet *and* cold."

Mordecai lay back on their packs and looked at the ceiling of their root-and-earth shelter. "So, I was thinking we should find Bellamy."

Kell watched a trickle of wayward rainwater slither along the dry dirt toward her boots from the entrance. "Denez told us not to interrupt whatever he's up to."

"But Denez failed to remember that Bellamy owes you," he pointed out.

Kell looked at him, confused. "What?"

"Bellamy. He owes you. He said so himself. You know, to atone for what he did. Remember? Denez asked if you had a request for Bellamy, but you were so angry about it all, you couldn't think of anything." Mordecai nudged her. "He's our only way into this."

"How do we find him? Where does he even live? We can't just walk in and demand to see him."

Mordecai shrugged. "Why not?"

Kell started to argue but stopped herself. Why not?

"What if we figure out where he is, dress up, and request an audience with him? Meet him."

"That's a lot of what ifs," Kell murmured, trying to puzzle through the plan. "And then what? We ask him to… help us get Simon and Tarquin out?"

Mordecai shook his head. "No, no. Can't do that. That'll definitely draw too much attention to him. We have to ask him something that is doable for him, something that won't seem out of the ordinary or make anyone become suspicious."

"He could have us arrested and forced to fight in the Munera," Kell offered. "Get us close enough to Simon and Tarquin—"

"And then what? I've never seen the Munera school, Kell, but I don't think they constructed it to be easily escapable, otherwise, Simon would have done so years ago." Mordecai thought for a moment. "Perhaps, though, that would be the other half of our request from Bellamy."

"What? That he get us out once we have Simon and Tarquin?"

Mordecai nodded. "It's not our best plan, but it is *a* plan." He leaned into her. "You know, it would be really useful if you could find Bellamy in his dreams or something."

"I… don't think I can do that. Denez said I have to have a strong focus to do that, something that ties me to him."

"Arguably, the last several years of your life tie you to him since he started everything."

"I'll think about it. I don't really have full control over the ability yet."

The following week, they picked up their pace, using rivers to travel faster when they could. One long stretch of river allowed them to travel a couple of dozen miles before they were forced to turned west again, angling for Eclat along the coast.

By mid-August, they had to start traveling along the main roads where automobiles, horses, and pedestrians traveled together. Mordecai kept his wrists hidden to avoid drawing attention to the black cuffs tattooed there and grew restless. Kell, too, felt uncomfortable traveling alongside, past, and with so many people. Trucks carrying goods passed them haphazardly, barely giving pedestrians and those on horseback a wide enough berth. Automobiles zoomed by, leaving clouds of dust in their wakes.

They finally entered the Lower District of Eclat near the end of August, the journey having taken them significantly longer than planned. Exhausted, Mordecai found them a small, local inn and bought a room for the night.

Worn from traveling, Kell stared at her belongings which now occupied the floor of their room. "We're going to need different clothes," she sighed. "Our garb is going to draw too much attention."

Mordecai continued to peer out the second-story window, his eyes observing the ragged, cobblestone street and its people below.

"Hey, you hear me?"

Mordecai glanced back at her and nodded.

Sensing that he was distressed, she joined him to see what he was looking at. Aside from the streets, rusting automobiles, and haggard peddlers, she didn't see anything out of the ordinary.

"You… grew up here?" he asked.

"Well, not *here* but, yeah, near the port."

Mordecai surveyed the street. "It's filthy."

Kell shrugged. "This one's pretty clean actually." She returned to her pack. "Tomorrow, we should go clothes shopping."

That night, despite her exhaustion, Kell sank into Mordecai's embrace, taking his kisses, touches, and love as eagerly as always. But when he went to sleep, she didn't. After struggling to settle her *satt*, she got up from their tiny bed and went to the window.

She was back in the Lower District. The port was a morning's walk from their inn. Did she dare return there to see what had become of everything? Tarquin wouldn't be there. What if someone remembered her and turned her in to the regulators? Frowning, she rested her head on the thin window pane.

Her body was heavy, tired. The last leg of their journey had been stressful. Urging herself back to bed, she slid in next to Mordecai and eventually slept.

She located Simon with ease in her dreams. Like a jolt of lightning, she felt herself surge through the city of Eclat, her essence winding up streets, turning, and coursing toward him. Once again, she found herself at the Munera school doors. She blinked and was standing inside Simon's private quarters.

She had been unable to speak to him since that first contact. Would he realize it wasn't a dream? With some reluctance, she approached his bedside. When her eyes lit upon his forehead, she gasped. Just above his right brow was a four-inch wound. Though it was healing and appeared to be a few weeks old, she could tell it had been bad.

"Simon," she said, kneeling beside him. "Simon." She touched his bare shoulder. "Hey."

He stirred and rolled toward her but remained asleep. "Kell…"

"What happened to your head?"

"Ini…tiation. Gives scar."

She caressed the wound, grimacing.

"Where are you?"

"I'm in Eclat," she replied, searching his face and body for other injuries. "The Lower District. It took us a while to get back. We've been traveling this whole time." She drew closer. "Hey, listen—Is Tarquin still with you?"

"He is."

"I need a way to enter the school. Can you think of anything?"

"Security… is high. Guards everywhere. The games are coming." He moved as if to reach for her, but his arm settled on the side of the bed. "The Council… is planning things. I don't know…"

"The Council?" She thought for a moment. "The Council of Ministers?"

"Yeah. Dockett says that something big is going to happen."

"Does it have to do with Bellamy?" She shook her head, realizing he didn't know who that was. "Never mind. I need—"

"Yes, Bellamy," Simon interrupted her. "But I don't… know any more."

Kell sat back in thought. "Where is he? Where is Bellamy usually? Here at the school?"

"No. At the palace… in the Upper District."

"Is it easy to get into the palace?"

"I don't… know."

Kell stood and paced his quarters, thinking. Denez's warning was loud in her head. Bellamy had a mission. Her sudden appearance might disrupt that plan. "Shit…" she muttered.

"Kellick," breathed Simon in his sleep.

She stopped pacing and looked at him.

"You're… a User?"

She considered him for a long moment and then nodded with a sigh. "Yeah. How do you know?"

"Tarquin."

She scoffed. It was unlike Tarquin to share such intimate information.

"You… killed… my family…"

"What?" she whispered.

"That day… at the market. The fire. I haven't seen… Mom and Dad since."

Heart pounding, Kell fidgeted. "Are you sure that they…"

There was a long pause before Simon cleared his throat. "No."

Kell nodded. "Fine, I'll go look. In the meantime, find a way to get us in."

"Who is… us?"

"Don't worry about it. I gotta go." Kell passed him a look once more and then left. In a blink of an eye, she was standing outside the school once more. She expected herself to wake. Instead, she peered northward.

Remembering what Mordecai had said about being connected to Bellamy, she tried to picture the young man in her mind's eye. Although her legs didn't move, her body zipped through miles of streets, crossed intersections, and surged up hills. She passed through enormous black, metal gates and manicured lawns before streaming up a set of stairs and into an enormous and opulent building.

She paused for a moment in the vast, marble and silver foyer, felt a tug to her left, and then coursed onward. She tore through rooms as a specter of Viterra until her body wrenched to a stop at the foot of a large, four-poster bed. Looking around to get her bearings, Kell took in the ridiculous lavishness of the room. Everything was made of marble and trimmed in gold. Flawless silk curtains rustled near the open balcony door.

Kell approached the bed but stopped as movement caught her eye. For a breath's moment, she forgot herself and worried she would be spotted. Her gaze settled on Bellamy's personal bodyguard who had sat up in his bed, his gaze searching the room.

She watched him before approaching the bed, glad that she had gotten the room right. "Bellamy," she whispered, leaning closer to the prince's sleeping form. "Bellamy."

There was a shuffling. Kell turned to find his bodyguard standing, an orange Arcane Circle under him.

"Hey, Bellamy," she continued, not turning away from the man's intimidating form. He was Bound? She searched his wrists but didn't find the markings there. No, he was Unbound. "Bellamy, Bellamy…"

"Hm?" hummed the prince.

"Hey, it's Kell," she said, not turning away from the bodyguard. "Hey, tell your guard to stand down. Please, hurry."

Bellamy's voice grew louder. "Marko." His words were slurred. "Ssstop. It's… Kell."

Kell watched the man with a topknot, gauging his reaction. When he didn't move or relax, she went on. "I'm using Viterra to speak with you in your dreams. Explain it to him. Hurry."

"Kell… using Viterra to talk… in dreams," the prince muttered. "I'm fine." He rolled toward her. "What'sss wrong? It's been a while."

Kell took a calming breath. "I'm in Eclat. Mordecai and I are. We need to get into the Munera school. Friends and family are being held there. We need to get in, get them, and get out. How can we do that?"

When Bellamy didn't reply, she looked back at Marko. The bodyguard seemed more interested than worried.

"Bellamy, focus," she said, reaching to touch him. Marko drew closer, reacting to her movements. How much he could sense, she didn't know.

"Sorry, think… ing." Bellamy sighed. "Who do you need… from the… uh, school?"

"Simon Ashway and Tarquin Fisk."

Bellamy's brows furrowed in his sleep. "Simon is a Champion."

"What?" hissed Kell.

"Simon is a Champion. It will be," he drew a long breath, "very difficult to re… trieve him. Why do you need him?"

"Remember that childhood friend you got arrested? That's him. He got sold to the Munera school. The other man, Tarquin, is my father." Kell leaned on the marble nightstand next to the bed. "I'm here to get them out."

Bellamy grimaced. "Now is not a good… a good time."

"I'm aware of what you're up to. Denez told me. But you owe me. Us, you owe *us*." She started to walk away, sidestepping Marko, who kept his gaze on the spot where she stood. "Mordecai and I are in the Lower District. We're going to be traveling up into the Middle District sometime tomorrow, probably by way of McManis Avenue. Figure something out."

"Wait, wait—"

From the corner of her eye, she saw Bellamy jerk awake. The scene around her vanished into black. Kell's mind became instantly conscious, and she opened her eyes. She glanced at Mordecai who was propped up on an elbow beside her in bed.

"Was that Bellamy?" he asked.

Kell nodded. "With Simon and Bellamy thinking it through, maybe we'll come up with something feasible."

"I feel bad putting Bellamy in such a compromising position," Mordecai murmured. "He's already got a lot going on."

"And according to Simon, the Council of Ministers is preparing to do something big, but he doesn't know what." Kell considered all that she had learned. "First thing in the morning, let's pack and head over to the port. I told him I'd check…" Her words caught in the back of her throat and she fell silent.

"We'll head out in the morning. How far is it?"

"A couple hours' walk. Not bad. We need clothes though. We'll draw too much attention in our Tribe gear." She stretched out beside him, kicking a leg out from under the blankets. "Simon had a huge gash across his forehead. It looked like it had hurt. He must have gotten it in the past few weeks."

"I heard you asking him about it," Mordecai murmured, caressing her hip.

"He said it was an initiation rite, done to create a scar." She frowned. "It's disgusting." She thought and then said, "Bellamy shared a piece of information that is going to make us getting Simon out of the Munera difficult. Apparently, he's a Champion."

"Oh."

"Yeah. That means he's well known and someone will know where he is at all times," Kell continued. She let out a long, exasperated breath. "This is becoming impossible."

"We have a plan for the morning." Mordecai kissed her shoulder. "Let's start there."

At dawn, they dressed in their most mundane clothes and headed southeast toward the port. Although Kell continued to muse on the night's events, she enjoyed watching Mordecai, who had only ever lived in Avives. The Lower District wasn't a tourist destination, but it was a different city and culture.

By midmorning, they were back in familiar territory, and Kell hurried him on, eager to get back home but not looking forward to discovering the fate of Simon's parents. As they followed the nasty, pothole-filled streets, Kell tried to come up with a plan for any number of situations, stirring herself into an anxious mess. Mordecai didn't seem to realize how unsettled she was because he was too busy grimacing at the filth and whipping his head around as he tried to take in the grotesqueness of the Lower District.

As the docks came into view, Kell's pace quickened; her heart thrummed in her ears. The sights, the sounds, the smells—everything was so familiar. Remembering her mission, she strained her neck to see the Ashway's slip. *Merry Maiden* was there!

She took off into a jog, her pack bouncing on her hips as she ran; Mordecai followed. The sound of her boots on the wooden docks was nostalgic. Panting, she came to a stop in front of the Ashway family boat. Seeing signs of recent work, she called into the cabin.

"Vera? Vera Ashway?" She dropped her pack next to Mordecai and ventured onboard. "Vera?"

"Yes?" came a familiar voice from the boat's bow.

Kell nearly sobbed with relief. She staggered along the side of the cabin; Simon's mother met her halfway. Taken aback by the raw emotion on Kell's face, Vera stopped, alarmed.

"Yes? May I help you?" Vera's frizzing hair was grayer than Kell remembered and her face was wrought with stress lines. She wore a dull, tattered dress whose sleeves were rolled past her elbows. Despite her apparent fatigue though, Simon's mother appeared strong.

"Vera, Mrs. Ashway…" Kell reached for her with a wet laugh. "It's me. Kell."

Vera Ashway's mouth fell agape as her eyes scrolled down Kell. "Kellick Fisk…" A laugh bubbled up from her throat and she embraced Kell with a cry. "Oh, Kell! Oh, sweet child. You're alive. Oh!" She hugged Kell, rocking back and forth in a manner all mothers inherently knew. "Oh, look at you." She held her at arm's length. "You're all grown up. Look how beautiful. Oh, Kell." Vera swept her into another hug.

It was another minute or two before both had calmed down enough to allow Kell to lead the way back to the docks. Spotting Mordecai standing patiently there with their packs, Kell drew Simon's mother closer.

"Mrs. Ashway, this is Mordecai. He's… my fiancé."

Vera immediately extended a hand to him, and they shook. "It's an absolute pleasure, Mordecai. Where are you from?"

"Avives," Mordecai replied with a handsome smile.

"That's quite a distance." She glanced at Kell. "So, you *were* in Avives."

"For a while, yeah." Kell looked around. "Mr. Ashway around?"

The fond smile on Vera's face faded. "He's… Actually, he passed in the Market Fire several years ago. I'm sorry you never heard."

Kell's heart sank. "And Simon?"

Vera's eyes misted over and she shook her head.

Kell exchanged looks with Mordecai. Making a quick decision, Kell took Vera's hand. "Could we go inside?"

Once seated, Vera hurriedly made tea for them. As the water heated, Simon's mother regarded Kell.

"Simon's alive," Kell said grimly.

Vera gasped and nearly fell to her knees. She caught herself on the counter and used it to keep herself erect. Hands shaking, she let out a few quick sobs of relief before looking to Kell. "Where is he?"

"That's… the bad news. He's at the Munera school. Been there for years. He's preparin' to fight in the Munera in a little over a month." Kell watched her before adding, "Tarquin's there too."

"Oh!" Vera straightened herself. "Oh, the whole port was in an uproar when the regulators came for him. Old man Montague killed one of them before they… shot him. So, Tarquin's all right?"

"As far as I know." Kell sat back in the narrow, creaking chair. "We're tryin' to find a way to get into the school, get them, and then get out. But that's provin' to be an impossible task."

Vera looked between them, a confused expression contorting her face. With a point of her finger, she asked, "And… why do you two think you are gonna be able to do that? Get them out? They've got guards and fighters and regulators. I've even heard rumors that the Containment Office from Avives is joining…"

"Kell's friends with the prince," remarked Mordecai. Kell threw him a frown though it wasn't quite a lie. "We're hoping to meet with him and see what he can do."

"Are you really? How?" asked Vera.

"I, uh, met him in Avives. Helped him out of some trouble. He said he owes me." Kell nodded. "So, I'm callin' in a favor."

The kettle on the stove began to whistle, prompting Vera to retrieve chipped cups and pour tea for them. "What I'm not understanding," Simon's mother continued, "is how you found out where Simon and Tarquin are when none of us could."

"My friend told me," lied Kell. "The prince. He mentioned Simon's name when he was talkin' about the Munera. And there's a list. He saw it and also remembered my father's named Tarquin."

Vera sat heavily on a nearby crate and sighed. "If what you're saying is true… I so hope it is." She looked between them, a small smile playing on her lips. "You look good, Kell. You really do. Where are you staying?"

"We were in a local inn last night," replied Mordecai. "We might head back there?" He looked at Kell.

Vera sipped her tea and then motioned eastward. "We've been keeping up *Polaris* for Tarquin. Been doing regular maintenance and keeping her clean. We can't always find someone to scrape barnacles off, but she's in working condition—like always."

Mordecai fidgeted. "Stay on the boat?"

Simon's mother smiled. "I even cleaned the cabin and washed the bedding so it would be clean for when he returned."

Kell mulled over the idea. It would prevent them from spending more money, and she could help keep an eye on the boat she had called home for most of her life. But Mordecai's discomfort was apparent. "Thanks, Vera. I'll take a look at her and then decide. Mordecai's from the city; he's not wild about boats or the sea."

"Well, if there's anything else I can do to help you two, just let me know. I'd like to be able to do something since…" Her face grew grave. "I've been waiting this whole time."

"Actually, we both need clothes. We've been travelin' for weeks. Do you know a good tailor in the Middle District? I'd buy from the Lower District, but where we're goin'… the quality's gotta be right."

"Ruth Ann's," replied Vera. "I'll draw you a map. Hold on." She hurried out of the cabin, leaving Kell and Mordecai alone.

"Kell, I can't sleep on a boat," he whispered into her shoulder.

"I know, I know. We'll just check on her and then get goin'."

He chuckled.

"What?"

"You've been talking with an accent since we arrived."

Kell frowned, having not realized it. Vera returned just then, spread a piece of wrinkled paper on the table, and began sketching a rough map of the area. Afterward, Kell led Mordecai down the docks to *Polaris*.

Swelling with pride, she looked at her boat, grinning, and reveled in the rush of nostalgia that surged through her. *Polaris* was just as beautiful as she remembered—rust, pock marks, barnacles, and all.

"You… lived here?" asked Mordecai.

Kell dropped her pack on the dock and lithely leaped onto the stern deck. She ran her hands over the chipped railing, noting the neatly coiled ropes, precisely stacked cages, and folded and lashed netting. Vera had certainly done work. "Yeah."

Kell went to the stern cabin door but found it locked. Figuring Vera had one of the keys but had forgotten to give it to them, Kell considered whether they should leave for the tailor. But she wanted to check on the innards.

With ease, she clambered along the corner of the cabin, using the scaffolding and rigging to pull herself up to the wheelhouse which was also locked. Hanging off the wheelhouse platform, she gazed out at the sea, which was an enticing blue-teal, ignoring the grime, refuse, and filth that crowded around the docks. She drew a deep breath of salty air and smiled. Her heart felt whole.

But more than that—she could feel Viterra here. The Flow here was powerful and extensive, expanding in all directions in varying degrees of density. It pulsed with life, a resounding sensation that coursed through her and filled her to the brim with palpable energy.

Remembering why she had actually scaled the wheelhouse, she reached under a hidden ledge, opened the small, metal box tucked away there, and retrieved the spare key. Holding one of the thin metal beams of the gantry, she slid halfway down and then dropped to the deck. She waggled the key at Mordecai who had the most unusual expression on his face.

"What?" she asked, unlocking the cabin door.

Mordecai smiled fondly at her. "Nothing. You belong here."

To Kell's surprise, the cabin did not smell familiar. On the contrary, it smelled of clean laundry and scented oils that Vera had undoubtedly added. Setting her pack at the foot of her bunk, she sat heavily on her bed and looked around.

The cabin was narrow, uncomfortably narrow. How had she slept in such a confined space? "So, this was my bunk," she told Mordecai, who loitered in the aisle. "And that's Tarquin's."

The bunks' blankets were neatly folded and tucked tightly underneath. Fishing hooks, tool boxes, glasses, pens, and other tools had been cleared from the table and counters and stored to prevent them from rolling around should a storm come up. Vera had fastidiously organized everything to make the boat stormproof—and Kell couldn't feel more loved.

Standing, she looked back at Mordecai. "Well? What do you think?"

Mordecai inched past her and went to the galley a few paces away. He regarded the sliver of counterspace, their one-burner stove, and bucket of a sink. "How did you live like this?" His eyes wandered around the cabin. "Kell, this is pitiful."

Kell smiled sadly. "You don't know what you don't know. My world was small. But I was happy. Tarquin was the best. We had so much fun and I learned so much. And Simon was there, and we played all the time and ran around and roughhoused." As she was reminded why she was back in Eclat, she said, "And I've gotta fix this."

"Come on. Let's head to the tailor."

Kell left *Polaris* with a final mournful glance over her shoulder.

The hike into the Middle District was not a pleasant one as the weeks of traveling combined with the stress of being back in old territory weighed heavily on Kell. She knew Mordecai felt similarly but for different reasons.

Early afternoon, they trudged up McManis Avenue to Ruth Ann's, sweaty and more than a little tired. Though they were dressed as travelers, not well-to-do Middle District citizens, the number of people on the streets and passing vehicles helped them to blend in.

Focused on the overhanging sign that advertised Ruth Ann's tailoring, Kell didn't realize someone had drawn close to her until Mordecai suddenly lashed out over her right shoulder. Kell flinched and ducked away.

"Sorry, sorry!" came a voice.

"Oh!" Mordecai relaxed beside Kell, the map in his other hand going limp.

Kell turned to find Bellamy smiling tiredly at them. "How did you— What are you—" Kell looked the prince over, utterly surprised. He appeared absolutely miserable. Although he was neatly dressed and his black hair set just so, the weariness on his face was painfully evident. She met his bodyguard's gaze and gave a small nod of acknowledgment. No one else was with them. "What are you doing *here*?"

"You said you'd be on McManis Avenue today," Bellamy replied.

"So, you've been waiting for us?" Mordecai asked.

The expression on his face grew, if possible, grimmer. "You need to get into the school to meet up with Simon and your father. And I need to go for… other reasons. I have an idea that'll get us both in there."

24

Plots

SIMON TRIED NOT TO APPEAR as though he were eavesdropping as he listened to Arden speak quickly to Dockett.

"What do you mean?" Dockett asked, glancing at the fighters training around him.

"He was assassinated. They found him dead this morning shortly after breakfast," replied Arden, lowering his voice. "Separately, his brother, the Duke of Farge, Augustine Trevarthen, has fallen gravely ill. Sounds like he was also poisoned."

Dockett fidgeted. "That makes Bellamy Trevarthen the regent and, should his pa not survive, next in line for the throne. Shit…" He looked at Arden. "And they don't know who's behind it?"

Arden glanced at Simon, who had all but stopped running drills, and said, "It's going around that the Council of Ministers is behind it, but no one's got any solid proof."

"With that kid on the throne, the games are doomed," Dockett seethed. "He's a pacificist, too weak-hearted." He motioned to Simon. "He'll never see combat!"

"This *just* happened," Arden argued, drawing Dockett away from the fighters, all of whom had stopped to watch the Lanista. "Let the nobles handle it. We'll deal with the fallout."

"And the kid? Bellamy?" asked Dockett. "What's he up to?"

Arden shrugged. "No one's seen him."

"Shiiittt…" murmured Dockett, running a tense hand through his hair. "King's been murdered weeks before the Munera. When this gets out, we're through."

The Lanista's partner patted his shoulder. "I'll keep my ear to the ground." And then he hurried off.

Returning to his block-and-cut drills, Simon allowed muscle memory to take over and thought about all that seemed to be coming to a head. The Munera, Tarquin's appearance, Kell's yet-to-be-confirmed presence in Eclat, the tension between the Council and the monarchy, and now the assassination of the king along with the attempted murders of the next two people in line. Bellamy most certainly had a target on his back. It was no wonder he had gone into hiding.

Late that afternoon, he caught up with Tarquin in the training yard, pretending to show the older man a few tips. Once others returned to their exercises and drills, Simon turned his back and, still holding the wooden practice sword close to them, spoke to Tarquin.

"I spoke to Kell again last night. She says we're supposed to be thinking of a way to get her in and us out." Simon maneuvered the wooden weapon as if trying to teach Tarquin how to properly block. "I don't think it's going to be possible—"

"Unless she gets arrested and sent here," interrupted Tarquin, trying to mimic Simon's movements in half-hearted attempts.

Simon glanced at him. The thought had occurred to him, but he hadn't wanted to bring it up. "She wouldn't make it here. Few women make it here."

"She doesn't have to stay here for forever." Tarquin sighed. "Look, I've been searchin' for ways to escape—I know you probably did, too, when you first got here—but security's tight right now."

"Then why are you wanting her to get in here with us?" Simon argued. "None of us will be able to get out!"

Tarquin leveled a look at him. "She's a User. If her talkin' to you in your dreams is somethin' she's learned, then I guarantee she's got other tricks up her sleeve. Kell's tough. Always has been."

Simon regarded him, surprised by the man's bold declarations and deep-seated faith in the girl he hadn't seen in years.

Tarquin continued, his huge shoulders glistening from the work he had been doing. "They have to move us for the Munera, right?"

"Yeah. We're transported together and then brought into the basement of the stadium." Seeing where he was going, Simon added, "We're cuffed. All of us. Escaping while on the way isn't an option."

Kell's father nodded. "Then at the actual games is when it will have to happen."

"That's cutting it… close," Simon muttered.

"So, we tell Kell—"

Tarquin stopped. Simon followed his gaze to find Dockett running toward the yard doors with Arden, his hair thrown back. A group of people had appeared in the training yard. From a distance, Simon could only make out three or four men and one woman. While the men wore opulent, navy and black three-piece suits sporting coattails, the woman was dressed in a narrow navy skirt, a white lace blouse with a high collar, and matching satin jacket. A wide-brimmed hat was perched atop her head at an angle.

As a whistle pierced the courtyard, signaling all to line up in attention, Arden sprinted back to the fighters. Simon, whose status allowed him to be as curious as he wanted, asked, "What's going on?"

"The prince is here." Arden glanced over the gathering fighters and then looked back at Simon. "This isn't going to be good."

Simon took his place first in line as Dockett's Champion. He searched for Tarquin and, after spotting him, returned his attention to the group that Dockett led across the courtyard. Once closer, Simon could discern Bellamy. Though dressed in the trappings of incomparable wealth, the prince appeared worn, ragged, and exhausted. His bodyguard, the man with the close-clipped hair, stood just behind Bellamy, his head on a swivel.

"Bow!" Dockett ordered.

As one, the long line of fighters bowed.

"And these are them?" asked an unfamiliar voice. Simon didn't dare peek at the prince's guests.

"Yes, they are," Bellamy replied. "Lord Dockett, may I present my dearest friends from Avives, Lord Mordecai Othonos of the Othonos family and his lovely wife, Lady Kellandry. They've traveled here to watch the Munera. When I mentioned that I knew your Champion, Lady Kellandry immediately asked for a meeting."

"I apologize if my wife's forwardness has interrupted your training," Mordecai kindly offered.

"Nonsense. Simon loves greeting fans," Dockett bubbled. "Simon?"

Simon straightened himself. The young man who had posed the query was tall, though not like Bellamy, and had his mane of dark hair swept back to reveal probing but cautious blue eyes. He appeared close to Bellamy's age and held himself in a similarly stiff posture.

Dockett joined Simon. "This is Simon Ashway, my Champion. He'll be fighting for us in the Munera in two weeks."

"And the mark on his forehead?" asked the young woman accompanying the prince.

Dockett discreetly nudged Simon, encouraging him to provide an answer.

Simon politely looked at her and froze. The face before him was both familiar and foreign, as if the woman had just stepped out of a distant dream to materialize in the physical world.

Kell!

He had glimpsed her in his dreams, but seeing his old friend standing in a sophisticated, ground-dusting dress, her form obviously feminine, struck him dumb. Light makeup colored her cheeks and lips and lined her eyes. She appeared soft, extremely approachable—and vulnerable. A torrent of emotions cascaded through him as he tried to decide how to proceed.

Brows folded upward in worry, Kell approached him, her skirts rustling around her. He could tell she wanted to touch him. "Does it hurt?" she asked.

Simon glanced at Dockett, flustered, and then cleared his throat. "Uh, no, Lady. It's an initiation rite. It marks a fighter as a certain Lanista's Champion. The Users'… uh, Champion is marked on his cheek."

Kell searched his face, resolve settling in her hazel eyes. She turned to Bellamy. "Majesty, could I meet with him in private? Is it possible?" Simon saw her swallow nervously before pulling her hands to her bosom in a most demure way. Her voice climbed into an even more feminine octave. "Oh, please, Majesty."

Bellamy, whose gaze had been on Simon, looked at Dockett. "Would that be permissible, Lanista?"

Dockett fidgeted. "I really don't like my Champion going anywhere unattended."

Kell glanced at Simon and then approached Dockett. Simon looked on in bewilderment; he didn't know this person. He didn't know this Kell.

"Please, Lord. I've traveled so far just to meet your Champion. I've heard so much about him and, admittedly, I've grown… to fancy him." Kell gently took Dockett's large, rough hand and lowered her voice. "I have a token for him but… I do not want to give it to him before everyone. It's too embarrassing. Please, Lord. From an admirer?"

Dockett grinned at Simon. "Perhaps Her Ladyship would like a demonstration of his abilities?"

Kell looked back, not at Simon, but at Bellamy and the dark-haired young man beside him. Simon noted the distinct fear and concern on her face. It was obvious she didn't know what to do.

"Wouldn't that be nice, Lady Kellandry?" prompted Bellamy.

Kell swallowed and turned back to Dockett. "What a lovely offer. That would be wonderful. Oh, do you think before that, I could look over the other fighters? My father-in-law, Lord Othonos, is quite the fan. He would be delighted to receive word of what I saw."

"Is he a betting man?" asked Dockett with a wolfish grin.

Kell chuckled. "He is, actually. Isn't that right, dear?" She peered back at Mordecai.

"Terribly so, I'm afraid," Mordecai replied with a winning smile.

Dockett shuffled uncomfortably but smiled. "I suppose there's no harm."

"Oh, I can't wait to tell my friend Vera!" Kell furtively glanced at Simon to make sure that he caught the name-drop before saying to the Lanista, "Thank you so much. You're too kind." She nodded to Mordecai who followed her down the line of fighters.

"A friend of yours, Majesty?" asked Dockett, turning his attention onto the young prince.

Simon watched Kell, awed by her performance. She was like another pers—He saw Kell step on the front hem of her dress and stumble forward. Mordecai grabbed her arm in time to keep her upright. In an almost comedic fashion, Kell straightened herself, adjusting her skirts before glancing back to see if anyone had seen her clumsiness and unsophisticated recovery. She caught Simon's gaze.

For the first time in years, Simon felt true mirth and amusement swell inside him. *There* was the Kell he had expected to see. She flashed a silly grin and then, holding Mordecai's arm tightly, strolled down the line toward Tarquin.

"So," said Dockett to Bellamy, "How are you holding up? Everyone's been wondering where you were."

Simon's attention turned to the prince whose face was stoic. "My uncle was just assassinated and my father is unlikely to make it through the evening. Please excuse me, I've been preoccupied."

"Then why are you here?" Dockett's voice was superficially friendly.

Bellamy didn't seem to miss it. "Because I am under no illusion as to who runs this country. I wanted to assure people like you and the Council of Ministers that I have no desire to interfere with the upcoming Munera." Simon saw the prince's amber eyes cut down the training yard to where Kell and Mordecai spoke with Tarquin. "It seems as though another fighter has piqued Her Ladyship's interest."

Dockett caught sight of Tarquin and sighed. "She *would* like him. He's hard not to take pity on. Please, excuse me." He gave a short bob and then hurried off to join Kell and Mordecai. All the other fighters, save Simon and now Tarquin, were still bowing.

Sensing someone's eyes on him, Simon found Bellamy studying him. There was something different in them, a kind of recognition that now illuminated their amber depths in a strange way. Bellamy approached Simon, his hands folded behind his back; Marko stayed a step behind him.

"I'm afraid this was my idea," the prince said lowly, turning his face away from the other fighters so his words wouldn't drift. "I've been with Kell and Mordecai for most of the afternoon. Kell was so desperate to get inside, to show you two that she was here..."

"Why are you helping her?" Simon kept his head bowed so as to give the appearance of deference to the noble.

"Because I owe her—and I owe you." Hearing Kell speaking more impassioned than usual, Bellamy sighed. "She's... a handful. Excuse me." He strode off to join the others, leaving Simon alone and away from the line of fighters.

The prince of Berceau owed her *and* Simon? What did that mean? How? Simon shifted his weight back and forth as he saw Kell speak to Dockett and then plea to Bellamy. Though he couldn't discern what was being said, he speculated she was begging the prince to buy Tarquin for her.

As Simon watched pieces of her familiar personality shine through the getup she wore, he remembered what she had said—that she would love to tell her friend Vera of his whereabouts. His mother. So, his mother was alive but not his father?

A twinge of dissonance reverberated through Simon suddenly, causing him abrupt discomfort. Kell was a User; she was the reason his father had been killed. She had caused the Market Fire.

Yet here she was trying to rectify the situation—with the help of the prince no less! What exactly did she hold over Bellamy to compel him to forgo his duties and safety and escort her there?

But it had been the prince's plan, not Kell's. So, what exactly was Bellamy hoping to accomplish by bringing her there?

There were so many what ifs, so many questions... Simon rubbed his chest absent-mindedly as that familiar tightening sensation spread there. Eevie called it anxiety or panic. He drew a long breath to settle himself and waited for their return.

A few minutes later, Dockett led the group back to where Simon waited. Despite recognizing that the Lanista's mood had turned foul, Simon remained silent, impassive. It was not his place to ask about such matters in front of others. Although Kell was struggling to keep her face pleasant, even Simon could discern the fury and frustration that tinted her eyes. She held Mordecai's arm in a death grip and carried the hem of her dress aggressively above her booted feet. Mordecai also seemed perturbed. Bellamy was doing a remarkably good job of maintaining an indifferent expression.

"Simon," Dockett snapped. "Grab, uh..." The Lanista glanced about in search of Arden. Upon spotting his assistant across the yard by the door through which they had come, Dockett waved him over. "It's been a few days since we had a mock battle. Why don't we—"

Simon interrupted him. "Sir, might I recommend something not so," he glanced at Kell, "bloody?" Dockett's eyes flashed at him, causing Simon to bow his head in subjugation. "Just… there's a young lady here. I wouldn't want to… upset her—"

"She's a fan of the games," Dockett replied, his voice warmer than the look in his eyes, "and of you. I'm sure she would appreciate a demonstration of skills from such a highly sought after fighter."

Simon tried to keep the concern from his face. "Just because she's a fan of the games doesn't mean that she's been so close to the, uh, fighting." The look on the Lanista's face made Simon recoil. Still, he continued, "Maybe I can show them—"

"Arden, bring me Esau."

Simon tried once more. "Dockett—"

The Lanista whirled on Simon. Though their relationship was usually amicable and Dockett regularly treated him like a student or a friend, the reality of their affiliation was far more complex. Whatever Kell and Bellamy had said had really upset him. And Simon was just adding to it.

Arden ran off toward the Users' wing while Dockett excused the other fighters, including Tarquin, for supper. As the Lanista spoke to the retiring fighters, Simon looked first at Kell and then Bellamy. He shook his head at the prince. "This isn't…" His chest constricted again. "This isn't going to go well." He started for the barrel of swords. As he passed Bellamy, he said, "Get her out of here. I don't want her to see this…"

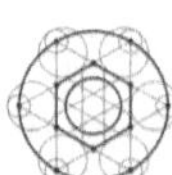

"Kell," said Bellamy, inching toward her. "You don't want to be here to see this. They've gone for a Bound. Dockett plans to have Simon kill him as a show of his skills."

Trembling, Kell watched Simon examine the swords. "Here? In the yard?" she whispered.

The prince nodded. "Simon's hands are tied. He must obey. After all of that with Dockett, I don't want to push our luck."

"If we leave during a demonstration by Dockett's Champion," said Marko softly, the first he had spoken since their arrival, "that's going to look suspicious to the Council of Ministers. Word gets around. I'm sure everyone knows we're here."

"I don't want someone to die because of me," hissed Kell, clenching Mordecai. She had initially needed his strength to ensure she wouldn't trip; now she was using him to keep herself from intervening. "This is stupid."

"We knew this was a possibility," said Bellamy.

"We can't leave," Marko added. "This is just as much a favor to you as it is a stunt for us. The Council must not think we're going to interfere with the games. We have to give our men time to plan and set up."

There was momentary silence between them before Kell concluded, "Then, we stay." The others nodded.

Simon returned carrying a sword. As he drew close, Kell saw Marko ease himself in front of the prince as a precautionary. Simon glanced at Dockett striding back across the courtyard and then at Arden who was returning with Esau. Pretending to show the sword to them, Simon spoke quickly, "Please leave. I don't want you to see this. *Please.*"

Kell's heart quivered at the rawness in his voice. Fortunately, it was Bellamy who replied. "We can't. More is at stake here than you realize. Please pay us no heed. We are aware of what is about to occur."

Simon's face turned pale as his eyes found Kell. "I'm sorry. I'm…"

She managed a pained smile but could otherwise say nothing. Mordecai trapped her cold fingers against his arm in a comforting gesture, but Kell could feel the tension in his hand.

A few minutes later, Esau and Simon faced off with one another. Esau was a short, middle-aged man with a bald spot atop the middle of his head that glowed in the late afternoon sunlight. His wrists were adorned with the tattooed handcuffs of a Bound individual. He wasn't gaunt, but he didn't look healthy. His eyes had dark, heavy bags under them and his skin was sallow. Unlike Simon, whose clothes were well-worn but of good quality, Esau was dressed in pauper's rags.

Kell watched as Simon stepped out of his boots and removed his thin shirt to expose muscled pectorals and strong, hard-cut arms. As he methodically rotated his sword in his hand, warming up his wrist, he kept his gaze off the onlookers.

Kell squinted against the hot setting sun, her heart hammering. A bead of sweat slithered down her neck. How could she stop this? How could she intercede without drawing suspicion to Bellamy or endangering Simon?

Kell startled as she felt a disturbance in the Flow around her. Two burning bands of red materialized around Esau's wrists. Mordecai also shifted uncomfortably as they felt the unevenness with which Esau drew from the Flow. It was a chaotic torrent, a sporadic jerking that left Kell nauseous. Now she understood how Renata and Terin had felt when she had first arrived and why her teacher had made her learn quickly how to create an Arcane Circle.

Esau began circling Simon, palms raised. The caution the man exhibited toward Simon worried Kell. Simon was obviously well-known and well-respected. He was phenomenally toned and light on his feet, as was evident by the quick shuffling he began stepping into.

Esau must have also known this because he did not venture closer.

"Let's go," Dockett called.

Simon glanced at the Lanista and then, his eyes hardening, feigned left and then darted to the right. He crossed the space between them with terrifying speed and slashed at Esau. The shorter man only barely dodged the attack, allowing Simon's sword to hiss through air. Kell felt another shift in the Flow and stifled a gasp as fire erupted from Esau's palms.

She had grown accustomed to seeing controlled fire, flames that moved in intrinsically wrong ways because they were being commanded to do so. The raging conflagration that exploded from Esau scared her into Mordecai's arms. It was unyielding, hot, and out of control.

But that didn't discourage Simon as he rolled under the spiraling flames and came up within killing range of Esau. The middle-aged man whirled just in time, setting off another blast of volatile flames. But Simon was inhumanly fast. He seemed to know what Esau was going to do before the man did it.

Thoughts racing and heart in her throat, Kell tried to come up with some way to stop the fight—to save Esau. She needed to draw everyone's attention from the fight…

Kell squeezed Mordecai's arm and looked up into his eyes. "Catch me," she breathed. Before he could respond, she wilted dramatically against him as she had heard women sometimes did in the heat of the day.

Mordecai cried with some theatrics, "Kellandry!" Holding her, he kneeled in the dirt.

"Stop the fight! Stop the fight!" called Bellamy, going to Kell and Mordecai. "What happened?"

Inside Mordecai's arms, Kell felt the heat of the fire disappear. She tried to keep the relief from her face as Mordecai frantically fanned her. "Call a doctor! Hurry!" His voice was raw. Kell wondered if he knew she was faking it. "Kellandry, dearest. Kellandry." Deciding that he was indeed privy to the ploy, Kell pretended to stir but remained otherwise lax. "It must be the heat. She's drenched," Mordecai continued.

Struggling some under her weight, he stood. Kell tried to hold herself stiffly to make it easier, but gathering someone, especially a young woman as solid as Kell, from the ground was not an easy feat.

Bellamy began unpinning her hat from her hair, his face close to her ear as he searched for the pins. "Keep it up," he murmured, his voice barely discernible.

Mordecai tried to adjust her so she was braced on his chest, but Kell defiantly allowed her head to hang at a precarious and wholly convincing angle. "Where should I go? Please?" he asked of Dockett.

"This way, this way!" called Arden.

Kell kept her eyes closed as they moved her through corridors, up a staircase, and down a carpeted hallway. When her neck began hurting, she pretended to wake, fluttered her eyes at Mordecai, and then limply rested her face against his chest.

She was eventually laid on a soft bed in a cool room with a fan. Momentarily, a woman's voice penetrated the commotion. "Enough, all of you. Let me through, let me through."

"You're a doctor?" asked Mordecai, standing at Kell's bedside.

"I'm Dr. Gray's head nurse. My name is Eevie," replied the woman. "May I ask all the gentlemen to please leave the room?

"I'm her husband," Mordecai quickly offered.

"I'm sorry. Decency requires that the men be out."

"Please, I'm just so, uh, worried."

"She's in good hands, sir. I promise."

Kell heard Mordecai cross the room. At the door, he said, "I'll just be outside should you need me."

"Yes, sir," replied the woman.

Determining it was time to recover, Kell stirred and then moaned slightly. She squinted at the ceiling and then wearily looked at the woman by her bedside.

"Hello, Lady. My name is Eevie. I'm Dr. Gray's head nurse. I see to the patients he is unable to attend to." Eevie's halo of blond hair was curled neatly along her head and revealed old blue eyes and a kind face. "What happened?"

"I… don't know." Kell brushed her head and blinked. "Where am I?"

Eevie touched her forehead and then her neck with a gentle hand. "It's possible you grew too warm outside in the training yard. The fabric you're wearing doesn't breathe well. Let's go ahead and get you out of that jacket, shall we?"

Kell didn't oppose. Lying back in her lacy blouse, she looked about the large room. It appeared to be for guests as it was exquisitely decorated and had quite a few amenities, including a large washing basin.

As Eevie checked her temperature and placed cool cloths on her forehead, Kell reviewed all that had transpired. Had Eevie not been there, she would have been grumbling in disdain. Fainting. What a stupid way to save someone's life.

"I heard you were observing young Simon," Eevie continued, wringing out a washcloth in a small nearby basin. "He's quite the fighter, isn't he?"

"Oh, yes," replied Kell with hollow enthusiasm. "He is, uh, indeed."

Eevie sat back. "Are you starting to feel better? The pink in your cheeks is fading. It looks like you grew overheated. Standing in that sun wearing dark colors will do that to you."

"Yes, well, I'm much more accustomed to the weather in Avives. It's milder there."

"Oh, you're from Avives." Eevie began packing her supplies. "I've heard it's wonderful there. Yes, I'm absolutely certain you're right." She retrieved Mordecai, who feverishly entered the room and rushed to Kell's side as a dutiful husband. "She's fine, just grew a bit too warm. Her collar was soaked with sweat." Eevie bobbed her head. "I'll leave you two alone. Should you need further assistance, please don't hesitate to request my service." She left, allowing Bellamy and Marko to enter. Kell was pleased when no one else was with them.

She sat up. "Did it work?"

Bellamy gave a tired grin. "Yes, it worked. Gave me a fright but yes, it worked." He stood at the foot of her bed. "You're sure you're fine?"

Kell rolled out of bed and stood beside Mordecai. "Yeah, I'm fine." Making sure to keep her voice down, she said, "All right, so what's the plan?"

"The plan?" Bellamy leaned on the bed frame. "We thank Dockett and leave. We've caused more than enough trouble. Simon and Tarquin both know you're here. Now, we leave and reconvene in a few days."

That wasn't what she wanted to hear. "So… I can't meet with Simon?"

"I don't think that's best," interjected Mordecai. She looked at him. "Did you see the Lanista? Simon is fully under his control. I don't want you getting in the middle of that until we have a plan." When Kell frowned, he added, "Simon learned everything he knows from that man. That man is just as deadly, if not more so. We can't go into this carelessly."

It was as if Mordecai had read her mind because she was most certainly ready to bust through the school with Viterra and finish what Renata had started all those years ago. Instead, she reined herself in and sighed. "Fine."

"Stay in here for another half hour," Bellamy said. "I'm going to visit the other two Lanistas to make my presence here seem more official. I'll collect you in an hour."

"Uh, Bellamy?"

The prince looked back at her.

"You're sure… you don't want us with you?" She glanced at Marko. "I know he's… gifted." A flicker of surprise crossed both Bellamy and Marko's face. "But he's only one person. Wouldn't it be safer to stay with us?"

The expression on Bellamy's face softened for the first time that day. "Thanks, Kell, but no. We'll be fine. You two, don't get into trouble." Marko opened the door but stopped in the doorway.

"What?" asked Bellamy, unable to see past him.

Marko stepped aside to reveal Simon, fully clothed. His face was taut with stress and his brows creased in worry. Upon spotting Kell, he nearly leaped into the room.

"I… came to check on her," he told Bellamy. "Docke—Lord Dockett said I could."

Bellamy threw Kell and Mordecai a look and then motioned Simon inside. "One hour," the prince reiterated over his shoulder as the door closed behind them.

25

Ludus Magnus

"IS SHE ALL RIGHT?" SIMON looked at Kell. "Are you all right?"

Kell shrugged. "Yeah, I'm fine."

"But you…" He glanced between Mordecai and Kell, confused. "I saw you…"

With a smirk, Kell said, "Yeah, it was just too hot. I passed out and couldn't watch, so the fight had to end, right?" When Simon didn't return the smile, she asked, "What's wrong?"

"The fight doesn't end just because a spectator fainted." Simon's voice was low. "That's not how showcases, demonstrations, or the Munera work." Kell fell motionless. "I'm standing here before you, not Esau. What do you think that means?"

"You killed him?" she whispered.

Simon glanced at Mordecai and nodded almost nonchalantly.

Kell sat heavily on the bed, her gaze falling to the floor.

"So… all of this was a ruse? The whole fainting thing?" Simon motioned to Mordecai. "I know the prince and his guard dog. Who are you?"

Kell watched as Mordecai crossed the space between them and held out his hand. "I'm Mordecai Othonos, Kell's fiancé."

"You don't have to keep playing; I know the story." Simon looked at Kell. "Who is he?"

She pointed at Mordecai. "Who he says he is."

The expression on Simon's face changed. "You're engaged?"

"Have been for several months now."

"Is it arranged?" he asked her and then Mordecai. "Was it arranged?"

Kell stood. "Arranged by who? By *which* of my parents, Simon?"

Simon ran his eyes over Mordecai before looking back at Kell. "Where the hell have you been?"

"It's a long story and we don't have the time." She joined the two young men. "We're leaving. I tried to have Bellamy buy Tarquin, but Dockett wouldn't budge. He won't sell any of his fighters so close to the games. We have to regroup."

"Oh."

Kell studied his face, the face she had dreamed of countless times. "Sorry for scaring… you." Tears of frustration abruptly filling her eyes, she stepped into Simon and hugged him deeply. "I've missed you so much. I'm so, so sorry. I couldn't…" A sob escaped her. "I couldn't be caught."

Simon's body was hard and his torso far broader than Mordecai's. But he felt like her childhood, like everything good that had ever happened to her. Hesitantly, he embraced her.

"I'm sorry," she cried softly. "Simon, I'm so sorry." She clung to him desperately, allowing the pent-up sorrow, guilt, and shame she had been carrying for years to pour out. Simon held her but didn't say anything. Pressing her face into his chest, she suddenly felt tired and old. "Do you hate me?"

Wiping her tear-streaked cheeks, she drew away to peer up at him. Simons' eyes were moist and red, but his cheeks were dry. When he spoke, his voice cracked. "I did… for a long time." A stray tear escaped his right eye, which he quickly wiped on his shoulder. "But I don't anymore."

She sniffed and suddenly remembering herself cleared her throat and stepped away. She was highly aware of Mordecai. "I'm-I'm really glad to hear that."

Kell saw Simon pass an appraising eye over Mordecai, as if to size him up, and then smiled stiffly. "Was Tarquin surprised?"

"Oh, he didn't recognize me." She played with the hem of her lace sleeve, her happiness fading as she remembered the expression on his face when her father had realized who stood before him. "Simon, I've gotta get him out of here. I can't leave…" She drew a long breath. "He's lost so much weight."

"He could stand to lose some more," Simon replied. Kell frowned deeply at him. "Sorry."

"No, he looks old, Simon. He's fifty-six this year." A spark of rage ignited within Kell. "What's Dockett think he's gonna do with an old man?"

"I got Dockett to bring Tarquin in."

"What?"

"Look, there are fighters and pro-fighters. Fighters are the criminals brought in to be used for training purposes and to eventually act as fodder in the Munera. Had I left him with the others, that would be his fate. Training with the pro-fighters, he gets better food and living conditions and has a chance of surviving."

"For a short while," Mordecai interjected coldly. "Right?"

Simon nodded. "Yeah, for a while."

"But he's not going to make it out of the games."

"Probably not," replied Simon.

Kell fidgeted, her mind racing. She was beside herself. Gytha would have chided her to find her *satt*, not to pursue action. But her impulsive desires compelled her to destroy the school in a magnificent burst of fire. Mordecai and Simon seemed to understand that she was struggling with a course of action and remained quiet.

Finally, begrudgingly, she said, "We'll leave when Bellamy comes back." She met Simon's gaze. "Thank you for taking care of him. I know you have his best interests at heart."

"Uh, yeah…"

Kell wandered past him to the mirror hanging nearby and began tidying her hair which was askew from Bellamy's attempts to unpin her hat. Having some space between the two tall men gave her a moment to breathe. Once her hair was a little neater, she turned to regard them. Mordecai, who had been staring out the western window, smiled tiredly. Simon appeared stoic, impassive. "Right." She retrieved her jacket from the bed and slid it on.

"Is—" Simon stopped as if to rethink his words. Kell looked up from clasping her jacket. "Is your fire stronger than Esau's? Is it…" He shrugged uneasily. "Is it the same?"

Kell exchanged looks with Mordecai before smiling. "It's not at all the same."

"Oh, it's different?"

"Yeah, much different."

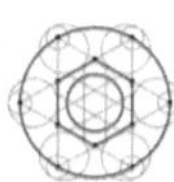

That evening, Simon ate with Tarquin but remained silent and pensive. He was excited by all that had occurred that day and relieved to know that his mother was alive and that Kell was, in fact, in Eclat, but he felt emotionally overwhelmed.

Kell's sudden appearance, the fact that the prince of Berceau was helping her, his killing of Esau, Kell's identity as a User, his father's death, Dockett's fury that—had they been alone—would have been unleashed on

Simon, Kell's engagement, the upcoming Munera and Tarquin's assured death… All of it was too much.

He tried to shake off the tightening in his chest well into the evening hours, pacing his quarters to avoid tears. But all attempts to calm himself were for naught and he sat heavily on his bed, weeping.

When he finally managed to contain himself, he rose and went in search of the one person who had always been emotionally available to him—Eevie. Unsurprisingly, he found her in her office in the infirmary completing paperwork.

"Simon," she said, glancing out the door. "It's late." She met his gaze, studied his face briefly, and then stepped aside to admit him into her office. She had exchanged her usual uniform for an ankle-length skirt and ruffled, powder blue blouse. Her short, wavy blond hair was tucked behind an ear. "What's wrong?" She closed the door behind him.

Simon opened his mouth to reply, but a quiet cry escaped his throat. Ashamed, he turned away, wiping his cheeks. Face burning from embarrassment, he tried to get a hold of himself.

"Hey, hey." Eevie's soft touch on his shoulder drew him back around. "What's going on? What happened?"

"I can't… keep doing this," he finally murmured thickly. "Eevie, I can't." Tears poured down his flushed cheeks faster than he could wipe them away. Clearing his throat, he turned away in humiliation. "Sorry."

"Ah, Simon." Eevie's gentle hands pulled him back. "Come here." She reached up to hug him but had to stand on her tiptoes to reach around his torso. She rubbed his back as he broke down in her arms. "Everything will work out."

Simon shook his head, unable to properly speak, and then sniffed. Although the pungent scent of antiseptic pervaded the room, he could still detect her mild perfume that lingered after a day's work. Eevie's hand slithered between them to caress his stubbly face as she shushed him.

It took Simon a minute or two to collect himself. Once his eyes were dry and his face cleaned with his sleeve, he suddenly became very aware of Eevie. Of how small she was compared to him. Eevie smiled up into his eyes.

Not knowing what he was doing, Simon reluctantly leaned toward her, his heart pounding. He expected Eevie to head him off and draw away. Instead, she stood very still, her eyes searching his before darting to his mouth. Understanding that that was a signal of some kind, Simon slowly, self-consciously, touched her waist and, after a moment's hesitation, pulled her closer.

Eevie's hands rested on his chest as she tilted her face up to his. Having never kissed a woman before, he cautiously pressed his lips to hers. When

Eevie reciprocated, fire rushed through him. He had never felt something so soft, so warm and intoxicating. Eevie caressed his face, running a thumb along his jaw before cupping it and bringing his face more forcefully to hers.

A surprised gasp escaped Simon. His hands clamped around her hips, crushing her against his form as he kissed her with less bumbling. Her body was so much thinner than his, so delicate. Were all women like that? Was Kell like that?

Eevie slipped her tongue between his lips, causing a groan to escape him, and then gently guided him to her desk. She gathered the papers there and then pushed him back onto the furniture. Pleased to do as she wanted, Simon leaned and then sat on the desk as Eevie fit between his legs.

For several long minutes, they kissed and touched. Drunk with lust, Simon put his hands wherever Eevie directed him to, fully infatuated with everything that she was.

"My quarters," she eventually panted, drawing away. "Come on." She straightened her blouse and skirt, both of which were askew, and then pushed her hair into some semblance of order. Simon wiped his lips and tried to hide his excitement as he followed her from the office.

Eevie's quarters were just down the hallway from the infirmary as she was on-call often and needed to be there at a moment's notice. Not a soul was around.

The moment Eevie opened the door to her room, Simon bore her through, gathering her in his arms as he kissed her. Somehow, he managed to close the door. They tumbled into Eevie's unmade bed.

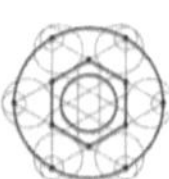

"You're mad," said Kell, sitting on the side of their bed. Bellamy had paid for a nice inn room for them in the Middle District. After a small meal, Kell and Mordecai had retired for the evening.

Mordecai threw his new jacket along the back of the winged chair situated in front of the hearth. "Not mad."

"You've been avoiding me since before dinner."

Mordecai braced his hands on his hips and gazed at the floor. "I don't know, Kell. I… I just don't know."

She watched him. "Is it about Simon?"

He nodded.

She fiddled with the hem of her blouse. When she had hugged Simon, she had felt Mordecai's eyes burrowing into her. "I'm glad we were able to

find him and Tarquin. I don't want either of them there. It makes me so…
angry seeing how Dockett treats them—all of them."

Mordecai paced the room, his brows furrowed. He didn't respond.

Kell stood and went to him, barring his path. "Hey, hey." She took hold
of his arms.

Mordecai jerked away, startling her. With a grimace, he murmured,
"Sorry, sorry." He sighed. "I'm… angry, Kell. I'm angry. And I don't know
why."

Hesitantly, she reached between them and took his hand. "It's the same
way I felt when I saw you with Terin those years ago." He met her gaze.
"Jealousy." She tightened her grip on him. "Mordecai, he's an old friend.
Someone I've been… dreading to meet again. And when I got alone with
him, I crumbled. I-I felt so guilty, so angry with myself, so… ashamed that
he's in this situation." Kell hugged Mordecai. "You're mine. I am yours.
We're a team—"

Mordecai kissed her hard, moving to grip her face with his hands. As
Kell bent to his form, his fingers slid to her hips, holding her tight to him.
She sighed into his mouth in contentment, her body reacting to his
forwardness and possession. Still kissing her, he lifted her from the floor and
deposited her on the bed.

"The clothes," Kell muttered, not wanting to dirty or otherwise harm
the garb Bellamy had purchased for them.

With a groan, Mordecai hurriedly began stripping out of his shirt. Kell,
however, struggled to disrobe and had to eventually have help. Only once
their clothes were off—albeit it on the floor—did Mordecai climb atop her
and remind her that she was engaged to be wed to him.

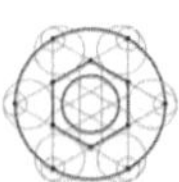

Simon awoke at his usual time prior to dawn. At first, he didn't know
where he was. The ceiling was unfamiliar and the room's scent was feminine-
smelling. In the dim light, he looked at Eevie who was asleep beside him,
naked. Remembering the previous night, he grinned in the darkness and
stretched. The prior day's troubles seemed distant, which suited him just fine.
Quietly, he dressed, glanced once more at Eevie, and then left.

He returned to training as if nothing had happened. He was in the
training yard warming up with the others, his soul and body feeling oddly
rejuvenated. He didn't allow upsetting thoughts to distract him from what
he knew he was good at.

He was fired up and remained that way well past lunch. He saw Dockett briefly after breakfast and almost regretted having argued with him the day prior. But the Lanista had taught him to let go of such things, so Simon did.

He had an amazing afternoon practice, completing drills with deadly precision and speed that even had Ferrik remarking about his prowess. Simon spent little time with Tarquin as he didn't want to be reminded about the stressors that surrounded him. All he wanted to do was focus.

Shortly before supper, he washed up and went to visit Eevie but was told that she was seeing a patient. Disappointed, Simon ate and then retired to his quarters for the evening.

The next day was much the same. He didn't see Dockett at all and so helped Arden train the other pro-fighters, including Tarquin. Just before lunch, Dockett finally made an appearance, striding across the training yard with his blond hair thrown back. Behind him two regulators led a hooded captive bound by iron cuffs.

A whistle sounded, and everyone in the yard stopped what they were doing and fell in around Dockett. Simon eyed the prisoner who was barefooted and had the form of a young woman. The shape of her breasts was visible beneath the thin shirt she wore. He searched the prisoner's wrists and, finding no tattoos, frowned in confusion.

"Simon, Simon!" called Dockett, motioning him over.

Sweaty and dirty from training, Simon passed his sword to Ferrik and approached Dockett, suddenly wary. The Lanista was far too excited.

Dockett swung a friendly arm around Simon's shoulders and looked out at the group. "So, the other day we had royalty in our midst. Yeah, it was real exciting. Couldn't believe it myself." His arm slid off Simon. "Why was the prince here? What on earth would a pacifist like him be doing in the place he hates most?" Dockett began pacing. "He told us some bullshit about the Council." That got some soft laughs from the group. "That he wanted to make sure the Munera went off without a hitch, blah blah…"

Simon glanced at the uniformed regulators, growing increasingly disturbed. When Dockett launched into impassioned rants, it usually meant something big had happened.

"Well, turns out that was only half true. See, he was actually escorting in reactionaries." The Lanista turned to study Simon whose whole body had gone cold.

Simon's gaze slipped to the prisoner once more, his heart beating wildly in his chest.

"Ah, and what's worse, Simon knew about it," said Dockett. All eyes turned to Simon who backed away. "Isn't that right, my Champion?"

"No, I… Dockett, I didn't know—Them showing up…" Simon stammered. "I didn't know they were going to show up like that."

"But you knew them, didn't you?" Dockett didn't allow Simon to respond. "Yesterday morning, after I received this information, I did some investigating and located the prince's partners. And now, just seeing the expression on your face, Simon, I know that everything my source told me was, in fact, true. Because," Dockett approached the prisoner, "my guess is, you know who is under here, don't you?"

The Lanista jerked off the burlap hood to reveal Kell. Her brown, shoulder-length hair was in disarray, and a nasty cut that decorated her left cheekbone bled sluggishly down her jaw. Wrath darkened her eyes.

Simon froze, torn between collapsing to the dirt and leaping upon Dockett with blind rage.

"A childhood friend, huh?" asked the Lanista.

At that moment, Simon knew who had betrayed him—Eevie. Cursing, he turned away, finding it difficult to swallow. He had tried to be as ambiguous as possible as he had talked with Eevie long into the night, but he should have known. Eevie was smart, and Dockett was smarter.

"So now she's here, Simon. And you know what's going to happen? We're going to work her until she breaks." The Lanista approached Simon, gathering his authority like a cloak. "And then, I'm going to throw her into the ring, and you and I are going to watch her be murdered for the viewing pleasure of the masses."

Simon lunged at Dockett but was interrupted by a force like a charging bull. He and Ferrik rolled in the ground briefly before Simon twisted his mentor into a powerful hold. "I will kill him," Simon declared, his voice strangled. "If you don't let her go now, I will kill him, and you damn well know I will."

Dockett considered him for a moment and then shrugged. "Eh, gotta do what you gotta do." The Lanista turned on Kell.

"Stop," Simon commanded. He released Ferrik, who remained prone nursing his shoulder, and then stood. "Dockett, stop."

Dockett leaned forward to gaze into Kell's eyes. "Traitorous bitch."

To Simon's horror, Kell spat at him. Dockett glowered at her momentarily before wrenching a hand back. Simon was on his feet, but knew he wouldn't be able to get there in time. From somewhere outside his periphery, he glimpsed a large shape moving fast. It took him a split second to recognize Tarquin.

Kell's father grabbed the Lanista's arm midair, halting the attack.

Unmoving, Dockett looked at him. "What are you doing?" His voice was low and dangerous.

"It's a girl," Tarquin said. "Who's cuffed. You manhandle a girl like that, she'll break before you can use her. Punish Simon."

The Lanista jerked his arm from Tarquin's grasp, his gaze returning to Kell. "Sure." He nodded to the regulators who uncuffed Kell. The Lanista gripped her hard, his knuckles turning white on her shoulder. Kell didn't so much as whimper. "Since she was so eager to buy you the other day, I think it's only fittin' that you return the courtesy. She's yours now, Fisk. She fucks up, you fuck up." He shoved Kell into Tarquin who caught her and then motioned to Simon. "And you, you will be sparrin' with her, daily. Doesn't matter that she's a woman, doesn't matter that she doesn't know jackshit about combat. You will fight her and you will make sure that she leaves your care bloody." Dockett whirled on the other fighters. "And if any of you so much as help her to her feet, I'll flog you. All of you. I'm tired of this bullshit! We are too close to the Munera to be fuckin' around like this! Now fuckin' get back to work!"

And with that, Dockett stormed off.

Simon fidgeted, his eyes darting from the other fighters to Kell to Tarquin and then, finally, to Ferrik. Realizing that he had threatened his mentor, the man who had taught him for years, Simon sheepishly approached him.

The dark-skinned man, still favoring his shoulder, passed a cursory glance over him and then walked off. "Ferrik," Simon called in defeat. But his mentor didn't look back at him.

Simon set his gaze on Tarquin, who was examining Kell's cheek. Realizing that he no longer had a need to keep his affiliation with Kell and Tarquin secret, he shuffled over to them. He opened his mouth to apologize but couldn't make himself utter a sound. He felt so old, so weary, and so defeated.

Kell reached through the space between them and tagged his shoulder with a surprisingly solid fist. "Don't worry." She tried to smile but only winced. "I'm toughed than I look." She glanced at Tarquin. "And now we're here."

"We?" asked her father.

"He got Mordecai too." Kell surveyed the training yard, oblivious to the state of her attire.

Simon glanced down at her visible cleavage and then out at the other fighters. Of the now forty-two pro-fighters, four were women, including Kell. He didn't like the idea of her sleeping in a dorm with all men. Simon was a Champion; he and Ferrik and a handful of others had earned private rooms. Kell would be bunking with the remaining fighters, including Tarquin.

"Kellick, this… isn't going to be easy," muttered her father. "Dockett is cruel, ruthless."

Kell nodded, gingerly exploring her cheek. "Yeah, I can see that."

Simon watched her, his brows furrowing in frustration and irritation. "Why are you not more upset about all of this?"

"Because I can start to figure out how to get you two *out*." Kell met his gaze. "I'll play the game—until I won't."

Something in her voice and the way she held herself made Simon whole-heartedly believe her.

26

Duel

KELL WASN'T PERMITTED TO VISIT the infirmary to have her cheek sutured. So she resorted to cleaning it with potable water. As the others left the training yard to break for lunch, Dockett's assistant, Arden, intercepted Kell, Simon, and Tarquin.

"Go run," he told Kell. "Five laps around the yard. No food or water today."

"Come on, Arden," Simon argued, stepping between him and Kell. "That's not fair—"

"And you, mind your goddamn business." With a fierce shove, Arden ushered Simon onward. "Get to lunch. Fisk, if she doesn't make the laps, you will run them for her." Tarquin only glanced at Kell. Arden pointed across the enormous yard. "Get to it. I'll be watching. Don't cut corners."

Kell exchanged looks with Simon and then turned and walked across the vast courtyard. When she found the path of packed dirt where others had tread, she set into a jog. Glad to be away from everyone, she ran the perimeter of the training yard, setting herself to focus first on the task at hand.

The ambush had been quick, but they had sensed it coming, as the inn at which Bellamy had housed them was made of ancient timber. Upon hearing the heavy footsteps reverberating up the staircase, Kell and Mordecai had prepared for the worst. She had not been surprised to see Dockett, but she had been shocked by how his accompanying men had handled her. She and Mordecai had agreed in advance not to use any Viterra or otherwise expose their skills and learning. That needed to be kept a secret until a moment of dire circumstances.

Kell ran her laps with relative ease before stopping near Arden slightly winded. Her skin crawled when Dockett's assistant ran his eyes languorously over her body.

"I said run," Arden scoffed after a moment. "Not jog. Go run them again."

"It's called setting a pace," Kell countered before she could stop herself.

Arden's fierce blow to the side of her head was fast and caused Kell to stagger to the left and then collapse to her knees. Her field of vision narrowed and her head pounded. Blinking, she held fast to the hot dirt until the world stopped spinning.

Arden grabbed her by her arm and lifted her from the ground. Sight returning, Kell glowered at him, murder swelling within her. "Talk to me like that again, woman, and you won't make it from this courtyard for the evening."

It took everything in Kell's power to keep her mouth closed.

Arden threw her to the ground. "Get up and run."

Kell dragged her feet under her, passed Arden a look, and then started running. She maintained an uncomfortably fast pace, but took the time to think about how easily she could torch Arden, how quickly she could bury him in the earth and smother him, how effectively she could suck the air from his lungs. The dark fantasies gave her great pleasure.

By the time she finished, fighters were returning from lunch. Kell passed Simon as he reentered the training yard. Though she caught his gaze briefly, she kept running, keeping her pace through the final lap. When she finally pulled even with Arden and Tarquin, panting, she folded over her knees.

Arden, however, was not a fan of allowing her to catch her breath and kicked her. Kell's legs collapsed under her. Unable to keep her temper in check, she screamed, "Touch me again and see what happens!"

Everyone in the courtyard came to a standstill; hundreds of eyes turned onto her. Snarling, Kell got to her feet and began dusting the dirt off her arms. She sensed movement from Arden, a change in the Flow of energy around her, and turned on the ball of her foot. Her stance wide and hands poised, she ducked under his groping arm, hooked her shoulder under his, and leveraged him over her. Having only practiced with Mordecai, Arden's weight was a frustrating surprise.

Though the action wasn't as smooth as she wanted, it had the desired effect. Arden crashed to the dirt with a yelp. Kell swung around, legs set in the base position for earth and metal traits and hands held before her. Renata hadn't taught them combat per se, but she had drilled into them that all the elemental traits were based off of martial arts and required certain indistinguishable skills. Balance, power, litheness, and an ability to read an opponent were vital to the control of Viterra. Sinewy strength helped create motion and direction and give purpose to energy. If Viterra was removed, all that remained was a variety of martial arts skills. She wouldn't want to be pitted against a trained fighter, but for the unsuspecting, she could put up a decent fight.

Arden's anger seemed to have been startled out of him. He stood, his eyes on her. "Where'd you learn to do that?"

"Doesn't matter, does it?" Kell replied.

Arden shrugged and then started across the training yard. "We're moving to weights. Let's go."

Kell relaxed. Straightening her shirt, she glanced at Tarquin. Her father drew close, his face grave. "That's not going to go unpunished," he murmured.

Kell followed Arden. "I know."

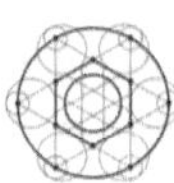

Simon did his best to ignore Kell and focus on his own training, but Ferrik refused to spar with him and many of the other fighters ignored him. Finally settling on something he could do by himself—conditioning—and having nothing else to look at as he did bucket squats, he watched Kell.

Though she struggled with the weights, especially since Arden made her lift twice and three times her body weight, Simon could discern that she was in remarkable shape. Her arms, which had been previously hidden by a lace blouse and jacket, were toned and strong. She didn't have rippling muscles, but it was apparent that she had been busy over the past several years.

She exceled at endurance and was light on her feet which became apparent when Arden made her run another ten laps for a snide comment. Simon noted with some amusement that since her earlier outburst, Arden had refrained from touching her again. He was certain Dockett would not be so amenable.

Arden worked her hard for the rest of the afternoon until the Lanista returned, calling to Simon. Suspecting what was to come, Simon steeled himself. "Get yourself and the young lady practice swords. I want a sparring match right now."

"She doesn't know how to hold a sword," Simon replied even as he turned to obey.

Dockett grabbed him. "Did I ask for your opinion? No. Now, get a damn dummy and break her."

Simon jerked his arm from the Lanista's strong grip and retrieved two wooden swords from a nearby barrel.

"Listen up!" called Dockett. The fighters, bearing varying degrees of sweat and dirt, gathered around him. "Simon here is going to show our newest fighter proper swordsmanship. Should anyone decide to intervene, I'll kill you where you stand."

Brandishing two wooden swords, Simon crossed the space that had formed by the ring of fighters and held out the dummy. Kell was just as sweaty and looked worse for the wear. Having had no food or water all afternoon, he could tell she was exhausted.

She wiped her forehead with the back of her arm and took the sword. She examined it for a moment and then tossed it into the dirt. "Kell," Simon muttered, pleading with his eyes, hoping she would understand that if she didn't pick the weapon up, she would be left defenseless. Kell only glanced at Simon before meeting Dockett's icy gaze.

"Don't want a weapon?" The Lanista shrugged. "That's fine." He approached Simon and prodded him. "Break. Her. Am I understood?" Simon shakily nodded. Dockett stepped out of the ring, squinting against the sun. "First one to the ground loses. No food or water until tomorrow morning. Let's go!"

Simon morosely regarded Kell. Compared to the men around them, she was small, as though she could be lost to a gust of wind. But the look in her eyes was frightening. She glanced at Simon in intervals as she leveled a malevolent glare at Dockett.

"I said, let's go!" the Lanista repeated with a clap of his hands.

Simon swung into stance two—sword reared back close to the body, left arm forward, and legs spread—in preparation to launch an attack. He was alarmed to see Kell move into a poised posture, her right leg forward and hands angled, sharp and strong. Her shoulders were cocked slightly and, to Simon, it appeared that she had every intention of fighting him.

He darted forward. Kell didn't move. She watched until the last moment when he brought the dummy sword over his head to strike her shoulder. She rotated out of the way, bending sharply to avoid the attack, and then swept a leg forward, connecting her knee to his left hip.

Pain blossomed there, and Simon snarled as he staggered to the side. The power behind her strike was alarming. Murmurs spread throughout the group, spurring Simon to collect himself. He may have fallen out of Dockett's good graces, but he was still Champion. Yet he didn't want to seriously harm Kell. The disparity in their strength, weight, and height was dangerous.

With speed, Simon whirled on her. When she dodged his first swipe, he dropped to a knee, spun around, and smashed the dummy into her left leg. The force of his blow threw her several paces, and she tumbled into the dirt. Simon stood, silently hope she was uninjured. He hadn't used his full strength, yet he had sent her flying.

Panting and hands noticeably trembling, Kell rose to her knees and then struggled to her feet. Her hair, which she had tied in a knot earlier in the afternoon, had come loose and stuck to her skin. Her face was grimy, and she didn't put her full weight on her left leg. But the fierceness and determination in her gaze was awe-inspiring and forced Simon to look at Dockett for direction.

The Lanista appeared intrigued, impressed even, as he stood there with his arms folded across his broad chest. He scrutinized Kell. "Where'd you study?" he finally asked.

Kell's gaze shifted to him.

"You've obviously been taught combat. Where'd you study?"

"I'm not telling… a piece of shit like you anything," Kell panted, gingerly shifting more weight to her injured leg.

Dockett pursed his lips and then jerked his head at Simon.

Grimly, Simon moved to stance four—a two-handed hold. He tried to force Kell to circle with him, but she resisted. Instead, she took a long breath and, moving her injured leg back, settled into a narrower posture, her hands steady in front of her but not in typical combat positions. She held them delicately, demurely even, as though she were preparing to pet a small, soft animal.

Simon considered where best to hit her to cause the least amount of damage. A strike to one of the arms would be good. Her injured leg was also an option. He wanted to avoid joints or vital organs.

Deciding he was going to go for an arm, he drew closer, sword at the ready. He held her gaze for a long moment and then lunged, bringing the sword down. At the last second, he altered its path and swung from the left. Kell seemed to know what he was doing because she had already started to step aside. She sideswept his weapon and then, pivoting, rammed an elbow into his chest as his momentum carried him past her.

Simon felt the air leave him but didn't stop. With more power than he intended to use, he struck Kell, taking her to the ground with him. Wheezing audibly in the dirt, he could feel Kell struggling under his weight—and wheezing. Simon rolled off her, still trying to find his own breath, and sat up. Kell lay on the ground, sobbing. Her injured leg shook horribly as she grasped the dirt between her fingers. Face flushed and hot tears streaking down dirty cheeks, she appeared entirely defeated.

Distantly remembering that this was a fight, he pulled his feet under him and stood over her. Kell laid a trembling arm over her eyes as new, fevered cries bubbled from her throat. Simon felt his heart break, her raw sobs opening a black chasm within him. He would never be the same.

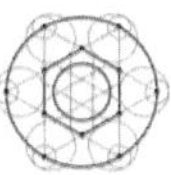

Lying in bed that night in the pro-fighters' communal dorm, Kell struggled to find her *satt*. She replayed her match with Simon again and again in her mind. Each time he struck her, a part of her childhood vanished. The power in his attacks was frightening and shook her to the core, yet she was positive he hadn't been using even half his strength.

All of her memories of them roughhousing on the docks had been replaced by one brutal fight. The strength in his arms, the speed in his gait and attacks, the power in his blows—she didn't know this person, and she didn't *want* to know this person.

She reached down and gently stroked her injured leg. It wasn't broken or fractured, but a vast purple and red bruise had begun to take form. Her skin there burned, and any time she put weight on it, she nearly screamed. She was sore from the tortuous training Arden had put her through and her back hurt from where Simon had collided with her, but none of that had made her break down in front of all those fighters.

A deep-rooted fear of Simon had commandeered her senses. She loved him and would always want what was best for him, but she didn't want to be near him. She didn't want to even look at him for the distress that he evoked in her.

She had matured next to Mordecai, who had always been sensitive, thoughtful, and introspective. She had grown accustomed to the strength, comfort, and stability he provided—and had perhaps taken it for granted. Mordecai was straightforward and direct, tender and thoughtful. He could be cunning and frequently came up with creative solutions to problems that could have been solved by more mundane responses. How he utilized Viterra often surprised and inspired her.

Comparing him to Simon made her viscerally disgusted.

Tarquin's form appeared at her bedside. Kneeling, he rested a hand on her arm. "You hurting?"

She glanced at the occupied beds around her. The room was long, boasting several dozen bunkbeds, and dim. Only a few dim lamps flickered. She shrugged. "Not too bad."

Tarquin seemed to understand. He looked over his shoulder at the others and then slid his hand under her rough bedsheet. Kell felt him press a bread roll into her palm. Kell smiled warmly; she would eat it in a little while.

A thought occurring to her, she leaned closer to him and spoke into his ear. "If I start talking in my sleep, wake me up." She met his gaze. "It's important. Don't let me keep talking. I might… reveal things."

Tarquin patted her. "Do you want me to try to get water?"

Kell turned, shielding her hand with her shoulder, and opened her palm. Water materialized there to glisten in the dim lamp light. Tarquin's eyes grew wide. With a tight squeeze of her fist, the water vanished. "I've been drinking all day."

"And food?" he whispered.

Furtively, Kell lifted her bed sheet to reveal tiny green vines growing from the hay of her mattress. She touched one to show him a pink strawberry. She pointed to another and mouthed the word "potato" to him.

Her father's mouth fell open briefly before he leaned forward and hugged her hard. The safety she felt within his enormous, familiar arms softened her heart considerably and did wonders for her spirit.

"I'm Unbound," she whispered into his bearded jaw.

Tarquin nodded and kissed the side of her head.

27

Threats and Consequences

AFTER EATING TWO POTATOES, WHICH she heated in her hands and ate under the sheets, and a variety of fruits and vegetables that she conjured into existence, she slept.

In her dreams, Kell crossed the courtyard, passed through the opposite building, circled the next training yard, and entered the partially underground prison where Mordecai and the other Users were kept. Following her instinct, she passed through the prison's metal door and wandered down the cold, cobblestone aisle to a cell.

She stood outside the wrought-iron door, her lips pursed, before stepping into it. Mordecai slept alone on a pile of hay. He had a ratty blanket under his head, that was it.

Kell lay beside him and stroked his face. When he stirred, she leaned forward and kissed his cheek. "You hurt?" she whispered.

"Not too bad. You?"

She thought about hiding everything from him, but they had shared too much pain over the years. "Simon hurt me pretty bad this afternoon. He... scared me."

"I'll kill him."

Though Kell relished hearing Mordecai's murmured threats, she fought to remain fair. "He didn't have a choice."

Mordecai snuggled closer, sighing into her. "What's the plan here? The games are in a week."

"I don't know… that I can make it that long," Kell muttered, touching his hair. She grinned. "I've pissed off too many people."

"What happened to *satt*?"

She scoffed. "Oh, that?"

Mordecai grew grim. "Find it, Kell. Keep it close."

"I'm trying. All of this is—"

Kell was jerked awake. On edge from the day's events, she very nearly reached for Viterra. Only when she recognized the large, rough hand as Tarquin's did she relax within his grasp.

"You were talking," he murmured.

"Thanks." Kell winced as her leg throbbed.

Tarquin patted her shoulder before returning to his bed nearby. Kell settled back. Worried that she had left Mordecai fretting, she urged herself to return to him in her dreams. But sleep eluded her, and she remained awake for hours.

The following morning, Kell could hardly walk. Her leg ached fiercely and her back was stiff. Limping, she joined the pro-fighters in the mess hall. She ate breakfast in silence with Tarquin, watching the others like a hawk. When Simon entered, she glanced at him and then returned to her meal. A few minutes later, he joined them.

Kell drank the rest of her stew, shoveled a semi-cooked egg down her gullet, and then hobbled off. She didn't have the composure to face him so soon.

Dockett visited immediately after breakfast to review all the damage he had done the previous day. Kell made sure to hide her limp as much as she could when she sensed his gaze on her. But when her injured leg gave out as she struggled with an oversized weight, her weakness was revealed. Dockett grinned widely and strolled over, his lanky arms swinging in time with his gait.

"Good morning," he beamed. "How are we this morning? Feeling good from breakfast?"

Sweating from the pain, Kell ignored him as she gathered herself. That was the wrong answer.

Dockett snarled a hand in her shirt and jerked her to him. Though she clasped his arms to better control her body, she could do nothing about the strength discrepancy between them. The Lanista searched her eyes and then let his gaze drift downward to her bare breasts which were now exposed. Kell fought the impulse to knee his crotch.

With a satisfied look, he released her and watched with predatory intent as she as the majority of her weight shifted to her injured leg. "Yeah, I'll break you. One way or another." He looked her over again. "What'd the prince call you? Killdry? Eh, doesn't matter. I'll break you. And then I'll watch Users kill you in the ring."

He liked power, Dockett did. He had access to young, easily influenced men and women. If he played it right, he could control them with fear, abuse, and threats. He was a more overt version of Father Legotis. Physical pain was how he garnered respect and maintained control.

"Can I get back to training, sir?" asked Kell flatly.

"Yeah, go do laps."

Kell crossed the training yard, hiding her limp with all the discipline she could muster. There was no way she could run laps; she could hardly bend her leg correctly. But she had to give the illusion that she was unbothered.

When she found the worn path along the perimeter of the training yard, she began to jog. Within two steps, her leg gave out again, crumpling beneath her. Kell tumbled forward, crashing to her knees in the hot dirt. Growling in frustration and humiliation, she pushed herself upright, gathered her feet under her, and then tried again, tightening her quads to give her aching leg stability. It helped some, but she had to stop after a dozen paces.

Panting, she glanced at Dockett who stood in the middle of the yard, arms folded and eyes set on her. Unwilling to give him the satisfaction of seeing her fall again, she acted as though she were adjusting her tattered hemline. Inside her pants leg, she forced a long, rigid vine to slither up to her thigh. As she stood, she placed her hand on her hips to continue drawing the stiff vegetation around her thigh. With precise finger movements, she wrapped it around her hip to give it support. When she next stepped forward, she found the pain still present but more controlled. She silently thanked Gytha and then tried jogging again.

It wasn't a pleasant experience, but she was able to lope around the track with some dignity. Eventually, Dockett lost interest in her and wandered off.

After four laps, Kell collapsed in the dirt on the far end of the training yard, wheezing. She was not in poor physical condition, but forcing anyone to exert that amount of physical energy was absurd. Of course, she reminded herself, Dockett and Arden weren't training her for their benefit.

Kell flopped a hand over her mouth and furtively gulped water. She tried not to imagine Mordecai and the odds he faced. While she could use small amounts of Viterra without the use of an Arcane Circle, thanks to Gytha's teachings, Mordecai couldn't—and would never be able to. How he was managing without food or constant water, she didn't know. But he was smart. He would figure something out.

Sensing a change in the air around her, she relaxed and peered up at a dark-skinned man approaching her. She recognized him from her interactions with Simon. His name was Ferrik.

Kell sat up to warily watch him. Ferrik was tall with beautiful black skin that glistened in the high sun. His eyes were just as dark, intelligent, and calculating. Like many of the fighters there, he wore nothing but pants to reveal chiseled abs and hardened shoulders.

"What?" Kell asked, placing her palm on the ground beside her. If he was going to attack her per Dockett's command, she would be ready.

To her surprise, he extended a large hand. Kell eyed him. "Come on," he said.

Kell hesitantly took it, and he pulled her to her feet.

"What's your name?"

"Kell. You?"

"Ferrik." He circled her once. When he reached to feel her arm, she jerked away. "You've trained. Where?"

"I didn't tell Dockett. Why would I tell you?" she countered evenly.

Ferrik's gaze was probing. "Because I'm his Champion's Dagger and because I can make your life a lot easier here."

She didn't know what the purpose of a Champion's Dagger was, nor could she speculate. All she had seen was Ferrik tackle Simon to the ground and Simon threaten to kill him. Their relationship didn't seem amicable. When she didn't answer, Ferrik pivoted in his questioning.

"You're... Simon's friend? A childhood friend?"

"Yeah. We grew up together." She glanced across the yard at Simon who was showing another fighter a series of steps with a dummy sword. She had to admit, he was quite graceful. It was as though he had been created for the sport.

"Along the docks?"

Kell looked back at Ferrik. "Don't lump me and Simon in together. He's been here for the past four years. I have not." Kell straightened her dirty clothes. "If you wanna do something, keep the other men off me. I don't have the time or mental energy to be gettin' pregnant." Hiding her limp, she walked off.

At lunch, Simon attempted to sit with her again. Just as she rose to leave, Arden called to her. Scarfing down the rest of her meal as she walked, she joined him outside. "We're going to the infirmary," the Lanista's assistant said.

Kell hesitated. "Why?"

"Ferrik said you needed it."

She glanced back at the dark-skinned man but didn't let any emotion show on her face. "I'll manage."

"That's not what he said. Come on."

Not wanting to cause another scene, she followed Arden across the training yard to the main building. After passing through some winding corridors, he escorted her into the infirmary. Rows of tables crowded the open space. A narrow hallway led to examine rooms.

"Eevie!" called Arden.

Momentarily, a blond in her late twenties appeared from an adjacent office. "Yes, sir?"

Arden nudged Kell forward. "I have a patient for you."

Eevie appeared bemused. "A… young woman…" She frowned, glanced at Arden, and then cleared her throat uncomfortably. "Lady Othonos, was it? How did—"

"Long story," interrupted Arden. "Look, young Simon gave her a thrashing. She's been limping pretty good."

"Oh, no," Eevie hummed awkwardly. She guided Kell into a private exam room and politely told Arden to wait outside. As the blond flitted about, Kell quickly removed the vine supports she had been using. Once she had her supplies, Eevie closed the door. "What… happened to your leg?"

Noting Eevie's discomfort, Kell said, "Got hit by a wooden sword."

"Uh-huh. And which leg is it?"

Kell pointed to her left leg.

"And you've a nasty cut across your cheek there. We'll get both taken care of. If you would, please undress."

As Eevie busied herself with antiseptics and whatnot, Kell slipped out of her pants. When the nurse caught sight of the injury, she gave a small gasp. Kell regarded the injury with mild interest. The bruise, which had spread, was wider than the span of both her hands and boasted a rainbow of vibrant, sickly colors.

Eevie reined in her reaction and then took a cloth and washed it and her cheek with some acrid-smelling liquid. Kell grimaced. Her skin hurt where Eevie touched.

"Can you put weight on the leg?"

"Some," replied Kell.

"I'm going to examine it now," Eevie continued. "Let me know if it hurts too much." She began prodding at Kell's limb, squeezing it and manipulating the muscle under her fingers until Kell whimpered. "Well, the good news is that nothing is broken. Unfortunately, there's not much I can do other than give you some pain medication. Something to dull the pain."

"Thanks," Kell muttered, putting her pants back on.

"Allow me to retrieve the medicine. I'll be right back." Eevie hurried from the room.

The nurse was far too nervous. The air around her was tense. How did she tie into everything? What was she hiding?

That afternoon, Kell hoped Dockett wouldn't make her spar with Simon again, but that was wistful thinking. She had seen how he had watched her throughout the day. He was out for blood.

"Let's go!" the Lanista called from along the ring of grim fighters.

Kell met Simon's gaze for the first time that day, and fear surged within her. Behind that familiar face was ungodly strength, cat-like reflexes, and limitless skill. He was twice her weight and as much as four times her strength. What did Dockett hope to—Kell knew the answer to that before she finished thinking it.

The fight was quick. She lost. All Simon had to do was aim for her injured leg. Though, he didn't use much power, the blow still crippled Kell, sending her to the ground panting and shaking. But she didn't cry. She had already mourned the fracturing of their relationship. She wouldn't give Dockett or the others the satisfaction of seeing that weakness again.

When Tarquin tried to help her back to the dorm, Dockett called him away, forcing Kell to limp across the training yard by herself.

She took a bucket bath that night behind a sheet which Tarquin held for her. She heated the water and washed her hair and body before drawing hot water into her palms and running it down her leg in a continuous loop of Viterra. It was heavenly. Once dry and dressed in the meager clothes she had been allotted, she rolled over and grew strands of creeping milk tassel in the hay under her blankets, something she remembered Renata doing the previous year.

Once the thin, spindly vines had risen around her arm, she tore the leaves off, dampened and then heated them, and then layered them on her wounded leg. The relief was instant, and she was able to sleep that night.

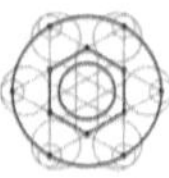

Simon sat on the edge of his bed, his heart murderous. Dockett's change in demeanor infuriated and confused him. How he treated and humiliated Kell shook Simon to his core, stirred black rage within him. On top of that, he was irate with Eevie.

Thoughts racing and heart thrumming in his ears, Simon rose and left his room. Striding down the hall, he whipped his anger onto his shoulders and allowed its weight to urge him onward. Although he passed numerous armed guards and regulators on nightshift, none paid him any heed as they knew he was a Champion. Somehow, he ended up in the infirmary. He checked the exam rooms and Eevie's office and, not finding her, stalked down the hall to her quarters.

Staring at the floor, he rapped on her door. There was movement from inside and Eevie called, "One moment."

Simon tried to control himself but was unsuccessful, for as soon as Eevie opened the door, he snapped it out of her hands. He pushed her back into her quarters, grabbed the door, and closed it.

"Simon," Eevie hissed, backing away. She was dressed in a modest, black night robe that boasted a gold clasp.

The door had barely clicked closed before Simon stormed across the room and grabbed her by the throat. "I trusted you!"

Holding onto his arm, Eevie struggled in his grasp. "I don't… I don't know what you're talking about."

Simon lifted her from the floor and threw her onto her bed. Eevie squealed in terror as he pinned her there. "You told Dockett about Kell! You told him—Do you know what you've *done*?"

Eevie's face shifted from fear to resolve, and she tilted her chin upward in defiance. "Yes, I told him."

Simon reared back to hit her but caught himself. With a roar of fury, he leaped off her and paced the room in a black rage, kicking her bureau as he passed. The leg of the luxurious furniture snapped off. Tears burning his eyes, he turned to glower at her. Eevie was perched on the side of her bed. "I trusted you… Eevie."

"You represent money, Simon. Dockett has staked his career on you. You've lasted longer than anyone else; you've done more than anyone else—"

"But you were always… taking care of me."

"Because you are money. I gave you what you needed." She smoothed the hem of her robe. "Dockett and I are partners. I make sure his fighters remain physically and mentally healthy. He does the rest. Every nurse in the infirmary is assigned a Lanista. Dr. Gray oversees everyone."

"But you—We slept—"

"I gave you what you needed." She rose and walked across the room to the door. "Now, get out. I know you were raised along the docks and in Dockett's care, but storming into a woman's private quarters, especially at night, is the height of poor decorum."

His fury ebbing, Simon trudged across the room. Eevie quietly opened the door. As he crossed the threshold, she gave him a scolding shove, ushering him into the hallway. The door clicked behind him.

Tears sliding down his cheeks and heart sinking, Simon stared at the floor. He had just attacked a woman. What was he becoming?

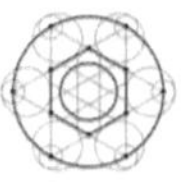

Kell didn't see Simon the next morning. Others seemed to miss him as well, but no one asked Arden or Dockett his whereabouts. Kell went through "training" by running more laps and doing weights before lunch. Her clever use of herbs from the previous night had greatly reduced the pain in her leg. Though it was still not pleasant to walk on, she could more easily hide her limp.

After lunch, she allowed Ferrik to teach her basic blocking exercises. Kell felt awfully clumsy with the dummy sword but tried so as to better understand pro-fighters' movements. Afterward, she joined the others to complete falling drills which, she quickly discovered, she did not like to do with an injured leg. Terin had worked with her and Mordecai for a summer, teaching them how to properly fall, but her techniques didn't seem to apply to the fighting styles Ferrik and the others utilized.

Late afternoon, a hush fell over the fighters. Kell, who was cooling off with Tarquin, spun around, alarmed by the sudden silence. Her eyes found Simon who stood beside Dockett, shirtless. He looked utterly defeated. His face was sweat streaked and filthy; his breathing was ragged; and the look in his eyes was distant.

"I want this," called Dockett, leaving Simon's side to pace in front of the fighters, "to be a wakeup call for some of you. I told each of you when you first arrived that we would be leaving weakness behind—mental weakness, physical weakness, character weakness. So, when I find residual, uh, deficiency, I'm going to beat it out of you. Or, in Simon's case, flog it out of you."

With a gasp of horror, Kell left the safety of the group and approached Simon. She felt Dockett's eyes on her.

"Simon here decided to exhibit some of that weakness last night, and he was punished for it," the Lanista continued.

As Kell drew near, she tried to connect with Simon, but his gaze was set across the yard. Steeling herself, she circled him. His back bore numerous raised abrasions that varied in color. Some leaked rivulets of blood while others appeared hot and angry. She couldn't count the number of lashes. Fingers trembling, she reached for his hand in utter horror but couldn't bring herself to cause him any more pain.

Settling herself at Simon's side, Kell turned to meet Dockett's gaze. The Lanista appeared amused, intrigued even. "I'll… kill you," Kell avowed. The silence around them deepened. Not a single body stirred. No longer aware of her injury, she approached Dockett, her eyes on his. "It won't be now. It won't even be tomorrow." She stopped in front of him, her body tight like a coil. Her fingers itched and burned. "But I'll kill you. And when I do, I want you to remember, in your final moments, my face."

Dockett's expression darkened. "Do you also want to be flogged? Because that can be arranged."

"You rose to your station because you are cruel, because you are brutal. You take," she motioned to Simon, "children, who are easily influenced, who can be manipulated, and you teach them how to kill. You control through fear, through pain, through-through torture! You leverage your reputation, your power, your money to cause *suffering*, to create pain! Who do you think you are, you rotting piece of shit!" Her voice cracked.

Dockett leaned closer to her. "I'm the one who's going to put you in a stadium, in front of thousands of people, and cheer at your death." He grabbed her chin with the intention to continue speaking.

But Kell struck his arm away with a powerful sweep.

Rage flared in the Lanista. "Simon, spar with her. Now."

"How about I spar with *you*?" Kell seethed. "We'll figure this out right here."

Dockett chuckled. "As much as I would like to pound you into the dirt, that's not a punishment. Having Simon do it for me is more," he waved a careless hand, "appropriate." He motioned to Simon. "Get it done."

The fear she had felt at their every duel thus far vanished. In its stead was raw resolve and torrential anger. She would not—could not—let Simon win; she needed to make a point to Dockett.

Simon hollowly took a dummy sword, his eyes everywhere that wasn't a human face. When Ferrik handed her one, she hurled it at Dockett.

The Lanista dodged with ease, amusement gone. "Take her down."

In her mind, Kell saw herself create an Arcane Circle and then strike her wrists to ignite her fields. From that stance, she positioned herself into an offensive posture, one that was a primary stance for flora traits. Like plants, she would be pliable but doggedly stubborn. She would curve and wind and then strike with surprising power. She would use the energy of the world around her and double it.

Hands angled in front in preparation to deflect, she widened her stance, shifting her weight to her back foot. Her leg screamed in protest but she ignored it.

Without flourish or much enthusiasm, Simon faced Kell, his sword held in a stance she had seen before.

"Go!" Dockett shouted.

"Sorry," Kell told Simon, lunging forward. Urging her tired body with everything she had, she darted at him. Simon swung half-heartedly. Still, Kell barely avoided it before whirling on the ball of her foot and sliding into Simon's personal space. He raised an arm to elbow her, but Kell tucked her head. She slipped a leg behind him and wrapped it around his knee as she took hold of his sword arm and pushed with all her strength.

Suddenly off balance, Simon staggered backward, taking Kell with him. Realizing she needed more force to compensate for his additional weight, Kell pushed into the ground, ordering the earth under her right foot to jut upward by an inch, propelling her with the power she needed. With a fierce cry, she threw him to the ground.

Panting, she stood over Simon, her hands still gripping his arm. He didn't move. Shoulders heaving, Kell turned to look at Dockett, as if to warn him that she was coming for him next.

"Supper!" called Arden loudly to distract from the upset that had just occurred. Everyone started to trail off except Kell, Simon, and Dockett. Ferrik and Tarquin also stayed behind.

As Simon finally sat up, Dockett scoffed and then stalked off.

Kell kneeled beside her longtime friend. She didn't know what to say to him. Of course he was hurt. Of course he wasn't all right. "Let's take you to the infirmary," she finally said.

Simon suddenly snapped from his daze and shook his head. "No, no. I'm fine." He stood shakily. Ferrik joined him and, exchanging looks with Kell and Tarquin, escorted him to the mess hall.

"Kellick," murmured Tarquin as they ate. They sat alone on the far side of the fighters' hall. "What's the plan here? We can't keep this up. You're pissin' off too many people."

"There are guards everywhere. The Munera is in three days. Making it to the stadium and then getting you, Simon, and Mordecai out is the plan," she replied. "And, if I get time, I'll kill Dockett along the way."

"Wouldn't it be easier to just, uh, blast our way out of the school?"

Kell paused mid-bite. "I met with Mordecai last night, well, dreamed with him. I didn't talk, but he did. Our other, more, uh, ambitious goal... is to get *everyone* out of the school, especially the Users." She looked at her father, her voice staying low. "If you think we have it bad here... It's nothing compared to what Mordecai's been going through. Once everyone's in the stadium, we'll all be in one place."

"How are you plannin' to get all them people out?"

"I'm gonna make a scene." She sighed. "I'm hoping Bellamy's also been busy and can offer some aid. He'll be there too."

There was silence between them before Tarquin said, "I'm worried about Simon. I've never seen him like this. I think it's all comin' down on him."

"Yeah." Kell picked at her rice.

That night, once she had bathed and most everyone was asleep, including Tarquin, Kell slipped out of bed and crossed the dorm to the door, acting as though she were going to the latrine. Once in the hallway, she ran the other way, her head on a swivel. Guards were posted along the outer exits, so she stayed indoors, sleuthing along corridors.

When she finally made it across the training yard to the main building, she drew herself into the shadows of the staircase that led to the second floor. Peering around the polished wood railing, she found several regulators milling about in the open space between the stairs and the infirmary.

She pressed her hand on the floor and, with precise discipline, urged a spindly but strong vine to creep along the floor, up the wall, and across the space to where a lantern, which was most often used to investigate outdoor alarms, burned on a marble table. She still wasn't comfortable manipulating metal, otherwise she would have thrown the lantern across the room. Straining against the effort, she urged the vine to climb the back of the table, slither to the lantern, and then push it off. The lantern shattered on the floor, spreading oil—and fire—everywhere.

The regulators startled horribly and went running to subdue the fire. Kell shook the Viterra from her hands, causing the vine to vanish, and then sprinted up the staircase, grimacing at the pain in her leg. She whirled to the left at the top and then jogged to Simon's door. She glanced around for prying eyes and then tested the doorknob.

The door opened easily under her touch. Simon's room was dark and smelled vaguely of sweat. The open window across the room caused a draft of warm air to pulse through, buffeting Kell as she tried to quietly close the door behind her. There was movement across the room.

Kell opened her palm and allowed a small kindling of fire to blossom there. The orange light illuminated Simon who stood beside his bed, alarmed. His eyes found her face first and then focused on the flame in her hand.

"Hey," she said.

"How did you…" He sat heavily on his disheveled bed, his eyes bouncing from her face to the ball of fire in her hand. After a long moment, he asked, "You're in control of it?"

She smiled and seated herself at the nearby desk. She shook her hand to rid it of Viterra and turned on the small, brass lamp there. "Yes, I'm in control of it." Grimly, she regarded him. "How are you feeling?"

As if suddenly remembering his current state, Simon slumped and his gaze shifted to the floor. When he finally spoke, his voice was raw. "I can't sleep. It hurts… so much."

"Maybe I can fix that." Kell stood and joined him at his bedside. "Can I see?"

With a shaky sigh, Simon turned his back to her. Dried blood left rusty tracks down his back; welts and abrasions of black, purple, and red adorned his shoulder blades, spine, and middle back.

Pursing her lips, Kell drew water to her hands and, using Viterra to keep it along her fingers, gently laid her palms on his back.

Simon flinched horribly and hissed, "What are you doing?"

"Just be still," she replied. She ran her water-coated hands down his back to cool and wash it, focusing first on the blood stains before moving to the raised, angry areas. After a minute, Simon sighed and leaned on his knees, his head bowed. His shoulders shook as he silently cried. Kell pretended not to notice.

Once his back was dry, she brought fire closer to him to study the wounds. She would use the same vine herb she had used on herself. There weren't enough open wounds to use helolium. "Give me a minute," she hummed, turning into the light of the desk lamp. Simon watched over his shoulder as she began to grow ivy in the palm of her hand. Slowly feeding Viterra into the slithering vine, she softly explained, "It's called creeping milk tassel. It's used for bruises, abrasions, swelling, anything that hasn't really broken the skin. I used it on myself yesterday. It helps a lot."

Simon only nodded.

After the vine coiled thickly around Kell's arm, she began picking the leaves from it. Once bare, the remaining spindles disintegrated into nothingness with a flick of her wrist. "Could I use this?" she asked, pointing to the cup on the desk. When Simon didn't object, she stuffed several leaves into it, conjured water, and then heated the mug between her palms.

"Where did you learn to do all this?" Simon murmured.

"What?"

"To… use stuff like this. I thought fire was the only thing Users could, uh, use."

"I did too. But I've had several teachers."

Simon's brows furrowed. "Where are your rings?"

Kell observed the steaming mug. "I still have them. I can use a little Viterra without them. But if I want to channel the Flow, I have to use the rings." She nodded to him. "Lie down."

Simon obeyed, groaning softly as the movement twisted his back. Once he was comfortable, his face turned toward her, Kell leaned over him and began drawing the heated leaves from the mug. Using Viterra to control them, she gently laid them across the worst of the welts, overlapping their edges for complete coverage.

Within the minute, Simon wound his arm around her hips and curled closer to her with a sigh. Tears of relief ran down his cheeks. Kell smiled, pleased. Once the majority of his wounds were covered, she let the leaves cool with the intention of replacing them once they had lost their immediate potency. In the meantime, she gazed down at Simon. In the flickering lamp light, she saw the boy she had loved all those years ago.

"The plan is to get everyone out at the Munera," she said, touching a runny leaf to check its temperature. "You included." When he didn't answer, she stroked his face with some hesitance. "Hey."

"Hm?" His voice was low, dreamy.

"Look at me," Kell commanded. Simon peered up at her, his blue eyes dark. "You have to make it through the next few days. Don't quit, not yet. Got it?" Simon searched her face for something that she couldn't know and then nodded. As she returned her attention to the leaves, she added, "And I wasn't making empty threats to Dockett. I'll kill him. He doesn't know how close he's already come to being scorched." She passed a smirk to Simon. "In my younger days, he would have already been ash."

Simon's arm around her waist tightened. "Have you been letting me beat you?"

Seeking to comfort him, Kell ran a gentle hand through his blond hair and scoffed. "No. You beat me fair and square. I haven't studied any type of combat."

"You haven't?"

She shook her head. "Everything I've been using so far is based entirely on traits, the movements used to control elements."

"What did you use this afternoon?"

"Flora traits. You must be like a plant—flexible, stubborn, enduring. You have to use the energy around you."

Simon sighed. "You've had good teachers…"

Suddenly missing Renata, Terin, Gytha, and the members of the First Whispered, Kell nodded. "Yeah, I have." She began pulling the leaves from his back.

There were several minutes of silence between them as she worked, much to Simon's relieved sighs. As she adjusted the layered leaves, Simon stirred beside her.

"Eevie… told Dockett about you."

Kell's hands hesitated over him. "What do you mean?"

"I… shared with Eevie about our background the day after you left… She must have told Dockett." He drew a long breath. "And then, last night… I confronted Eevie, uh, in her quarters. I wasn't… in the right mind. Of course, she told Dockett."

"And that's why you were flogged?"

Simon nodded, his face pressing into her thigh with shame. Kell finished settling the leaves. The fear and disdain their "sparring" matches had instilled in her vanished. The young man beside her was Simon—alone, scared, in pain, and betrayed by the world.

After passing warm, fire-heated hands over his back to reheat the leaves, she started to stand, but Simon didn't let her go.

"Please, stay," he murmured groggily. "Just for a little while."

Kell sat back down. "Yeah."

The soft breeze that played through the open window was pleasant and made Kell sleepy. But she fought off her fatigue by constantly rewarming the leaves. When, after a half hour, she considered their medicinal properties used up, she coaxed them from his back and deposited them out the open window.

Simon appeared to be asleep. Dismayed and distraught by all that she had seen, heard, and suffered, Kell felt compelled to impart warmth—something she was sure he had gone without for years—to her friend. She brushed his hair once more and then leaned down and kissed the top of his head. When she drew back, his chin tilted upward. In the dying light of the lantern, she saw his eyes open. The arm he had kept around her waist slithered up to her face and brought her lower.

"Thank you," he whispered into the space between them before lifting himself to kiss her. His lips were chapped and tasted salty.

Kell drew back, panicked, aware of the inappropriateness of her intrusion. She had come to heal an injured friend but now found herself alone in a dorm room with a man other than her intended.

Simon searched her eyes before pulling her back to him.

If it had not been for her desperation, her need for intimacy, she would have wrenched away. Instead, she drew a long breath and deepened the kiss, opening to him. The whimper that escaped her throat alarmed her; she couldn't stop her body from reacting. The heated excitement that rushed through her veins was such a welcome reprieve from the torment and stress she had experienced over the past several days.

Simon perched on the edge of the bed and cupped her face, his hands rough and calloused. Kell folded into his hard embrace, intrigued by the broadness of his chest and arms. His taste was new, warm, and not unpleasant.

It took her a moment before she came to her senses. "Hey, hey," she whispered, halting him.

Breathing hard, Simon looked at her, his eyes dilated. His arms were carved works of rock-hard art.

Keeping her gaze away from the rest of his body lest she be further tempted, Kell shook her head. "I can't…"

He sat back and cleared his throat. "I know."

Heartbeat ringing in her ears, she stared incredulously at the blankets. The realization of what had just nearly happened settled on her shoulders heavily.

Simon must have seen the look on her face because he murmured, "Sorry."

"No, I'm sorry… I shouldn't have…"

"I… was too forward…" His words sounded hollow.

Kell met his gaze and then stood, both aroused and guilty. She shifted uncomfortably beside the bed before saying, "I gotta go."

Simon reached through the space between them and took her hand. He held it for several long seconds before saying, "You could stay." His grip on her tightened. "I want you to stay."

Kell peered into his blue-black eyes. Torment, defeat, and desire vied for prominence within them, and she found Simon silently pleading with her. When she didn't say anything, he reeled her closer until she placed her hands on his shoulders.

Still seated on the bed, he embraced her, wrapping his arms around her middle and burying his face in her stomach. "Please, Kellick…"

Her name on his lips nearly broke her. The rawness in his voice shook her. Kell cleared her throat as she gently caressed the back of his head. "I shouldn't be here." She began to untangle his arms and back away.

Simon stood, following her.

Kell stopped him, placed a firm hand on his chest. "No."

The hurt in Simon's eyes shamed her.

Looking to redirect his attention, Kell said, "Promise me you'll make it to the games. Yeah?"

He simply nodded.

28

The Day Before

HIS BACK STILL HURT THE following day, but the pain was far more manageable. Feeling as though his soul had been reborn, Simon held himself proudly as he strode into the training yard. The Munera was two days away. He had to get back into the mindset and provide enough cover for Kell.

To his surprise, Ferrik met him. The older man passed a searching gaze over him and then held out his arm. "You good?"

Simon took it with deliberate strength. "I'm good. You?"

His mentor nodded and motioned to the other fighters who had paused briefly to watch the exchange.

After that, Simon began stretches and morning drills with renewed vigor. His back ached constantly as the movements pulled the abrasions and welts, but compared to the previous day, it was wholly tolerable—thanks to Kell.

As he warmed his muscles, he peered about the field. He found her watching Tarquin demonstrate sword movements using a dummy sword. Simon grew grim as he realized she probably had an ulterior motive for studying the stances. Kell had no intention of ever holding a sword; she had no need for one. But every fighter there in the arena would have one.

Tarquin passed the dummy sword to her, and Simon watched as she lithely settled into a stance that no sword fighter in their training yard had ever taken. He remembered what she had said the night prior—that she had not studied martial arts, that her movements came from controlling the elements. Lost in thought, he allowed his gaze to shift to the ground and memories of the previous night to flood his senses.

She looked strong and indomitable in the yard, but pulled against him, she was surprisingly small and all female. After deciding that he liked her fingertips on his bare skin, he had tested the waters to see if she would be receptive to reciprocation. Of course, her hesitance had been expected. But the glimpse of enthusiasm he had tasted in her and her subsequent throaty whimper had sealed it for him.

Kell had been his best friend growing up. They had roughhoused, swam, and worked side-by-side for years. But *she* had been a *he*... Perhaps this new dynamic as friends of the opposite sex would play into his favor.

A thought occurred to Simon. He sighed as he realized that there had been no bumbling or awkwardness between them. Some other man, probably that Mordecai fellow, had had the opportunity to bed her already.

He chided himself for getting upset over something so silly and returned his attention to his stretches.

Kell had given him something he had lost a long time ago—his humanity. He had seen the hate and fear in her eyes over the past week, yet she had come to him in his hour of need. She had cared for him, loved him, healed him. He smiled. For years he had felt as though pieces of him were being chipped away by his time at the school.

He watched as Arden approached her. Kell frowned at the assistant and then, with a huff, half-limped across the field to the track. Though she had tied the majority of her brown hair back into a knot, tendrils of it had escaped and now hung limply around her sweaty face.

Simon glanced at the other fighters and, finding none of them watching, returned his attention to her. Midway to the track, he saw her kneel, as if to adjust her pants leg. Knowing her secret now though, he saw her press her palm to the ground next to her foot. He couldn't discern what she was doing exactly, but he knew she was using... what had she called it? Viterra.

When she returned erect, her gait was smoother and more even. With only a slight grimace, she broke into a jog and started around the track.

Dockett visited them midmorning to check on the fighters, encouraging them not to overwork themselves, and then motioned to Simon.

Not at all eager to be alone with the Lanista again, Simon cautiously followed him to the mess hall. In the threshold there, Dockett paused as if to collect his thoughts. "Your back bothering you?"

Simon shrugged. "Not really."

Dockett turned him around and examined the marks. Simon flinched under his probing fingers. "Hm, it's healing fast. *Real* fast. Looks good." The Lanista circled him until he was gazing at Simon. "I hated doing that to you, kid. But you can't go laying hands on women."

Simon nearly retorted in Kell's defense but managed to keep his mouth shut. "I know. I was out of line."

Dockett nodded and placed a hand on Simon's shoulder. "In two days, it's you and me. Yeah? Everything we've been working toward—money, fame—all of it's gonna culminate at the games. And you and me, we gotta be on the same page. Yeah?"

"Yeah."

The Lanista cupped Simon's jaw. "You're still my Champion. We gotta show everyone what you're made of. Come on. Let's have a good session this afternoon and then rest."

Dockett turned to leave, but Simon stopped him. "I don't want to fight Kell today. All right?" The Lanista frowned. "You want me focused on the games, stop pitting me against her. We grew up together. I can't… keep hurting her like that. Please." As Dockett considered him, Simon added, "It's the last day of training."

"Fine." The Lanista whirled around. "I'll pit her against someone else."

Simon knew he couldn't argue.

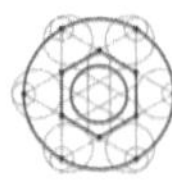

That afternoon, Kell found herself circling Ferrik, who towered above her. He was built differently than Simon with willowy limbs and a long coal-colored body that shimmered in the hot September sun. She hadn't seen him fight before but knew he was as good as Simon, perhaps better. Simon had called him a mentor.

Deciding she needed to stick to something she was most comfortable with, Kell decided to utilize water traits, her strongest suit. Much like flora traits, water traits had to be fluid and flexible, but that's where the similarities ended. Water was not stubborn, it became what it needed to be, it went where it needed to go. It could be soft and trickling or raging and concussive.

The movements water traits employed were ebb-and-flow type motions, actions that took surrounding energy and doubled it. Kell was not looking forward to trying to throw Ferrik as she suspected he was far wiser and more cautious than Simon.

Unlike flora traits, which waited on energy to come into play, water traits were more proactive, and so, with some hesitancy, Kell lunged several paces toward Ferrik with the intention to attack but called it off upon seeing the unflinching expression on his face.

Cursing under her breath, she backed away. She had been right; Ferrik was more evenly tempered and well-trained. He wasn't impulsive like Simon, who would have prepared to counter or reacted in some way. Ferrik watched her.

Feeling out of her element, Kell tried to decide what to do. She didn't know how to attack without Viterra. Dodging, evading, and throwing were all well-known tactics and had forms to accompany such skills. But to strategically attack, she needed Viterra. She wasn't accustomed to striking human flesh, even if she had hit Simon a handful of times.

Simon.

She glanced at him. But the moment she did, she sensed Ferrik move. In two large strides, he was on top of her. Kell deftly blocked a strike to her face by pushing it down and to the side. The power in his blow numbed her arms. Ferrik followed the assault with two more rapid-fire punches. Kell dodged one before taking the second across the face. Though the attack glanced off her cheekbone and grazed her nose, the force stunned her.

She staggered backward into a nearby fighter, who caught and steadied her. Her vision blurred and her ears rang. She wanted to lie down. But a shift in the surrounding energy warned her.

Without seeing the incoming attack, she dropped her left shoulder and turned her head to the side. Ferrik's blow struck the fighter supporting Kell. Realizing Ferrik was close, she wrenched to the side, dropping her knee to the ground, and drove her elbow into the side of Ferrik's outer thigh, hitting the nerve she knew was there. Less gracefully than she had hoped, she scrambled away in the dirt on her hands and knees as Ferrik, grasping his injured leg, attempted to kick her.

Sensing incoming movement but unable to properly see it, Kell drew Viterra into her left palm and leveled a layer of rock-hard earth against Ferrik's hardened foot. Though his brutal bunt connected, it struck the plate of dense, hardened soil first before collapsing Kell's arm and sending her rolling. Still rattled from the blow to her head, Kell loss consciousness briefly.

She woke a few seconds later to someone frantically tapping her cheek. Disoriented, she blinked up at Simon, squinting against the harsh sunlight. There was mild conversation as the other pro-fighters were dismissed for the day. Holding her head, she tried to make sense of what had just happened.

"You all right?" asked Tarquin, kneeling beside her.

Momentarily, a pair of shadows appeared. Kell tried to look up at them, but the action alone made her dizzy.

"Training is finished for today," said Dockett, peering down at her. "The day before the Munera, everyone rests. Use the time to pray." Kell saw the Lanista give Simon a look before loping off after Arden.

"You hardly ever attack," remarked Ferrik, still looming over her. With Simon's help, Kell sat up and gingerly touched her face. When she pulled her fingers away, there was blood. "Did your combat school not teach you to strike?"

"No." Gathering herself, Kell stood, urging her body to cooperate. She met Ferrik's gaze. "Because I was never taught to fight using martial arts."

"But you used it, just now. The nerve along the leg—"

"Is a well-known weakness to many doctors and herbologists. My teachers were *not* combat instructors." Feeling as though she had been run through an extensive field of brambles and then thrown along a white-water river, she started for the dorms.

That night, Kell slept fitfully. Knowing what was coming, she drank three cups of the herbal concoction Renata had taught her to brew years prior. A single cup could ease menstruation cramps. Three cups of the potent brew delayed her period for a week. Not wanting to be cramping and bleeding as she fought for her life, she drank the nasty blend with hardened discipline.

The following day, she didn't feel great. Her body was worn. Though she had also laid creeping mild tassel on her face to control the swelling and pain, she felt ragged. When Tarquin declared that she had a fever, she decided to stay in bed for the morning like some of the other fighters.

She ate lunch with Simon and Tarquin and then went back to bed. Simon eventually woke her early evening, much to her dismay. After eating snacks and bathing, Kell allowed Simon, who had free rein of the heavily-guarded facility because of his status, to escort her to his quarters where they could visit without others listening.

Once the door was closed, Simon sat on his bed.

Kell leaned on his desk, wearily. She shouldn't have returned to his room, but she was too far beyond caring. "So, what'd you wanna talk about?"

He chuckled uneasily. "Why do you think something's bothering me?"

She passed him a frown. "Because you're fighting tomorrow."

He glanced at the floor and then nodded. "Yeah, but you are too." His brows creased in worry. "How are you feeling?"

She sighed. "Not well. Everything on me hurts. I've been making every herbal cocktail I can think of and applying medicines when I could, but…" She looked at him and smiled grimly. "I've not ever felt this beat up before."

Simon fidgeted. "Are you going to be all right tomorrow?"

"I don't really have a choice, do I?"

"No." He stood and crossed the space between them. Kell didn't move, not because she wanted him to be so near but because she quite frankly didn't have the energy to adjust her position. Simon touched her cheek and then flattened his hand across her forehead. "Your fever's gone down. That's good."

His fingers trailed down the side of her face before he cupped her jaw. He studied her face, tracing the skin under her bruises and cuts with a delicate thumb. "I must have been really dense to have not realized you were a girl."

His finger grazed her lips before he moved to her hair, continuing his exploration of her.

Kell sighed into his touch, feeling more sleepy than aroused. Only when his hand ventured down her shoulder and passed over her breast en route to her hip did a lightning bolt of lust rock her core. She squinted at the floor as her head pounded under the intense effort of her heart.

Simon gently drew her hand into his and then leaned forward and kissed her forehead. The heat of his breath mixed with the remnants of the fever made her feel delirious. His cheek resting atop her head, he said, "I know you're engaged. But do you think… if everything works out, you would be… willing to reconsider?"

"Simon…"

He slipped a large arm around her back and embraced her. "It was always supposed to be us, Kellick. Look how well we fit together."

"You don't know anything about me. All you know is who I am in here. You don't know what I've done, where I've been…"

"Then tell me." He drew away to meet her eyes. "Please."

Kell tiredly trapped his hand against her skin. "I'm engaged to Mordecai. We've been together for years—"

Simon kissed her, one hand on her face and the other on her waist, holding her captive. Kell struggled for a breath's moment before she decided the energy it required was too much. She sighed into his mouth and then kissed him back, drawing herself against his body. Her head hammered painfully with the thrumming of her racing heart.

After a moment, Simon sat on the bed, drawing her to him. Logic and reason eddied from her weary mind. She straddled him, kissing him as his hands traveled up and down her body. When he tugged at her threadbare shirt, she raised her arms. It was on the floor in the next instant.

Simon kissed her chest and shoulders, his rough hands on her breasts and hips. Kell's loud gasp as she settled firmly into his lap startled her from her excitement. She stiffened in Simon's arms, a cry bubbling up from her throat.

"What?" Simon stopped, real worry on his face. "Did I hurt you?"

Kell slid off him and curled up on his bed, folding in on herself. Hot tears came suddenly, and she buried her face in her hands. Mordecai's loving gaze swam to the forefront of her mind—his charming smile, his quiet comfort, his enduringly tender touches, his laughter and ecstatic mirth, and, of course, his hurt and disappointment. She couldn't betray him; she loved him too much. Simon was heady lust and desire, but Mordecai was love.

The bed shifted as Simon lay down beside her, but she didn't look at him. She could hardly contain the sobs that wracked her drained body. She felt beyond delirious with heat.

With a strong arm, he corralled her into his embrace, tangling his legs with her own, and curled her head under his chin. Crying harder, Kell let it all out—her frustration concerning her relationship with Mordecai, her fear and dread of tomorrow, her confusion about the future, all of it.

After a few minutes of intense sobbing, what little energy she had left was gone, and she slipped into a deep sleep.

She dreamed.

Her mind traveled not through the winding corridors and courtyards of the school but down the elegant streets of the Middle District until she found a way out of the city. Like a stinging, zipping bolt of lightning, she rocketed past suburbs and farms into the nearby forest. When she was suddenly wrenched to a stop, she looked about in confusion. It was far too dark as it was the night of the new moon.

Sensing a familiar presence, she followed an almost indiscernible trail into a patch of vegetation that looked natural, but Kell knew better. Recognizing Renata's work, she entered the makeshift shelter and kneeled beside her teacher. "What are you doing here?"

"Kellick," the old woman muttered in her sleep, turning toward her. The creases in her face deepened. She made a motion as if to reach for Kell, but she was not immune to the paralysis of sleep. Instead, Kell took her hand. "Oh, Kell. What's happened to you?"

"Mordecai and I are in the Munera school. We were arrested and thrown in here." Kell tried to sound more upbeat. "But the good news is we've got Simon and Tarquin. The plan is to—"

"Listen to me," Renata interrupted with the curtness of someone who was awake. "Terin and the reactionaries are outside the city. I came to stop them." The old woman spoke more fluently than all others Kell had previously talked to in dream form. "The country's elites are gathering for the games. Terin and the reactionaries are planning to interrupt the games."

"Security is tight," Kell said. "That's why we've not tried to escape. We're waiting to do so at the Munera."

Renata scoffed. "You have more power than every fighter in that school. Why not just—"

"Because we're not just trying to save ourselves," Kell replied gravely. "Everyone here is a prisoner. And none more than the Users. I've not spoken to Mordecai in several days, but I dread seeing him tomorrow. My time here has been rough, but I've been with the pro-fighters. Mordecai's been imprisoned with the Users. What if he…" Kell's throat closed around her words.

"You're wanting to… save everyone? Where-where would you take them? Where would they all go? You're being naïve as always, Kellick. You've got to think. I know great injustice is being done there, but getting you and Mordecai and your friends out is priority. Get out *then* plot to help the others." Her grip around Kell's fingers tightened. "I know you have been suffering—I can feel it—and that your world is what you see around you, but more is going on in Berceau."

"Then… what should we do? Avives' Containment Office has come in as extra security. They were stationed around the school earlier this evening."

Renata was silent for a long moment before saying, "I don't want you to tangle with the Containment Office. Combat with Viterra is one thing, stopping gunfire is another." She thought again. "Go to the Munera tomorrow. Grab Mordecai and your friends and get out."

A thought occurred to Kell and she asked, "What about Bellamy? He's supposed to be there tomorrow. I was hoping he'd be able to help us."

"Help *you*?" Renata's face grimaced as she tried to laugh. "If anything, *you* will be helping *him*. Tomorrow is going to be a shit day, Kellick. There's no easy way to put it. I'm going to do my best to head off Terin and the reactionaries. I don't want more civilian deaths because of our people. Get yourselves out of the Munera. If Bellamy needs help, give it to him. He's all that's preventing our people from being completely wiped out in the coming years." She squeezed her hand again. "Remember, when you fight, you make sure your opponents know who they're dealing with. Now go, you've somewhere else to be."

Before Renata had even finished speaking, Kell was being drawn back to Eclat. In the blink of an eye, she was at the imperial palace. Darting upward as the world moved in slow motion around her, she landed on the balcony of Bellamy's private quarters. Like a flash of light, she found herself standing at the foot of his bed—except it was empty.

She stared at it for a moment and then, feeling a tugging sensation from farther away, submitted to it, allowing it to drag her deep into the palace. Through vast rooms of marble and finely decorated halls, past exquisitely folded drapery and gold-flecked furniture she soared until she came to an abrupt halt at an inconspicuous door. She blinked and she was inside, at the bottom of a set of lengthy stairs. Kell looked up at the spiraling staircase overhead before venturing into the bowels of the palace.

She eventually found Bellamy and Marko, both asleep on hard cots and surrounded by bags of personal effects. It appeared they were preparing to leave.

"Bellamy," she murmured, kneeling beside him. Unsurprisingly, Marko woke suddenly and rolled onto his feet beside his cot. He created an Arcane Circle and ignited his fields. "Bellamy, tell Marko it's me."

"It's Kell," Bellamy muttered. Marko relaxed.

"The reactionaries are in the city," she reported. "Renata's come to intervene."

"Where the… hell are you? I've been looking everywhere for you two."

"We were arrested last week. Dockett figured out who we were. We've been at the Munera school ever since."

"I *knew* that plan was too risky," Bellamy seethed with impressive control of his speech. "I shouldn't have… taken you."

"But I've found Simon and my father."

Bellamy grumbled indistinctly.

"The Containment Office is here at the school."

"I know. They'll be… at-at the games tomorrow too."

"Where? In the stadium?"

"I'm unsure." Bellamy sighed. "Things are precarious right now. My father died the other night. Kell, I'm… in line for the throne. The coronation is next month. Marko and I have been changing where we sleep every night because assassins are after us. He stopped an attempt just two days ago while I was giving a speech. I have several dozen men preparing to overthrow the… Council of Ministers, but until the coronation, I'm not safe."

"Will you be at the games tomorrow?" she asked.

"I have to be. I'm… the reigning monarch."

Kell smiled grimly. "We'll see you there then."

"What's your p-plan?"

"Make a scene and escape."

Bellamy smiled. "Knowing you, that'll be easy—making a scene."

"Perhaps I'll include you in the drama," she replied fondly. "It is our intention to provide help tomorrow if you need it. But our priority is escaping the ring."

"As it should be," Bellamy replied. "If Renata fails… and the reactionaries reach the Middle District… there will be blood. Bound or not, people will die. T-thousands will die, Kellick." His voice grew grave. "For the sake of… the future of this country, we cannot let them get to the stadium."

She touched his hand. "Command us, Bellamy."

The new king squeezed her hand. "See you tomorrow. Good night, Kellick."

29

Preparations

SIMON STARTLED AS THE DOOR to his quarters slammed open and the overhead lights flickered on. "Simon!" called Dockett gleefully. "Let's go, my boy! The day is here—"

Simon tried to shield Kell who had also jolted awake.

The Lanista leaned in the doorway and said with a wolfish smile, "I was wondering where she was at roll call last night. If you wanted a doxy, I would have found you a prettier one. My Champion deserves it all."

As Simon drew a sheet over Kell, who was still partially nude, he stood, bleary-eyed. It was far too early for Dockett's antics. The sun had not yet risen; not even the birds were awake. "What time is it?" he finally managed.

"Three-thirty," Dockett beamed. "Let's go, let's go. We've got shit to do." Simon grabbed his shirt, which Dockett quickly snatched from his hands. "Don't worry about that. You'll be wearing better things today."

Simon glanced at Kell, who sat on his bed, the sheet wrapped around her shoulders. Her hair was tussled and her eyes red. The swelling of the right side of her face had gone down, and she looked almost normal, save the crusty gash that extended across her cheekbone.

"You, get back to the dorms," Dockett commanded. "Arden's waking everyone now."

As the Lanista excitedly led Simon from the room, Simon looked back at Kell in time to see her slip into her shirt and then take a long breath, allowing her hands to rise before her and then fall, palms-down, as if she were pressing something toward the ground.

He had heard her talking the previous night, visiting with people in her dreams as she had done with him. The air around them had shifted, had become denser and charged, the change palpable even to Simon. With rapt attention, he had watched her seemingly one-sided conversations, his hand never leaving her waist. Though he gathered she had spoken to Bellamy, the new king, he couldn't discern who else she had visited. All the same, it was evident that much was going to happen today and that Kell, no matter how he hated to admit it, could take care of herself.

He needed to worry about what awaited him. He was still a Champion and had numerous sponsors, who had been financially supporting his training and upbringing, betting on his skills. No matter what Kell's plans were today, he needed to win the Munera at all costs.

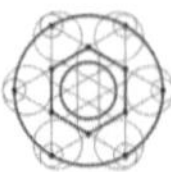

Shortly after sunup, Kell found herself shackled and being led to an open-air van that waited outside. All of the pro-fighters were set to travel together while the regular fighters, who would be used as fodder in the games, and the Users were to be bused in separately. Simon, the fighters' Champion, the Users' Champion, and their partners were ushered into a separate vehicle behind the pro-fighters.

Perched on a bench next to Tarquin, Kell squinted against the light of the September morning sun as the van shifted gears and exited the alleyway adjacent to the school. She was not prepared for the crowds nor for the sudden cacophony of cheers that erupted as the van turned onto the main thoroughfare. Kell couldn't help but gape as she turned to look over the trailer's railings at the hundreds of people gathered along the streets. Women flapped handkerchiefs at them as men took their hats and gave the passing entourage hearty waves.

Several young ladies ran alongside the van, throwing flowers at the predominantly male fighters and blowing kisses at them. Children squealed and jostled each other to see the fighters, especially the Champions.

As the van churned up the main street toward the stadium, Kell caught a faint scent on the air—smoke. No one else seemed to notice it. Breathing deeply to ensure that her senses were correct, she stood, bracing against Tarquin. In the distance toward the Lower District's suburbs, she saw thick tendrils of smoke coiling into the air. It had to be Terin and the reactionaries.

Troubled, she sat back down and leaned into Tarquin to explain what she knew and what she had just seen. Her father only nodded, concerned.

Splendidly dressed nobles and women wearing elegant dresses of lace and satin that trailed the ground greeted them outside the stadium and added to the menagerie of flowers that had come to bedeck the van's trailer. Kell was relieved to be rid of the crowds when the van finally pulled into a gated access drive that was heavily guarded by armed regulators and men dressed in burgundy suits. Though people's cheers and well wishes could still be heard, the empty space around the vehicle allowed Kell to better collect herself.

After some discussion, Dockett and others finally began unloading the pro-fighters. Shackled together, the fighters had to move as one and wait for each other to step from the trailer. Only once everyone was out did the procession follow Dockett through a side door.

Kell shivered as a deep chill pervaded the passage. Her attire, and that of the other four women, was similar to their male counterparts'. Because the male fighters were shirtless, she and the other women were allowed bandeaus to cover their bare breasts. Like the men, she wore loose beige pants with ample knee space that fit tightly around her ankles. All were barefoot.

Dockett led them up a sloping hallway and into a large room with benches and an extensive water closet. The walls were adorned with mirrors. As they entered, Arden unlocked each of their shackles. Kell followed Tarquin in, eager to get to Simon, whom she could see on the other side of the room talking with Ferrik. When she glanced at her passing reflection though, she stopped mid-step.

The young woman gazing back at her appeared exhausted, worn. Purple shadows hung under her eyes. Although she had done her best to knot her hair at the back of her head, pieces of it had already fallen, giving her a half-crazed appearance. Her face looked as though she had fallen headfirst into a thorny tree. With a dismayed sigh, she moved on.

"One hour," called Arden before closing the door behind him.

Kell observed the others, hoping to garner information on how they were to behave or what they were to do. Simon and Ferrik, and a few others, seemed to understand that now was the time to stretch and warm up. The room was unusually large and lavish, but with forty or so fighters gathered there, it was cramped.

Kell desperately wanted to go to the bathroom because she felt like she was going to be sick, but someone was already in there throwing up the meager breakfast they had scarfed down. She looked at Tarquin. Her father was pale, his face taut with stress and fear as he tried to stretch his bulky shoulders. He didn't seem to sense her worried gaze.

Awkwardly, Kell shuffled to the rear of the room and sat against the wall. Realizing now was the time to gather herself and reestablish her *satt*, she folded her legs, rested her hands in her lap, and focused on her breathing.

Initially, her nervous heart jumped sporadically in her chest, but with some time, she was able to calm it. She remembered sitting next to the river with Gytha, listening to the water bubble through the nearby reeds. Using that as a focal point, she gently urged her mind toward composure.

"Stretch," advised Georgie, a fighter with whom she was familiar. "They're going to call us soon."

"Thank you," she replied. Keeping her gaze low, she slowly rose and performed light stretches.

A few minutes later, the door opened and the pro-fighters began filing out. Kell didn't see Simon or Ferrik leave at the head of the group. She was hardly aware of herself as she fell into line, her father ahead of her.

At the door, Arden passed each fighter a sword. When Kell approached him, he eyed her and said, "You have to have it to enter the arena. You can throw it down once the games start." Without a word, Kell took the offered weapon, grimacing at its weight, and followed the others into a queue in the hallway. No longer in the isolation of the prep room, the sound of a distant female announcer could be heard echoing throughout the arena. The dull roar of the audience shook the stadium.

Tarquin turned to her. "Here." His voice trembled. He offered her a thin leather thong. "Found it… earlier." He motioned to her hair. "For you…"

Kell passed her sword to him and gratefully tied back her hair. When Tarquin returned her sword, she saw his hands shaking. Shamefaced, he turned away from her. Her *satt* wavered. She had never seen her father so frightened, not even the day he had hauled her out of Eclat.

Kell took his arm and slid her hand into his. His normally warm palm was clammy. "Stay close to me," she said. He nodded unsteadily before looking down the line as the door at the end of the hallway opened.

"Never conquered!" shouted Arden from behind them.

"Always feared!" the fighters roared in response.

The distant rumble of an elated audience evolved into a maelstrom of cheers and cries, the magnitude of which floored Kell. Ahead, she saw Simon and Ferrik jog into the sandy arena. The line of fighters followed their cue. Tarquin headed out with Kell right behind him.

The scale of the event shook Kell to her core. As she ran over the sand, she looked up at the thousands of people perched on continuously running marble benches that spiraled ever upward and seemed to curve toward the sky the higher they went. It was evident by their trappings that everyone present—well, at least those with the best seats—was affluent. Men, women, and children of all races and nationalities screamed and cheered, broadcasting their approval and excitement.

In the center of the arena were enormous palisades, several feet tall, adorned with nondescript white packets. At least thirty of them were spread out across the sand.

Kell lined up beside Tarquin, her gaze shifting to the other side of the arena which boasted a dais and terrace. Though it was quite a distance away, she was certain she could discern Bellamy there. The other fighters, those who had not been trained and who had been kept as prisoners for their past transgressions, were let in next. Kell glanced at them briefly but remained too overwhelmed by everything to note much more than their evident fatigue and raggedness.

As a woman's throaty voice soared over the stadium, Kell continued to take in her surroundings. There was plenty of sand—probably for the fire, Kell concluded. Her gaze fell on Simon who looked like the perfect chiseled statue of a warrior, his eyes on the dais. At first surprised to find the welts on his back gone, she realized they had been strategically covered with makeup. He had shaved his face and wore his sword at his waist with pride. The slash across his right brow also appeared faded, but it could have just been makeup.

"Now, let's meet our challengers!" called the female announcer, snapping Kell from her thoughts.

The intricately decorated door across the arena opened. Men and women boasting thick tattooed cuffs on their wrists filed out with far less enthusiasm than the pro-fighters. Jeers erupted throughout the stadium, horribly startling Kell. Boos echoed around her. The hatred of the masses was terrifying.

Searching the line of newcomers, Kell spotted a familiar form—Mordecai. Despite his disheveled appearance, he seemed just as alarmed by the cries of disapproval that swelled around them. Across the distance, she saw his gaze shift from the stands to the fighters gathered in the arena. To catch his attention, she stepped away from the others as if antsy to get started. Mordecai saw her and gave her a single nod.

"Now, his Majesty, Bellamy Trevarthen, King of Berceau, will bestow a blessing of good fortune on today's Munera and her fighters," announced the purring woman on the speaker, quieting the scornful cries.

Kell looked at Bellamy as he approached the microphone. She could only barely make out the elegant robes of purple, red, and gold that he wore. "Thank you, Madam Parthemos. Best of luck to you, fighters… and Users. Remember, never conquered—"

"Always feared!" chorused the fighters around Kell.

"Thank you, Your Majesty," said Madam Parthemos, reclaiming the microphone. "Our first event is the Proving Trial. Users and fighters must face each other in an arena equipped with volatiles. Those standing at the end of ten minutes may move on to the next event. Users and fighters, you may take the field. Await my signal to begin."

Kell saw the Users, of which there were fifty—Mordecai included—turn as one and run along the northern side of the arena. They spread out, some hiding behind the palisades while others remaining in the open. Realizing that combat was about to start and remembering herself, Kell stole a look at the pro-fighters to figure out what she was supposed to do. Seeing Georgie, Giles, and others she recognized fan out, she did the same, encouraging her father to stick close to her.

"Begin!" commanded Madam Parthemos, her voice accompanied by a loud boom of drums.

30

Unbound

A CONCUSSIVE EXPLOSION REVERBERATED THROUGHOUT the stadium as a palisade near the middle of the arena erupted into flames. Kell cowered not from the sound or the heat but from the abrupt nausea that rose in her as the energy across the sand wildly fluctuated.

Another palisade exploded, and the audience gasped and cheered. A layer of white smoke rose from the smoldering ruins. Kell dropped her sword into the sand, her eyes darting about in search of Simon or Mordecai.

But the entire arena had been thrown into utter chaos. She could hear nothing except the audience and the hiss of flames as torrents of Viterra gushed forth from desperate Bound prisoners. Fighters, both professional and amateur, were everywhere, seeking cover or lunging after Bound individuals in pursuit. Kell thought she saw a blur of blond that was Simon but couldn't be sure.

A putrid scent passed her face and, knowing instinctively that it was the pungent odor of burning flesh, she began heaving. But nothing came up. The smells, the sounds, and the kaleidoscope of constant but erratic movement from those in the arena were overwhelming. But it was the undulating upheaval of Viterra that made her feel violently ill and unbalanced.

"Kell, Kell—Kell!" Tarquin's voice cut through her panic. She hadn't realized she was holding her head until she saw Tarquin's enormous form maneuver in front of her.

Her father hurriedly dragged her to her feet, his sword in hand. "Come on, come on," he huffed, leading her toward where familiar pro-fighters were working together to stave off attacks.

Kell made it a few steps and then, unable to control herself, braced on her knees and vomited, getting rid of everything she had eaten that morning and then some. Distantly, she heard scattered laughter throughout the crowd.

"Kell!" shouted Tarquin, pacing before her in defense.

"Yeah!" Kell wiped her mouth and shakily rejoined him in time to see two Bound prisoners peel away from the palisades and head toward them. She didn't have the time to steel herself before the two—a man and a teenage girl—unleashed fire.

Kell shoved Tarquin one way as she darted the other. The girl's torrent of flames followed Kell, heating the sand around them.

Terrified, Kell searched for cover. Spotting a nearby palisade, she lunged for it, forgoing her initial suspicion of the barricades. She needed time to collect herself, to not feel so ungodly ill.

The flames stopped.

Kell peered around the barrier but didn't see her opponent.

Suddenly, a force like an unfettered ship slamming into a pier struck her, driving the wind from her lungs. A muscled arm wrapped around her and lifted her clear from the ground.

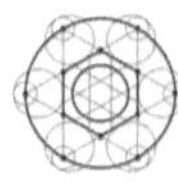

Panting through his panic, Simon carried Kell away from the palisade.

First rule of combat in the arena—don't be anywhere near the palisades.

The adrenaline pumping through him made her weight inconsequential. When they were far enough away, he unceremoniously dropped her into the sand and then went racing after the teenage girl who had been prowling around the other side of the palisade.

Body taut and coiled, Simon evaded her first stream of raging flames by rolling on a shoulder before feigning a change in direction. She fell for it. As he closed the distance between them, he saw the horror in her eyes. Her hands came down in front of her, and a familiar hiss erupted around them. With a mighty cry, Simon swung diagonally, his sword passing through her arms with brutal precision.

The girl's dismembered hands dropped into the sand as she staggered backward. Simon ran her through with his sword, quickly ending her suffering. Remembering that Tarquin was still under attack, he whirled around and went sprinting toward the large man who was only barely dodging flames.

Simon saw Kell scrambling toward the old fisherman, but compared to her at that moment, he was lightning. Tarquin's opponent saw Simon incoming and flung a conflagration toward him, heating the entire area. Focused, wholly intent on what he was doing, Simon ducked out of the way and then leaped over a bubbling swath of sand. He landed a few paces from the man and then, sensing the air fluctuate, rolled.

Heat tagged his lower back and singed the hairs there. Using the sand to stop his momentum, he rushed forward with a grunt. As the man leveled his hands at him, Simon realized he had messed up. He had been singed before. Not badly, but enough that large patches of hair had been burned off. The stinging pain was never pleasant, but he could usually push through it. Coupled with the lashings he had recently received, however, the agony that erupted along his back was crippling. He hadn't been fast enough.

Simon caught movement over his opponent's shoulder and darted to the right. With brutish strength, Tarquin cut the man from shoulder to hip, disemboweling him in a single stroke and slinging blood across the sand. On his knees, sword still in hand, Simon nodded his thanks to Tarquin and then grimaced in pain.

Kell joined them, her face pale and eyes hazy. Despite the searing agony that wracked his body, Simon could tell she was only partially lucid. She appeared disoriented, sick. She was barely holding it together, and something in him told him that what ailed her was somehow related to Viterra.

"We've got eight minutes left," he panted, standing. He did what he could to hide his discomfort from the crowd. "Kell, hey."

She looked at him, her eyes not fully focusing on his face.

A blast of fire at their one o'clock between a User and a pro-fighter had Kell staggering into her father, her hands visibly trembling. She tried to vomit again but only spat onto the sand. She shook her head as if to clear her mind, to will away whatever was crippling her.

"She's been unsteady since it started," Tarquin shouted. "Been throwin' up and—"

"What's wrong with her?" he shouted to Tarquin.

Her father shook his head. "Don't know. She's unsteady on her feet, been throwing up. Don't know what's going—"

"Simon!" shouted Ferrik. Even from a distance, Simon could discern the blood smeared across his mentor's pants.

"Watch her," Simon ordered. "And stay close to me." He started across the sand. Tarquin and Kell followed.

He needed to trust that Tarquin would watch his back. He couldn't let them—

Simon collided headlong into a man who had just sprung out from behind a palisade, not in attack but in retreat. Glimpsing red rings on the User's wrists, Simon instinctively reared back to attack.

"Simon!" the man cried.

Simon broke from his combat-induced trance to regard the User. Mordecai had a wild look about him, a stark difference from how he had appeared two weeks prior. His black hair was oily and matted to the side of his head; his face appeared slightly gaunt with dazed eyes ringed by purple circles. Like Kell, he looked ill, only somewhat lucid. His clothes were tattered and blood-stained. And two glowing rings of red hummed on each of his arms.

Simon didn't have a chance to process Mordecai's sudden appearance because Ferrik lunged from behind a palisade and swung, throwing Mordecai into further retreat.

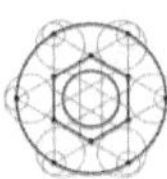

A familiar tug at the Flow around her drew Kell from her stupor, her eyes flickering in an attempt to focus as the world around her dipped and bucked. She knew that pull, that sensation. Feeling faint, she leaned heavily on Tarquin, the ground periodically meeting the sky in her vision.

She closed her eyes for a moment, took a long breath, and then opened them again. Before the earth rolled under her once more, she caught sight of Mordecai—fighting for his life. Absolute terror steadied her as she processed the scene.

Simon was half-heartedly circling Mordecai as Ferrik jabbed, feigned, thrust, and lunged. With every sword swing, Ferrik drew closer to Mordecai, even as Mordecai loosed precisely-aimed blasts of fire. The fear in his eyes was heartrendingly apparent. He hadn't had time to ignite an Arcane Circle.

Yet another pro-fighter joined the circle, bating Mordecai as if he were a wild animal.

"Morde…cai…" whimpered Kell, her voice closing around her words.

She had had enough.

She could take no more torture, no more cruelty, no more pain or death.

She had endured for the past few weeks because that was what had been needed to get her here.

Renata's words rang in her ears. *Remember, when you fight, you make sure your opponents know who they're dealing with.*

Drawing herself upright, Kell stepped away from Tarquin. Though she could hardly make sense of the movements of the fighters around her, she could feel the sand shift beneath her feet. Assuming a position she had used countless times over the past several years, her right leg crossed and toe touching the sand, she drew a swift circle around her and struck her wrists, igniting two brilliant bands of blue along each of her arms.

The world around her stop spinning. In fact, everyone and everything in it fell shockingly still.

The firmness of the Arcane Circle under her was reassuring. The debilitating nausea that had plagued her since the onset of the first event was gone. In its place was swelling confidence and an intense desire to assert herself in an unjust world.

Glancing first at Simon, whose mouth was agape, she shifted her gaze to Ferrik. The tall, onyx-colored man seemed unsurprised, understanding even, as if this sudden reveal confirmed what he had suspected.

"Away from him," Kell said, moving into an earth stance. She motioned to Simon. "You too."

As the fighters retreated, Mordecai joined Kell. Breathing hard, he braced on his knees to catch his breath. "You couldn't have done that sooner?" he panted, his voice breaking.

Kell looked back out at the arena where fiery eruptions continued to set off explosions and the scent of blood tainted the air. She had become numb to the noise, to the crowd's sounds of pleasure and contempt. "Ignite your fields when you can. We're done here."

"Yeah."

"As long as those palisades are around," said Tarquin from behind them, "it'll be too dangerous."

Though the roar of the crowd managed to break through the mental barrier she had erected, she breathed, found her *satt*, and then with forceful strikes that utilized her forearms, the backs of her hands, and fists, she commanded the earth move.

The arena began to tremble, at first a low rumble, before swelling to a violent tremoring. The audience screamed as those in the arena paused their life-or-death duels to discern what was happening.

Screams of "She's Unbound!" and "Run!" reverberated through the stadium as onlookers began scrambling out of their seats.

Kell directed the earth throughout the arena to rip open to reveal black, yawning chasms that strategically swallowed the palisades and separated fighters from Bound prisoners. Great waterfalls of sand poured into the abysses she made, draining parts of the stadium. When her gaze found Simon once more, she twitched her fingers. The sand around him shifted, and he was drawn on unsteady legs to Tarquin.

"Users," announced Madam Parthemos. Kell looked up at the terrace along the eastern grandstand that held the most important of nobles and aristocrats. Kell felt Mordecai start drawing from the Flow as he ignited his circle. "Anyone who can kill that Unbound will instantly be granted their freedom alongside a sizable monetary reward." Kell thought she heard Bellamy yell at the president, but the microphone was cut off.

"What's the plan here?" asked Tarquin as the remaining Bound prisoners in the arena—a total of fourteen—began making their way toward them, leaping over crevasses and making crystalized bridges out of scorched sand. In the meantime, the fighters retreated, knowing they would not be partaking in the battle. The two nearest Bound prisoners were already within range.

Kell changed traits, opting for her specialty. Pressing downward in a sharp movement, she conjured ice, which began circling her in a controlled twister of razor-sharp shards. She met her opponents' gazes. The first appeared far older than most; the second looked oddly familiar.

"Ambrose?" she whispered, recognizing the scar on his eyebrow. She looked back at Simon. "Ambrose?" He nodded grimly. She felt both of the men dip into the Flow, their techniques carelessly allowing energy to surge around them in an irrepressible rush. "Ambrose!" she shouted. But it was already too late.

A maelstrom of out-of-control flames vented from them. Not wishing to kill Ambrose, Kell converted the ice to water and loosed a powerful jet, turning his flames into hissing stream and hurtling him backward several paces. In the split second that followed, Kell switched stances, moving fluidly to fire traits. Unleashing weeks of pent-up anger and frustration, her blast of brilliant orange flames met the man's, cutting through the fire with lethal accuracy and power. She struck him in the chest, driving the Viterra into him like a sword.

"Kidane!" Simon suddenly screamed. "Stop!"

Kell sensed a dramatic shift in the Flow and the consequential draw of an alarming amount of Viterra. Wildly, she wheeled on the man Simon had called Kidane, who was flanked by several other Bound prisoners.

Dread took hold of Kell. Impending doom, like how she felt when *Polaris* was sitting in the trough of a monster wave that seemed to grow forever skyward, choked her. It was inevitable, unescapable.

Renata's smug expression from years ago flitted into her mind.

"So… you said that you and Madam Nicolea had come to an understanding? What… does that mean?" Kell had asked shortly after the Containment Office destroyed Renata's first home.

"I sent her and her men running into the forest, of course," Renata had replied with a wolfish grin. "If you fight, you make sure your opponent knows who they're up against. Nobody wants to face off with an Unbound."

"Aren't you worried they're going to come after you?" Mordecai had queried, concerned.

Renata had cackled. "And do what? I can turn this whole forest against them. And they know it."

Kell glanced down at the sand beneath her Arcane Circle. Knowing what she needed to do, she shifted to air traits, positioning her body sideways to her opponents. With an open palm extended toward their attackers and a fist stationed firmly at her waist, she stepped forward, urging Viterra into the air around her. With sharp arm movements but fluid hand gestures, she called forth wind.

Great gusts whipped to life around her, spraying abrasive sand outward. Moving her hands upward, she commanded the wind to take the form of a whirling cyclone, tucking herself, Mordecai, Tarquin, and Simon within the safety of its eye. Fiery explosions ricocheted off the cyclone and twisting rivulets of fire were sucked upward as her adversaries attempted to dismantle the growing maelstrom.

Kell turned her attention on Kidane, who appeared to be the most immediate threat, and directed the earth beneath his feet to open. Kidane leaped away, escaping the gaping fissure with astonishing litheness. Kell gave chase. With a surge of energy, she thrust Viterra into the ground, causing it to swell to life. Enormous, spindly tentacles of sand materialized around Kidane and lashed to his ankles. Even when he fell, he continued to thrash, sending smoldering waves of fire everywhere.

Panting, Kell kept a tight grip on the man as she fought to control both earth and wind. She had practiced using more than one trait at a time while with the First Whispered, and it had always been difficult, even on a small scale. But now their survival depended on her ability to maintain a disciplined hold on the raging elements.

Kidane was pulled into the earth, kicking and screaming, a flaming conflagration of panic and desperation. The moment the top of his head disappeared, Kell slammed the earth closed and then returned her focus to the remaining others. Upon spotting their retreat, she calmed the sandstorm, settling herself with a final breath—

A burst of exquisite pain erupted along her right side followed by the loud thwack of a firearm.

Kell toppled, the momentum of the bullet dragging her body a pace or two forward. Wheezing audibly, she curled in on herself, digging at the sand. Hot gushing wetness seeped down her stomach and hip. The pain was on another level.

Stunned, she drew a hand away. Her fingers were wet with crimson blood. Simon slid into the sand beside her and lifted her in a single motion. She cried out as the movement jarred her.

"Simon…" she breathed, trying to focus on his face but instead looking up at the azure sky. "What… happened?" He didn't answer. "It hurts…" Her vision tunneled briefly, frightening her from her daze. "Simon!"

"Take her, take her," Simon said to someone. Tarquin's enormous arms folded around her.

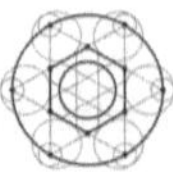

"Did you get him?" Simon called, peering up at the elevated stands where a man in a burgundy suit bearing a rifle had just collided with Mordecai's boulder.

A whistle pierced the air from across the stadium. Though Simon thought it just another response from the crowd, Mordecai seemed to find special meaning in it because he turned and ran, urging Tarquin to follow him. Simon followed. As they drew closer to the fighters' gate, he could make out Bellamy, the new king, accompanied by three others.

Simon glanced over his shoulder at the remaining fighters, who stood idly in the middle of the arena with the Users, and then up at the stands just above the gate. His eyes found Dockett. The Lanista had a look of unadulterated rage on his face. Simon had never before seen such a malevolent expression on a man. He held Dockett's gaze as they passed underneath.

"Let's go, let's go," shouted Bellamy, turning to run down the sloping hallway. He had foregone his imperial robes and opted for boots, a fine blouse, and slacks. In his hand was a sword, which surprised Simon.

Marko, his guard who led the way, bore orange bands of glowing energy on his arms and a circle under his feet. He was Unbound too? The other two men Simon didn't know or recognize.

"She needs help," Tarquin huffed, hugging Kell to his chest. Blood dripped on the floor behind him. "She's bleedin' too much."

"This way," Marko instructed, taking them not out the external door Simon was accustomed to but turning down another corridor and climbing stairs.

Coming around a blind corner, Simon couldn't see what lay ahead of them, but he knew Marko had come across an opponent as the glow of fire illuminated the stairwell. Tarquin turned his back to the heat, covering Kell as Mordecai drew a wedge of the wall outward with a swift kick to act as a shield. Bellamy ducked behind it as well. The floor rumbled.

As the cacophony raged on, the young king turned to examine Kell. Panting, he pulled his silken shirt over his head and, with Tarquin's help, tied it around Kell's bloody waist. When he knotted the sleeves, Kell hissed and briefly came to, snarling.

"Kell, apply pressure. Press on it. Harder, like this," he instructed. To Tarquin, he added, "I know of a doctor. Once we get out, we'll take her there. There's a bridge that connects to the stadium. It's mostly used by high-ranking nobles. We'll leave through there." He turned to Mordecai and Simon. "Marko, Rohan, and Jeremiah will cut a path through. You two bring up the rear. Don't let anyone come up behind us. We need a route back if something happens."

Simon nodded, his gaze flickering to Kell. Her face was ashen and knotted in horrible pain. Realizing this was his most important task yet, he looked at Mordecai.

The man appeared worse for the wear but also seemed to understand the significance of what needed to be done. Resolve settled in Mordecai's eyes.

"They're moving!" Bellamy called.

Mordecai withdrew the stone shield, and the group hurried onward though the labyrinth of corridors, passages, and stairs under and around the stadium. Much of the passing décor, signage, and embellishments of the stadium blurred together.

As they ran on, Marko and his comrades continued to blaze a trail through regulators and private guards.

"Tarquin!" shouted Mordecai suddenly, snarling a hand around Tarquin's meaty arm. A moment later, the door to their right was blown open by an enormous venting of fire. A barrier of ragged stone rose from the floor with a snap to shield Simon, Mordecai, and Tarquin. Flames licked the wall, promising no escape. Brandishing his sword, Simon prepared himself for battle.

Beside him, Mordecai gave a short three-chirp whistle which reverberated down the hall. A response, presumably provided by Bellamy, sang back.

"What's happening, what's happening?" asked Simon, realizing that they were communicating.

"They're waiting for us." Mordecai glanced at Kell and then at the sopping silk blouse that dripped blood onto the flagstone floor.

"What're you thinking?"

Mordecai met his gaze, his eyes suddenly possessing that same sharp intelligence they had exhibited upon their first meeting. Drawing a few swift breaths, hardening himself, Mordecai whirled away from the barrier. Hands positioned before him in a stance similar to one Simon had seen Kell hold, Mordecai slid a foot forward and then angled it, first to the left and then the right, before kicking straight up with remarkable flexibility and power.

Enormous, verdant vines erupted around him and leaped at the attackers beyond the stone blockade. Unlike Kell who utilized all her limbs in unison as she wielded Viterra, Mordecai's arms remained nearly motionless. His footwork, however, was phenomenally quick and precise. A knee jab followed by a lateral kick, which required him to spin on his heel, seemed to provide instruction to the rampaging vines.

When fire roared around them to fend off the attacking vegetation, Mordecai shifted positions and began utilizing solid, flatfooted kicks to direct stones to disengaged from the surrounding concrete. When a perfectly square boulder went soaring through the air past him, the flames disappeared.

Simon watched him, impressed. Very few, if any, of the pro-fighters could move like that. Even after being imprisoned for two weeks, Mordecai had the strength and grit to push forward. Simon dreaded meeting him when he was well.

Once the barricade was lowered, Simon was not only able to see Bellamy and the others waiting for them around the corner but the extent of Mordecai's assault. There had been three Containment Officers, all of whom had been using that Viterra stuff. One middle-aged man hung from a tangle of gnarled and thorny vines, his limp body squeezed so tight that a blood oozed down the viny spindles. The other two men were bloody smears under enormous rocks of cement and marble.

"Come on," Mordecai shakily panted, passing his victims to rejoin Bellamy. Tarquin and Simon followed.

Along the eastern side of the stadium, the group finally emerged on an open-air pavilion where patrons normally gathered to visit and drink prior to and immediately after the games. Instead of nobles, they found a collection of men and women in burgundy suits—the Containment Office of Avives.

Simon and Mordecai turned to observe their rear as Bellamy addressed the woman dressed in a crimson suit. "I am King of Berceau, Bellamy Trevarthen. Let us pass."

"I am Elpida Nicolea, Director of the Containment Office. We've been formally asked to arrest you and to destroy those in your company."

"By whom?" demanded Bellamy.

The madam smiled. "We both know who."

"We need to get her out of here," muttered Mordecai, eyeing the burgundy-clad men moving to cut off their escape. "Kell's lost too much blood."

Simon rhythmically gripped his sword's hilt. "I'm all ears—"

An explosion from somewhere down the vast open corridor reverberated through the building, shaking the walls and marble columns around them. The three officers stationed near Simon and Mordecai turned as one to see what had happened.

Sensing Mordecai move, Simon also lunged forward, sword reared in preparation to attack. One of the men managed a brief wall of fire but Simon slid underneath it and swung with all his strength. He felt his blade bite into the man's legs, a kind of crunch-crunch sound. In the next movement, he slashed diagonally upward, cutting a second man from hip to navel before reaching the limit of his reach.

But Mordecai, who had already taken care of the third officer with a marble slab, was there, ready to finish it. With a fierce downward kick, he loosed a precisely angled jet of flames that followed the trajectory of his kick and tore into their opponent. Still bouncing lightly on his feet, Mordecai searched for more attackers.

Farther along the corridor, brackish smoke billowed into the arena and laid cover for silhouetted forms of fast-moving people. As fighting broke out between the Containment Office and Bellamy's men, Simon and Mordecai prepared for battle with the newcomers.

Bellamy suddenly appeared beside them, whipping them around. No words were spoken as they followed him out the pavilion's doors. When a burgundy-suited man attempted to stop them, Mordecai met his torrent of fire with his own, driving the officer back as Bellamy and Tarquin, carrying Kell, cleared the door.

His training kicking in, Simon darted past the battling streams of blistering fire and attacked, slashing with brutal precision. The officer collapsed before his flames dissipated. Together, Simon and Mordecai charged through the doors onto the attached open-air trestle bridge that connected the stadium to another building Simon had not seen before.

To his surprise, Simon found Bellamy and Tarquin standing motionlessly several paces from the door. Mordecai at his side, Simon joined them, panting and confused. "What? What's wrong?"

Bellamy, who was also winded, plainly pointed over his left shoulder. Simon turned to find Dockett perched atop the upper level, a dozen or so armed regulators with him, their rifles leveled at the group.

Dockett leaned on the marble railing with a grin. "Figured you'd be coming out this way."

"This has nothing to do with you," Bellamy called, carefully turning to peer up at the Lanista.

"The hell it doesn't. I just lost millions because of that girl." He jutted a vehement finger at Kell. "Come on, *Your Majesty*. We both knew this was gonna be the last Munera. Half the Council's gone." He chuckled. "You've been working hard. Too bad the Containment Office couldn't get their hands on you."

Simon watched the Lanista, the man whose tutelage he had been under for years. Dockett appeared as though he was coming unhinged.

"Let's call this what it is—a draw," Dockett continued. "Give me the girl and Simon, and I'll let you go on your way, destroying the country and such."

"No," seethed Bellamy.

Dockett shook with rage, his face taut with white fury. "I will—I'll— Take aim!" The regulators beside him, dressed in their cobalt uniforms, raised their rifles as one.

"Wait! I'll go!" interrupted Simon. "I'll go."

"What? No," Bellamy barked, turning on him.

"I'll go—"

"I don't want *you!*" screamed Dockett, his voice breaking. "I want that fuckin' girl!"

"No." Mordecai's answer was so low that even Simon wasn't sure he had heard it.

Mordecai stepped away from Tarquin and Simon, drawing the regulators' aim. The glowing black circle under him hummed intensely, projecting an eerie light around him. An indiscernible wind shifted his hair and tugged at his clothes as he drew a deep breath, mimicking the same upward and downward palm motions Kell had displayed before shifting his weight to his back foot.

"Kill them," Dockett demanded suddenly with a strangled scoff.

A volley of gunfire resounded. Simon startled horribly, but his eyes never left Mordecai. With speed he didn't know the man possessed, Mordecai kicked upward and then, tilting his body to the side, spun his other foot around. Several muted thuds followed in the ensuing half-second. Mordecai straightened himself and then stepped back into a new stance, his legs set widely. A cache of bullets appeared around him, dancing in the air, ready to strike.

Wildly, Simon peered upward to find all of the regulators slumped along the marble rim, blood seeping from various bullet wounds. Dockett, who had not been in line alongside the officers, was the only one alive. Gaping,

Simon glanced back at Mordecai, whose eyes burned with wrath, and then at Dockett.

The Lanista gawked. "You… But you're Bound."

"Metal is my specialty," Mordecai snarled.

"Kill… him…" whispered Kill, squinting up at Dockett. "Morde… Kill him."

Dockett didn't have the opportunity to respond, to run. With a final stomp, Mordecai sent a single bullet whirring through the air. Dockett reared back as it struck him in the forehead; his body went limp and he toppled over the marble railing. Simon jerked Tarquin and Bellamy away. The Lanista hit the bridge with a sickening crunch, dead.

As if on cue, an explosion from inside the pavilion rocked the entire building and blew the iron-and-wood doors off their hinges. Great clouds of toxic smoke poured out, sending Simon and the others scurrying backward.

"Let's go!" shouted Bellamy, turning to run.

A snaking vine as thick as an arm slithered along the ground from within the pavilion, chasing them with intent. Simon chopped off the tip with a quick swing. But the vine regrew instantly—and sprouted four more writhing creepers.

Mordecai swung around, unleashing a potent hiss of fire that sizzled the vines, and then shouted, "Terin!" When there was no immediate answer, he called out again.

The wriggling green tentacles of vegetation glided back through the threshold. Momentarily, a handful of figures emerged from the smoke, seemingly unbothered by the noxious air.

"Simon," Mordecai muttered, motioning for him to get behind him. Not knowing what was going on or who the newcomers were, Simon edged closer to Tarquin and Kell.

A young woman in her early twenties separated herself from the others and approached their group. She was fit and boasted a toned and bronzed body. Braids close to her scalp kept her black, kinky hair out of her face but allowed a halo of puff to form at the back of her head. Her teak-colored eyes were cold, calculating. But dressed in men's clothes, she looked more like a fisherman's son than a new enemy.

"Mordecai." The woman named Terin regarded the group, her gaze landing on each person for a moment. Despite her fierce appearance, when she next spoke, it was with some concern. "What happened to Kell?"

"She was, uh, shot," replied Mordecai. Simon could hear the nervousness in his voice; that, of course, put him on edge. "Containment Office."

Terin glanced at Simon and then at Tarquin and Bellamy. "And them? Who are they?"

"Friends," Mordecai quickly replied. "All prisoners. We're just trying to get out, but…" He motioned to Dockett's body behind them and to the pavilion. "It's not been easy."

"Besides Kell and the three that got in the way inside, are any of you Unbound?" Terin asked, her voice even.

"What?" snarled Bellamy.

Mordecai barred his way with a strong arm. "Kell's hurt—bad. Please, we need to go. Look." He motioned to the blood that still leaked down Tarquin's legs.

Terin gestured to Simon and Tarquin. "You call them friends, but they look like fighters."

"Yeah, they were prisoners, like us. They've been helping us." Mordecai turned and pointed to him. "This-this is Simon. Terin, Simon. *The* Simon. Remember?" He turned to Tarquin. "And Kell's dad. Come on. We just need to go."

Terin's gaze fell on Kell. "Where are you taking her?"

"To a doctor," Mordecai replied. "My friend says he knows a good one."

"Renata…" Kell's voice was weak. Simon looked back at her, surprised she was awake. "Where… is she, Terin?"

Terin scoffed and then whirled away. "How should I know?"

31

Truce

KELL BREATHED DEEP, THE PAIN that had been nagging her a distant ache. She tried to swallow but found her mouth torturously dry and her lips cracked. Her eyes refused to open and her body disobeyed any command to move. Having no energy to fight the fatigue that swaddled her, she allowed herself to drift back to sleep.

The next time she woke, it was dark—and she had the horrible need to relieve herself. Taking a rattling breath, she struggled to sit up. Pain bit into her side, causing her to collapse back on the bed. Someone must have heard her because the sound of feet padding down a corridor drew her attention to the open doorway across the quaint room.

A middle-aged man with a handlebar mustache carrying a lantern appeared. Glancing at the floor, he weaved his way to her and took a seat at her bedside.

"I'm Lachlan Fitzgerald, a doctor and a friend of His Majesty. You were brought to my clinic a day and a half ago." A set of round glasses perched on his hawkish nose reflected the dancing flame of the light. "How are you feeling?"

"Thirsty," she managed.

Lachlan left the room with a smile, stepping strangely toward the door. Realizing that he was maneuvering around something, Kell rose on her elbows to peer over the side of her bed. She had thought the room was of moderate size, but with Simon, Mordecai, and Tarquin sprawled out on the floor, snoring in various intervals, she couldn't help but smile.

Lachlan returned with a cup of water and a robe since she was completely nude. He helped her sit up, asking, "How's the pain?"

"Fine," Kell lied, grimacing. She eagerly sucked down the entire glass and then another.

"I want to do an exam." Lachlan increased the brightness of the lantern and then moved the stethoscope, which he had returned with around his neck, to his ears. "Breathe." The skin around her wound pulled painfully; the doctor didn't miss her response. "Yes, it will be painful for a while. You're very lucky. No organs were damaged. Just muscle and tissue."

"Can I see?" Kell asked, her voice hoarse.

"Of course." Lachlan eased the side of her robe over and held the lantern a closer. "You can see, it went in just above your hip on the back and went upward. I did a thorough exam and several tests to make sure no pieces were left before suturing the wound closed. It's going to take time to heal. We use these muscles here for everything—sitting, standing, getting up."

There was a rustle and momentarily Mordecai stood beside the doctor, bleary-eyed, his black hair a haystack.

"I'll heal though, right?" she whispered, glancing at Mordecai.

Lachlan gave a noncommittal shrug. "You'll heal, but you'll probably always have those scars. For now, I want you on bedrest for the next two weeks. No moving around at all." Kell frowned deeply. "Ah yes, His Majesty warned me about you," the doctor added with amusement. "If you want to recover sooner, stay in bed. Give your body time to repair itself." He rose from the stool situated at her bedside. "It's just past midnight. Do you need anything from me?"

"I have to pee so bad," Kell uttered with no qualms about decency.

"I can help with that," replied Mordecai.

To him, Lachlan said, "Do not let her bend or sit by herself. She will tear the sutures. Also, she's still groggy and won't be stable. Hold her at all times; do not leave her unattended."

Mordecai nodded and offered his hands to Kell. Sitting up was one thing; urging her body to stand was another. Seated on the edge of the low bed, her robe open down the middle, Kell struggled to pull her legs under her; they felt like limp fish.

Lachlan watched Mordecai maneuver her to her feet. "Good, one step at a time," he instructed. "Let her get settled."

Kell clung to Mordecai's arms with all her strength, her fingers digging into him as she inched across the room. When Lachlan appeared satisfied with her progress, he left, disappearing down the hallway.

"This way," Mordecai muttered, guiding her at a snail's pace in the opposite direction down the corridor. There were numerous other closed doors, but the building remained silent.

The bathroom at the end of the hallway was roomy, possibly to accommodate uncoordinated or injured patients. Kell squinted against the light as Mordecai closed the door behind them and steadied her.

Kell regarded herself in the mirror above the sink and then scoffed. "I look rough."

"You look better than you did," he replied, holding her from behind but taking care not to touch her wound.

Grimacing as she shifted her weight, Kell moved to the toilet. Deciding it would be best if the robe wasn't on, she slipped it off her naked body. With solid arms, Mordecai gently lowered her. After doing her business and taking care of herself, Kell pulled on Mordecai to lift herself. But the pain it caused her was terrible, and she slouched on the toilet momentarily.

"Here, here," said Mordecai. He went on her uninjured side and provided a sturdy base, pulling when she did. Once she stood, he dressed her in her robe and balanced her as she inched toward the sink. He offered her a wet cloth to wash her face, holding her hair back while keeping her wavering body upright.

Kell braced on the sink for a moment and looked back at him in the mirror. "I don't... remember much. What happened? How did we get out?"

"Let's get you back to bed and I'll explain," Mordecai replied with a soft smile.

Kell had to rest on the way back to the room, bracing heavily on Mordecai. Her legs threatened to give with no warning and the minute steps made her breathing come in rasps.

"Take your time," he whispered, his support a constant warmth that bolstered her. "I have you." She felt like crying; never before had her body been so ragged. It scared her. Silent tears streaking down her face, she started to move again, but Mordecai stopped her after a single step. "Hey, take your time."

"I'm..." She was so tired.

"Focus, Kellick. Don't think about anything but getting back to bed." He gave her an encouraging squeeze. "Come on."

Kell sniffed loudly and then shuffled onward. Their bedroom door was open; the light from the lantern poured into the dim hallway, a welcoming sight. Upon appearing in the open threshold, Kell saw movement across the room. Simon sat up to watch them in alarm.

"What's going on?" he asked, his gaze searching her and then Mordecai.

"Bathroom," Mordecai replied, guiding Kell back to the bed. With tender hands, he slowly lowered her onto the bed's edge, not letting her go even when she sat, his arm pinned against her uninjured left side to provide stability.

Kell sat panting for a long moment before drying her tears on the shoulders of her robe.

"Ready?" Mordecai whispered. She nodded. As she moved her legs into the bed and started to recline, he placed a knee over her, keeping his other foot on the floor, and then, hugging her shoulders to him, helped her go down smoothly. Kell whined as a twinge of pain reverberated along her entire right side. "Relax, relax."

"I'm trying," she growled, clenching his arms.

Mordecai chuckled. "You're not. Un-unclench—Kellick, look. Unclench. There, *there*."

Kell melted into her pillows, heart hammering. Staring up at Mordecai, she said, "Tell me. What happened?" He shifted to the stool next to the lantern and began answering her questions. Periodically, Simon would insert information from his seat on the floor nearby.

"And I told you to kill him?" mused Kell, trying to remember everything. Most of it was a blur of flames, smoke, and loud noises that had punctuated her delirious state.

Mordecai nodded solemnly. "And I did. Turned his own bullets against him."

Kell took his hand. "Thank you."

"But that… wasn't it," interjected Simon, standing. He looked down at her. "There was another group there at the stadium."

"Yeah…" Mordecai met her gaze. "Terin was there. She was destroying the entire building and killing everyone inside, even Bellamy's men. She came after us too. I recognized her Viterra and called to her. She stopped."

Kell looked between him and Simon several times. "And?"

"Well, she let us go," Simon said.

"You asked her about Renata," Mordecai continued.

Kell's eyes grew wide. "What did I say?"

"You asked her where Renata was. And… she said that she didn't know." Mordecai grimly held her gaze.

"Well, she actually said, 'How should I know?'" clarified Simon.

"'How should I know?'" Kell repeated, dread filling her. "Renata went to stop the reactionaries. I haven't…" She looked at Mordecai. "Terin wouldn't… She wouldn't…"

"She's doing a lot of things," Simon went on. "I was talking to the doctor. He told me the Lower District's in flames; been that way for three days. Vines took over the Middle District two days ago. They… went after the palace yesterday."

"And nothing from Bellamy?"

Both shook their heads.

Weary and fading quickly, Kell struggled to keep thinking, plotting, planning, wondering. Mordecai caressed her face, prompting her to look at him. "Go to sleep—and find them." He gestured to Simon. "You're safe here."

Kell's gaze shifted to Simon who nodded in grim agreement. "I'll..." She drew a long breath, allowing her eyes to drift to the ceiling. "I'll find them."

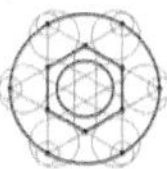

Kell fell asleep fast. Simon left to use the restroom and stretch his legs. When he returned, he found Mordecai still seated at Kell's bedside, his gaze on her hand, deep in thought.

"If we don't lock her down fast," Simon said, seating himself beside Tarquin, who still snored softly, "she'll run off to save people."

Mordecai stood and crossed the room. "Come with me."

No longer sleepy, Simon obliged, following him down the hall of the private residence to the steep staircase which they had carried Kell up days earlier. Simon regarded Mordecai from behind, keeping in mind how fast the black-haired young man had moved days prior.

Mordecai led him through the kitchen to the rear patio where they had supped earlier that evening. The doctor's private garden was beautifully manicured and well maintained by an on-staff gardener.

With a tired sigh, Mordecai sat in a patio chair and propped his feet on the adjacent chair. Rubbing his face with weary hands, he finally looked at Simon who sat across the table. "How's your back?"

"Rare," replied Simon. Though the doctor's medicines had definitely helped, he was still stiff. Burns on top of flogging stripes were remarkably painful.

"I bet." He adjusted himself in the chair. "So, yeah, you're right. We can't..." Mordecai nodded. "Kell will figure out where Renata is—"

"And who's Renata?"

"Our teacher. She took us in—and Terin—and trained us. Taught us the New Knowledge." Mordecai waved a hand. "We lived off the land in the middle of the forest for several years with her and then moved to the mountains with the First Whispered this past year. The point is Kell will kill for her, and so will I. But..." He drew a long breath. "Terin is her first. Renata sees Terin as a daughter. I just don't know that, uh, Terin views their relationship in the same light."

Skipping over all the new information Mordecai had just shared about their past, Simon asked, "You think Terin killed her?"

Mordecai propped his face on his hand, his gaze set across the garden. "I hope not. But if she did, we're going to have some issues."

"Why?"

"Terin's Unbound."

"So? Kell is too."

Mordecai looked at him pointedly. "Terin is powerful. She has a personal vendetta against Berceau and intends to dismantle it." His gaze shifted to the ground. "But she's not a bad person. Just troubled. Angry with the world—and rightfully so. Life's... not been easy for her, or us."

"Do you agree with her?"

Mordecai looked at him. "I want the world to change. I want everyone to just... live. It shouldn't matter who you are. But I don't want it to change at the hands of Terin and the reactionaries. She paints everyone with a broad brush and believes that everyone who can't access the Flow should be killed. That means you, Bellamy, Tarquin, anyone who can't in some way evoke Viterra." He sighed. "Honestly, we're lucky she let us go. She killed... Bellamy's men." Mordecai shook his head. "Even Marko. He was Unbound as well. But she killed him with... ease."

Simon recalled Mordecai's tense responses to the bronzed woman. "Is she... so much stronger than Kell?"

Mordecai nodded. "She's not just stronger; she's older and more experienced. She's been with Renata longer—studied more, practiced more. Kell was flagging in the arena, riding right up to her limit. Terin," Mordecai gave a shrug, "could have killed them, all of them, with a single blow. Easy."

Alarmed, Simon asked, "And your teacher couldn't stop her?"

"Don't know. Terin's response doesn't bode well." Mordecai regarded the garden. There was silence between them for several minutes.

Simon glanced at Mordecai periodically, aware that not only was he Kell's partner and fiancé but that he clearly had more worldly experience. In addition, he was a User, the enemy whom Simon had been trained to maim and kill. The black tattooed cuffs peeking out from under Mordecai's long sleeves kept Simon on guard. He greatly disliked being alone with Mordecai.

Eventually, Mordecai cleared his throat and met Simon's gaze. "I'm not going to pretend like there's no ill will between you and I because we both know there is."

Simon conscientiously worked to hide his surprise.

"But seeing the predicament we're in right now, I don't really have anyone else I can turn to." Mordecai traced a pattern on the table before saying, "When Kell learns where Renata is… would you come with me? To get her?"

Simon scoffed to better conceal his discomfort. "I'm not going to be much good against any of your people."

"That's exactly why I want you with me. Because you know how to fight them. Terin's Unbound, but the majority of the people with her are Bound. She's gathered thousands of Bound, inciting riots in Avives and encouraging everyone to stand against government entities." Mordecai thought for a moment before continuing grimly. "I haven't told Kell, but I'm pretty sure my family was ousted earlier this year from Avives—or killed. Terin's done a lot of damage in Avives, and now she's in Eclat."

Simon peered out at the garden and then up at the faint sliver of the silver moon. "You trust me?"

"Not really."

Simon didn't move.

"But I can't ask Tarquin to come with me. He'll slow me down. And I don't much want to make that journey on my own…" He sighed in dark amusement. "I'm good but not that good."

"You don't know anything about me. I could turn on you," Simon mused. He wasn't astute when it came to relationships and communication, but he could sense the caution with which they maneuvered around one another.

"I know more than you think," replied Mordecai, his voice even. "Over the years, Kell's… dreamed about you often. She set our house on fire once in her sleep, screaming your name. Even then, I suspected you and I would meet one day." He tapped his foot for a moment and then said, "I also know that she loves you. Sometimes, I worry she loves you too much." Simon looked at Mordecai and found him gazing across the table. "And I know you love her."

Simon fidgeted. "Did she tell you that?"

"No." Mordecai looked back out at the garden. "You did." The calming hum of September cicadas punctuated the silence between them. "The way you move around her, how you look at her."

Simon waved a mosquito away from his ear in an effort to appear unbothered by the conversation. "And what if that were true?"

His face illuminated by the moonlight, Mordecai appeared mature, solemn. "Did you bed her?"

Unprepared for such a straightforward question, Simon froze. "No."

"But there was something?"

After a moment, Simon nodded. "She… wouldn't… She stopped us." Suddenly concerned that Mordecai might take his anger and frustration out on Kell, he added, "I was… hurt bad. Dockett flogged me earlier this week. Kell came to use that Viterra stuff. She grew these vines and heated them and… it helped a lot. I was distraught and I took advantage of her."

"Just the once?"

Heart in his throat, Simon didn't answer.

Silence expanded between them before Mordecai stood. "I see." He stretched and then looked at Simon. "So? You willing to grab Renata with me or what?"

"What? Just like that? You're not angry?"

Mordecai braced his hands on his hips; he was tense. When he spoke, his voice was low, gritty. "We've been together for years. We grew up together. Yeah, I'm… pissed. But there's not much I can do about it right this minute, is there? Kell's hurt; our teacher has disappeared; Terin and her horde are tearing through the Middle District. I've… got to do something." He drew a long, calming breath and then turned and held his hand out across the table. "So, you in?"

Simon stood and took it. "I'm in."

32

Searches

WITH A SILENT HUFF, KELL glowered at the wood-plank ceiling overhead. She hadn't found Renata. She had looked all over the Middle and Upper Districts where Terin had recently been, but still found no trace of their teacher.

Tarquin appeared over her; he smiled, an odd expression on his usually stoic face. "How are you feelin'?" His voice was hushed. Given the taste of the light coming through the pulled curtains, it appeared to be morning.

"I couldn't find Renata." She blinked to urge the brain fog away.

"Dr. Fitzgerald said he wanted us to get him when you woke. I'll be back." Her father lumbered across the room and slipped through the ajar door.

Turning her attention onto herself, Kell swallowed and tried to sit up. The pain wasn't nearly as bad as it had been the previous night, but it was still debilitating. After silently struggling, she managed to pull herself into a seated position. From there, she could survey the floor where Simon and Mordecai slept in piles of disheveled blankets.

Taking the moment of privacy, she discreetly pulled her robe away to survey her wound. The sutures, of which she counted five just above the top of her hip, were crusted with dried blood and old medicine. With ginger fingers, she dabbed at the first suture and immediately regretted it. Whimpering, she clenched her fists until the pain began to ebb.

Tarquin returned with Lachlan. "Get those boys awake," the doctor said. "I'm tired of stepping around them." Although Mordecai stirred at Lachlan's words, Simon remained motionless.

As Tarquin nudged them awake, Lachlan took a seat next to Kell and pulled open the curtain to let in wondrous sunlight. "How are you feeling?

315

You've managed to get yourself upright. Now, I'm going to have you lie back down. Can you do that on your own?"

Kell lay back, grimacing. When she was flat again, she sighed in relief. Lachlan pulled aside her robe, exposing her right flank and breast, and scrutinized the wound. "Little pokes here," he murmured, gently touching the sutures. Kell whined but otherwise remained still. "Tarquin, could you come help me roll her?"

With Tarquin's assistance, they rolled her onto her left side so the doctor could examine the entry site along her back. Fists clenched, for the position was quite uncomfortable, Kell waited. When they rested her on her back again, she relaxed.

"Everything looks surprisingly good." Lachlan glanced at Simon and Mordecai. "That being said, you cannot be pushing yourself. Getting up, sitting down—everything we talked about. You have to take it easy and give your body time to recuperate."

"How long will it take to heal?"

"It's as I said last night. Two weeks of bed rest. After that, we can reevaluate." Lachlan flashed her a most serious look when she opened her mouth to argue. "If you undo my work, I'll be quite cross with you." He stood. "Breakfast is ready. I'll have Linda bring you a plate. You boys are welcome to eat in the dining room."

The moment the doctor was gone, Mordecai turned on Kell. "Well? Where is she?"

Kell shook her head. "I couldn't find her. I looked everywhere in the Middle and Upper Districts—"

"That's not how you usually find us," he interrupted. "You're usually drawn to us—"

"I know. But that didn't happen. So I started looking in the Middle and Upper Districts where Terin last was." Kell lifted a knee. "I couldn't find her."

"Maybe she's not in the area?" Simon offered.

Mordecai pointed at him. "That, yes. If Renata were hurt, she wouldn't be hanging around in the city."

Kell grew grim. "If she were badly hurt, she wouldn't be able to go very far."

"What if she just left the city after everything with Terin?" Mordecai speculated. "You know she hates it here. She wouldn't spend any more time in it—"

"Then why couldn't I find her?" Kell stubbornly pushed herself upright. Fighting through the pain, she said, "Every time I trace someone in my dreams, it's a-a feeling. I follow the feeling and end up where I'm supposed to be. But I didn't get that last night."

"What if she's… not alive?" Simon cautiously offered.

"No," replied Mordecai as Kell shook her head. "No way. Renata is a master. She wouldn't so easily be taken down—"

"You said yourself that Terin is powerful," Simon countered, looking between them. "And she has other Users with her. Can your master take on her *and* the others?"

Chewing her lip, Kell exchanged looks with Mordecai.

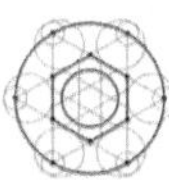

After a cold shower—to prevent the burns on his back from searing—shaving, and dressing in clean clothes, Simon went downstairs with Tarquin to eat. He didn't like leaving Mordecai alone with Kell, but given her state, he was certain nothing was going to happen between them.

He and Tarquin ate breakfast with a few other patients who were mobile and sat outside on the rear patio to sip tea, a pleasure he had not had in many years. Tarquin sat with him to admire the flowering garden and watch patients mill about.

"Lachlan told me most of the people he's treatin' right now are here because of the reactionaries. They were injured in the attacks this week," said Tarquin. Simon nodded in thought.

Both watched a middle-aged woman shuffle across the grass with the aid of a nurse to an azalea bush adorned with bright, pink blossoms.

"We can't let Kell escape."

Simon chuckled, but when he looked at Tarquin, he found her father solemn. Clearing his throat, he apologized and agreed. "Mordecai and I were talking about that last night. This Renata-thing will drive her to action."

"Yep," replied Tarquin. He looked at Simon. "So, what's the plan?"

"Once she knows where Renata is, me and Mordecai'll go get her."

Tarquin regarded him and then sipped his coffee. "You all right goin' alone with Mordecai?"

Unable to hide his true feelings from Tarquin, Simon grimaced. "Not really." He leaned on his knees and gave a short laugh. "I just really hate him."

"Well, you're vyin' for the same woman."

"Is it that obvious?" Simon asked. He glanced at the old fisherman. "You got nothing more encouragin' to say about it?"

Tarquin sipped his tea thoughtfully and then shook his head. "Not really. I'm on Kell's side. Whatever is gonna keep her in bed and out of action." He looked at Simon. "So if that means you two cooperatin', then I'm all for it."

Simon sat back in mild distress. "He's a goddamn User though..." He glanced at Tarquin when the man didn't reply. Seeing the solemn look on his face, Simon swallowed. "I'm sorry, Tarquin. I didn't mean—"

"Kell's a User," Tarquin said lowly so others couldn't hear. He met Simon's gaze. "Arguably, she's more your enemy than Mordecai... with her bein' Unbound and all."

"Yeah, but that's... Kell," Simon argued half-heartedly. "She's..."

"My daughter."

"Sorry. Really. I didn't... I'm sorry. Truly."

Tarquin took the pot between them and poured more Earl Grey tea into Simon's cup. "Every User's got a mother and father that loves them. Kell and Mordecai ain't no different. All them people you and I killed the other day... they had parents, siblings, children..." He sat back and thought over his own steaming cup. "Think on that, Simon."

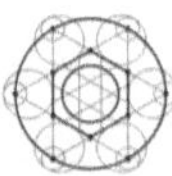

"I talked with Simon last night," Mordecai said, steadying Kell as she attempted a sponge bath in the bathroom. "Talked for a while actually."

Kell fumbled, her heart, which was already racing from the effort, leaping in her chest. "About?"

Mordecai's hands remained gentle. "You two." Gripping a rail, she turned to look at him. He met her gaze with a sad smile.

"I'm... so sorry," she whispered.

He chuckled, glancing down at her nude, ragged body before his face folded into pain. "I knew it was a possibility with you two living... and being so close to each other. But I hoped... And then you stopped visiting me in my dreams, and I..." He met her gaze, his eyes moist. "Do you still want to be engaged to me?"

Kell's legs trembled under her. Unsteadily, she took hold of his arms and edged into his embrace, tears of frustration and hurt swelling in her eyes. "I'm sorry." Mordecai hugged her, though it felt more like he was keeping her upright. "I'm sorry, Mordecai," she whimpered.

He buried his face into her neck, gripping her wet hair with a free hand. "Kellick."

"I'm yours, Mordecai." She winced as pain shot up along her injured flank, but she didn't dare bring it to his attention. Instead, she clung to him, her cheeks wet with more than just bathwater. "I love you. I'm yours. Always." Mordecai pulled away to press his forehead to hers. "I'm sorry for making you worry."

"You're sure?" he asked, holding her gaze.

Kell kissed him. Mordecai sighed lovingly into her mouth, his arms strong around her and his hands tender. He must have felt her weakness returning because he gently guided her to the little stool left near the tub and sat. Kell straddled him to keep from twisting her side and, panting from the effort it took her to just move around, she kissed his neck. Mordecai held her close, seemingly uncaring that she was getting his clothes wet.

Simon was passionate, was virile and intoxicating. His body was hard and muscular. When he kissed her, she felt as though she could hardly keep up with his enthusiasm. He was hungry for physical contact and love and wanted every part of her all at once. Of course, she liked kissing him, and just thinking of his rough hands coursing over her body ignited within her a deep fire that ached for him. But the depth of their relationship felt shallow.

Mordecai, on the other hand, was like a smoldering fire—low, hot, even, and constant. He didn't have the same physical prowess as Simon, but he had the emotional maturity of someone twice his age. When he held her, she felt settled, as if she had always belonged there in his arms. She could rely on him, count on him to be there at the exact right moment. He was friendship; he was love. He was home.

Kell eventually finished bathing. Mordecai not only continued to hold her steady but provided kisses and touches that had not been shared earlier. By the time they returned to the room, Kell was starved. Only Tarquin had returned from breakfast to tidy up.

As Mordecai and Tarquin got to know one another, Kell voraciously stuffed her mouth with as much food as possible. Sadly, the plate she had been allotted had not come with much food—doctors' orders, according to Tarquin—and she was left hungry.

She watched Mordecai for a while, liking how he so easily chatted with her father, before feeling drowsy. The window near her bed was open, and a soft breeze wafted in, carrying with it the scent of blooming flowers. Coupled with the voices of the people she loved, Kell slipped off to sleep.

Her dreams were erratic, flitting from one scene to another, never lighting long enough for her to grow comfortable. She searched disheveled alleys and vine-barricaded roads and scanned abandoned shops with broken windows and half-burnt townhomes, her desire to locate Renata swelling with each passing minute.

Growing distraught by what that could mean, she roared down a street in the Middle District, zigzagging like a bolt of lightning. Suddenly, she was pulled to a wrenching halt before a building, a familiar sensation. She looked up at the apartment complex whose outer frontage was marred with burn marks and windows were overtaken by spindly ivy, thorned vines, and tree branches that weaved in from the street.

Cautiously, Kell entered the building, ducking under a large, leafy bough before, blinking, she appeared at the base of a set of stairs. The interior was wrecked. Doors stood open to reveal the personal lives of people who had once lived there; thorny bushes, small flowering trees, poisonous vines, and green grass overran every aspect of the building, giving it an eerie, dystopian feeling.

Kell blinked and found herself at the top of the first set of stairs. Like the second floor, individual apartment doors stood open. People bearing tattooed handcuffs milled about on this floor, however, talking quietly and freely using the utilities and personal effects of those who had been there before them. Some slept while others sat in the grass and chatted. The third floor was in a similar condition, so she continued upward.

On the final floor, she was compelled down a hallway to a secluded door that must have been the building owner's residence. Kell passed through it and stood just inside the doorway, surveying her surroundings. While the rest of the building had been taken over by nature, this room was completely devoid of such greenery.

Kell crossed the room in one step. The apartment was large and spacious, and it appeared that nothing in it had been disturbed. Moving decidedly slower, she made her way to a bedroom. Once in the doorway, she found a familiar figure stretched out along a four-poster bed—Terin.

Swallowing, Kell approached. Terin rolled to face her, as if she sensed Kell's presence in her sleep.

"You look rough," Kell murmured, stopping a few paces away. She was cautious; she had never learned what Terin's third field was.

"You're… one to talk," Terin replied.

It was true. Kell didn't feel amazing, but equally accurate was the fact that Terin appeared worn, stressed. Her hair was dirty and her usually warm, golden skin was sallow. She had multiple injuries that, though minor, most assuredly were draining her.

"What are you doing, Terin?" Kell regarded her, angry but wary. "Half of Eclat's gone."

"I'm working on… *all* of it."

"But for what? What are you hoping to achieve?"

Terin drew a long breath and shifted in her sleep. "They will know our pain. They will know how we have… felt for decades."

Kell drew closer, her head cocked in interest. Terin's words troubled her, but there was something there that Kell had not felt before. It was as though Terin were trailing her fingers in the Flow, disturbing it just enough to create tiny ripples in its course. "And how many people have you killed?"

"Not enough," Terin replied through gritted teeth.

Kell chose her next words carefully. "And did you kill them like you did our prey when we were hunting? No mercy, just unnecessary brutality?"

"Enough!" snarled Terin, a gushing torrent of Viterra rushing from her. Kell felt the immediate need to fall silent. "You don't know... *anything* about me. You don't know anything about the world. You never have."

Kell just stared at her sleeping form. What could she say to convince her former teacher to choose a different path? *Was* there anything? "Renata told me she was going to meet you here in Eclat. Have you had a chance to talk with her?"

Terin's face contorted in fury though she remained asleep. "You... are trying my patience, Kellick. You and Renata both. Go away."

Kell fidgeted as she once again felt the weirdest desire to obey. Still, she resisted. "So you met with her? What did she say?"

"Kellick," growled Terin, her fists clenching the bedding around her.

"No, *you* listen!" argued Kell. "You're using your power to—"

"Leave, *now*!"

Viterra lashed around Kell's limbs and began dragging her backward out of the room. Digging her feet into the floor, Kell fought. "You have to stop! You're better than this. Renata taught you better than this!"

Terin rolled away. "Go away!"

As if fighting a gale-force wind, Kell hunkered down against the onslaught. "Where is she? Where's Renata?" She dug her toes into the floor and leaned into the rush of Viterra. "Where is she?"

Just when Kell thought she wouldn't reply, Terin muttered, "Somewhere near the Lower District docks..."

Kell was hurled out of the building. With a cry of surprise, she startled herself awake. Pain bloomed along her side as she sprang up in bed. Hissing, she doubled over. Simon joined her.

"What happened?" With calloused hands, he helped her lie back.

"Terin," Kell panted. "It was Terin. But I-I know where Renata is. The docks. She's somewhere near the docks." Laying an arm across her face, Kell stared up at the ceiling. "Renata's near the docks."

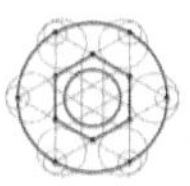

Simon looked back at Mordecai who had just reentered carrying a lunch tray. "She's at the docks," he told the black-haired man.

"Who? Renata?"

Simon nodded, holding his gaze.

Mordecai delivered the tray of food to the bedside table and studied Kell. "You reek of Viterra. What happened?"

She looked at him. "Terin. I found Terin."

"Kellick." Mordecai sat on the stool there, his sudden fierceness and frustration compelling Simon to step away. "You can't do—"

"I didn't know it was her until I got there," Kell argued.

"We still don't know what she can do."

Kell sighed. "She used a lot of Viterra. Scared me real bad."

Mordecai braced on his knees in thought. "But she told you that Renata's at the docks?" Kell nodded. With a sigh, he stood and motioned to the door; Simon followed him.

"Wait, where are you two going?" Kell tried to sit up but winced. "Hey, Simon. Mordecai!"

Simon slipped into the hallway and watched as Mordecai turned in the doorway. "We'll be back. Don't leave that bed. Got it?"

"Mordecai!"

Simon saw Kell already trying to swing onto the floor. Hearing footsteps, he turned to find Tarquin jogging down the hallway. "Keep her there," he told Kell's father. "We're going after Renata."

Tarquin fondly handled the side of Simon's head and then clapped Mordecai on the shoulder. "Be careful." He hurried in and immediately barred Kell from standing. Her snarls of frustration followed Simon and Mordecai as they hurried down the hallway.

33

Simon and Mordecai

"HOW FAR ARE WE FROM the Lower District docks?" asked Mordecai as they jogged down a beautifully manicured avenue. Bellamy had previously brought them via automobile. Now on foot, Simon could fully appreciate the affluence of the area.

"If we keep this up, we'll be there by evening," Simon replied. Mordecai fell into step behind him, reaching an easy but steady pace.

The streets were relatively empty, a consequence of Terin's encroaching faction of reactionaries. Shops and restaurants boasted barred windows and doors, and few people were out. As they turned onto a main thoroughfare, Simon suddenly slammed to a stop, grabbed Mordecai's shirt to keep him from proceeding, and directed him into a nearby alleyway.

"What?" Mordecai asked, panting.

"Regulators."

"So?"

Simon lifted one of Mordecai's arms and pointed at his exposed tattoos. "Eclat's under attack by Users. You fit that description."

As Mordecai rolled down his sleeves and buttoned his cuffs to hide his wrists, he sighed. "So, what do we do?"

"We can't take the main roads to the coast." Simon glanced down the alleyway at the brick-laid street running parallel. "Come on."

For the next several hours, they weaved through alleys, ducked under bridges to avoid being spotted, and slipped between buildings that made Simon feel far too claustrophobic. Eventually, their path was blocked not by regulators but by enormous swaths of wild and gnarled vegetation that had overtaken buildings, crumbled streets, and rendered apartment complexes, shops, and cafés to poisonous forests of destruction. It was silent save the periodic chirping of frivolous birds as they claimed the area in the name of nature.

Hands braced atop his head, Simon regarded the ruins. He had witnessed Kell's power in the arena and had learned what it is to truly fear a User. But the extensive damage that spread before them now was incomprehensible.

Hearing movement nearby, Simon looked back in time to see Mordecai complete a circle and strike his wrists. Red, glowing handcuffs blazed to life around his arms as a black Arcane Circle illuminated under his feet. Simon stepped away. Mordecai lithely brushed his boot along the ground in an arc and then inched forward.

Fire ignited several paces ahead of him and then raced toward the tangle of knotted vines. The flames hit the vegetation—and nothing happened. Simon wanted to urge him to really blast the jungle wall with a plume of fire but kept silent as Mordecai seemed to grasp something that wasn't immediately apparent to Simon.

Just as fluid as Kell but wholly different, Mordecai shifted stances and, softening his tense hands, gently and slowly lifted a knee, balancing on one foot. Eyes scanning the verdant barrier, he dropped his foot with a commanding power and then slid forward. The vines slithered away, recoiling from the roads. Grass receded into a tumble of bricks as trees shied into the surrounding disheveled buildings.

Relaxing, Mordecai looked back at Simon with a grin and then started down the razed street, keeping the Arcane Circle under him active. Simon followed, not eager to be alone with a User.

By late afternoon, they were in the Lower District, which had taken substantially more burn damage than the Middle District. It seemed Terin and her people had started off burning everything before she had turned to creating horrific vistas of wild foliage. The first row of rundown flats they came across was blackened but relatively intact. Everything after that, however, was in complete ruin.

Ash drifted on the wind; the streets were barren. Every block was nothing but ghostly structures of charred wood and brackish bricks. Some buildings were completely gone. Simon paused to take in the scene.

"What is it?" asked Mordecai, joining him.

Simon motioned to the line of blue-green that sparkled along the horizon. "I've… not ever been able to see the sea from here. All the buildings were usually in the way." A soft breeze stirred the ash around them. "There's nothing left. Where did… the people go?" He glanced at Mordecai who wore a grim expression. "She wouldn't have killed *everyone*, would she?"

Mordecai drew a long breath. "Terin has always been very good at, uh…" He rolled a charred piece of rubble under his boot. "Kell always hated hunting with her because of the way she killed animals." He nodded and then motioned to Simon. "Yeah, she probably did…"

They hurried along the disheveled streets, keeping an eye on the surrounding abject destruction. Though Simon didn't like traveling in the open with a User, journeying to the docks without any type of protection irked him more, so he kept his thoughts about Mordecai to himself.

They passed a few people picking through rubble, but no attention was paid to the two young men keeping pace.

Simon expected regulators to be roaming the streets, but none ever appeared. Shopkeepers, clerks, tanners, morticians, butchers and bakers, delivery boys, tailors—all of them were gone. Periodically, a single person would emerge from the debris to continue raking through the devastation. Only once did an older man with a bleeding gash across the top of his head take a moment to really scrutinize Mordecai and Simon. Eyes bulging and mouth agape at the sight of Mordecai's rings, the man clambered clumsily over crumbling rocks to escape. Growing ever uncomfortable with Mordecai's presence, Simon ushered them on.

When they reached familiar territory around sunset, Simon leaned heavily along a retaining wall to rest. Mordecai joined him, sitting a little too close. Simon casually inched away, acting as if he were studying something, but he should have known better.

"Are we going to have a problem?" asked Mordecai.

Simon grimaced and then stood, uncomfortable. "Look, I've spent the past several years learning to kill Users. I can't act like I love hanging out with you."

"You didn't mind sleeping with Kell," Mordecai retorted bitterly.

"I didn't sleep with her." Simon paced for a moment. "And she's different. She's Unbound."

Mordecai's response was curt. "She's not."

"She doesn't have the tattoos."

"She still pulls from the Flow in the exact way that I—"

"It's different. She's different."

"No, you can overlook it because you love her."

Simon held his gaze, his temper flaring.

Mordecai regarded him. "If I had wanted to kill you, I would have done it already."

Though he knew the words to be true, Simon still didn't like them spoken aloud. "I could say the same thing," he countered.

Mordecai gave a shrug, which caused the tension between them to diffuse, and then shook off the Viterra, ridding himself of his red cuffs and Arcane Circle. "We're here so Kell doesn't have to be. I can suffer through it." He watched Simon.

"Yeah," Simon eventually said.

The dark-haired young man ran a hand along the ashy retaining wall and then examined his dirty fingers. "I don't want to have to ask this but… can I count on you should we run into trouble?"

Simon stared out at the horizon. After a long moment, he sighed. "Yeah." When he glanced at Mordecai, he saw him nod in relief.

They continued toward the coast.

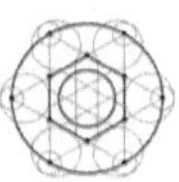

"What are you saying?" Kell asked, her heart sinking.

Bellamy pursed his lips. "I'm saying that the biggest threat to the reactionaries right now isn't me or my military. It's you and Renata."

"Why… do you think that?"

The new king appeared grimmer than usual. "We intercepted a messenger. She was coming back from running word to another half of the reactionary group." Bellamy stood at Kell's bedside. Although he wore commoners' clothes and a sword along his waist, the way he held himself betrayed his status as a noble. "She's sent men to the docks. The only people in Eclat who can possibly thwart her assault are you two. But as far as I can tell, she doesn't know you're here. So, rest—"

"Simon and Mordecai," Kell blurted, looking wildly at Tarquin. "They left earlier today for the docks. Terin knows I'm too injured to make that journey and that I'll send Mordecai to collect Renata. Mordecai's not Unbound, but he's trained. He has the discipline and power to cause problems for her." Kell swung her legs out of bed and stood.

Bellamy swiftly caught her as the floor rose up to meet her.

"Bellamy, you have to—No, I just got them back—I gotta…" Kell gripped the young king, her heart in a frenzy. "She knows I'm hurt. She knows I can't do anything. Please, we have to go after them."

"And do what, Kellick?" asked Bellamy as Tarquin started to argue with her. "What can you do? You can barely stand."

Kell slid to the floor, Bellamy's hands bracing her so she didn't hit too hard. He was right. What could she do? Renata had already tried and failed. What chance did Kell have stopping Terin?

Kneeling beside her, Bellamy said, "Look, Simon and Mordecai got a good head start. I bet they were moving fast, right?" Kell nodded, utterly frustrated with her weakened self. "Have faith in them. Once they're with Renata, they'll be safer."

That wasn't possible. "I haven't been able to contact Renata. I don't know… where she is or what's happened to her. What if she's really bad hurt or-or even… dead? Then they'll be in the harbor with no protection. And Terin will have sent her strongest—" Unable to bear the heartache, Kell grabbed hold of the bed and drew herself to her knees.

"Kellick, stop," Tarquin demanded, going to her. "You're gonna make everything worse."

Turning her fierce gaze onto her father, she said, "I've stayed out of Terin's way for most of the year. But I'm not going to," Kell stood, "let her…" She held her wound as a sharp pain seared across her flank. "Let her take away everything that *I've* fought for."

"I don't disagree with you," Bellamy replied, "but you have to approach this rationally. If you go down there in the shape you're in, you're going to distract Simon and Mordecai. Both of them will be more worried about guarding you than finding Renata." Kell met his amber gaze, knowing that he spoke the truth. "We're preparing—"

A distant explosion rattled the room.

The king nodded. "We're preparing an assault of our own to push the reactionaries out of the Middle District. Let's see how everything pans out. Give it until morning. Rest and see if you can gather information."

"What do you plan to do?" asked Tarquin.

With a sigh, Bellamy backed away from the bed. "Well, my first mission was to come here and warn you about the information we intercepted, and I didn't want to take any chance of your whereabouts getting out, so I came alone."

In a city overrun with Bound seeking to kill any and all involved with the government, Bellamy was either really brave or supremely foolish. Remembering that he had lost his bodyguards, Kell asked, "Have you found someone to replace Marko?"

Pain fleetingly crossed the king's face before he hid it. "No, I haven't." He drew a steadying breath. "From here, I'm meeting up with a company of men to the west."

"By yourself?" Kell sat on the edge of her bed.

"Yes."

"I don't think that's a good idea either, Highness," added Tarquin.

Bellamy chuckled albeit darkly. "This sword isn't for looks."

"Swords can't defend against fire," Kell's father argued.

"Tell that to Simon." Bellamy held his hand out to Kell. Confused, she laid her fingers in his palm. "Stay safe, Kellick Fisk." He kissed her hand. As Kell withdrew, uncomfortable by the formality of his actions, Bellamy turned to Tarquin. Kell's father started to give a stiff bow, but the king stopped him by offering a handshake. Surprised, Tarquin took it. "Kell and Renata are our most valuable assets right now. Don't let her out of your sight."

Bellamy crossed the room. "I'll send a trusted messenger if I can't come again. Good night."

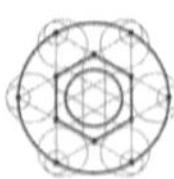

Though they had intended to make it to the docks by midnight, Mordecai declared he needed a break. He was still recovering from his stint in the Munera school. "Here," he called, leading Simon to the remnants of a brick wall whose surrounding structure had burned through. He shone a weak flame over the area.

Simon recognized the standalone butcher's shop on Porter Road and searched the shadows beyond the dancing light for evidence of life. But most of the building had been razed, leaving only steel beams that were haphazardly held together. Overhead, the waning moon continued its magnificent journey across a star-studded sky made all the more brilliant by a lack of city lights.

As Mordecai pulled together a makeshift shelter comprised of surrounding vegetation, Simon surveyed the area, listening to the nonstop rumble of explosions that pealed across the northwestern horizon. Mordecai created a fire—with a few more steps than Kell—and then went to a trail of dense grass that had miraculously sprouted between the cobblestone road. He removed his boots and socks and then shuffled his feet along the ground.

More annoyed than intrigued, Simon wandered over to see what he was doing. As Mordecai moved, touching the heel of his foot one way before sweeping his toes over the grass, chutes of green rose to glisten in the firelight.

"What are you doing?" Simon finally uttered.

"I'm Bound," Mordecai replied. "I can't use my hands like Kell." With a small smile, he ground his entire foot into the grass suddenly. The plant sprouted quickly, growing a full foot in a few seconds and forming lavender flowers. As the flowers bloomed and then withered, Mordecai turned to another area and called forth more vegetation.

In silence, Simon watched him, trying to reconcile all that he had seen and learned over the years regarding Users with the scene before him.

Mordecai wasn't angry or anxious, afraid or hateful. He was forcing plants to grow with his feet, an absurd accomplishment. Simon fidgeted as an uncomfortable thought visited him. What if this was the nature of most Users? What if the beasts he had trained against, learned to kill, and fought weren't as evil as he had been led to believe?

"Do you hate people who aren't Users?"

Mordecai crouched beside the largest of the plants. "No." Wrapping his hands firmly around the green stalk, he jerked. He came away with an enormous bundle of potatoes. Flashing a smile, he asked, "Hungry?"

Sometime later after gorging himself on coal-fired potatoes, half a tomato, several handfuls of strawberries, and roasted carrots, Simon flopped backward onto the grass and sighed in contentment. Mordecai also reclined, satisfied. After a hard day of running, both had needed replenishment.

With a stomach full of fresh fruits and vegetables, Simon couldn't help but feel grateful for Mordecai's skills. He still wasn't pleased to be sharing a fire with him, but he supposed there were worse allies.

"I'll take the first watch," Mordecai eventually said, sitting up. "Sleep. I'll wake you."

Slightly more trusting, Simon crawled into their makeshift shelter and slept.

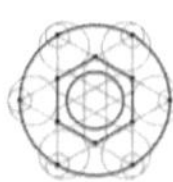

Kell didn't find Renata that night, nor did she visit Terin again. Instead, she found herself near the mountains. She knew where she was instantly. Standing beside Gytha, who was asleep in her yurt, she considered why her dreams had brought her so far from Eclat. Still, her talent had not yet led her astray, so she kneeled beside her friend.

The blond immediately rolled over to face Kell, her eyes remaining closed. "You've gotten good," Gytha said.

"Not intentionally," Kell replied. She looked about the yurt, her heart yearning for its familiarity.

"So? Why are you here?" Gytha's voice was lucid. If not for her eyes, Kell would have thought she was awake.

"I... don't know." Kell sat on the ground beside her. "Usually, I've been thinking about someone and my dreams take me to them. But I haven't been thinking about you."

"Tragic," Gytha joked. "Did you find your friend?"

"Yeah, I found him and my father, but... a lot is happening in the capital right now."

"I've heard."

This surprised Kell. "What have you heard?"

"A quarter of the city's been razed. Thousands have been displaced—"

"Half of the city has been burned, another quarter of it is nothing but a wild forest," Kell corrected. "And people displaced? Gytha, there's no one here. They've all been… killed. Hundreds of thousands."

Gytha was quiet.

"Renata went after Terin—and then she disappeared. I can't find her anywhere."

The blond softly snorted in amusement.

"What?"

"Renata never told you her ability?"

"No." Kell frowned. "And I never thought to ask."

"It's concealment. How do you think she was never found after so many years in the forest?"

"Well, the Containment Office found her."

"No, the Containment Office found you and Mordecai. She just happened to be with you two." A smile tugged at her lips. "My guess is Renata is purposefully hiding herself."

"Why?"

"Terin."

"But she already… met with Terin, right?"

"If you say so. Let me ask you something, Kell. Who do you think is Terin's biggest threat right now?"

"Me and Renata."

"And Renata knows that. Of course, she's hiding."

Kell sat back, hugging her knees to her chest. "So? How do I find her?"

"*You* don't. Let your friend find her. He's not connected to Viterra, right?"

"Who? Simon?" Kell frowned in confusion. "I don't understand."

"Renata's hidden from those connected to the Flow. Not from normal humans. He can find her."

Kell gazed across the yurt in thought. She had entrusted both Mordecai and Simon with the task of locating Renata. But how was Simon supposed to find someone he didn't know?

Gytha seemed amused. "You're injured, Kellick."

She looked down at her flank. Though it didn't bother her dream self, the wound was still realized in the surreal form. "I was shot."

Gytha's right hand inched toward her, and Kell took it. Her voice grew serious. "Remember your *satt*." Kell felt herself drawn in an uplifting torrent of Viterra. When she looked down to thank Gytha, the blond was no longer there. As she watched, the First Whispered nomadic village grew small below her. The surrounding landscape soaked in moonlight swallowed them whole, and Kell wheeled back toward Eclat.

Like a star streaking across the sky, she traversed the lands as a constant stream of energy until she slammed into the one person who she needed most—Mordecai. She landed lightly next to him and surveyed where he and Simon had made camp. She was unsurprised to find Simon awake, sitting next to a smoldering fire.

Kell crawled into the little shelter Mordecai had constructed and lay beside him. Mordecai turned into her with a contented sigh. "I just visited Gytha. She told me Renata can conceal herself. But only to those who have access to the Flow."

"What does that mean?"

Kell heard movement and peered out the shelter at Simon, who had leaned back on his hands to listen to Mordecai. "It means that Simon's gonna have to be the one to find her."

"But he doesn't even know what she looks like..."

Kell sat up as Simon stood and drew closer to the shelter, his head cocked. Grinning, she told Mordecai, "Tell Simon I say hello."

"Kell says hi," Mordecai sighed, laying an arm across his chest, still fully asleep.

Simon scoffed in mild amusement. "Who don't I know?"

"Tell him Renata," Kell instructed.

"Renata," Mordecai iterated.

"Tell him to hold on."

"Hold on."

Kell thought for a moment. "I don't know how he's going to find her. She could be anywhere."

"She could have left the city," Mordecai offered.

Kell braced on her knees. "But why could I talk to her all those nights ago? I don't understand."

"Maybe she wasn't concealing herself at... that time?" he suggested. "She was trying to find Terin. She hoped... Terin would find her."

"How far are you two from the docks?"

"I don't know."

Kell motioned to Simon. "Ask Simon." Mordecai repeated her question.

Simon stood and peered out at the area. "We're at the butcher's shop on Porter Road. So, maybe—"

Kell saw his gaze fall on something straight ahead and his body go rigid. "Mordecai, something's wrong. Simon's acting strange. Wake up. Go to him. Wake up—"

Kell was thrown back into her body in her room at Lachlan's private medical facility.

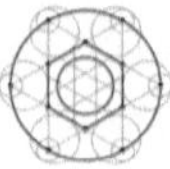

"Evening, Simon."

Simon studied Ambrose and his cohorts in the light of the campfire. "What are you doing here?"

The even expression on Ambrose's face changed as Mordecai joined Simon, his sleeves rolled to expose the black tattoos on his wrists. "Could ask you two the same. What are you doing in the Lower District?"

"Did Terin send you?" asked Mordecai.

His long, straw-like hair pulled back in a horsetail along the nape of his neck, Ambrose appeared gaunt, like usual. But the way with which he held himself had changed. It appeared that he had been given authority as the others, of which there were about a dozen, were situated around him. "Why are you with him, Mordecai?" Ambrose asked. "He's a pro-fighter; he was training to kill us."

"Then why'd you go after Kell?" Simon asked. "She's one of you too!"

Ambrose's brows furrowed. "What are you talking about?"

"Kellick Fisk, you attacked her in the arena."

"Tarquin's kid?" Ambrose appeared genuinely confused. "What are you talking about?"

"The girl you were ordered to attack in the arena." Remembering that Ambrose had only known Kell as a young boy, he said, "Kell's a girl. The Kell that grew up on the docks with us—she was the girl you attacked the other day. She even called to you, trying to make you stop."

"Oh." Ambrose looked between Simon and Mordecai. "I didn't hear her."

"There's a lot going on here that you don't understand," Simon continued.

Ambrose held up an impatient hand. "Actually, I don't wanna hear another word from you, Simon. I'm finished listening to anyone who doesn't respect Users."

"Then respect yourself and stop calling yourself a User," countered Mordecai. "It's the name given to us by those who can't draw from the Flow."

"Why *are* you with him?" Ambrose inched forward, motioning to Simon with disgust. "You're one of us."

Mordecai scoffed. "I'm not."

"Look at your wrists."

Simon ran an eye over the Users around Ambrose. All thirteen were relatively young and appeared in good physical shape. He recognized a few from the arena.

"I'll ask again—Did Terin send you?" Mordecai prompted.

Ambrose eyed him as those around him murmured. "How do you know Terin?"

Mordecai created an Arcane Circle and then ignited his fields. "She was one of my teachers." The black light under his feet radiated energy that made Simon, who was becoming more sensitive to it, shift uncomfortably. The hair on his arms stood up, and he backed away. "Now, why did she send you to come meet us tonight?"

Ambrose looked as though he were considering an answer before another User stepped in front of him, red, glowing cuffs materializing on his wrists. "Doesn't matter," he replied. In the next moment, violent flames erupted from his hands in a flash of hair-singing heat.

Mordecai blocked the fire with a rush of movement, positioning himself in front of Simon, before returning a heated stream of orange flames. "Come on, come on!" called Simon, grimacing against the heat but nonetheless pulling on Mordecai's shirt, urging him to run.

Mordecai cut off the attack, and together they turned to run, sprinting down the alleyway to the rear-connecting delivery lane. As torrents of fire followed them, Mordecai headed the flames off with rapid kicks that exuded fiery plumes of Viterra so strong that even Simon could discern their power.

They reconnected with the main street and ran hard. Unsurprisingly, Ambrose and the other Users were right behind them. Shots of fierce fire flew past them as their attackers attempted to tag Mordecai and Simon. Spurred by adrenaline, Simon felt a deep-rooted need to turn and fight. He was a fighter, a Champion, and yet he was running.

As they ran past the scorched and mangled shell of an old automobile, Mordecai slid to a halt. Simon staggered a few paces past. "What are you doing—"

Mordecai made a few sweeping motions, swung a leg around in an arc behind him, and then leaped upward and kicked. The blackened frame of the car screeched from its resting place across the bricks and went hurtling down the street, toppling two Users in dramatic fashion. As their screams spooled into the air and their comrades looked on in shock, Mordecai pointed to a nearby warped lamppost with his knee and made a jerking movement.

The pole wrenched to the side with a loud crack and then spun through the air with impressive speed. Explosions of collaborative fire stopped its progress, even as Mordecai groaned and leaned into the motion, urging the pole onward. When it was unceremoniously swept to the side and charred, Mordecai caught Simon's gaze. They ran.

Despite their speed and the confusion Mordecai's prowess with metal had caused, Ambrose and his allies remained close behind. Though they stopped trying to scorch Simon and Mordecai from the rear, they continued their pursuit.

"Here, here," hissed Simon, drawing Mordecai into an alleyway that he knew connected to another street. Glimpsing Mordecai's haggard breathing and the way he held himself, Simon felt his confidence ebbing. It was eleven against two; there was no way they were coming out of this alive.

On the adjacent street, Mordecai turned around and stomped the ground hard with his boot, sliding his foot forward in a sharp movement as he did. A ten-foot wall of hard-packed earth sprang up at the end of the cobblestone alley, closing it off. Even as Ambrose and the other Users set it afire and crimson flames licked the top of the wall, Mordecai made symbols in the dirt with the toe of his boot and then crouched. Gaze set on the object materializing just outside his Arcane Circle, he inched his boot forward.

Simon anxiously glanced at the wall of earth behind them. It was holding, but Ambrose and the others would find a way around it.

Panting, Mordecai grinned and, in a single movement, kneed the air as he stood. The object leaped upward, gleaming in the light of the fire that burned from behind the barricade. A sword clattered to the bricks at Simon's feet. "A gift," Mordecai wheezed.

Grateful, Simon hurriedly took hold of the weapon. It was an exact replica of the swords he had handled for years. "Come on." Simon led the way down the street, the sound of their pounding feet and harsh breathing the only noise between them.

After several minutes of uninterrupted running, Simon felt himself start to relax. But he knew that was how fighters got themselves killed; they grew complacent, too sure of themselves or their surroundings. Thus, he kept a vigilant eye on the shadows, growing jumpier by the minute.

He desperately wished Mordecai would rasp quieter so he could better hear impending danger but he kept his thoughts to himself. They ventured along Robinson Lane, past the skeletons of apartment flats and shops. Black ash stirred in the wind; the lack of noise disturbed Simon.

But it was that silence that focused his senses, that made him aware of the slight shuffling that emanated from the intersecting delivery lane a block away. He nudged Mordecai and led him across the street away from the sound, his eyes searching the darkness for bodies he could sense were present. To his credit, Mordecai remained quiet and attentive. He seemed to have picked up on what Simon had keyed on.

When the scuffling grew louder, they froze. Momentarily, a grubby white dog appeared from the alley, his wiry fur soot-streaked and filthy. The dog paused mid-step, his ears pricked not in their direction but westward. At that moment, Simon realized he and Mordecai had been deceived. The alley directly adjacent to their current location illuminated with fire.

As Simon turned to run, Mordecai whirled on heel and vented an enormous plume of fire to counter the oncoming attack. The ensuing result was an explosion that lifted Simon from his feet and threw him into the street. Mordecai, similarly, was toppled and sent rolling across the uneven bricks.

Catching sight of Mordecai's state, Simon scrambled up. "Stay alive," he panted as he darted into the darkness, sword in hand. He couldn't face Ambrose and the Users head on. In an alley, their fire would be focused by the high walls of the remaining structures. But if he could draw them to the other side and engage them in combat one or two at a time, perhaps he could even the numbers.

Behind him, more fire bloomed from the middle of the street as Mordecai fought back. Simon sincerely hoped for his own survival that Mordecai could hold his own.

He cut the corner at the block down the street and sprinted hard along the adjoining road. The sound of his boots on the ground was loud to him, but compared to the inferno that roared behind him, he was sure he could go unnoticed. From outside the battle, it appeared as though gods were warring in the Lower District as walls of flames fought for prominence and the earth tremored.

Simon sprinted down yet another street. Even from a distance he could discern Ambrose and the other Users gathered at the junction of the alley and the road; they were ghoulish silhouettes with shadows that danced on the surrounding bricks.

Simon squared his shoulders and tensed his body as he charged headlong for the Users. He expected them to turn their attacks onto him, but Mordecai was doing an impressive job keeping their attention. In fact, at least two of the Users appeared discouraged by the power that was being thrown back in their faces. Their hesitancy only further spurred Simon.

Sword held at the ready, Simon darted from the cover of a scorched automobile frame, moving with deadly speed. The nearest User saw him but didn't have a chance to announce his arrival as Simon swept his sword with fatal accuracy in a downward arc, cutting the young man from neck to groin. Before his victim fell, Simon ran his sword through the belly of the next and ripped it outward.

Low to the ground, he charged two more Users who were retreating from the alley with an injured comrade supported between them. They saw him, but none could do anything but cry out in surprise as Simon ran his blade through the hurt man. Whirling to avoid a punch, he pulled his blade across the attacker's back, cutting deep before yanking upward. The third man he slashed with ruthless speed, blood showering him in a fine mist.

By then, it had become evident that Simon was attacking from the rear. As half of Ambrose's force turned to defend, Mordecai's assault grew in fervor and desperation.

Simon evaded a haphazardly thrown stream of fire and lunged, drawing his opponents into the street. Though he felt flames lick his arms, he pushed through the pain, constantly striking, slashing, and thrusting; he never stopped moving or risk being burnt alive. In the span of a few seconds, three more Users fell.

A blazing river of fire ignited near him, but Simon was already in motion, intent on leading the Users away from Mordecai. The earth suddenly shrugged, sending Simon and his pursuers stumbling. Simon struggled to keep his feet under him as the ground quaked and naked structures swayed around them. The brick road beneath him curled, rippled, and then jerked.

Curious as to what had happened but still determined to put distance between himself and the Users, Simon peered over his shoulder as he continued to run. He glimpsed Mordecai exit the alleyway, aglow in a black light like a demon. Simon had to admit that he was an imposing figure. The way with which he moved, so unlike Kell, was intimidatingly purposeful. The whirling kicks, twists, and quick footwork Mordecai implemented was unnerving; Simon was glad they were on the same team.

Simon vaulted through the open window of a shop, rushed across the lobby, and then slid out the side door into the delivery lane. With the earth now more stable, three Users broke away from Ambrose and his battling partner to give chase. They set the shop aflame. Simon found some satisfaction in the fear he saw in their faces as he stepped back into the street. He was sure he looked like a wrathful spirit covered in drying blood, blond hair matted and askew.

From down the street there came a whistling. Recognizing the sound, Simon ducked as an arrow whirred past him and embedded itself in a man's throat. Before anyone could react, another arrow had been loosed from the shadows to take down yet another User.

Simon tried to draw away from the middle of the street, but given the proximity of the roaring inferno, he had nowhere else to go. He turned to meet the newcomer, his sword at the ready and eyes feverishly searching the shadows beyond where the light of the fire reached. Someone had a bow. It wasn't a typical weapon that many knew how to use these days. Had Terin sent reinforcements?

The remaining User, who stood in shock next to his dead comrades, looked first at Simon and then out into the dark, his eyes wide. With a cry, he threw a long tendril of curling, seething fire that punched its way past Simon down the uneven street. A moment later, an arrow found its target in his chest. The User staggered and then collapsed.

Simon crouched near a lamppost, refusing to turn his back on the archer. After a moment, a dark figure strode into the light. Simon fell still. "Ferrik?" he breathed.

Ferrik, his lanky and onyx-colored mentor, regarded him with a smile. "Simon."

"I—" Simon looked back at the walls of fire still ricocheting farther up the street. "I gotta—"

Ferrik set his bow and quiver down and withdrew a sword. "Let's go."

Confidence soaring and heart full, Simon turned on heel and ran back up the street, Ferrik by his side.

34

On the Move

THE BATTLE HAD MOVED. MORDECAI'S duel with Ambrose and his partner had shifted northward. Appearing on the scene, Simon took in the chaos. Mordecai had stumbled across the private textile manufacturer on Surrey Lane. Spindles, bolts and screws, various tools, and other metal objects of indiscernible origins whirled around him in a maelstrom. Molten slugs covered the ashen ground around Ambrose, evidence of Mordecai's deflected attacks.

Though Mordecai was obviously flagging, so were Ambrose and his partner.

Ferrik allowed Simon to take the lead, staying just out of sword range. Ambrose's partner, a twenty-something-year-old with round glasses, whirled on them, his eyes suddenly wide. As Simon drew his fire, Ferrik came charging in from the right. Surprised by the fighter's appearance, their opponent turned his flames onto Ferrik, but the tall man was fast and had not been in battle.

The moment the bespectacled User's flames hissed into nothing, Ambrose faltered. Wheezing audibly, he held his hands up in immediate surrender. Simon relaxed in consideration of his admission of defeat. But Mordecai wasn't so merciful. With a kick, he sent a spindle through Ambrose's neck.

Ambrose staggered to the side, blood spilling down him. His panicked eyes found Simon. A second later, a shower of other tiny metal objects passed through him like a flock of starlings through the dusk sky. Ambrose crumpled into a heap.

Mordecai dropped to the ground with a strangled whimper, flopping limply onto his back. Wheezing loudly, he just lay there, struggling to breathe.

Around them, fire burned, illuminating not only the devastation but the blood that coated Simon.

Simon hurried over and kneeled beside him. Mordecai's rings were gone as was his Arcane Circle. His body shook and his hands trembled violently from the effort he had exerted. In the light, Simon could see patches of burned skin along the man's arms.

Exhaustion suddenly hitting him as well, Simon fell onto his butt and sat staring at the ground between them. They had just defeated thirteen Users—together. Simon was elated.

There came a muffled huff next to him. Simon glanced at Mordecai, noting the streaks of tears that tracked down his cheeks. After a moment, Mordecai covered his eyes with his palms and cried silently. Not knowing what to do, Simon just sat with him.

It didn't take long for Mordecai to calm himself. "I can't... keep lying here," he murmured, sitting up. He held his head. "We need somewhere to rest—"

Catching sight of Ferrik, who had been hanging back several paces, Mordecai tried to jump to his feet. But all he managed to do was tangle his legs under him and go crashing back to the ground.

"He's fine, he's fine!" Simon hurriedly assured him. "He just helped us."

Still wary, Mordecai staggered to his feet; once upright, he wavered there, squinting at Ferrik.

Simon tiredly intervened. "He's fine. This is Ferrik. He's my mentor."

Mordecai braced on his knees, looking at Ferrik in intervals. "Ferrik..."

Simon saw his eyes roll up into his head as his body tilted at an unnatural angle. Surging forward, he caught Mordecai's shoulders, the man's dead weight carrying them both to the ground. Mordecai's body and clothes were sweat ladened.

"Come on," Ferrik said, crouching near them. "We need to find a place to hide."

After the man collected his bow and quiver, he helped Simon lift Mordecai. They carried him beyond the private shop two roads over to a neighboring brick factory whose walls remained semi-intact. They didn't dare enter for fear of running into more trouble. Instead, they sat out back of the building, remaining tucked away beside a charred delivery truck.

Once Mordecai was safely hidden among the long grass, Simon flopped down beside him and stretched out, weary. "So?" he asked, looking at Ferrik's dark form. His mentor peered out at the horizon. "What are you doing here? How'd you find me?"

"I escaped around the time you did. Got weapons from the armory and left." Ferrik leisurely paced. "But I hung around the arena, not really knowing where to go. It started getting dangerous to be there. The military's gotten involved, and I didn't want to be anywhere near them. I saw a group of Users heading out toward the coast and thought I'd see what they were up to." He looked at Simon. "I guess they were coming after you."

Simon sat up. "No. Not me." He pointed at Mordecai. "Him."

"And the girl? Is she alive?"

"Yeah, she's alive."

"So, why are you out here with," Ferrik motioned to Mordecai. "He's a User."

"Because he's Kell's… fiancé. And because I told Kell I'd help him find their teacher." Simon braced on his knees. "We've only gotten as far as we have because of him. The city's a jungle, a complete hellscape, and his… stupid abilities…" He looked at his mentor. "I'm glad to see a familiar face. I've not liked hanging out with a User."

Ferrik sat nearby. "The girl's a User."

Simon nodded gravely.

"Did you know?"

"Yeah. But seeing it is different than knowing about it." He looked at Ferrik. "Do you know what happened to Dockett?"

"No, I assumed he ran."

Again, Simon pointed at Mordecai. "He killed him. The day we escaped, Dockett had a unit of regulators head us off, and Mordecai just… killed him. Turned his own bullets against him and…" Conflicted feelings arose in Simon, forcing his words to trail off as his thoughts turned inward.

At the time, his relationship with Dockett had become strained and contentious. But it hadn't always been, and Simon felt… sad? Confused? Angry? Dockett's death elicited something from him, something that made him want to blame Mordecai.

But it had been Kell who had given the command; she had been the one to demand that Mordecai kill the Lanista. Simon couldn't fault Mordecai, who had had almost no interactions with Dockett, for listening to his significant other. Now that a few days had passed and Simon wasn't seeing Dockett's leathery face daily, he almost missed the Lanista. Almost.

Ferrik sighed. "I knew he was close to his end."

"Why?" grunted Simon.

"Kell. The way she looked at him—I've never seen such murder in someone's eyes before, but," he nodded, "I figured if anyone could find a way, it'd be her."

"Even before you knew she was a User?"

Ferrik nodded solemnly. "She's fast, disciplined, tough for a woman. She only lacked strength. But with, uh—"

"They call it Viterra," Simon supplied.

"Yeah, she'd be unstoppable."

"Well, her sister is who's been destroying the city, so…"

"Sister?"

"Not a blood relation, but the woman who heads the reactionaries—Terin—was a student alongside Kell. They share the same teacher."

"Then we need to get rid of the teacher," Ferrik concluded.

"No, not what we're here to do. Their teacher tried stopping Terin, and then Terin turned on her. Terin's the one who sent those Users after us. She wants Kell, Mordecai, and their teacher out of the way… Gone."

"I see." Ferrik thought before saying, "Then, I'll help you."

"Why?" Simon bluntly asked. It wasn't that he didn't trust his mentor, but what did the man gain from helping them?

"Because you need my help."

"That's… it? That's the only reason?"

"For now."

Simon considered him and then added, "Kellick, Mordecai, their teacher, Tarquin… anyone associated with them… They're off-limits. I need to know that—"

"I'm not going to turn my sword on them," Ferrik concluded evenly. He looked at Simon. "Dockett's training has been as effective as he touted it to be though, hasn't it?"

Simon nodded somberly. Only his mentor knew and understood the mental gymnastics Simon went through to work alongside Mordecai.

"You have my word," said Ferrik.

Immensely grateful, Simon smiled into the darkness. "Thank you."

While Ferrik stood watch into the morning hours, Simon knocked out beside Mordecai. Only when the sun was well above the horizon did Simon finally muster the discipline to get up. He grimaced at the sight of his clothes, which were stiff with blood. In the light of day, he appeared grotesque.

"Any problems?" he asked his mentor.

"No, nothing. It's been quiet." Ferrik nodded toward Mordecai who had not moved. "Should we… try to wake him?"

Simon leaned over and touched Mordecai. "Hey." When he didn't stir, Simon shook him, at first gently and then with more fervor. "Hey!"

Mordecai finally roused, his eyes bleary and unfocused. Squinting against the sun, he moaned and weakly rolled toward Simon. "What happen—" His gaze fell first on Simon's blood-streaked face and then on his filthy clothes.

"You, uh, fainted," Simon said, ignoring his reaction. "We," he gestured to Ferrik, "carried you a ways but then had to rest."

Mordecai sat up, holding his head. "Did anyone else come?"

Both Simon and Ferrik shook their heads.

After methodically clenching and unclenching his hands, Mordecai stood. He wavered on his feet and then, once he was steady, looked at them. "I can… conjure water and food. Do you want me to try?"

"We're getting closer to the docks," replied Simon, seeing the way Mordecai stood. The man was obviously not recovered. "You don't… look like you're up to the task."

Mordecai frowned but didn't argue.

Simon led the way down the charred street. Now that they were deep within the Lower District, the remnants of once-rampant fires pervaded the landscape. Blocks of apartments, single-story flats and shops, and factories had been razed to toppled piles of detritus. Though Simon would normally have welcomed the sea breeze, all the wind did now was kick up ash that made them cough and odors that caused Simon's stomach to knot up.

The streets were empty; the lots of burnt buildings were empty. It was as if the city had been touched by a raging volcano and its inhabitants melted into the surrounding inferno.

Simon periodically and furtively looked back at Mordecai to gauge his state. Though it was apparent that Mordecai was trying to stay focused, he was flagging. Once they found Renata, they would need to rest for a while.

After two and a half hours of diligent walking, they finally made it to the waterfront. Though much of the docks was gone, several slips still remained, boats and all. Nostalgic and heart hurting, Simon led them down the docks to the familiar boat moored in its designated slip.

"What are we doing?" whispered Mordecai, looking about.

"My boat," Simon said, fondly tracing the boat's shape and rigging with his eyes. "Home."

Unsteady on his feet, Mordecai looked about. "What boat?"

Simon pointed to the forty-foot fishing boat docked in front of them. "This one. Right here."

Mordecai's eyes were looking in the right place but…

"This one." Simon lithely leaped onto the boat's railing.

Brows furrowed and mouth agape, Mordecai studied him. "How are you… doing that?" To Ferrik, he asked, "Can you see it? The boat?"

Bewildered, Ferrik nodded.

Hanging onto a rope, Simon gazed at Mordecai. Had the battle earlier somehow damaged his eyes or his brain? No, that couldn't be right. Mordecai had shown no issue navigating toward the waterfront. What else—

"Renata!" Mordecai suddenly cried. Grinning at Simon, he said, "Remember what Kell said? You'd have to find Renata because she's concealing herself."

"But this is my family's boat. I can see it, and Ferrik can too—"

The door to the inner cabin swung open to reveal, to Simon's delight, his mother boasting a pistol. A fierce expression on her face, she looked first at Simon, who was covered in varying shades of blood, and then at Ferrik and Mordecai. "Get off my boat," she seethed.

"Vera—" Mordecai began as Simon jumped to the deck from the railing ledge.

Frightened, Vera swung the pistol toward Simon, but he easily caught her thin arm, trapping the weapon over her head. "Mom. It's me. It's Simon."

Vera's eyes grew large as she staggered out of his grip. "Simon."

Simon glanced down at himself. "Sorry I look… like this. We ran into trouble—"

His mother dove into his arms with a strangled cry. Simon desperately grasped her. Though her comparative size startled him, her smell was the same as always. "Oh, my boy," she sobbed, squeezing him. "Oh, oh!" She peered up at him. "Look at you. Oh, Simon."

Simon held her, tears of happiness leaking down his cheeks. He had thought he would never again see her.

"Where have you been? My child, my boy." Vera drew away just enough to survey him once again, running a rough hand down his jaw and then along the scar above his eyebrow. Her smile faded as her eyes searched his. "Life has not been kind to you…"

Simon held her hand to his face and shook his head.

She finally turned to Mordecai and Ferrik. "Mordecai, you're worse for the wear."

Surprised, Simon looked between them. "You know him?"

"Yes, he and Kell visited several weeks ago before they went to find you." Her face fell as she started to look around. "Where *is* Kell? Is she—"

"She was injured earlier this week. She's resting in a hospital in the Upper District," Mordecai supplied. He grinned. "She was not pleased that we came without her."

"No, I can imagine not."

"Actually," Simon took his mother's hand, "we're looking for someone."

"Mordecai," called a gravelly voice from within the cabin. With a glance at Vera, Mordecai hurried past them. Curious, Simon followed with his mother and Ferrik.

The main cabin of *Merry Maiden* was virtually unchanged. The small family table, which doubled as a map desk, took up much of the central area.

The room smelled pleasantly of drying herbs, which hung along the open windows. Separate cabins occupied the space on either side of the main cabin.

Simon found Mordecai kneeling beside the bed Simon had once called his own, hands clasped around an old woman's gnarled palm. "Renata," Mordecai breathed, kissing her knuckles.

"Oh, stop it," the old woman muttered from her prone position. "I'm not dead."

Mordecai continued to fawn over her, brushing back her frizzled, gray hair before kissing her forehead. She was wrinkled like the trunk of a live oak tree with heavy jowls and sagging skin around her cheeks. But her gray eyes were brilliantly fierce and sharp.

"You're exhausted," she said, running a fond hair through Mordecai's hair. "You fought so hard last night." Mordecai nodded, his adoring eyes on her. "You didn't have to come."

"Kell's been looking for you," he replied.

Renata sighed. "An unintentional consequence of my ability. We're hidden from Bound and Unbound. But I knew one of you would find me if I stayed *here*." The old woman leveled an appraising eye onto Simon. "So, you're Simon. Bit of a mess, aren't you?"

Simon shuffled awkwardly into his quarters, smiling. "I haven't had time to clean up."

Renata guffawed, her eyes running the length of him before shifting back to Mordecai. "I get the sense you two make a good team."

Mordecai smiled grimly at Simon over his shoulder.

"And your friend standing in the main cabin there—Who's he?"

Vera stepped aside to admit Ferrik. The old woman's face hardened and she nodded. "A pro-fighter, huh?"

"Yes, ma'am."

Holding onto Mordecai, she pulled herself upright. Simon saw her grimace as Mordecai seated himself on her bed to brace her. "Well, this is quite the gathering."

"What happened?" Mordecai asked softly. "How did Terin…"

"When she and the other reactionaries arrived here along the docks, I tried to talk to her, to dissuade her from continuing." The old woman's gaze slipped to the bedding around her as her face folded into fury. "She sicked two dozen Bound on me." She nodded. "She intended to kill me. And she tried to kill you as well."

Mordecai pursed his lips. "Yeah, she did."

"Kell, where is she?"

"A hospital in the Upper District," Simon provided.

"In the… Upper District." Renata looked between him and Mordecai. "She should have come with you two."

Mordecai glanced at Simon before saying, "She was badly injured. She really shouldn't—"

"Kell's tough," Renata interrupted. "You should have brought her." To Mordecai, she said, "She's safer with you around. You keep her from doing stupid things."

"Well, she's with her father," Mordecai argued half-heartedly.

Renata was already shaking her head. "You know how stubborn she is. She'll do as she pleases."

Ignoring the old woman's comments, Simon asked, "Do you think Terin will go after her?"

"She came after me."

Simon met Mordecai's gaze, prompting the black-haired man to hesitantly say, "Kell met with Terin… in her dreams."

Renata looked at him in alarm. "She didn't."

"The other night. She said it was an accident."

"Does Terin know where she is?"

Mordecai looked at Simon. "No, I don't think so."

"No," confirmed Simon.

Renata squeezed Mordecai's hand. "If I felt you drawing from the Flow last night, so did Terin. She knows you bested her lot. She'll send more. And she'll go after Kell."

"Do you think you're putting yourself too much into this girl's mind?" asked Ferrik from the doorway. Seeing his petit but strong-willed mother next to the enormous man, Simon was amused. "She's trying to take over the palace right now. Why would she weaken her forces to go after one or two people?"

"Because she knows we don't agree with what she's doing," replied Mordecai. "Even if she overthrows the government and razes the capital, we pose a threat to her. We can interfere at any moment and upset all that she's… done."

"And we've… left Kell," mused Simon grimly, "in the Upper District where Terin is currently battling Bellamy's military…"

"If she doesn't draw from the Flow," offered Renata, "Terin won't be able to find her."

Simon met Mordecai's gaze, certain they were thinking the same thing. When it came to Kell, using Viterra wasn't a matter of if, but when. "I'll go back for her," Simon said the same moment Mordecai opened his mouth to volunteer.

"Neither of you is going anywhere," Renata replied sternly. "I know you're fond of her, but you forget that Kell is first and foremost my student. She can hold her own against Terin if she needs to."

Mordecai fell still. "Kell was shot, Renata. A regulator shot her while we were in the arena."

The old woman was silent for a long moment before finally sighing. "Like I said, she's first and foremost my student. She can hold her own against Terin."

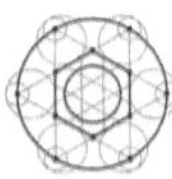

Kell spent much of the day fidgeting and staring out the window as she listened to the sounds of distant battle. She could vaguely feel the disturbances in the Flow, but the fighting was so far off, she began to ignore it, opting instead to worry about Simon and Mordecai. After warning Mordecai the night before and urging him to wake up, she had felt great draws of Viterra. Had Terin caught up to them?

Kell tried to pace the empty room—Tarquin had gone to find them more clothes—but her wound bothered her too much. Still, she stubbornly shuffled about, her thoughts consumed with the two men she loved more than anything.

Sometime mid-afternoon, an enormous boom shook the private hospital, causing dust and debris to rain from the ceiling. Tarquin, who had been napping nearby, startled awake as Kell swung out of bed. "Time to go," she muttered.

Her father helped her dress in cotton pants, a button-down shirt, boots, and a cap, which she tucked her hair under. As the rest of the hospital evacuated, Tarquin guided her down the hallway to the first floor where nurses helped patients as Lachlan gave urgent directions. They were apparently waiting for trucks to carry the incapacitated.

Panting from the effort, Kell waited under the front porch awning with Tarquin, her eyes set on the great plumes of smoke that rose just a few blocks away. Gunfire suddenly ricocheted down the street, causing the patients and nurses to cower. Tarquin dragged Kell to the safety of a brick column as the tops of the neighboring buildings were illuminated with the unmistakable light of rampant fire.

More gunfire.

Lachlan's shouts grew angry as he hollered for nurses and asked after the status of the vehicles.

"We gotta leave," Tarquin muttered, clutching Kell. "We can't stay here. They're too close."

As if to emphasize the fact, a torrent of angry red and amber flames vented down the street that led to the private hospital, shattering the windows of buildings along the way. A collection of pops followed as imperial soldiers attempted to mount a defense before scurrying in the opposite direction. More fire exploded after them, stretching down the street toward the hospital.

"Let's go." Tarquin started to lift Kell, but she resisted. "We gotta go." He looked down at her as she pulled from his grip. "Kellick."

A frightened and sobbing nurse staggered by, carrying several rolls of bandages in her trembling arms. The patients on the veranda who could stand were retreating into the hospital, fearing for their lives. Those who were unable to walk or move were left to weep openly or struggle to their feet. Lachlan was losing control of the situation. Kell held her father's gaze for a long moment before, sighing, he motioned her on.

Kell limped off the front porch, holding her wound. It wasn't hurting badly, but she suspected if she did too much, it soon would. Standing before the hospital, she gazed down the street. The pristine buildings had caught fire. Although most of the population in the Upper District had already evacuated, a few citizens remained, rushing out of the flats, coughing and crying.

Sensing people nearby suddenly draw from the Flow, Kell steadied herself and then, once she was sure she was balanced, created an Arcane Circle and ignited her fields. As Terin's reactionaries appeared on the street to survey the damage they had done, Kell stomped and then, gathering Viterra under her, pushed the energy through the earth, causing a violent ripple in the neat brick road. It bypassed the fire victims before crashing into the reactionaries.

Twisting her arms and moving forward, her stance wide, she gave direction to Viterra, commanding it with precise movements to ensnare. Enormous, thorny vines erupted from the disrupted bricks to latch onto the reactionaries.

Fire broke out as they fought off the vegetation, but this time, Kell wasn't unbalanced or upset by the onslaught of out-of-control Viterra. She had braced herself for it. Arms moving, striking, blocking, and thrusting, she directed the vines to snarl around the reactionaries, tying their hands to their bodies.

Unfortunately, three got away and went fleeing down the street. Kell thought about going after them but stopped as she felt her knees give beneath her. Suddenly weak, she sat on her Arcane Circle, panting. The bricks beneath her swam in her vision. More annoyed than anything else, she pushed herself to her feet. After scrutinizing her vicious vines and their victims who continued to squirm in their thorny embrace, Kell turned to limp back to the hospital.

"She's… Unbound," someone said as hushed words were passed between patients and staff. Kell swept her gaze over them, weary.

Tarquin joined her and immediately offered his arms for support.

The harsh whispers and anxious looks didn't stop as they approached the veranda. In fact, those who could backed away.

Tarquin helped Kell lie on the polished wood of the porch and then turned on everyone there. "So what if she's Unbound?" he snarled. "She just saved all of you. They're not all bad, yeah? Stop bein' so pigheaded and get over yourselves."

Kell watched her father with a tired grin before closing her eyes.

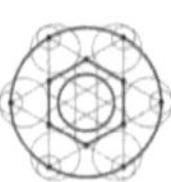

"No."

Simon looked up from supper, his eyes flicking to Mordecai. "What?" he asked, seeing the expression on Mordecai's face. "What's wrong?"

"Kell," he whispered, frozen over their meager meal.

Simon stood. "What happened? Is she all—"

"She used Viterra." Mordecai also stood and looked back at Renata who had remained in her room. "Something's happened at the hospital. I have to go."

"Hold on, Mordecai," Renata advised, moving to the edge of her bed. Vera hurried to help her stand. Weakly, Renata joined them in the main cabin. "It wasn't a lot, the Viterra she drew. It's possible it wasn't an attack."

"But Terin will know where she is now," Mordecai replied, moving toward the door.

"Mordecai!" Renata barked.

Simon winced at the authority in her gritty voice. It was no wonder Kell and Mordecai listened to her. She had the air of a wise teacher. Even Simon, who had just met her, was inclined to show deference to the old woman.

"Calm down. Find your *satt*." Renata shuffled to his chair which Vera held steady and then sat. Bracing on the table, their teacher leveled a steely eye on Mordecai. "You're not going to help her by trekking all the way back to the Upper District. You *will* help her by resting and regaining your strength." Renata glanced at Simon. "The both of you."

Mordecai paced in the open doorway of the main cabin before looking at his teacher. "Renata, she's…"

"I know," the old woman replied. "Find your *satt*."

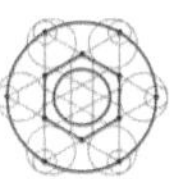

The vans eventually made it to the hospital shortly after eight o'clock, but they were charred and sported varying degrees of damage. Kell doubted how far they would get. The worst of the patients were promptly loaded up as others looked on helplessly and tried to edge in where they could.

Kell and Tarquin watched from the far side of the veranda, knowing full well that they were not going to be offered transportation. "So, what now?" asked Kell.

"We wait," Tarquin replied.

"Terin knows where I am now."

Tarquin nodded, peering up into the purple sky. "Do you think… we should leave the hospital and try to make our way to the Lower District, meet up with Mordecai and Simon?" He didn't look at her which meant he was worried. "Can you make that trip?"

"I can make it," Kell replied. "It'll be a slow one though."

Tarquin nodded and, spotting Lachlan, waved the doctor over. Lachlan appeared utterly beside himself with exhaustion and stress. He had seen Kell just like the others but didn't seem to have any qualms about drawing so near.

"We're leavin'," Tarquin said. "There anything you can give her to help with the pain?"

Lachlan studied Kell, his gaze distant, and then nodded shakily. "Yes, yes, there is. One moment." He was gone for but a minute before hurrying from within the hospital, carrying a small bag with him. He withdrew a small vial and a large syringe bearing a long needle. "I can dose her right now, but I can't give this to you. Others… others need it."

"Will it make me sleepy or disoriented?" asked Kell. Lachlan gave a noncommittal shrug to which she nodded. "Then let's not." With a tired smile, she held out her hand. "Thank you, Doctor, for caring for me."

Without hesitation, Lachlan took her hand. "Take care of yourself. I hope we see each other again." The doctor passed her a fatigued smile, shook Tarquin's hand, and then hurried back to his responsibilities.

Tarquin at her side, Kell started down the perpendicular road, heading south.

35

Converge

TO KELL'S DISMAY, SHE DID not dream of Mordecai or Simon or even Renata that night after she and Tarquin settled behind an opulent house with a garden. Instead, she found herself wandering the torn streets of Upper Eclat, scrutinizing the extensive damage.

Eventually, she came across rows of barricades lined with the same packages she had seen on the palisades in the arena, the ones that exploded when exposed to fire. Hundreds of them blocked every street.

Kell passed through them, following her instinct, that deep tug behind her navel that always guided her. Spotting a familiar crimson and navy standard, she bolted to the tents gathered under it. When she didn't find Bellamy there, she began searching the area. She was led to a wealthy apartment building nearby. In the blink of an eye, she stood at the foot of his bed, which was someone's living room sofa. He was alone, save the guards outside his closed door.

Kell sat wearily against the sofa and stared across the room. "What progress have you made?" she asked. "Where are we at?"

"We've managed to hold them off from most of the Upper... District and have started to take back... parts of the Middle," Bellamy murmured. "Where are you?"

"We had to evacuate the hospital. The attacks got too close. I had to intervene. Lachlan and his staff and patients have also evacuated." Kell leaned her head back with a sigh. "What of Terin? Have you seen her?"

"No. Her forces seem to be losing direction. We... haven't faced Terin herself in over a day."

Kell thought. "So, what does that mean?"

"I don't know."

Mind suddenly whirring, Kell stood. "Hold on, I'll be back."

The room around her shifted in a kaleidoscopic blur. As if tumbling from the stars, she was jolted to a halt along the docks she had once called home. Why… the docks? Staring, she tried to understand why her gift had brought her there. No one was there. Yet she had been drawn to the Ashway family slip. Their boat wasn't even there…

A thought occurring to her, Kell approached the empty slip. "Mordecai!" she shouted, searching the empty space in front of her. "Mordecaiii!" Though she could only discern dark water, she felt a disturbance in the Flow.

Momentarily, Mordecai appeared from thin air. But he was clearly standing on something as he wasn't on the water. Kell grinned. They had found Renata. Mordecai wavered on his feet, his eyes closed and his head lolling. Kell moved to his side in a single stride. Holding his hand, she said, "Lie down. Careful."

Still asleep and clumsy, Mordecai leaned against the doorway and sank to the deck. Once he was prone, Kell sat beside him, touching his hair and face. "You're hurt," she whispered.

"Yeah, big fight."

"And Simon?"

"He's fine. He saved… my life."

Kell kissed Mordecai's face. "I just talked with Bellamy. He says he hasn't seen Terin since last night. That wouldn't worry me if he hadn't also said that the reactionaries are growing disorganized. He and the military are starting to regain the Middle District."

"Where are you and Tarquin?"

"We left the hospital. Fighting was too close. We're making our way to you. But we're easily two days away. There's no way I can complete the journey in one fell swoop."

Movement in the doorway caught Kell's attention. She startled, clambering away from Mordecai at the sight of Ferrik. "What is he doing here?" she gasped.

"Who?"

"Ferrik!"

"He helped us last night," Mordecai replied.

Ferrik studied Mordecai, only the whites of his eyes visible in the dark night.

"And you trust him?" she asked.

"Yes, we trust him."

Kell approached Ferrik who was tight like a spring. "Tell him you're talking to me and that I'm watching him right now. It's a form of Viterra."

Mordecai did as she said. Ferrik frowned deeply and replied, "Tell her to stop."

"Well, tell *him* to go back to bed and stop eavesdropping," Kell retorted.

Mordecai guffawed. "Kell says stop eavesdropping then."

Slightly amused, Ferrik retreated into the main cabin. "I don't like him being around you," Kell said, rejoining Mordecai. "You don't have to reply because he'll hear you, but I don't like that he's with you."

"I know, but according to-to Simon, we wouldn't… have made it out of that fight without him."

Kell paced the invisible deck, watching the waves beneath her. "Do you think Terin's lost her desire to fight?"

"No," replied Mordecai. "That doesn't sound… like her."

"But why would she retreat when she was so close to the palace, to Bellamy? It doesn't make sense. She's been ruthless, killed thousands. Why now? Why stop now?"

"Kellick?" called Renata suddenly. The boat beneath Kell appeared, and Renata's mind unfurled before her. Like a specter born of fog, Kell invaded the main cabin and slipped into the adjacent room where Renata slept. "What did you talk to Terin about the other night?"

"Why?" asked Kell, bewildered.

"Stop arguing. What did you talk to her about?"

Kell worked to remember the encounter. "I asked her what she was hoping to gain and if she intended to keep going. I really, uh, angered her. I don't know how, but she threw me out. She pushed me out of her dreams. No one else has been able to do that."

"Terin's third field… gives her the gift of absolute obedience. Whatever she says, you must do."

Kell sat heavily on her teacher's bed. "That's how she's pulled all of this off. Even if people didn't want to fight, she just commanded them to… and they had to obey. That's horrible!"

"It's much worse than that," Renata replied, sighing briefly in her sleep. "There are far worse things that can be done with absolute obedience."

Kell's brows furrowed. "She could have ordered the military to surrender. She could have commanded everyone to… die or something. Why hasn't she done that?"

"Her gift has limits, just like yours."

"Bellamy says they're regaining ground, that her reactionaries are growing unorganized. He says they haven't seen her in a day."

"Did you say anything else to her?"

Kell looked at her teacher. "Did I do something wrong?"

"Well, you very plainly pissed her off. Who else can scold her but you?"

Kell frowned. "What?"

"Who else can identify with her but you?"

"We're not… the same…" Even as she said it, she knew it was wrong.

"Who else close to her has experienced the cruelty of a system… meant for only those without access to the Flow—but you? You touched a nerve, Kellick."

Kell stood and began pacing the room. "You're speculating. Guessing."

"Am I? Who called Terin out for her inhumane hunting methods? Who scolded her for flirting with Mordecai? Who pressured her into bettering her water traits? Who argued with her about whatever inconsequential foolishness she did on a daily basis?"

Heart hammering, Kell gazed at her teacher.

"She's angry, Kellick. Angry… and hurt."

"I don't get it. What's your point?"

"You touched a nerve and now all of her hard work is unraveling."

Kell was silent, still not piecing together what her teacher implied.

"You can be so dense someti—She's coming for you, and us, but mostly you. All of us are a threat to her, but none more than you."

Resuming her pacing, Kell replied, "Terin's six years my senior. She's better at all traits. Also, she wasn't recently shot. What are you wanting me to do?"

"You accessed the Flow earlier. She knows where you are—"

"Where I *was*. We're on the move."

"Get to us as quickly as you can. We're stronger together."

Kell stopped pacing. Staring at the familiar floor, she asked, "Do you think… we'll have to fight Terin?"

"Terin's not in the right mind, Kell. Someone in the right mind wouldn't have been able to slaughter thousands… Ask me how I know."

Kell kneeled at her teacher's bedside and pressed her forehead into the bedding. "I don't want to do this anymore, Renata. I don't like fighting. I don't like using Viterra like that. It's not… natural. It feels dirty."

"I know. But until Terin is brought under control, it can't be helped."

"I wanna go home," Kell whispered.

Renata swallowed. "Me too."

Drawing a long breath, Kell pulled away and stood. "Please, keep them safe until I get there."

"I'll do my best."

Kell took a step back. Her surroundings blurred momentarily before she was standing beside Mordecai who was still asleep on the deck. "I'm coming. Hang in there."

"Yeah."

She regarded *Merry Maiden* and then added, "You could go out to sea for a while. She'd have a harder time finding you."

"We're not leaving without you," Mordecai replied.

Kell had known that was going to be the answer. "Right. I'll hurry."

She leaped off the boat and landed inside the living room where Bellamy slept. "Simon and Mordecai found Renata. They're at the docks in the Lower District. Renata thinks Terin is coming to hunt us."

Bellamy grumbled in his sleep thoughtfully.

"Also, she told me that Terin's third field allows her the ability of absolute obedience."

"What's... that?"

"If she tells you to do something, you must do it."

"That's... not good."

"It's how she's been controlling the reactionaries. Bellamy, the Bound that she's been using... they've not had a say in the matter."

"Can she use the ability on anyone?"

"I'm unsure," replied Kell. "Renata said she has limitations but didn't explain what those were." She sighed. "I'll try to check on you again tomorrow night."

"Kellick?"

"Hm?"

"Knowing you're... out there... helps. More than you can know." Bellamy's lips twitched into a smile. "I... intend to thank you properly someday."

Kell scoffed. "Then let's finish this. I wanna go home."

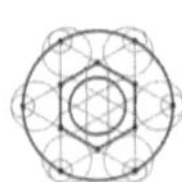

After sleeping restlessly, listening to Renata's one-sided conversation with Kell, and tossing in heated frustration, Simon rose and went to the wheelhouse. Though dawn was still a few hours away, he was wide awake. Seated at the helm, his feet propped on the dashboard, he gazed out at the dark horizon.

He couldn't decide if he was uncomfortable because he was once again aboard his family's boat or if he was anxious for what was to come. Resting his head on his hand, he allowed his thoughts and worries to consume him.

Sometime later, soft footsteps behind him were preceded by the soft glow of a dim lamp. Simon turned in the chair to look back at his mother. She appeared relieved. "Your bed was empty," she whispered, hanging the lamp on a hook overhead. "I was worried."

Simon gave an apologetic smile. "Sorry."

"Couldn't sleep?"

He drew a long, weary breath. "No, but that's not a new occurrence."

Vera slid her hand under his jaw to turn his face to her. She studied him in the lamplight with a bothered expression, her eyes searching his. "Kell said you were sold to the Munera school. Does that mean... you just participated in the Munera?"

He nodded.

His mother embraced him tightly, pulling his head to her bosom. She kissed his hair. "Oh, my child." Simon tried to keep his throat from closing up with emotion. Eevie had offered him glimmers of maternal gentleness over the years and had looked out for his well-being. But this was different. "I'm so sorry, Simon," Vera cried into his hair.

Simon clung to her and, unable to keep the tears at bay, wept silently in his mother's arms. He couldn't tell her all the horrible things he had done during his training. He wanted to spare her those images.

Eventually, they both calmed. Sniffing, Simon wiped his eyes and cleared his throat. "I'm surprised," he said softly.

"About what?" replied Vera, cleaning her face on her nightdress.

"You saved a User. Renata, she's a User."

His mother nodded. "Yes, I saved her. She appeared one evening on the docks, looking for the Ashways. I saw she was horribly injured, burnt. Before I even took her in, she told me that she was a User."

"But you still took her in, even after everything they did to the docks?"

Vera nodded. "She told me that she was a User but that she could hide us from others." His mother sighed and leaned against the helm. "She was an old woman, injured. And she didn't have cuffs. So, I agreed. Then I got her in and she told me that Mordecai and Kell were her students."

Simon fiddled with the hem of his clean shirt. "And now you know Kell's a User?"

"Yes. But she's different. All of them are—Renata, Mordecai, Kell..." Vera studied him. "Was it difficult finding out she's one of them?"

Passing his mother an annoyed look, Simon sighed. "Yeah, but not for the reasons you think." Sensing her waiting gaze, he continued. "For years, I trained to kill Users. Exercises, drills, mock battles, everything was to prepare us to kill Users." He shrugged. "And now I've been working with them, fighting alongside them. And Kell... She's Unbound." He stared at the dashboard. "But I don't hate her; I can't hate her. I..." He chuckled. "I don't even hate Mordecai anymore. And he's Bound." Distressed, he leaned into his hand. "Fuckin' Dockett."

"All of it suddenly made more sense," said Vera, "when Renata told me that Kell was her student. How Kell had mysteriously ended up in Tarquin's life, why he raised her as a lad, why they had run when the fire…" His mother turned away as if distracted by something on the horizon, but Simon saw her wipe her face.

"You know?" Simon whispered. She looked back at him, her eyes moist. "You know about the fire?"

Vera gave him a wet smile. "It wasn't hard piecing everything together…"

There was silence between them for several long minutes as each fell into their own thoughts. Eventually, Simon said, "I'm… in love with her. I asked her to leave Mordecai last week." He looked at his mother and then pursed his lips. "But she's not going to. And I can't even hate him because he's saved my life too many times!"

"You can be grateful and still view him as a rival," his mother kindly offered with a smile.

"Right," Simon replied. "That'll go over well."

"You and Kell have always gotten along well—even when you didn't know she was a girl."

He looked at her, suspicious. "Wait, did you know?"

"Well, yes. I suspected, and then one night, Tarquin came barging in, asking specifically for my help. I mean, when was the last time that man ever asked anyone, much less a woman, for help? But I went with him. Kell had started her monthly cycle and thought she was dying."

Simon frowned. "What's that?"

His mother grinned fondly at him.

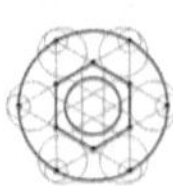

The following morning after conjuring and cooking breakfast, Kell followed Tarquin south. Knowing that Terin could track her if she used Viterra, Kell limited how much she relied on it. Only when necessary, she pulled apart vines and pushed away fallen debris. Though she felt stronger, she grew winded easily, and they were forced to break often.

Near midday, they rested to place medicinal herbs on Kell's wound. Afterward, she napped in the cool grass next to an apartment complex that had been overrun with enormous trees whose boughs shifted pleasantly in the summer breezes. Tarquin woke her an hour or so later, and they continued.

Midafternoon, they had to take a longer break as Kell had grown too weak. She slept for several hours, trusting that her father would wake her if she were needed. She eventually woke sometime around supper.

Squinting against the sun, she stared south. She could discern the sparkling horizon of the sea. Frowning, she looked at Tarquin. They hadn't made much progress. "Two days?" she muttered. "We'll be lucky if we get there in a week."

"You're hurt," Tarquin replied, following her. "What'd you expect?" He sighed and looked east. "Too bad they're not at the Middle District harbor. That would have—"

Kell whirled on him, her eyes wide. "How far is it?"

"What? The docks?"

"No, the Middle District harbor!"

He motioned eastward. "A few miles down the road from here. Couple hours of walking." Seeing the expression on her face, he frowned. "What are you thinkin'?"

"That taking a boat might be much faster."

Tarquin opened his mouth to argue but stopped. After a moment, he smiled. "It would be much faster, wouldn't it?"

With renewed purpose, they set off east, working together to navigate around snaking roots and barricades of dense vegetation. Not wanting to reveal her location to Terin, Kell stopped using Viterra all together, which significantly slowed their progress. Still, it gave her and Tarquin the opportunity to talk and reconnect after so many years of separation, and though tired, Kell relished it.

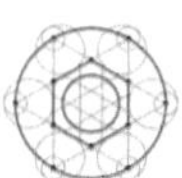

Simon paced the wheelhouse, his gaze set northward over the disheveled docks coated in the pink of dawn. Where there had been smoke, gunfire, and evidence of ongoing battle in the Upper and Middle Districts, there was nothing. What was going on? Had the palace been overrun? What had happened to Bellamy? Maybe the fighting was over? He didn't dare hope.

What was to become of the capital once everything settled? Eighty percent of its people had been displaced or killed. Even he knew the upper echelons of society couldn't survive without the lower and middle classes. He didn't envy Bellamy and the monumental work that he faced.

When Simon eventually returned downstairs, he found Mordecai hovering guardedly around Renata as she took a few tentative steps toward the family table. Vera watched with worried eyes as the old woman reached a chair and sat. Letting out a sigh of relief, Mordecai glanced at Simon and shook his head. Renata was healing but not fast enough. The burns she had incurred to her legs and hips were responding to the herbal treatments the old woman had implemented, but they would take time to heal.

"Have you been tending to your own burns?" grumbled Renata, looking at Mordecai and then at Simon. "Both of you?" The two exchanged looks and shrugged, causing the woman to sigh in exasperation. "Mordecai..."

"We've been busy," he replied. "I didn't want to access the Flow and draw attention to our position."

"You are hidden. All of you are," Renata replied sternly. "I'll extend the concealment. Go out on the deck and grow emberweed, plenty of it for everyone. Go, now."

Simon saw Mordecai furtively look first at Ferrik and then at Vera, who was making tea and breakfast, before slipping out the rear door. It occurred to Simon that Mordecai was well aware of the precarious position he and his teacher were in; it was no wonder he had become so protective of Renata, especially in the presence of Ferrik.

"I didn't hear from Kellick last night," Renata said, looking at Simon. "And neither did Mordecai."

Simon shook his head. "Me either."

Renata laid a wrinkled hand on the table and tapped in thought. "The night before she said she and Tarquin were traveling... Simon?"

Startled by his name on her lips, he looked at her. "Yes, ma'am?" She regarded him. Behind her gray eyes was wisdom, intelligence, and a lifetime of experience.

"What is she up to?"

"Ma'am?"

"If you were traveling with her and needed to get from the Upper District to us, where would you go? Where would Kell go?" Before he could answer, she continued. "She hasn't been using Viterra, which means—"

The old woman froze, her eyes growing wide.

"Renata?" whispered Simon, alarmed. "What? What is it?"

At that moment, Mordecai burst into the main cabin, hair thrown back. "Terin," he panted. "She's here."

In a distressing transformation, Renata slumped in her chair, her normally stern face folded in fear and pain. "We're concealed," she whispered, as if trying to convince herself. "She won't be able to find us..."

Everyone fell still as a feral scream echoed down the docks. A soft sob from Renata followed.

Simon looked at Mordecai, unsure of what to do or say. *They* were the Users; *they* should be the ones to handle Terin. But Renata was clearly not in a state to do so, and sending Mordecai out there to face an Unbound alone was a death sentence.

"What do we do?" quavered Vera, holding the kettle, her hands trembling. She peered out a narrow porthole. "She's… Everything's on fire."

"We leave," Simon asserted. He turned and started up the stairs to the wheelhouse.

"Simon, Simon!" called Renata, her voice strangled. He peered back down the staircase at her to find her shaking her head. "Don't leave the docks."

"Why?" he snarled.

Mordecai was the one to reply. "She'll see the wake and use the water to kill us. She'll… sink the boat and… trap us underwater."

Bracing on the overhead beam, Simon looked between them. "Then what the hell do we do? We can't just sit here!"

"We'll stay hidden," Renata concluded shakily. "I'll keep us hidden—"

"No, Simon's right." Mordecai glanced out the window; the glow of brilliant flames illuminated his face. "Vera, how much fuel do you have?"

"Some," Simon's mother replied.

"Enough to make it to Avives?"

"Oh, no. Not that much."

"But enough to get you a couple of miles out to sea?"

"Mordecai," barked Renata, suddenly struggling to stand.

Mordecai motioned to Ferrik as he turned to open the cabin's forward door. "Don't let her leave."

Renata was on her feet now. "Mordecai!"

"I'll buy you time." He met Simon's gaze. "Once I'm off, start the boat and go."

Renata's voice cracked. "Mordecai!"

The expression on Mordecai's face was grave. "Get her out of here." And then he slipped out, closing the door behind him.

"Please, Simon." Renata reached across the table to him. "Please, go after him. She'll kill him." The raw desperation in the old woman's voice spurred Simon to action.

"Mom, start the engines. Get out of the harbor *fast*." Simon crossed the room. "Ferrik, stay with them."

His mentor held him still with a strong hand. "I'll go with you."

Simon sincerely considered the offer before saying, "No, I need you to stay here with them. They'll need protection… if we fail."

"Then I'll go and you stay," his mentor replied.

Lips pursed in thought, Simon thought of Kell and what she would want. "No, I'm familiar with Mordecai." He grabbed his cleaned sword and snapped the forward cabin door open. "I'll go, you stay. Keep them safe for me."

His mother's plea followed him onto the forward deck. Brandishing his sword, he leaped onto the lopsided dock to find Mordecai barefoot finishing an Arcane Circle. When he struck his wrists, two glowing bands of red materialized on each arm.

The harbor was on fire—again. What had been overlooked during its previous razing was aflame. Already thick, black smoke spilled into the warm morning air, obscuring the sun. Flames as high as buildings roared along the neighboring streets as the remains of the Lower District were indiscriminately torched. And in the middle of it all, standing along the brick street directly adjacent to the docks, was Terin, a ferocious silhouette spewing destruction as she leveled the surrounding block.

Simon swallowed, the hair on his arms standing on end. Kell's power had been frightening, but the rage that vented from Terin compelled him to run. Even from the docks, he could feel the searing heat; it scalded his already burned skin and made a vicious sweat break across his body. How were they supposed to stop her?

Behind them, a roar erupted from *Merry Maiden* as its engines revved to life. Simon saw his mother in the wheelhouse as she looked over her shoulder and then slammed the throttle. The Ashway family boat surged backward, spraying water across its stern as Vera aggressively reversed.

"Simon!" Mordecai shouted, returning his attention to Terin, who had spotted them and was now surfing across the bricks and shoddy cobblestones toward them. Mordecai dragged his foot across the wooden docks and then kicked toward Simon. Water collided with Simon, sweeping him a few paces to the right. Drenched, he looked at Mordecai, confused. "Same as before. Find a way behind her. I'll hold her off."

Realizing Mordecai was trying to provide him with some defense against the heat, Simon turned on heel and sprinted down the docks in the opposite direction. He was relieved when Terin didn't even acknowledge his departure. Glancing over his shoulder, Simon glimpsed Mordecai go through a sequence of fluid motions that culminated with several kicks. Water sprang from the slip behind him to shoot at Terin as more surrounded Mordecai in a protective shield.

Terin knocked the water away with a fiery fist and then loosed a blast of orange flames. Steam erupted around them with a hiss.

Knowing he didn't have much time, Simon skirted the smoldering docks, dodging falling debris and grimacing as flames licked his skin. Between the smoke and the steam, he could hardly discern Terin and Mordecai. But the rampant fire that continued to spill from a central point gave him a good enough idea.

Running faster than he had ever moved in his life, Simon raced across the blackened bricks, leaped onto a fallen support beam, and charged Terin from behind. The moment he was almost within striking range, Terin turned, dropping her right shoulder. Knowing what was to come next, Simon dodged, rolling behind her.

Mordecai took the opportunity to send an anchor's chain whirling through the air at her. With deadly skill, Terin ducked in a spin and vented fire at him in a concussive explosion.

Sword gleaming in the surrounding fire, Simon thrust the weapon at her in that split second. But Terin was fast, fluid, and wholly Unbound. She swept the blade to the side with a thick vine, which had materialized between her hands, and then kicked. Although Simon dodged the counter, his sword missed its mark; the sudden empty air in front of him broke his commitment to the attack, leaving him open.

He sensed her move, saw her hands instruct with precise gestures the Viterra that he felt rush in around them. Realizing with dread that he couldn't get out of the way quick enough, he lashed out with a kick. His boot caught her hip, disrupting her balance and sending her staggering. Simon met her teak-colored, unhinged gaze before seeing a spark in her palm.

Dockett's voice suddenly tore through his mind. *The legs!*

Simon dropped low and darted forward, sweeping his sword. A cloud of fire erupted between them—and then suddenly vanished. Face tucked, Simon peered over his arms to find Mordecai wrapped around Terin, a muscled bicep wound around her neck. As he cranked down on her, strengthening his hold into a strangle, he dropped to his knees. Terin crumpled with him.

She fought him for a breath's moment, and then, with a snarl, formed a thick, eight-inch-long thorn between her fingers. Simon was already moving, drawing his sword back to deliver the final blow. But Terin was fast. With brutality Simon had only ever seen in the arena, she wrenched the organic dagger back and drove it deep into Mordecai's flank. Before he could release her, she had wounded him three more times.

Mordecai collapsed on the charred docks with a gasping cry, blood soaking his clothes. Sword bared, Simon moved in front of the injured man. He knew he couldn't defeat Terin; he didn't stand a chance, not when she could call any element to her. Panting, he tried desperately to think of how they could escape, his eyes never leaving Terin as she coughed and sputtered.

"Go," Mordecai groaned. "Go, Simon."

"No!" Simon seethed. "I won't!"

There was a thud, a distant reverberation along the docks, as if someone or something had just landed. Though Terin looked to see what had made the sound, Simon could not afford to take his eyes off his opponent. The expression on Terin's face changed, and she relaxed and turned away from him.

Simon reared back, muscle memory spurring him to action. She was no longer guarded. He could attack, swiftly and precisely. It would—

"Don't!" came a familiar voice.

Simon looked toward the end of the docks at Kell who stood aglow in blue light, all three fields and Arcane Circle alit. Ashamed relief spilled over him. He had never been so happy to see her. As Terin stalked away, Simon kneeled beside Mordecai and began checking him.

"Shit…" Mordecai wheezed as Simon rolled him over. His hands came away coated in thick blood. "She… got me."

Warily looking back at Terin, Simon ripped Mordecai's sopping shirt off, no longer being gentle. He needed to stop the bleeding, fast. "Where?" Simon breathed, searching the man's left flank. Mordecai pointed a trembling finger first at his abdomen and then his left thigh. "Damn it!"

Simon pulled his own shirt off and began holding pressure on the abdominal wound, drawing a strangled hiss from Mordecai.

"Hold this, hold this," Simon instructed, pushing Mordecai's shirt into his hand and pressing both against the man's thigh. "Hard, as hard as you can." Wildly, Simon looked about. Where could they go? There was literally nothing, no one. Panic forming in his throat, he peered down at Mordecai. "Hey, you gotta stay awake. Yeah? Don't close your eyes."

"Yeah," Mordecai murmured, semi-conscious. "It… hurts… a lot though." His eyes fluttered. "Si-mon… If I don't make…"

"No, nope, nope." Simon looked over his shoulder, terrified. What could he—

Fast, heavy footsteps interrupted his thoughts. Searching the flames, he spotted an enormous figure barreling toward them. Simon scrambled to his feet in preparation to defend them, but as the man's form grew more familiar, Simon cried out in relief. "Tarquin!" The sound of his voice cracking scared him. "Tarquin!"

Kell's father joined them, sliding along the uneven wooden planks of the dock. "How bad is it?" he asked, dropping a bag alongside him.

"He-he was stabbed. I don't know—She did it so fast—I…" Simon began applying pressure again which caused Mordecai to curse and flail under his blood-slick hands. "I don't know what to do—Tarquin, help. Please. Help."

The enormous man dumped medical supplies from the bag and began going through them. He passed rolls of gauze, bandages, and tape to Simon before peeling away the soaked shirts. With swift hands, Kell's father jerked Mordecai's pants down to his knees to better scrutinize the thigh wounds. After a moment, he leaned over Mordecai. "Hey, hey, I got you, boy. Come on. Stay awake. There's a lad. Let's go. Come on. Simon, talk to him."

As Tarquin worked on Mordecai, Simon looked back at Terin and Kell who appeared to be speaking.

"What… what's happening?" Mordecai murmured between gasps.

"I don't know, I don't know." Simon passed Tarquin more gauze watching Kell and Terin. He felt a tug on his pants and looked back down at Mordecai.

"Thanks," Mordecai whispered. He grimaced as Tarquin cinched down a bandage. "I… didn't want to face her… alone."

Simon gripped his shoulder comfortingly. "You're braver than I am."

36

Synchrony

KELL TRIED TO KEEP HERSELF focused, intent upon Terin who appeared like a fiend. But her gaze kept slipping toward the familiar figures along the docks, one of whom was prone. Even from a distance, even with flames eating away at everything in the vicinity, even with smoke billowing into the sky and embers soaring ever upward, she could discern Tarquin and Simon's frantic movements.

Terin raised a hand and pointed her palm behind her at the men, a silent threat.

"Terin, please," Kell begged, inching closer. Her mentor held her gaze. "Please…"

Terin's hair was singed and her clothes frayed and burnt. The way she held herself was not quite right, as if she no longer cared for proper posturing when it came to the traits. The look in her eyes was wild and raw, reminding Kell of a lone coyote they had once cornered. There was wrath there and plenty of hatred, but something else—desperation.

"You won." Kell held her hands out to show that she wasn't going to do anything. "You won. You beat us. You got… Renata and… Mordecai. You beat us."

"No!" Terin screamed, startling Kell. "That's *not* what I want!" She panted, her body tense and fists clenched. "I want… you dead. You—This is all *your* fault!" Kell backed away. "Everything was going well before-before you—You invaded my mind! You—"

"I can't control it!" Kell argued. "The dreamwalking, I can't control who I go to—"

"Kneel."

A wave of Viterra rushed over Kell, adding weight to her shoulders and pushing her down. With a growl, she fought the command, struggling to remain standing, but her knees were already bending. "Terin!" Kell cried as she felt one knee touch the wooden planks of the docks.

"Kneel!" Terin screamed.

Kell crashed to the docks with a yelp as Viterra stacked upon her. Breathless, she held herself on all fours, her arms trembling from the effort. She couldn't so much as raise a hand. "Terin, please," she whispered. "Don't do… this." She heard Terin approach but couldn't lift her head.

"You've always been a nuisance. *Always.* You run your mouth and insert yourself where you don't belong. You and Renata—the both of you—stand between me and conquering the capital, all of Berceau," Terin said evenly. "Once you two are out of the way, I'll rebuild—"

Kell felt a shift in the air around her. Fighting the command she had been bestowed, she glanced up in time to see Simon leap off an upturned support beam. With phenomenal strength and speed, he tore downward, his sword splitting the space between them. Though caught off guard, Terin managed a step back. That single step saved her life as the tip of Simon's blade bit into the flesh above her right breast and torn down to her navel.

Simon whirled on the ball of his foot, his body gathered under him like a coil, and swept at her legs with the bloody sword. But Terin was already ahead of him and had drawn a plank of wood from its nails with a flick of her hand to stop the attack.

Suddenly free from Terin's command because her attention was elsewhere, Kell scrambled upright. She could sense her mentor drawing dangerous amounts of Viterra from the Flow. Kell rammed into Simon, sending them tumbling over the edge of the docks into the water. Gripping his arm, she also began pulling from the Flow. The moment they broke for air, Kell created a barrier of ever-shifting water around them.

As fire ricocheted off it, she drew herself and Simon onto the water's surface and pushed, heaving them away from the docks in an enormous wave of water. Confident Terin would follow and leave Tarquin and Mordecai, she began forming a plan of attack.

Widening her Arcane Circle so Simon could stand there with her, she jerked off her shirt and shed her stockings and boots, allowing the articles to sink into the sea around them. Adjusting her soaked bandeau, she watched as Terin stepped off the docks and began calmly walking toward them along the water's surface.

"If I give you a boost, can you swim back?" Kell asked.

"What are you planning?"

"You wounded her. I think we're on more even ground now. Get back to Mordecai and Tarquin."

Simon glanced down at her healing wound and then, with a pained expression, pulled her to him and kissed her hard. All that Kell sensed in his tense lips was fear, anger, and desperation. She returned the brief kiss, fervently thankful for his support and strength.

Without another word, they drew apart. She gave him a nod, stepped back, and then in a sweeping movement, drew a wave toward them. Kell gestured for Simon to take a breath, which he did, before she enwrapped him in a column of water and sucked him beneath the surface. Her gaze set on Terin, who had paused her advance to watch, Kell maneuvered Simon under the water toward the docks. When she felt a change in the water depth, she brought him to the surface in a single motion, hoisting him onto the sloping docks with a spindly tentacle of water. Simon looked back at her and then hurried off to where Tarquin still sat beside Mordecai.

Relieved that Simon was no longer in Terin's immediate range, Kell settled herself into a water traits stance, drawing from the Flow to create a whirring shield of salt water. She hoped maintaining a steady rush of water around her would make it more difficult to hear Terin's commands.

Terin regarded her and then, her strides becoming longer and faster, charged. Water gathered before her fists to form solid ice. Realizing Terin intended to make this a close-combat battle, Kell lashed out with several rapid strikes, converting sections of her liquid shield into frozen ballistics that zinged through the air like arrows loosed from a bow.

Terin dodged two, absorbed another, and struck three others down, her pace unchanged. Kell knew the time for her match against Terin had arrived. Making a split-second decision, she dropped her shield of water and dug deep beneath the sea's surface. Arms strong, hands willowy, and legs pliable, Kell called on the forest of kelp she knew hugged the bottom of the boating channel, jerking it free with broad gestures.

With Terin approaching, she sent the tangle of living kelp at her opponent, manipulating the aquatic vegetation to trap Terin's hands and arms first and foremost. As Kell danced backward along the waves, struggling to keep the wild and frenetic fronds around Terin, she considered what it was she was supposed to do in the end with her mentor. Did Renata wish her to be killed? Captured?

Terin loosed a raging fireball of Viterra that spread outward across the sea's surface, effectively scorching the kelp to ash. Kell shielded herself behind a curtain of water and grimaced as steam erupted.

She couldn't beat Terin; there was no way.

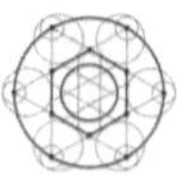

"Do something," Mordecai moaned, sitting up. "Simon."

Simon looked on in horror as an explosion erupted around Terin, the blast of heat so powerful that they could feel it even along the docks. "There's... nothing I can do," Simon admitted, his gazed following Kell as she escaped the cloud of steam and streaked across the sea's surface. She crashed through the mild harbor waves, a constant swell of water under her as if she were surfing. All the while, Terin pursued, a mixture of fire and water spilling from her in great rushes of Viterra that made even Simon shudder.

"Mordecai, don't," chided Tarquin.

Simon felt Mordecai grip his leg and looked down at him.

"Get me up," Mordecai snarled through gritted teeth, his hands trembling.

Simon exchanged a look with Tarquin before helping him to his feet. Heavily bolstering Mordecai, he kept the man steady for a long moment, his eyes once again seeking Kell.

The battle was spiraling out of control. In the few seconds Simon had looked away, Terin had gained the upper hand. From the docks he heard Kell scream as a flailing column of scalding water, the result of Terin mixing fire and water, sent Kell toppling across the harbor. She landed in a pile atop the tempestuous water, struggling to get her legs under her.

Mordecai shifted his weight forward. "Help me," he demanded with more determination.

Tarquin joined Simon, and together they started for the docks' edge.

Kell was flagging. Her movements were slow and heavy. The quickness with which her shoulders rose and fell revealed how out of breath she was. "Shit," Simon cursed, spotting rivulets of pink leaking down her flank from her reopened wound.

As Terin gathered fire around her, steam spewed into air. Kell took an unfamiliar stance which caused Mordecai, who was stepping over a downed support beam, to say, "Not good, not good."

"What?" asked Simon.

"She's trying to use metal." Mordecai pushed himself away from Simon and Tarquin. "She's... bad at metal."

"Then why is she usin' it?" asked Tarquin.

Wavering on his feet, Mordecai stumbled forward before he caught himself. "Because Terin... is bad at it too." He drew a long, slow breath, his palms rising and falling in sync with his shoulders. His body stopped teetering; it grew still. Ready to catch Mordecai, Simon remained directly beside him.

With a strangled grunt, Mordecai swung his left leg around him to create a circle and then struck his wrists. The red cuffs appeared emblazoned around his arms as the foreboding black Arcane Circle ignited beneath his feet. Though the violent rush of Viterra around Mordecai frightened him, Simon didn't move. Right now, Mordecai was the only one who could help Kell, and Simon needed to make sure he didn't fail.

Mordecai swept a bare foot outward, skimming the rough wood, before drawing his knee to his chest with a pained groan. His balance remained solid. With a quick breath, he kicked upward and then spun around, lashing out with his other foot. An enormous TW anchor equipped with several feet of rusty chain rose from the water. Simon recognized it as old man Montague's since it was adorned with his initials; it had been lost nearly a decade ago due to Montague forgetting to bolt it to the reel.

Panting, Mordecai held it for but a moment and then with a visceral shout, he whirled around and kicked, rotating with unexpected strength. The sixty-five-pound anchor and its length of chain streaked across the water with speed that rivaled the icy ballistics Terin and Kell had exchanged.

Upon realizing the anchor's trajectory though, Simon gasped, grabbing for Mordecai. It was hurtling toward Kell.

In that moment, Simon thought Mordecai had just sentenced her to death. But Kell seemed to sense its approach. Using what strength she could muster, she whirled as Mordecai had just done, drawing the anchor, its chain, and momentum around her like a meteor circling Earth's orbit. With an extended arm, she flung the anchor toward Terin.

Terin flailed to evade the bombastic projectile. Though the anchor missed her entirely, the chain wrapped with intent around her hips. In the next second, she was jerked backward by the weight and sucked underwater.

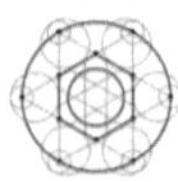

Panting, Kell fell to her hands and knees and stared at the water shifting beneath her. She hurt. Everything on her hurt, but none more so than the throbbing wound just above her right hip. Tears in her eyes, she pressed on the injury. Her hands came away bloody. Swallowing hard, she looked across the sea where Terin had disappeared.

Was that it? Was it over?

She remained unmoving for several long moments, trying to comprehend all that had just transpired. She could hardly process it. She sat on her Arcane Circle and looked back at the docks where Simon kneeled with Mordecai. Tarquin waved at her.

Kell meant to return the gesture but fell still as a great surge of Viterra suddenly blossomed beneath her. The Flow around her grew erratic. Scrambling to her feet with a cry of pain, she staggered backward to search the water which had begun to bubble and boil. "No, no, no," she whispered. She had nothing left. She couldn't keep going.

A geyser of seawater erupted some thirty feet from her. Inside it was Terin, seemingly unscathed.

Kell gaped, unable to understand how someone could have so much power. Terin was truly Renata's disciple.

She heard a shout from the docks and looked to find Simon motioning for her to run.

Run?

Run where?

Legs trembling, Kell tried to form some sort of stance, but she was wiped, utterly exhausted. Terrified, she took a few tentative steps back, Terin's name on her lips.

There was nowhere to run, nowhere to go. Nothing to do…

You are able to do because you believe you can. Denez's voice was strong in Kell's head. *How you perceive Viterra and your own abilities influences how you are able to use them.*

"How I… perceive Viterra," she muttered, looking at the glowing rings of blue around her arms. Her gaze drifted to the Arcane Circle, rough and reassuring, under her feet. "*Satt.*" Her thoughts turning inward, Kell relaxed.

Viterra was drawn from the Flow, the inherent stream of energy that ran through everything—earth, rock, flora, water, fire, ice, wind, even ore. Viterra was a part of everything. It was in the waves gently bumping Kell's feet; it was in the heat of the sun overhead. It was in the kelp forests that extended for miles out from the harbor, and it was in the innumerous fishing hooks, anchors, and other metal paraphernalia that littered the sea bottom. Viterra was in the wind that buffeted Kell's salty hair and in the rocky wavebreaks that protected the harbor.

Kell looked at Terin.

Viterra connected everything, even opposites like fire and water, earth and wind, metal and flora. Such interconnectedness meant that mastery of one element meant mastery of all elements. Remembering Gytha, Kell grew still.

She could picture them sitting next to the river, the water trickling by pleasantly. Gytha, her long blond hair plaited, standing and lithely dancing across the gentle current. *All of the elements belong to us.*

Despite the raging inferno that churned around Terin, Kell remained motionless. Fear seeped out of her until she regarded her former mentor not as a rampaging, hellish beast intent on destroying everything around them but as a young, tortured woman whose life had been torn asunder from an early age. The more Terin accomplished, the more dissatisfied and angrier she became.

Taking one last, calming breath, Kell shook the Viterra from her hands. Though her rings disappeared and the Arcane Circle beneath her feet vanished, she remained poised atop the water's surface. As the heat from Terin's attack swelled, it seared the parts of Kell's skin that had previously been burnt. Still, Kell didn't move.

Her former mentor was unhinged, panting and gasping like a dragon. Her once glorious halo of black, puffy hair had been reduced to singed ringlets that hung at odd angles. Her clothes were scorched and hung heavy with seawater on her frame. Blood continued to seep into her shirt and drip down to the hem. Her movements were no longer methodical, fluid, and purposeful. She acted with vehement desperation, as if failure in her killing of Kell would, in fact, signal her own end.

As waves of fire pulsed across the choppy water, finally reaching Kell, she raised a palm to the onslaught. The moment the Viterra licked her fingers, she forced it away, the stark stances of fire traits providing a foundation for her new revelation.

"All of the elements… belong to me," Kell whispered. A curtain of seawater rose to keep the encroaching fire at bay as kelp intertwined with strands of algae to form a living shield.

Upon realizing that her fire was being withstood, Terin switched to ice, hurling infinitely sharp blades over the harbor's waves. But the flora at Kell's command stopped the missiles with ease, snapping them inches before their intended mark.

Gale-force wind tore across the open sea, whipping the waves into frothing whitecaps that emanated from Kell. Viterra surged under her as she asked the multitudinous fishing accoutrements and manmade metals that besieged the bottom to join her. Anchors, chains, hooks, rods, propeller pieces, bolts, and more rose from the depths to hang menacingly beside her, despite the raging wind.

As Kell continued to fend off frozen missiles and blasts of fire, she started toward Terin. She didn't know what she was supposed to do, only that she needed to get to the young woman flailing through sets of traits.

Only when Terin vented a large flux of fire around herself and Kell nullified it with a slight pass of her hand did Terin back away. Using the thick stipes and fronds of the kelp to continue to push away attacks with minimal effort, Kell watched her former mentor—the crazed look in her wide eyes, the anger and hatred that contorted her face.

"Stop!" Terin suddenly shouted, holding a hand out.

Kell felt the rush of Viterra that accompanied her command.

"Stop, don't move!"

Kell stopped, not because absolute obedience made her, but because Terin had asked it.

Panting and body still coiled in preparation to attack, her mentor regarded her.

"Can we… end this?" asked Kell. "I'm tired and hurt, and you're hurt. And I'm… I just don't want to fight you."

Terin's gaze met hers, and for a moment, it seemed she would consider Kell's request. Ultimately, however, she shook her head. "No, this is only over when you and-and Renata are dead."

"And then what?" Kell laid the water to rest and let the kelp relax upon the waves. The wind around them settled. "Then what will you do? You kill us and then you… what?"

"The capital will fall."

"Eclat's fallen!" Kell barked, waving a hand at the razed city. "It's gone. *You* did that. Thousands of people, killed. Thousands more displaced. *You* did that. Eclat's fallen." She composed herself. "So, you've gotten what you wanted—revenge on-on every person, every woman, every child. Everyone." When Terin didn't reply, Kell continued. "I… *killed* people, Terin. I burned dozens of blocks of the Lower District. Renata destroyed half of Eclat when she was younger." She lowered her voice. "So, why would we let you do the same thing?"

"Because you don't have a choice," she seethed, murder tinting her eyes. "Kellick, die."

Viterra slammed into Kell, ushering her a few paces back. The command was piercing and struck her with such force that she was left struggling to breathe. As she stumbled backward, her lungs no longer drawing air, she grasped for the one thing that had been a part of her life since the day Tarquin had found her—water.

Dropping to her hands and knees, she urged seawater to mercilessly tangle around Terin's legs. Terin thrashed at the water, trying to command it away, but her efforts were all for naught. The moment the woman opened her mouth to screech in sheer panic, water invaded her, cruelly driving in to fill her lungs.

Kell felt Terin's Viterra slacken and then dissipate as the woman was pulled under the surface for good.

37

Coming to Terms

PANTING, KELL REMAINED MOTIONLESS, THE waves lapping against her legs. The expression of pure terror that had consumed Terin's face would haunt her.

Distantly, she recognized the steady drone of a boat engine, but she couldn't take her eyes away from the spot where her mentor had disappeared. Kelp drifted around her, spiraling lazily outward, no longer under her control. Kell reached forward to touch the water with a few fingers, her gaze searching the deep blue depths. Terin was gone.

A seagull overhead cried, breaking her trance. Stiffly, she sat back on the water and leaned on her hands. Chin tilting upward, she squinted at the sun. Though the air held traces of smoke, the scent of seawater was powerful.

As she took a long breath, she lay back in the waves until she floated on her back, the buoyancy of the saltwater keeping her afloat with ease. Ears underwater, she could hear the waves on her face and the grinding gears of a boat slowing.

She felt a familiar sensation as her teacher drew the water around her up and over the lip of the Ashway family boat. Eyes closed, Kell waited until she felt the hard deck under her. After a moment, she peered up at Ferrik and Renata. The pro-fighter appeared mildly concerned, but Renata was crying.

Her teacher's tears confirmed her dark reality. Kell grimaced as she felt her eyes sting—not from the saltwater—before resting an arm across her face. A sob erupted from her throat.

Renata scooped her up with strong arms and hugged her, her strangled cries melding with Kell's sorrow.

"S-sorry," Kell managed, clutching her teacher as tears rolled down her cheeks. "I'm sorry, Teacher!"

Renata didn't shush her or try to comfort her. They both understood and mourned the tragedy that had just occurred. Renata just held Kell, her arms shaking periodically from grief and effort.

Eventually, Vera brought out a rough blanket and wrapped it around them as they were both soaked. Ferrik stood silently nearby, observing. As Vera fired up the boat engines from idle, Kell leaned into Renata until they collapsed together on the deck. She took her teacher's hand and held it between them, her face curled into the old woman's damp bosom.

They weren't far from the docks, but for Kell, for whom time seemed to have dilated, the ride back was long. By the time Vera killed the engines, Kell was half-asleep, tangled in a blanket with Renata. "Come on," her teacher softly urged.

Kell weakly sat up. A hand came into her field of vision and, without thinking about it, she took it. Ferrik drew her to her feet and held her steady as she wavered there.

There came a commotion as Simon leaped aboard the boat's bow, slipped along the side railing, and tackled Kell in a mighty embrace. Still not fully processing everything around her, Kell stood weakly in his arms as he kissed the side of her head and hugged her fiercely. When he pulled away to gauge her, she found she had a hard time focusing her eyes on him.

"Tarquin!" he called over his shoulder. Simon scooped her up, blanket and all, and shouldered his way into the main cabin. "Mom, tell Tarquin to bring the first aid here. Ferrik, help him get Mordecai onboard."

Simon took her to his narrow quarters and sat on the bed with her.

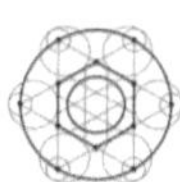

Knowing this would likely be the last time he had her to himself, Simon clasped Kell to him, kissing her tangled and salty hair reverently. He couldn't stop himself from muttering the first thing that visited his lips. "I love you *so* much." He didn't expect a response; still, her lack of a reaction hurt. Her unblinking gaze remained set on the corner of the room.

Nevertheless, he kissed the side of her head numerous times as he rubbed the blanket with gentle hands to dry and warm her. Renata joined them, limping significantly. When Simon started to stand, she motioned for him to remain seated.

Tarquin came in, supporting Mordecai who could barely walk.

"Here, Tarquin," Simon's mother said, offering a thick blanket. Tarquin deposited Mordecai atop the blanket on the floor before turning for Kell, the medical bag slung over his shoulder.

Simon kissed Kell once more before stretching her on the bed. As he backed away, he glanced first at Mordecai and then at Renata.

"Vera, would you help?" Tarquin murmured, sitting on the side of the bed. Kell stared up at the ceiling, seemingly unaware of her father's presence. As Tarquin and Vera crowded around Kell and began scrutinizing her reopened wound, Simon watched, his heart hammering. He felt so helpless, so unnecessary.

A strong hand on his shoulder brought his attention to Ferrik, who had been standing in the doorway. His mentor gave a nod and then left the main cabin. Simon glanced at Kell to find her hissing in pain and then followed Ferrik outside.

Standing on *Merry Maiden's* stern, Ferrik peered out at the horizon of open water. "Now's not the time," the onyx-colored man said when Simon joined him.

"For what?"

Ferrik motioned to the cabin. "She's not here."

Simon only partially grasped what he was saying but, like when he lied about understanding a technique, Ferrik seemed to sense this and continued. "Do you remember the first User you killed?"

"Yes…"

"She just killed her sister. She's not emotionally here right now." Ferrik flopped a fond hand on his shoulder. "Give her time."

Looking to change the subject, Simon cleared his throat. "Thank you for helping."

"I didn't do anything."

He looked at Ferrik grimly. "I entrusted my mom to you. You did plenty."

His mentor scoffed, though Simon could tell he was secretly pleased, and then turned to regard the ruined harbor. The docks were in disarray; the Ashway family slip was nowhere to be seen. His mother had parked alongside the only remaining upright poles and still-standing but slightly sloping dock. "What now?" Ferrik asked. "What happens now?"

"I… don't know." Simon leaned on the boat railing. "There's nothing left of the Lower District." Memories of his childhood flooded him. "Eclat's done for."

Ferrik sighed. "I think that depends on your friend the king."

Simon nodded, turning his gaze to the boat Kell and Tarquin had arrived in which bumped lazily against a half-sunk support beam.

The king…

A thought occurred to him. "We'll head back to the Upper District. Regroup with Bellamy."

Ferrik passed him a muted smile. "Sounds like a plan."

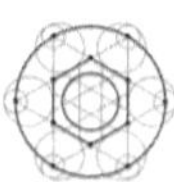

Once they transferred fuel and supplies from the stolen vessel to *Merry Maiden*, they set off for the Middle District port. Because the Ashway family boat was significantly older than their getaway ride, the going was slow. Kell took the opportunity to sleep, soundly. Though she wanted to stay by Mordecai's side, she simply couldn't keep herself upright or conscious.

Vera woke her briefly around supper to feed her a thin, tasteless soup. Kell ate what she could, used the restroom, and then limped back to the room she shared with Renata. She could feel her teacher's eyes on her, but she could comprehend nothing more than the hollowness in her heart. Grimacing in pain, she flopped unceremoniously onto the floor and quickly went back to sleep, her body craving rest.

She dreamed horrible, visceral dreams that featured Terin being killed again and again, each more violent than the last. With a strangled cry, Kell finally jerked herself awake. Panting into the still darkness of their shared quarters, she stared at the ceiling. The look in Terin's eyes, the way she had thrashed and flailed, the absolute fear that must have overwhelmed her…

A cry erupted from Kell's throat. She covered her face as great, heaving sobs wracked her body, pulling from her the remains of her strength. Large hands wrapped around her and sat her upright. Gasping and crying, Kell continued to weep into Simon, shaking so hard from the effort that she thought she might vomit.

When, in fact, bile creeped up her throat, she struggled to her feet, using Simon as a brace, and raced clumsily into the small galley where the sink fed out to the sea. She threw up into the sink, her whole body shaking. Between crying and vomiting, she gasped for air until finally a cold sweat broke over her.

When she finally calmed, she became aware that she had not been holding up herself; Simon had. Arms splayed on the counter, Kell panted for a moment and then glanced at him. His face was mercifully void of judgment or emotion. "Done?" he whispered.

She nodded weakly and croaked, "Water?"

"Wait a few minutes," he replied. "Let your stomach settle." When he turned to lead her back into Renata's quarters, Kell stopped him and motioned to the forward door. Simon momentarily deposited her at the table, retrieved a blanket, and then escorted her to the bow of *Merry Maiden*. He wrapped the blanket around her clammy skin and helped her sit against the outer cabin wall.

Kell numbly slid to the deck. Simon sat beside her, the pressure of his arm around her comforting. Utterly worn, Kell slumped against him, her gaze fixed on the dark night sky.

Had she done the right thing? Had she tried every possible solution to get to Terin, to make a difference? She had talked with her, argued with her, appealed to her, and fought her. Was there anything else she could have done that could have produced a different outcome?

As she reviewed all that had transpired, running through the gruesome details in her mind—yet again—she slowly sunk into Simon's lap. Though it wasn't comfortable, she didn't have the energy to move.

With gentle hands, Simon lifted her into his embrace and held her there, using his knees to keep her from slipping. As Kell settled against his chest, she found his warmth made her exceptionally sleepy. Clutching his shirt to make sure that he, too, didn't disappear, she went back to sleep.

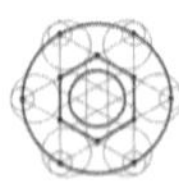

The sound of the engine shifting to a lower gear and the consequential jerk woke Simon. Breathing deeply, he peered up at the pink light of dawn and then inched Kell, who was already tucked against him, closer. Unable to remain sitting on the hard deck for so long, Simon had laid them down once she had fallen asleep. With the blanket wrapped around her and Kell's weight pressed firmly against him, he had fallen asleep with ease. He had slept in worse places at the Munera school over the years.

Eventually though, he needed to get up because his shoulder ached. Not wanting to disturb Kell, he sat up, keeping his back to the wall, and angled his legs over her to keep her from sliding. Stretching his neck and gingerly touching his shoulder, he winced. Medical attention had been on Renata, Kell, and Mordecai. His back and shoulders hurt.

Looking out, he saw the Middle District port a couple of miles away, a collection of pale dots against a backdrop of gray and green.

Simon looked down at Kell who was curled against him, her arms tucked to her chest. Her blanket was mostly trapped under her, exposing the pale blue dress his mother had clothed her in the previous night. Though she had managed to briefly bathe, her hair was still knotted and coarse from the salt water, not unlike how it had been when they were growing up.

Obsessed with her strength, resilience, and perseverance, Simon reached down and brushed stray tendrils from her face. Unable to help himself, he ran a thumb along her cheek and then sighed. He had to stop doing that to himself.

Eventually, there came a shuffling sound from within the cabin. Momentarily, Tarquin emerged with Renata. Though the water was relatively smooth, save the occasional bump, Tarquin kept a secure arm around the older woman.

"Did she sleep?" the woman asked.

"After she finished…" He gestured to indicate vomit. "Yes, ma'am. She slept."

Renata nodded in grim approval. "Thank you for taking care of her." She scrutinized him for a moment and then looked out at the looming port. "I'm in no condition to help her right now. And neither is Mordecai. I've already tasked Tarquin with finding a doctor. I must also charge you."

Simon looked between them. Tarquin appeared solemn. In the early morning light, the white in his beard and hair was more prevalent, and Simon saw his age. "With what?"

"Kell needs to see Bellamy. Immediately."

"I agree that we need to meet up with the king, but…" He frowned. "Kell can hardly move."

"That's why I'm asking you to find him and bring him to port." Kell's teacher held his gaze. "I know you hurt, Simon. I can see it in your eyes, but you two are the only ones capable right now."

"Then send me and Ferrik," countered Simon.

Renata shook her head. "No, Bellamy knows you. He'll trust anything—"

"I've met Bellamy two or three times," Simon interrupted. "I don't think that will lead him to believe what I have to say. I'm a pro-fighter. I'm… everything he hates."

Renata leveled a steely gaze at him. "Bellamy is the one who asked for your arrest that day in the market. The kid who turned you and Kell into the regulators? That's him." Seeing the revelation and subsequent anger on Simon's face, the old woman added, "Kell already gave him quite the thrashing for it years ago. Myself and another had to break the fight up before she killed him." Simon relaxed. He supposed that bit of information helped a little. "Bellamy knows Kell, and he knows you. Bring him to port at once."

Tarquin steadied Renata as a wave bounced the boat.

Perplexed, Simon looked between them. "What am I missing here? What's going on?"

"Bellamy needs her," Renata concluded. "It was decided months ago when Bellamy began his campaign to overthrow the Council. Kell is to be the bridge between the Old and the New." She nodded. "He *will* come for her."

"Oh." Simon glanced down at Kell to find her awake and staring at the wall.

38

Offer

SIMON SET OFF ONCE *Merry Maiden* was docked along the reeds that clustered the overgrown docks of the Middle District port. He and Tarquin walked together for a while before splitting up. As Tarquin headed northeast along the same path he and Kell had taken the day before, Simon went northwest.

Though his body was tired, he pushed himself, maintaining a steady pace until he was forced to pick around stints of thick jungle-like vegetation that cluttered the streets and alleyways. Near midday, he heard voices and the sound of hooves on brick. Coming around the corner of a half-crumbled building, he met several dozen uniformed men leading horses that were burdened with chopped boughs, bound clusters of enormous vines, and other assorted vegetation.

Before he could enter the work area, Simon was briskly halted. Four men detained him, binding his hands in front of him, and led him away to a collection of tents. Even as Simon tried to explain who he was and why he needed to speak with the king, he knew it was futile.

He was handcuffed to a solid tentpole and left to wait. Irritated, he searched the area for a familiar face. He didn't know many people in the military, but he knew several regulators who had been regular guards at the school. Maybe they would be helping out.

An hour passed. He tried a number of times to stop someone, to plead his case, but no one would listen. Since he was the only non-User foolish enough to still be in the city and was dressed in poor clothes, he was a person of suspicion.

Circling the post in frustration, he continued to scan the passing men, looking for insignia that marked an officer. Eventually, a woman's voice reached his ears. Simon fell still as dread swelled within him. Momentarily, Eevie strolled by, escorted by two officers.

Unable to escape or hide, Simon waited for her to spot him. The moment her eyes fell on him, her gait faltered and her conversation suddenly became stilted. The two officers she was with noticed and glanced at Simon. "Do you know him?" one asked.

Deciding he was going to head off her response and appeal to her—otherwise, he would be detained indefinitely—Simon held her gaze. "Eevie, I have a message for His Majesty. I'm acting as a messenger. I was the only one who could make it. Please."

Eevie regarded him for a long moment, searching his face with surprisingly soft eyes. "He's a pro-fighter from the Munera school." She gave a small, charming smile that immediately made Simon dubious of her intentions. "What he says might be true."

One of the officers approached Simon, sizing him up as he approached. "What's your name, kid?"

"Simon Ashway."

"Simon Ashway… one of the Champions?" The officer, a middle-aged man with a handlebar mustache and neatly trimmed goatee, looked him over, wide-eyed.

Eevie joined him. "He's got the mark above his brow."

"What message have you for the king, son?"

"I'm sorry, but I've been tasked with delivering it only to him," replied Simon. "Please understand. It's urgent. He knows my name; he knows who I am."

The officer held his gaze for a long moment before nodding. "Very well. I'll send for His Majesty." He frowned. "How did you end up out here? Who sent you here?"

"I'm not at liberty to say."

"Mh-hm." The officer glanced at Eevie and his colleague. "Let us hope that your name alone is more important than the king's deliverance of Eclat."

Simon smiled grimly. "I guarantee it."

The officer hollered at a private who hurried off. As the mustachioed officer and his colleague continued about their business, Eevie hesitated, hovering near Simon anxiously. "Miss Thornburgh?" the officer inquired.

"Simon is an old acquaintance. I'd like to stay with him for a while, if you have no immediate need for my assistance," Eevie replied, her blue eyes enormous. With a curt nod, the two officers left.

Pulling on his cuffs, Simon growled, "What are you up to now?"

"I could ask you the same thing," Eevie replied evenly. She was dressed in her usual uniform of an ankle-length dress adorned with an apron. Her blond curls were pinned under a white nurse's cap. She carried a leather bag across her back.

"I'm not lying." Simon peered out at the men continuing to cut and haul vegetation. He couldn't help but think that Kell and Mordecai could easily handle it all. "I have a message for the king."

"Since when have you been on speaking terms with His Majesty?"

"A lot's happened in the past two weeks." He glanced about and, seeing that they were mostly alone, added, "I see you've climbed the ranks *quickly*. How many men did you sleep with to get—"

"I didn't—" Eevie peeked uncomfortably over her shoulder. "It might come as a surprise to you, but I'm a nurse—a *good* nurse. And there are injured soldiers. Dr. Gray and some of the others were absorbed by the military to help keep up with the number of wounded." She ran her eyes over him. "You look… worse."

He grinned. "Like I said, a lot's happened."

Eevie folded her arms to her, her chin stubbornly tilting upward. "And your friend? Lady Othonos?"

"What of her?"

Eevie shrugged. "Is she still alive?"

The playful spitefulness with which he had been addressing her vanished. In its stead was anger and a fierce desire to protect Kell at all costs. "You will know of her soon enough."

Eevie's brows folded together. "What's that supposed to mean?" When he didn't reply, she sighed and drew closer. Simon stepped to the other side of the pole. Eevie searched his eyes. "I didn't know Dockett was going to go after her."

"What else did you think he was going to do with that information, Eevie?" Simon growled. "Dockett isn't—wasn't—a forgiving person."

Eevie fell still, her eyes wide. "What do you mean *wasn't*?"

"Dockett's dead. He was killed the day of the Munera."

"You-you saw it?" She gasped. "Did *you* do it?"

An automobile screeched to a halt beyond the tents. Simon saw a familiar figure leap out of the vehicle and begin striding toward him.

Eevie reached between them and took his arms. "Simon, what happened? What happened to Dockett?"

"Simon!" called Bellamy, his black hair blown back.

"My friend killed him," Simon told Eevie, his attention turning to the king.

"Why is this man shackled?" Bellamy boomed to the nearby soldiers. "Release him at once!"

Simon glanced at Eevie as he was freed to find her hands covering her mouth.

"Simon, come." Bellamy began drawing him away.

With a sigh, Simon went to Eevie whose cheeks were wet with tears. "Sorry you had to find out like this. His death was... quick."

"How?" she whispered.

Simon frowned in thought. How was he to explain that Mordecai had killed him by hurling a bullet at him? "He was shot."

"By a regulator?"

"Like I said, a friend of mine killed him. That's it." He regarded her trembling fingers and then laid a hand on her shoulder. "I'm sorry." With that, he followed Bellamy to a private tent.

"What was that about?" asked the new king as they entered.

"She was Dockett's, uh, friend. I just told her he was killed."

"Ah." Bellamy surveyed the mostly empty tent and then looked at Simon. "Well?"

Setting aside Eevie's sudden appearance, Simon calmed himself. "It's done. Terin is dead."

"How?"

"Kell."

Bellamy began pacing in thought. "And where is she?"

"That's why I'm here. Renata sent me. They're at the Middle District port. On my family boat."

The king stopped his frantic movements and worriedly looked at Simon. "And why isn't Kell standing here in front of me?"

"She was hurt. The whole event has taken... a lot from her. Renata wants you to come to the boat and speak with Kell." Simon watched to gauge his reaction.

As Bellamy considered the request, he nodded to himself, his mind apparently whirring. "At the Middle District port, correct? Did Renata provide a timeframe?"

"No... sire," Simon replied, remembering to whom he spoke. "She was confident that you'd come once I passed the message."

To his surprise, the king chuckled. "Well, she's not wrong. I'll make arrangements." As he started for the door, Simon stopped him.

Not sure if he was permitted to mention it but concerned for Kell's future nonetheless, Simon said, "Renata mentioned that you were planning to... use Kell? That it's been planned for a while?"

Bellamy regarded him. "Yes?"

Chiding himself to tread carefully, Simon continued. "Kell is… a dear friend. I don't want her to suffer more than she already has. And I will do anything—to anyone—to safeguard her."

The young king smiled. "Oh, good. We are in agreement then. Come along. We need to find a way to port."

Bewildered, Simon stopped him again. "You're-you're serious?"

"Yes, of course. Why wouldn't I be serious?"

"Because you had me and Kell arrested," Simon replied. A spark of fire ignited within him, but he remembered what Renata had said, that Kell had already punished the king for his transgressions. Imagining Kell landing punches on Bellamy's weary face pleased him.

"Oh, yes, that." Bellamy's smile faded and he straightened himself in front of Simon. "Kellick made it abundantly clear to me how my actions… impacted those involved. I have since done everything in my power to make it up to her. I intend to do the same for you. If you'll allow me."

Holding his amber gaze, Simon nodded. What else was he supposed to say to the king of Berceau?

The expression on Bellamy's face softened. "Come on."

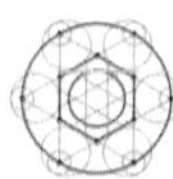

Kell remained as still as possible, holding steady globes of fire next to Lachlan's hands so he could better see the curved needle he pulled through Mordecai's flesh. Although all the windows were open to admit light, her flames remained necessary. Kell glanced at Mordecai who was staring up at the ceiling, jaws clenched.

"You two can be on bedrest together," Lachlan remarked, throwing a wink at her. Kell smiled but otherwise remained silent, focusing on staying still. "You've been especially helpful. Perhaps I should hire you to work in the operating theater." In mock bravado, he continued, "And here is my assistant fire holder, Kellick Fisk."

"I don't think your colleagues will find my presence as comforting as you seem to," replied Kell dully.

Lachlan glanced at her, his mustache twitching. "I'm sure we will change their opinions." He untwisted thread and said to Mordecai, "Whoever bandaged you saved your life. They did an expert job."

"It was… Tarquin," Mordecai muttered. Though Lachlan had administered a local anesthetic, Kell knew Mordecai could still feel much of the doctor's poking and prodding.

Some twenty minutes later, Lachlan sat back with a sigh to study his work. As he had done to treat Kell's abdominal wounds, he had stripped Mordecai nude. With the additional punctures in his thighs, it had just made sense. The doctor laid a soft blanket across Mordecai for modesty and turned to Kell. "Let's look at you."

"Why?" Kell grumbled.

"Because you appear worn, like you've been doing the exact opposite of what I told you to do. Did your wound reopen?"

Mordecai answered for her. "Yes."

Kell threw him an annoyed look.

With a sigh, Lachlan called Vera into the room to help Kell undress. Kell winced and grimaced as the doctor drew out the torn thread and injected a local anesthetic in preparation to re-suture the wound.

"Mom!" came a familiar voice from the outer deck followed by heavy footsteps.

"Hold on, Simon," Vera called, bracing Kell.

Though the anesthetic was working, it didn't prevent Kell from feeling the tugging. Gnashing her teeth, she clung to Vera with a whimper.

"The doctor's working on Kell," she heard Ferrik tell Simon.

"I brought Bellamy," Simon called through the closed door.

"I'm not going to work any faster just because His Majesty is here," Lachlan replied over his shoulder, seemingly unbothered. By the time he was done, Kell was panting and covered in a fine sweat. The doctor bandaged it, giving further instructions for care, and then stepped outside.

Once back in the dress Simon's mother had loaned her, Kell sat on the edge of the bed to catch her breath. Mordecai tiredly watched her but remained quiet. She drew a long breath, struggling to find her *satt*. When, as she tried desperately to calm herself, she felt her heartrate increase, she buried her face in her hands. Hot tears slid down her cheeks.

Vera kneeled in front of her and took her hand.

Frustrated because it seemed like her composure so easily fractured of recent, Kell swiped at her eyes and nose and regarded Simon's mother through blurred eyes.

Vera seemed as though she wanted to say something, but the words stayed in her throat. After a moment, she leaned forward and kissed Kell's forehead. "Take your time," she whispered. Vera left, closing the door behind her.

Tears still running down her cheeks, Kell met Mordecai's gaze. From his prone position, he took her hand and squeezed her fingers lovingly. "We'll get through this."

Kell nodded though she couldn't force herself to believe it.

As Simon's mother busied the men, Kell closed her eyes and clung to Mordecai. Several minutes passed before she felt composed enough to leave the sanctity of the room. She imparted Mordecai a kiss and then left.

When she opened the door, she expected the others to be waiting for her at the main table. Instead, she found them standing on the rear deck, talking cheerfully. The familiarity of Bellamy's form elicited from her surprising relief. Feeling stronger, she joined them, passing Lachlan as he examined Renata in her room.

Simon, of course, was the first to meet her gaze and smiled fondly at her. He slipped past his mother and went to her, offering his arm. Kell gave a small shake of her head before turning her attention to Bellamy. The new king greeted her, a large smile spreading across his face. "Kellick," he beamed.

Before she could decide which was more appropriate, a bow or a curtsey, Bellamy crossed the deck and embraced her. The hug was brief but confused her. Bewildered, she watched as he drew away, pulled her hand to his lips, and kissed it. "How are you feeling?"

"Uh, well enough, I guess." She glanced at the others. Vera was smiling pleasantly, but Ferrik, Tarquin, and Simon seemed solemn.

"I'm pleased to hear that." Bellamy looked her over with mild amusement. "You do appear—"

"You're acting strangely," Kell interrupted. "Why?"

Bellamy scoffed. "I am not."

"You've not ever hugged or-or kissed me. And since when did you speak so properly to me?"

The king grinned. "Since you saved the capital."

"Oh."

Bellamy glanced at the others, amused. "Yes, oh…" He drew a long breath. "I have a proposition for you. Well, for you and Mordecai. But I hear he is currently incapacitated."

"What proposition?" She looked back at Simon and Ferrik. "Can they know of it?"

Bellamy shrugged, a most un-king-like motion. "I don't really care. It doesn't concern them."

"Thanks, Majesty," Simon muttered good-naturedly.

The king leveled a smile at him. "No, your time will come soon enough."

The look on Simon's face made Kell smile, the first true one she had shown in days.

Bellamy began pacing. Dressed in a long-sleeved navy blouse, white breeches, and knee-high boots, he didn't belong on the rusting *Merry Maiden*. "Eclat is in ruin; the Council of Ministers is fractured—my own doing, I'm afraid; and society as we know it has collapsed. All because of a girl." The king stopped and looked at her. "I want you to help me rebuild it."

"Rebuild what?"

"All of it. Everything. I want you to help me rebuild Berceau."

Kell frowned deeply and, before she could stop herself, asked, "Why?" Bellamy seemed to have expected this response because he only smiled. "Why would you need my help when you have thousands of men at your disposal?"

"Because you know both the Knowledge of Old and New." Bellamy regarded her. "You will be the bridge between what was and what will be."

Kell thought, looking between the others. "Who told you? Simon?"

"Tell him what?" asked Simon, sincerely confused. Tarquin shook his head as well.

Kell glanced at Ferrik and then back at Bellamy. "How did you know that I can... use both forms?"

"Denez told me," Bellamy beamed.

"But I hadn't... What did... When did he tell you?"

Bellamy thought, his hands on his waist. "Maybe four or five months ago. I rode out to meet him outside of Eclat."

"But I was still training then. How could..." Kell's sentence trailed off as she realized that the First Whispered must had known long ago that she would be capable of drawing from the Flow using both the Old and New Knowledge. "They knew," she concluded.

"Yeah, they knew you'd become a master of both," confirmed Bellamy. "We discussed it those months ago to figure out what your accomplishment would mean for Berceau and the First Whispered. They want you to represent them on the Council of Ministers."

Kell gaped. "What?"

"The seat that the First Whispered once had on the Council, I've reopened it. And it's yours. Along with the living arrangements, special privileges, and title that comes with it." Bellamy held her gaze, a smile tugging at the corner of his mouth. "Of course, those *benefits* extend to Mordecai as well should you wed him."

"But I'm not... Bellamy, I'm not a First Whispered. How can I represent them? Denez would be better suited—"

"Denez doesn't want to set foot in the capital, much less hold a government position. Besides, we're going to need people well-versed in the New Knowledge to teach those Bound who will be returning to the city. I'm hoping Mordecai might help with—"

"But there are so many other people more qualified than me! I'm just a-a fisherman's daughter. I don't—"

"Kellick." The king's voice was even. "Berceau is changing. We can't maintain the divide between those who can access the Flow and the mundane like myself. You will bring balance. Denez has agreed to counsel you so that you accurately represent the Tribe and its interests, but your specific background, education, and training make you the perfect candidate."

Kell regarded him for a long moment before asking, "Are you just wanting me to fix the city?"

Bellamy laughed. "Well, that might be part of it. Yes." He reached between them and took her hand. "I don't need an answer right now. I don't even require one next week. Promise me, however, that you *will* consider it."

"I promise."

He squeezed her hand and then looked at Simon. "*Now* it's your turn." Simon joined Kell. "I have two opportunities for you. You may choose whichever you would like to pursue or neither of them." The king grew solemn. "I'm in need of a new bodyguard. Someone to ensure that myself and others remain safe. This would be a long-term position that would allow you to continue using your training and expertise in a beneficial manner. *Or* I can elevate you to officer status within the imperial army. With both positions, you will be afforded special privileges, substantial pay, and pension."

Simon blinked at him. "A bodyguard or-or an officer?"

Bellamy grinned with a slight grimace. "I can't tell you how much the pay would be yet as my government is currently in turmoil and everything has been upended. But rest assured, both of you," he nodded to Kell, "will be well cared for."

Kell watched Simon from the corner of her eye. He was thinking, his gaze darting between Bellamy and the horizon and the deck. Finally, he asked, "What about Ferrik?"

"Who?"

Simon pointed at his mentor who stood near the cabin.

"Simon, don't," Ferrik chided half-heartedly.

"Ferrik's been my mentor for years. Everything I learned, I learned from him and Dockett," argued Simon. The expression on Bellamy's face hardened as he regarded Ferrik. "He helped us get down to the docks, to get to Renata. Without him, Mordecai and I wouldn't have made it."

"Allow me time to consider it," Bellamy replied. "I came here prepared to make you and Kellick offers. I'm not—"

"What is a former pro-fighter going to do?" Simon interrupted. "Where is he going to go?" He rejoined Ferrik. "With the Munera no longer running, you're going to have pro-fighters on the streets looking for ways to survive. Do you want to end up facing off with him somewhere down the line."

Bellamy repeated himself calmly. "Allow me time to consider it."

Before Simon could continue to argue, Ferrik nudged him. "Thank you, sire, for your consideration." Ferrik gave a polite bow. "I look forward to hearing from you."

The king drew a long breath and looked back at Kell. "I would invite you into the city, but you might be more comfortable here given the military presence in the streets."

"We couldn't move Mordecai anyway," Kell replied.

"I'll send for food and supplies." He peered at the surrounding docks and then out at the water, growing grave.

As the king fell deep in thought, Kell took stock of herself in the late afternoon light. Her body was worn, ragged. But something stirred within her. Denez had known—all of the First Whispered had known—that she would be able to master the Knowledge of Old. The Tribe leader had even reached out to Bellamy and discussed what such a development would mean for their people. Denez was placing the Tribe in her hands.

"Recovery is going to take years," mused Bellamy more to himself than to anyone else. "We'll have to rebuild *fast* and provide incentives to encourage people to return. Many of our tradesmen fled to Avives. Others headed to Chantis. There was a mass exodus… and slaughter. We have to start rebuilding the lower and middle classes immediately. And the—"

"Bellamy?"

The king looked at her.

"The Bound who were part of Terin's… campaign," said Kell, "can't be punished."

She expected him to push back, but Bellamy sighed. "Agreed. Unfortunately, I'm walking a fine line, Kellick. They took part in the destruction of the entire city—"

"They were *made* to take part in the destruction of the city," Kell corrected. "They didn't have a choice."

"Right, Terin's gift…"

"I felt it," continued Kell. "It was terrible. She… commanded me to die. And my body… listened to her. I couldn't fight it. If she gave the others orders, they couldn't have disobeyed had they even wanted to."

Bellamy leaned against the railing. "Everyone is gunning for revenge."

Kell met his gaze. "It has to stop. The cycle has to stop."

He nodded. "It has to stop." The king regarded her thoughtfully before saying, "Rest up, Kell." He stood and straightened his blouse with a curt gesture. "We have work to do."

Kell gave a short bow. "Yes, sire."

Epilogue

Simon edged closer to Bellamy, unsettled. The people of the First Whispered were odd. They gestured with the minutest of motions, and their faces remained impassive, stoic. Their light-colored eyes were intelligent and inquisitive, and nothing seemed to escape their attention.

"You'll grow accustomed to them," the king said, sensing Simon's discomfort.

Simon glanced at Ferrik who gave an almost indiscernible nod of agreement. They were used to reading people, predicting movements, and understanding cause and response. But these strangers were different. Nothing seemed to ruffle them. Their reactions to noise, conversation, disconcerting news, anything that would have elicited more excitement or enthusiasm, were not what Simon expected. "You lived with them?" Simon murmured into Bellamy's shoulder.

"Perhaps I should leave you two with them for a year and see how you get along," replied the king with a wry smile.

It was a glorious late-July afternoon. The skies overhead were a breathtaking shade of deep azure and were decorated with joyous, puffy white clouds. Although it was hot, a cool breeze swept down from the mountains to usher away summer sweat. Lush, rolling meadows of green expanded in all directions up to the gorgeously clear mountains to the north that stretched to greet the infinite blue.

Pale, cream-colored yurts dotted the area; paths of depressed grass where traffic was heaviest were most evident between the yurts and social gathering spaces.

Though they had arrived at Heim—which Simon learned was what the village was always called no matter where it was located—around midday, their sudden presence hadn't altered the activities of the day. As Bellamy spoke at length with Denez, Simon and Ferrik, both of whom were supposed to be safeguarding the king, watched the First Whispered. When Bellamy wanted to continue his conversation in private with the Tribe leader, he excused Simon and Ferrik, leaving them outside a yurt.

A woman with a long plait of platinum blond hair paused in passing, her arms full of robes. "You're… Simon?" she asked, bright blue eyes shining.

Startled, he nodded.

A gorgeous smile spreading across her face, the woman replied, "I'm Gytha. I'm Kell's teacher, well, one of her other teachers. It's a pleasure to finally meet you."

"Oh, uh, it's nice to meet you too," Simon replied, painfully aware of how attractive she was. Gytha carried herself with a confidence that he hadn't seen in many women. Clearing his throat, he searched the surrounding area. "Have you seen Kell and Tarquin? Or even Mordecai? I thought they'd be here by now."

Gytha chuckled, her laughter a tinkle of chimes. "They're here. Tarquin is helping down by the river. Mordecai went out to hunt earlier with the others. And... no one is allowed to see Kell right now."

Simon grew solemn. "Why? Is she hurt?"

Gytha held up the long navy robe in her arms. "She's preparing for the ceremony. See you boys tonight." With a flirtatious smile, she bid them goodbye and strode off to a yurt situated far from the others.

Ferrik nudged Simon teasingly. "You're drooling."

Simon elbowed him hard in return, both embarrassed and amused. Looking to change the subject, he said, "I didn't know the ceremony was happening today."

"Yeah, it'd be nice if Bellamy shared a bit more," Ferrik agreed. They turned to watch as a handful of middle-aged women, quietly talking among themselves, made their way to the yurt into which Gytha had disappeared. Nearby a young man casually lit a firepit with a single wave of his fingers. He fanned it briefly with a low but steady stream of air before beckoning for the earth to deliver to him a pot.

"It's... second-nature to them," Simon eventually said. Ferrik nodded.

Half an hour later, a group of First Whispered appeared across the meadow. As they drew closer, Simon saw that they had three large bucks strung between them as well as an assortment of other game. Mordecai, who was lively talking with another young man, carried three brown rabbits over his shoulder.

Dressed in loose pants and barefoot like the others in the hunting party, Mordecai looked strong. He had cut his black hair short, which made him look older, more mature. Even from a distance, Simon could discern two, red scars along the left side of his abdomen. For all their rivalry, Simon was glad to see him as the last time he had visited with Kell's fiancé had been in April.

As the hunting party strode into the village, others came to help with the game. Mordecai passed his kills to a pre-teen boy before he continued speaking with his friend. Simon watched them, intrigued. While Mordecai was animated and used his hands to speak, his comrade remained impassive.

His friend said something and then motioned toward the yurt where Bellamy was. Mordecai's eyes lit upon Ferrik and then Simon. Grinning, he hurried over. "Simon!"

Amused by Mordecai's enthusiasm, Simon took his strong hand and then hugged him. Still smiling, Mordecai turned to Ferrik and shook his hand as well. "It's good to see you, Mordecai," Simon's mentor said, warmth tinting his voice. Simon smiled. Ferrik liked Mordecai more than he let on.

"When did you three get in?" Mordecai breathed, a fine layer of sweat coating his skin.

"Just a while ago," Simon replied. "You've been busy."

"Yeah, well…" Mordecai breathed deeply and looked about. "A lot's going on."

"We didn't realize the ceremony was tonight," said Ferrik. He glanced at Simon. "Bellamy doesn't tell us anything."

"That's not true," interjected Bellamy, exiting the yurt with Denez. Mordecai's greeting to the king was more polite. "Mordecai, how are you?"

"Good, really good."

Bellamy chuckled. "I don't think I've ever seen you in such high spirits."

"I'll leave you four to catch up," said Denez with a smile before meandering off.

"How's Kellick?"

Mordecai glanced about Heim. "She's really well."

"Is she nervous?" the king asked.

Mordecai shrugged, still smiling. "I'm sure she is, but I haven't seen her in two days."

"Two days?" asked Simon, confused. "What's she doing?"

"Studying and preparing." Mordecai motioned to the isolated yurt on the far side of camp. "She'll do fine."

"Well, we look forward to seeing her tonight," Bellamy said.

"That makes the both of us—" A whistle sounded over the camp, causing Mordecai to turn and look, searching. Simon saw another young man waving to him near the river. "If you need help with anything, come find me, yeah?" He loped off.

As the sun settled in the west, tucking behind the tips of distant mountain ranges, the village came abuzz with excitement. Several bonfires around Heim's perimeter were lit; another two were set ablaze in the main social area. The smell of food that permeated the air made Simon salivate. Nevertheless, he stayed faithfully by Bellamy's side, observing the frantic preparations.

Eventually, a drum and whistle duet began playing at twilight. Simon and Ferrik followed Bellamy to a designated location near one of the central bonfires. Mordecai and Tarquin joined them. As others of the Tribe fell in, Simon noticed the black symbol on their foreheads that had been painted for the occasion. A single line stretched over their brows from temple to temple. Five thinner strokes that looked like the rays of a sun peering over a horizon stretched up to their hairlines.

"What's the symbol mean?" he murmured to Mordecai.

"The six elements—fire, water, flora, earth, metal, and wind," he replied.

The First Whispered formed a pathway from the isolated yurt on the other side of the camp to the space between the two bonfires. As the shrill cries of the flute soared above the steady drumming, the Tribe fell still. Denez, accompanied by four others, strode into the space between the two fires. Those with long hair, male and female, wore it freely.

Simon craned his neck to watch Kell and Gytha step from the yurt. Gytha wore her usual short-sleeved tunic. But Kell was dressed in a ground-sweeping robe of deep navy that boasted long, intricately decorated sleeves. Her hair was pinned atop her head. Though she peered straight ahead, the expression in her eyes was old, distant, as if she saw everything and nothing.

The music stopped suddenly.

Gytha moved in front of Kell and then unclasped the robe. As she drew the garment from her shoulders, Kell's gaze didn't waver. Simon gaped as Kell's nude form was revealed. She was adorned in dark whorls and complex swirls that had been painstakingly sketched onto her bare skin. Every inch of her bore some coiling, curling, or looping pattern, except her face. Her face remained unembellished.

As Gytha melded into the darkness behind other Tribe members, Kell remained motionless, the expression on her face stoic. A single stroke of the drum signaled for her to move. Gaze set in the distance, she walked a few paces, the epitome of ethereal beauty.

Simon took her all in, his eyes lingering boldly on her painted breasts and thighs, but felt no arousal. The old look in her eyes, the way with which she held herself, her gait, the lack of movement in her hands and arms—all of it was unfamiliar and beautiful.

Kell stopped as the drum quieted. As she slowly turned to her right to meet a middle-aged man, she cupped her hands before her. Simon didn't know it was water that had pooled in her palms until the man flourished a gleaming tendril of the fluid into the air between them. It expanded and then looped around Kell's hips. She didn't move.

Once the water swirled in a constant and controlled stream around her, skimming her skin but never touching it, he stepped back into the line. After a slight bow, Kell continued walking between the lines of First Whispered.

The next time the drum stopped, she turned to the left. To Simon's surprise, Renata, all four of her fields and Arcane Circle already ignited, stepped forward with a slight limp. Kell once again cupped her hands, and a leafy vine grew there. The old woman used the same dramatic motion, gesturing the vine into the air. It twirled and then contracted before settling atop Kell's head as a verdant crown.

Despite the special moment, Kell impassively bowed and then moved down the line.

The next member of the Tribe drew the metal Kell conjured into the air, created eight rings of the raw material, and then clasped them along Kell's forearms and ankles.

As she drew near, Simon could discern the sweat on her brow as it glistened in the firelight.

Kell gave another First Whispered a handful of earth, which she was forced to keep circulating just above the water around her hips. Now even with Simon and the others, she stopped just short of the two bonfires. Gytha met her with a conjured gust of wind.

As the wind buffeted Kell, she raised her hands toward her and then, as Simon had seen her do before, gently turned them palm-side down and breathed out, a kind of settling gesture. The wind calmed. Though it was apparent no one was supposed to express any type of emotion throughout the length of the ceremony, Simon saw the slightest of smiles twitch Gytha's lips as she stepped back to return to the others stationed between the two bonfires.

Kell approached Denez, prompting the leader to flourish a hand to create fire, further illuminating her face. He held it between them and then jerked it outward. A blaze erupted over Kell like a cape unfurling in the wind. Simon fidgeted, the heat drawing unexpected instinctual responses in him. Ferrik leaned into him comfortingly.

Denez made a gesture, and the roaring flames calmed as he looped them around Kell's shoulders. The fire drifted around her like a magical cloak fluttering in an invisible wind. The Tribe's leader watched her as though he were searching for something, waiting for something.

After a minute of pure silence, he smiled and then stepped forward and touched his forehead to Kell's. Tears spilled down her cheeks and a soft cry slipped from her throat. Denez handled her fondly before he took a brush from one of the other men. Crying, Kell worked to keep herself still as Denez drew upon her the symbol of the First Whispered.

When he was done, he returned the brush to its owner and then gestured for Kell to face everyone. "*Pad er buid.*"

Kell cried harder as the bonfires that had been set up around the village burst into torrents of whirling fire that shot up into the sky in a magnificent display. The village converged on her, cheering and clapping. The water and fire around her vanished when Gytha swept her into a bear hug, lifting her from the ground.

Before Kell disappeared into the folds of welcoming arms, her friend helped her slip back into her robe.

Smiling, Simon exchanged looks with Bellamy, Tarquin, and Ferrik. The king grinned as he clapped, obviously pleased, while Tarquin discreetly brushed tears from his face. Mordecai had disappeared into the celebrating group. Simon himself swelled with pride. Even though he didn't understand it all, even though he would never be able to participate in such a ceremony, he was thrilled for Kell and wanted to envelop her in an all-consuming hug. But her new family swept her away as the drum-and-flute twosome once again began.

Heim celebrated long into the night. The next time Simon saw Kell later in the evening, she was adorned in several crowns of vibrant flowers and surrounded by Gytha, Denez, and others of the Tribe. Mordecai, who had been instructed not to be around Kell, stood nearby, drinking an alcoholic beverage made of fermented fruit and watching.

"Why don't they want you near her?" asked Simon, finishing up a second bowl of hearty venison, wild rice, and an assortment of vegetables.

"Because I'm not Tribe—yet," he replied, smiling, his eyes never leaving Kell.

Simon felt a mild surge of jealousy pulse through him but pushed it away. "I heard that if you wed, you become Tribe." He clapped Mordecai on the shoulder. "Good for you, Mordecai."

Mordecai's gaze slipped to the nearby fire in thought before he turned to Simon who was mid-bite. "Thank you."

Bewildered, Simon shrugged. "What for?"

Mordecai held his hand out to him. "For being her confidant and friend." He held Simon's gaze, the meaning clear. "You're important to her, so you're important to me."

Simon slipped his spoon back into his bowl and shook Mordecai's hand, his grip firmer than it probably needed to be.

Mordecai grinned. "I like you better as an ally than an enemy." He released Simon and motioned between them. "You and me—we make a good team."

Simon couldn't argue with that. They had taken out over a dozen Users together and distributed substantial damage to an Unbound. "So?" He peered out at the First Whispered as they milled about, ate, and talked. "When do you return to Eclat?"

"Don't know. It depends on Kell. I don't know the laws for a newly-minted Tribe member."

Simon glanced at him. "Have you tried to contact your family back in Avives?"

"Earlier this year I did," Mordecai replied. He drew a steady breath. "Surprisingly, they are still alive. I was so certain that Terin had… But my mother responded. I'd like to eventually take Kell to Avives to meet them."

Simon frowned. "Why?"

Mordecai didn't have an answer.

"Didn't they… drop you off at an orphanage or something?" Simon chuckled. "You should wait until Eclat has been restored and then invite them as a personal guest of the king of Berceau." He motioned to Bellamy who was chatting with Tarquin and Ferrik nearby. Hearing his name, the young king paused in conversation. Simon pointed at Mordecai. "We're going to invite his family to Eclat later. Let them see what happened to the son they abandoned."

Bellamy smiled wolfishly. "Of course, your family is always welcome to visit my court." A distant smile on his face, Mordecai sipped his drink, his eyes searching the crowd for Kell.

Simon exchanged amused looks with Bellamy. He found he got along well with the king and often joked with him in private. Ferrik, who was fifteen years their senior, was more reserved in his interactions, but Simon knew he greatly enjoyed his new position alongside him.

Though members of the Tribe continued to drink late into the night, Mordecai eventually retired to a bachelor's yurt after helping Renata. When Bellamy grew tired, he led Simon and Ferrik to their private quarters. As Simon was preparing to close the door, he glimpsed Kell leaving the village, the long robe she still wore drifting behind her in the moonlight. "I'll be right back," he told Ferrik who nodded.

He swept a glance around the village—no one was paying attention to him—and then jogged out into the surrounding meadow. He stopped several paces from Kell who stood motionlessly in the cool, summer grass. Tendrils of light-colored blossoms spilled down from the floral crowns she wore.

Simon didn't think she knew he was there as she peered up at the moon and took a deep breath. With a smile, she turned to him. "This'll be… the last time," she said, "that you and I will meet alone."

Adorned in cascading ivy and flowers and the paint on her forehead smeared, she looked like a wildling that had just wandered from the forest. Grinning, Simon drew near, his hands in his pockets. He glanced up at the stars before saying, "Congratulations, Kell. I'm happy for you. Truly, I am."

She held a painted hand out to him, and he took it. "I'm… really glad you're here." She squeezed his fingers. "Having you and Bellamy… and Tarquin… and Renata here…" A tear slid down her face, and she wiped it away with mild annoyance. "My family."

"Yeah." Simon gingerly drew her into his arms. Kell hugged him, resting her head on his chest. She smelled strongly of fragrant blossoms, greenery, and wood smoke. Simon kissed the side of her head. "I love you, Kellick."

"I know," she whispered, her voice thick. She drew back to see his face, her fingers reaching between them to stroke his jaw. "I love you too. And I always will." With a small smile, she stepped back farther so that all that remained touching were their hands. Swallowing, she said, "I look forward to working with you, Simon Ashway. Don't be a stranger."

Simon studied her face, taking in all that she was. This was their goodbye to what could have been. This marked the moment their relationship would change, *had* to change, to accommodate their new roles within Bellamy's administration.

Unable to say anything else, Simon smiled into her eyes and kissed the back of her hand with a short bow.

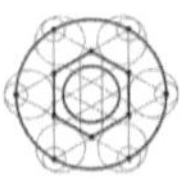

Simon was eager to leave Heim. Already two days had passed since the ceremony, and still, the Tribe acted as though the initiation had happened just hours prior. Everyone drank and ate—no matter the time of day—and music often sporadically erupted followed by dancing and jovial singing. Simon vaguely wondered where the odd, distant people he had known prior to the initiation had gone.

"We're leaving tomorrow," said Bellamy as they wandered the outskirts of the village that afternoon. "I've been gone long enough."

"Will Kell and Mordecai travel with us?" asked Ferrik.

Bellamy snorted, a frown spreading on his face. "No."

Simon shared a glance with Ferrik. "Why… do you say it like that?"

"Well, Kell's not due back in court for several months," the king replied moodily.

"What? Why?" Simon paused as he remembered what Mordecai had said—something about laws.

"She must remain in Heim until she's completed her initiation *tasks* which, according to Renata, will take her a while. So…" Bellamy drew himself up. "I've already spoken to Denez; supplies are being readied. We'll head out after dawn."

Simon went to bed relieved that night.

The following morning, they rose in the dark and began packing their horses. Denez and three others, Gytha included, came to see them off. As Denez spoke with Bellamy and Ferrik visited with the others, Simon stood off from everyone. Gytha joined him.

She smiled warmly at him, her hair braided over her shoulder in an intricate plait. Her blue eyes were bright and inquisitive but sharp, as if they could perceive his every thought. "She's already gone off for her first task."

"Who? Kell?"

Gytha nodded.

"What… does she have to do?"

"Survive the mountains for a week."

Simon gaped at her. "Survive… Did anyone go with her?"

Gytha tilted her head in confusion. "No, why would someone go with her?" When he didn't respond, she added with a smile, "She is First Whispered. She doesn't need anyone's help. She'll be fine."

"When did she leave?"

"Late last night."

Realizing that Gytha spoke truth and that Kell would indeed be fine, he relaxed. He got the feeling that when Kell returned to Eclat, he wouldn't know who or what she had become. And he was fine with that.

Gytha folded an arm behind her back and grinned up at him in a most attractive way. "I've enjoyed meeting you, Simon."

Blind-sided by the flirtatious way she held herself, Simon stammered over his words. "Yeah, it was, uh, nice to meet you too."

Her eyes briefly raked over him before she held her hand out. "I'm sure we'll see each other again."

"Oh, uh." That puzzled him. Was she not aware of the distance between Heim and the capital? He took her hand gently and felt something akin to a shock of lightning pass between them. "That might be difficult, but, uh, I would be pleased to, you know, see you again."

Gytha chuckled, allowing her fingertips to grace his wrist. "Take care of yourself." And with that, she strolled off, her gait strong but leisurely. Simon watched her, bewildered, before looking at Ferrik and the other First Whispered who had watched the interaction with apparent amusement. It seemed Gytha had come just to see him off.

The journey back to Eclat was long and arduous. By the time they arrived three weeks later in the capital, Simon was ready for a bath and a bed. Although the Upper and Middle Districts had begun rebuilding, albeit slowly, no work had been done on the Lower District. Because of this, he had long since moved his mother and the family boat to the Upper District port. He had offered to buy her a house near the palace with the money he earned working as Bellamy's bodyguard, but Vera had politely refused—just like Tarquin had, despite *Polaris* being utterly destroyed.

Though Eclat was still in disarray, word had gotten out that the reactionary group was disbanded, and so throngs of people had returned, hoping to pick up where their lives had left off. Some were successful, but the majority were not.

In the Upper District, much of the roads and buildings remained untouched. Even in parts of the Middle District, everything was as it once had been. But the internal infrastructure of the country was a mess, something Simon was well aware of given that he was everywhere that Bellamy was for more hours a day than he slept.

The political intrigue and fancy high-stakes maneuvering Bellamy regularly engaged in went over Simon's head. All he had to keep track of was who was an immediate and dangerous threat to the new king. Day in and day out, Simon and Ferrik flanked Bellamy to his every appointment, meeting, meal, and outing. Their quarters were directly adjacent to the king's, ensuring that they could be there within a moment's notice.

When they weren't acting as Bellamy's bodyguards, Ferrik and Simon trained together, working on scenarios they thought they might encounter while in a meeting or when out and about.

As the summer drew to a close, Simon grew restless. His work was monotonous; nothing of interest ever happened around or to Bellamy. Though the king was not well-liked, especially by the elites, his new Council was strong—and growing stronger. The people he chose were not aristocrats or affluent political heads, but individuals who were aware of the trials the country faced.

Kell no longer visited him in his dreams, but Simon knew she spoke often with Bellamy in his. He frequently heard him through the wall chatting familiarly with her throughout the night.

A year after that fateful Munera in the first week of September, Bellamy gathered his Council in its meeting chamber. With Ferrik and Simon beside him, he cheerfully greeted the others, prompting bewildered looks from ministers. "I asked you here this morning because I received word that our representative of the First Whispered will be returning shortly to fill her post."

The king looked out at the twenty or so ministers. "I'd like to introduce you to her."

"Her?" questioned Madam Parthemos, whom Bellamy had been obliged to give a cabinet position because of the power she wielded among the elite. "The position is being filled by a woman?"

Bellamy braced on the long table centered in the middle of the room, a smug look on his face. "Yes, *her*. Lady Kellick Fisk."

There were murmurs from the male-dominant Council, but it sounded more like discussion rather than outright disagreement. Bellamy listened, his eyes furtively flickering to Simon, before he said, "So, let's go meet her." Simon and Ferrik followed him from the room. The ministers fell in behind them, talking among themselves. Simon cocked his head to listen, as was his job—to protect the king from potential threats.

"Let them speculate," Bellamy said confidently. Simon glanced at him to find the king smiling. "My ace has returned."

Outside the palace grounds, glittering automobiles awaited them on a pristine brick driveway. Bellamy clambered in; Simon and Ferrik joined him. As their vehicle pulled away, Simon saw the other ministers climb into additional automobiles. "Where are we meeting her?" He tried not to sound excited.

"We are meeting *them* at the Munera school," Bellamy replied. "Kell's not alone." He sighed in apparent relief. "This is the first and last time I'm letting her be on leave for so long."

Still confused by Bellamy's excitement, Simon asked, "Why... do you say that?"

Peering out the window, Bellamy explained, "The truce between those who can access the Flow and us mundane folk remains delicate. It's hard for either to stay truly neutral given all that's happened over the decades. I've already blocked legislature presented by certain aristocrats. The damage Terin and her reactionaries inflicted still drives people to want to make Bound and Unbound suffer. With Kell at my side... I hope to keep everyone in check. She's the bridge."

"You're putting a lot of stock in her," Ferrik offered evenly.

Bellamy scoffed. "She knew what she was agreeing to. Still, if you two could be extra vigilant, I would be most appreciative. I expect Kell to head off any attacks, but she's not familiar with the ministers and their caprices."

The drive to the Munera school was a relatively short one. When they arrived, Ferrik stepped out and surveyed the area first before allowing Bellamy to exit the vehicle. Simon joined them on the stairs that led to the front of the school. As a rush of emotions swarmed him, he tried to keep his face stoic. Even so, he couldn't hide his discomfort from Ferrik who nudged him fondly.

The ministers arrived after a few minutes and gathered along the bottom of the stairs, chatting amicably. Dressed in their dark, three-piece suits, they looked as though they were preparing to pay their respects at a funeral. Even Madam Parthemos, whom Simon abhorred, was dressed in deep navy and blended in with the other ministers. A newly renovated clock tower to the north showed nine o'clock.

Spotting movement down the street, Simon called Bellamy's attention to it and then positioned himself before the king, his hand on his sword. His mentor likewise maneuvered a few paces in front of them to head off a possible attack.

A whistle pierced the air. Relaxing, Bellamy returned a similar whistled greeting and descended the stairs to the street. "Ministers, this way, please," he said, striding past the parked automobiles. "Gather here." He motioned for them to stop once on the bricks.

Simon hung between the king and the ministers while Ferrik slowly paced the street, his gaze set on the newcomers making their way to the school. When Simon glanced over his shoulder, he spotted not just Kell, but Mordecai, Renata, Gytha, and a few other fair-haired First Whispered.

Bellamy met them with Ferrik by his side; Simon stayed near the ministers. The entire group, of which there were half a dozen people, wore Tribe blues and appeared utterly out of place within the structure of the city.

Eventually, the king led the group to the ministers. Simon caught Kell's eye, and she grinned. Though it had been several months since they had last seen each other, she looked different—older, more mature, more self-aware and confident. Aside from two braids on either side of her head, her dark hair remained free-flowing, a scandalous detail the ministers would no doubt remark on later. Her attention turned to Bellamy as the king introduced her.

"Ministers, this is Lady Kellick, Representative of the First Whispered. With her is Lord Mordecai Othonos; Master Renata Logiadi; and Tribe Members Gytha Andottir, Aethel Vikardottir, Vidkunn Hreinson, and Vigot Bjalkson."

Simon's gaze shifted to Gytha, whose mouth twitched at him in greeting. She was still as beautiful as he remembered. His excitement seeing her rivaled his enthusiasm of being back with Kell, and that revelation surprised him.

Kell moved forward to mingle with the ministers, politely introducing herself with strong handshakes. She didn't wear a dress or skirts as women were expected to, especially in such diplomatic situations; she was clothed in a long tunic, breeches, and supple, knee-high boots. Still, she somehow exuded formality in the way she held herself and how she moved. Simon noticed that she had picked up some of the Tribe's isolated and minimalistic mannerisms, which seemed to keep the ministers on edge.

"Majesty?" asked Madam Parthemos, sidestepping Kell.

Bellamy, who had been jovially speaking with Renata, turned to meet the stiff-shouldered woman. Simon saw the expression on the king's face change. "Yes?"

"Is there a reason we've asked the *representative* to meet at my—the school?" Madam Parthemos asked, her voice curt.

"Ah, yes. Thank you. Yes, there is a reason, quite a good one." Bellamy left Renata to insert himself beside Kell and place a hand on her shoulder, a motion that did not go unnoticed by the others. "Lady Fisk recently made a recommendation." He glanced at Simon and Ferrik. "She suggested we tear down the school." The ministers were silent. Bellamy smiled. "Oh good— adamant agreement. Lady Fisk, if you—"

"I *beg* your pardon?" snarled Madam Parthemos. Simon moved closer to Kell and Bellamy. He was well aware the woman could exact no bodily harm on either of them, but she represented trauma he had undergone during his formative years. He would not let her anywhere near the people he held most dear. "How dare you think you—"

To his surprise, Kell stepped between them, placing a gentle hand on Simon's arm. She seemed to sense and understand his concern. "Madam Parthemos, the Munera school is a relic of the past that promotes brutality, cruelty, and separatism," Kell said, her voice calm. "Surely, as a civilized society, we are better than that."

If Madam Parthemos could breathe fire, she would have snorted flames all over Kell. As it were, she cleared her throat and politely replied, "The school is a capitalistic venture that brings not only economic prosperity to the country but entertainment to hundreds of thousands—"

"At the expense of the lower classes," interrupted Kell. She drew closer to the woman and lowered her voice. "I know what went on in the school. I was in the arena. Have you been in the arena?" When she didn't reply, Kell added, "Perhaps you should experience the *pleasure* of fighting for your life before the masses. What do you think, Simon?"

"I would pay a large sum of money to bear witness to that," Simon growled, the thought a satisfying one.

Kell nodded. "As would I." She suddenly smiled pleasantly at the school's former owner. "As much as Simon and I would enjoy seeing you struggle, the event itself would be dismal entertainment, I'm afraid." Kell held her gaze. "So, I recommend to His Majesty that we tear down the school."

Madam Parthemos fanned herself, perhaps to show that she didn't care, and said, "My school is expansive. It'll take years—"

"It normally would," Bellamy graciously supplied, "but Lady Fisk and her guests have agreed to help." To the rest of the Council, the king asked, "We will be tearing down the school posthaste. Does anyone else have reservations like Madam Parthemos?" There was silence. "All in favor?"

Nearly every hand went up accompanied by a chorus of "ayes."

Bellamy turned to Kell and gestured to the enormous school. "It's yours."

Kell glanced at Madam Parthemos, who was silently seething, and then looked at Simon. "Bellam—Majesty, could I borrow Simon?" The king motioned for him to leave his service.

Bewildered, Simon strode after Kell as she rejoined the others. Mordecai held his hand out. Simon took it, glad to see him, and then greeted Renata respectfully. The old woman reached between them and tapped his face with rough fingers; her eyes twinkled.

Kell drew Gytha forward, against her hushed protests. "Simon, you remember Gytha."

Gytha blushed through a smile and held out her hand for a handshake. "I told you I'd see you again."

Simon took her hand, brought it to his lips, and kissed the back of it. "So you did," he replied, his eyes lingering on hers. When he finally looked at Kell, he found her grinning teasingly. He sighed through pursed lips. "What do you need me for, Kell?"

Clearing her throat, Kell took hold of Simon's arms and turned him to face the school. "I was hoping you'd help me."

He frowned. "How?"

Kell exchanged looks with the others. Mordecai and Renata created Arcane Circles and struck their wrists to ignite their fields. Gytha joined Simon as Aethel, Vidkunn, and Vigot positioned themselves nearby.

Smiling, Kell slipped her hand under Simon's fingers, her palm toward the earth. His enormous hand resting atop hers, Simon glanced first at Bellamy and then at Gytha and Mordecai. "Ready?" Kell asked.

"W-what?" Simon startled as a surge of Viterra swelled under them. It had been months since he had last felt such a sensation, but he hadn't forgotten it. Although the hair along his arms rose and a shiver spread down his spine, it was no longer an unpleasant feeling. Marveling at the power that streamed in around him, he looked at Kell, who grinned mischievously up into his face, her hair drifting around her in an undetectable wind.

Kell raised her hand—and Simon's—and made a quick gesture. Her arm remained tense, solid under him. The earth around them began to rumble, to shake and quiver. He sensed the power moving through her; its immediacy made it feel as though it were his own. Alarmed by the overwhelming sensation, he started to step away. Gytha took hold of his other hand and held it at her side, her focus set on the enormous building before them.

"Renata!" Kell called over her shoulder.

Renata stepped forward with a fluid stomp and then extended her arms in a slithering motion. Thick, sinewy vines erupted from the earth to strangle the columns, crash through the roof, and squeeze the structure into debris.

Simon felt unsteady as he sensed a change in the Viterra. Mouth agape, he glanced at Gytha whose infinitely blue eyes were squinted in effort as she helped exact precise destruction. The earth under the school cracked and then tore open.

Another flux in the Flow drew Simon's attention to Mordecai as he took a few steps back and then swung a kick sideways, rotating in midair. Metal scaffolding, beams, and pipes exploded from the building. As Vidkunn fell in beside Mordecai, the metal that had made up the school gathered in a clamorous sphere overhead, leaving rubble and wood below.

Kell nudged Simon. "Ready?" She didn't give him a chance to respond. A roar of Viterra billowed around them, shaking Simon to his core as brilliant orange and amber flames vented from Kell. The power he felt behind the conflagration was controlled, disciplined, and cleansing. For the first time in his life, Simon felt utter exhilaration being at the epicenter of the blaze.

With a shout of delight, he watched as the place of his tormented upbringing was reduced to a raging inferno. He could feel Gytha, Mordecai, and the others partaking in the destruction, but he couldn't tear his eyes from the glorious scene. The heat from the school's obliteration roused Simon into a solemn grin.

Kell turned her hand over and, intertwining her fingers with his, looked up at him. "You're free," she said loud enough for only him to hear. Simon's gaze shifted back to the seething fire and the reaching black smoke that spiraled into the sky. He was free, not from just the games, but from the mental torment that had plagued his dreams and made him jumpy any time the Munera was mentioned.

The place where he had spent five years of his life learning to kill was now a simmering pile of expansive debris that reached several square blocks.

"Thanks, Kell," he whispered, squeezing her hand.

Kell extracted herself from his grip as he continued to watch the smoldering mess. It took him a moment to realize that Gytha still held his other hand. When he tried to pull away, she didn't let go. Instead, she smiled and leaned into him, her weight new but comforting.

He could move on.

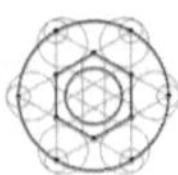

"Theatrical," murmured Bellamy into Kell's shoulder as she rejoined him, his gaze still set on the blaze. Vidkunn, Aethel, and Vigot were suppressing the fire as Mordecai and Renata separated the metal and began organizing it on the street for future use. The rising smoke was already a quarter of what it had been.

Kell glanced at the ministers, taking in the varied expressions on their faces. "But effective," she replied quietly to the king.

Bellamy's expression grew solemn. "We have a hard path ahead of us. It's as I was telling you last week. Already there have been clashes in Avives. I heard just last night that several Bound were executed. The Council wants to—"

Kell lightly punched his arm. "Stop."

The king frowned. "This isn't going to be easy, Kellick."

"Never thought it would be." Seeing his continued displeasure, Kell sighed and gestured to the ruins. "We've made the first step."

"And what's the second step? And the third? And fourth?"

Kell pointed to the remains of the school. She felt the others start drawing Viterra alongside her, following her lead. The earth yawned open, allowing the refuse to spill into a chasm. Numerous blocks of burning rubble dropped into nothingness below the raw lips of tremoring earth.

Stepping away from Bellamy, Kell urged the ground, which had enveloped the ruins, to sew shut. As it mended itself, dust puffed into the sky instead of smoke. Renata and Vigot took several steps forward, moving the Viterra around them in unison before commanding it to a new form.

Lush grass bloomed across the cleared expanse. Flowers erupted in explosions of vivid colors as trees suddenly sprouted from the earth and stretched upward as if awakening from a deep sleep. It took but a minute for the picturesque landscape to materialize within the heart of the capital.

Panting from the effort, Kell turned to look at the ministers. "We're here to make Eclat better than it was. To make the lives of the people living here better than what they were. Are you going to help?"

The ministers looked between themselves before a familiar face emerged from the group—Doctor Lachlan Fitzgerald. "Let's get started," he said, his handlebar mustache twitching into a smile.

Kell met Bellamy's gaze, grinning.

Acknowledgments

As much as I want to take complete and utter credit for this book, I could not have done it without the support of a dedicated group of people.

Firstly, to Michael Smith, science fiction author and friend—your feedback on each of my books when they haven't even reached beta-reader stages is invaluable. I rely heavily on your critiques and appreciate the time and effort you take in picking apart the mess that early drafts tend to be.

To my beta readers: Kimberly Endo, Dana Shanell, Lora Cannon, and Natasha Raymon—sometimes, your feedback is more important than even an editor's! You help decide what I've written is worth your time and emotional energy. I am thankful.

To my husband, Dakota—You give me the space and time I need to pursue my craft. You push and encourage me, make me shift my paradigm to come at plot problems another way. Knowing you're behind my every step gives me the courage to push forward.

And to Japanese composer Takashi Ohmama who wrote the music for "Mobile Suit Gundam: The Witch from Mercury" (2022)—You don't know me, but your music made several appearances in the mental film of this book. Much appreciated.

About the Author

Kara has worked toward becoming a Young Adult (YA)/New Adult (NA) fiction author since she was thirteen. Her first book, *The Empress' Consul*, was first published in 2013.

Kara currently works as an independent book editor for self-publishing authors and as a freelance graphic design artist. She holds a Master of Arts in Communication from the University of Arkansas with a special emphasis in ESL education and mass media. She also holds double Bachelor's degrees in International Relations and Asian Studies.

When she is not writing her own books, Kara enjoys listening to soundtracks from a myriad of shows and movies, watching anime, reading romantasy, playing piano, and beating her husband in video games.

Follow Kara on social media!

www.karadwilson.com
www.facebook.com/karadwilsonbooks